OTTO PENZLER PRESENTS
AMERICAN MYSTERY CLASSICS

THE TRAGEDY OF X

Ellery Queen was a pen name created and shared by two cousins, Frederic Dannay (1905-1982) and Manfred B. Lee (1905-1971), as well as the name of their most famous detective. Born in Brooklyn, they spent forty-two years writing the greatest puzzle-mysteries of their time, gaining the duo a reputation as the foremost American authors of the Golden Age "fair play" mystery. In addition to the Queen books, the pair wrote four novels in the Drury Lane series under the Barnaby Ross pseudonym, of which *The Tragedy of X* is the first. Besides co-writing the Queen novels, Dannay founded *Ellery Queen's Mystery Magazine*, one of the most influential crime publications of all time.

Otto Penzler, the creator of American Mystery Classics, is also the founder of the Mysterious Press (1975); MysteriousPress.com (2011), an electronic-book publishing company; and New York City's Mysterious Bookshop (1979). He has won a Raven, the Ellery Queen Award, two Edgars (for the *Encyclopedia of Mystery and Detection*, 1977, and *The Lineup*, 2010), and lifetime achievement awards from NoirCon and *The Strand Magazine*. He has edited more than 70 anthologies and written extensively about mystery fiction.

This is a work of fiction. Names, characters, places, and incidents either are the product of the author's imagination or are used fictitiously. Any resemblance to actual persons, living or dead, businesses, companies, events, or locales is entirely coincidental.

Published in 2025 by Penzler Publishers
58 Warren Street, New York, NY 10007
penzlerpublishers.com

Cover image: Andy Ross
Cover design: Mauricio Diaz

Paperback ISBN 978-1-61316-669-7
Hardcover ISBN 978-1-61316-668-0

Library of Congress Control Number: 2024950104

Printed in the United States of America

9 8 7 6 5 4 3 2 1

THE TRAGEDY OF X

ELLERY
QUEEN

writing as
Barnaby Ross

Introduction by
OTTO
PENZLER

AMERICAN
MYSTERY
CLASSICS

Penzler Publishers
New York

INTRODUCTION

During what is often called the Golden Age of the detective novel, the years between the two World Wars produced some of the most iconic names in the history of mystery. In England, the names Agatha Christie and Dorothy L. Sayers continue to resonate to the present day. In America, there is one name that towers above the rest, and that is Ellery Queen.

If pressed, mystery readers would struggle to say whether that name resonates more as the name of the author or of the character. That famous name was the brainchild of two Brooklyn-born cousins, Frederic Dannay (born Daniel Nathan, he changed his name to Frederic as a tribute to Chopin, with Dannay merely a combination of the first two syllables of his birth name) and Manfred B. Lee (born Manford Lepofsky). They wanted a simple nom de plume and had the brilliant stroke of inspiration to employ Ellery Queen as both their byline and as the name of their protagonist, reckoning that readers might forget one or the other but not both.

It evidently worked wonderfully, as evidenced by the pronouncement of Anthony Boucher, the mystery reviewer for the

New York Times: "Ellery Queen *is* the American detective story." It would be impossible for any reasonable person to disagree.

However, while still caught up in the first excitement of their earliest publications, they had additional plans, one of which was to create another memorable character. They succeeded with the eccentric genius Drury Lane.

Dannay and Lee combined to write a letter to the reader in the 1940 reprint of *The Tragedy of X* (originally published in 1932), coming out of their secret closet to admit that they had written four novels about Lane. That letter is included in this edition and you will be fascinated by their ingenious plan to promote these novels as well as those about Ellery Queen.

The Queen and Lane figures are diametrically opposite, with the young Queen an urban man-about-town, relatively normal aside from the snooty snobbery (of the early adventures), while the elderly Lane is somewhat remote, eccentrically living in a rural castle with a staff of retired actors who he dresses as characters based on Shakespearean roles.

The authors saw fit to open this first Drury Lane novel by providing a long biography of the former actor with an excerpt from the 1930 edition of *Who's Who of Drama* listing the highlights of his extraordinary career.

Deafness forced the wealthy actor to leave the stage and retire to his magnificent manor, named the Hamlet, a castle overlooking the Hudson River, surrounded by his old friends. His most important retainer is Quacey, a hunchback who was his loyal wigmaker and makeup man for more than forty years.

Lane's detective career begins when he solves a case without ever leaving his home, making deductions merely from the information he gleans from newspapers. While that first letter, sent to the New York Police Department and the district attorney, was unsolicited, D.A. Bruno and Inspector Thumm soon come to rely on him to clear up their most baffling cases.

While the Drury Lane series had success, as evidenced by the large number of reprints they had in the 1930s and 1940s, they never managed to approach the enthusiastic following enjoyed by the Ellery Queen character. The series ended after only three more novels: *The Tragedy of Y* (1932), *The Tragedy of Z* (1933), and *Drury Lane's Last Case* (1933), an excellent bibliomystery involving the theft of Shakespearean manuscripts from the fictional Britannic Museum on New York City's Fifth Avenue.

The authors worked together for more than forty years on novels, short stories, and radio dramas. Dannay was a copywriter and art director for an advertising agency while Lee was writing publicity and advertising material for a motion picture company when they were attracted by a $7,500 prize offered by *McClure's* magazine in 1928; they were twenty-three years old.

They were informed that their submission, *The Roman Hat Mystery*, had won the contest but, before the book could be published or the prize money handed over, *McClure's* went bankrupt. Its assets were assumed by *Smart Set* magazine, which gave the prize to a different novel that it thought would have greater appeal to women. Frederick A. Stokes decided to publish *The Roman Hat Mystery* anyway, thus beginning one of the most successful mystery series in the history of the genre. Since the contest had required that books be submitted under pseudonyms, the simple but memorable Ellery Queen name, born out of necessity, became an icon.

The success of the novels got them Hollywood offers and they went to write for Columbia, Paramount, and MGM, though they never received any screen credits. The popular medium of radio also called to them and they wrote all the scripts for the successful *Ellery Queen* radio series for nine years, from 1939 to 1948.

In an innovative approach, they interrupted the narration so that Ellery could ask his guests—well-known personalities—to solve the case because, as he told them, they now had all the necessary clues. The theories that were offered were almost invariably in vain so the program would then proceed, revealing the correct solution. The Queen character was also translated into a comic strip character and several television series starring Richard Hart, Lee Bowman, Hugh Marlowe, George Nader, Lee Philips, and, finally, Jim Hutton.

While Lee had no particular affection for mystery fiction, always hoping to become the Shakespeare of the twentieth century, Dannay had been interested in detective stories since his boyhood. He wanted to produce a magazine of quality mystery stories in all sub-genres and founded *Mystery* in 1933 but it failed after four issues when the publisher went bankrupt. However, after Dannay's long convalescence from a 1940 automobile accident that nearly took his life, he created *Ellery Queen's Mystery Magazine*; the first issue appeared in 1941 and remains the world's leading mystery fiction magazine to the present day.

Although Dannay and Lee were lifelong writing collaborators, they had very different personalities and frequently disagreed, often vehemently, in what Lee once described as "a marriage made in hell."

Dannay was a quiet, scholarly introvert, noted as a perfectionist. Lee was impulsive and assertive, given to explosiveness and earthy language. They remained steadfast in their refusal to divulge their working methodology, claiming that over their many years together they had tried every possible combination of their skills and talent to produce the best work they could. However, upon close examination of their letters and conversations with their friends and family, it eventually became clear that, in almost all instances, it was Dannay who created the extraordinary plots and Lee who brought them to life.

Each resented the other's ability, with Dannay once writing that he was aware that Lee regarded him as nothing more than "a clever contriver." Dannay's ingenious plots, fiendishly detailed with strict adherence to the notion of playing fair with readers, remain unrivalled by any American mystery author. Yet he lacked the literary skill required to make characters plausible, settings visual, or dialogue resonant. Lee, on the other hand, with his dreams of writing important fiction, had little ability to invent stories, although he could improve his cousin's creations to make the characters come to life and the plots suspenseful and compelling.

The combined skills of the collaborators produced the memorable Ellery Queen figure, though in the early books he was clearly based on the best-selling Philo Vance character created by S.S. Van Dine. The Vance books had taken the country by storm in the 1920s so it was no great leap of imagination for Dannay and Lee to model their detective after him. In all candor, both Vance and the early Queen character were insufferable, showing off their supercilious attitude and pedantry at every possible opportunity.

When Queen made his debut in *The Roman Hat Mystery*, he was ostensibly an author but spent precious little time working at his career. He appears to have had unlimited time to collect books and help his father, Inspector Richard Queen, solve cases. Although close to his father, the arrogant young man is often condescending to him as he loves to show off his erudition. As the series progresses (and as America's appetite for Philo Vance diminished), Ellery becomes a far more realistic and likable character.

One characteristic of the Queen novels is an opening situation in which a murder is committed that appears so confounding that it may be insoluble. If it weren't, the police would handle it and not have to bring Ellery Queen to the scene to help them figure out what happened, how it was achieved, and who did it.

The tantalizing puzzles created by the Ellery Queen writing team are irresistible to anyone who enjoys fair-play detective stories, no matter how outré or impossible they may seem.

We selected *The Chinese Orange Mystery* as the first book in the American Mystery Classics series because it features one of the most extraordinary scenes in the history of mystery fiction and have continued publishing Queen detective fiction ever since, *The Tragedy of X* being the tenth book by these remarkable authors.

We are confident that you will agree that these have been the right choices—with more Queen novels tempting us. After you have read one or two, you will understand why the London *Times* wrote that "Ellery Queen is the logical successor to Sherlock Holmes."

—Otto Penzler
New York City
July 2025

An Open Letter
TO THE READER

Dear Reader:

Nine years ago two young men, who had been collaborating under the single pen-name of Ellery Queen, were persuaded by certain persons and events to write a new series of mystery stories.

The result of their supplementary labors was the creation of *Mr. Drury Lane,* an aged Shakespearean actor with wonderful sleuthing powers.

Obviously the series celebrating the exploits of *Mr. Drury Lane* could not be publicly attributed to Ellery Queen, since the Ellery Queen books celebrated the exploits of *Mr. Ellery Queen.*

So the two young men fashioned a second pen-name; and the introductory book of the *Drury Lane* tetralogy, "The Tragedy of X," burst upon an unexcited world as written by one "Barnaby Ross."

Now to all intents and purposes there was no relationship between Ellery Queen the author(s) and Barnaby Ross the author(s). Each was published by a different house; around each was hopefully woven a great deal of mumbo-jumbo and secrecy;

in fact, in one phase of that duo-pseudonymous period in the public lives of the two young men, they actually glared at each other across many unfriendly lecture platforms, each secure behind the barricade of a domino mask . . . one posing as Ellery Queen, the other as Barnaby Ross, and both pretending furiously to be bitter rivals in the field of mystery authorship. Not all the things they said to each other in the curious hearing of lecture audiences from Maplewood, New Jersey to Chicago, Illinois were complimentary, thus by sheer sculduggery preserving the illusion, of rugged individualism.

Nevertheless, a cunning clue has always existed which, if spotted by the alert armchair-detective, would unquestionably establish the relationship between Ellery Queen and Barnaby Ross, and would expose the vile deception they practised upon the trusting public these last nine years.

For if you will turn to the *Foreword* of "The Roman Hat Mystery" (the first book written by and about Ellery Queen), you will find on page x, lines seventeen to twenty-two, the following remarkable revelation:

> "It was said, for example, at the time of his brilliant detectival efforts during the now-ancient *Barnaby-Ross* murder-case, that 'Richard Queen by this feat firmly establishes his fame beside such masters of crime-detection as. . . .'"

It was from this apocryphal excerpt that "Barnaby Ross" was selected when it became necessary to create a new pen-name—so that Barnaby Ross was really born in the year 1928, at the time the *Foreword* to the first Queen book was written, although it was not until the year 1931 that he was publicly baptized by his fathers and moved into a house of his own.

So now it can be told: Barnaby Ross was, and is, and will forever be . . . Ellery Queen; and *vice versa.*

A word about *Mr. Drury Lane.* We've always kept a soft spot in our hearts for the old coot, who was half ham and half ruffed grouse . . . mountebank and genius, and quite the most extraordinary detective who ever lived (except, perhaps, one who shall be nameless).

Like his brother (weren't they sired by the same Machiavellian young men?), *Mr. Drury Lane* stems from the deductive school—that special branch of which makes a fetish of fairness to the reader; so that in "The Tragedy of X," as in the *Tragedies* to follow, you will find all the clues given to you before the dénouement is reached.

So in this solemn hour of resurrection . . . *Vive Drury Lane!*

Sincerely,

"Ellery Queen"

Friday the 13th of September, 1940
New York

List of Scenes

Something About

MR. DRURY LANE

EXCERPTA COMPILED FOR THE PUBLISHER
BY MR. CHARLES GLEN FROM PRELIMINARY NOTES
ON HIS UNFINISHED LANE BIOGRAPHY

Excerpt from Who's Who of the Drama, *1930 edition:*

LANE, DRURY, actor; *b.* New Orleans, La., Nov. 3, 1871; *s.* Richard Lane, American tragedian, and Kitty Purcell, the English music-hall comedienne; unmarried. Education, privately tutored. First stage appearance, at the age of 7; first important rôle at the age of 13 in Kiralfy's "Enchantment," Boston Theatre; first featured at the age of 23 in "Hamlet," Daly's Theatre, N. Y.; in 1909, in Drury Lane Theatre, London, gave longest "Hamlet" run of consecutive performances until that time—24 longer than previous record established by Edwin Booth. *Author:* Shakespeariana, The Philosophy of Hamlet, Curtain Calls, *etc., etc. Clubs:* Players, Lambs, Century, Franklin Inn, Coffee House. Member of American Academy of Arts and Letters. Honorary Member, French Legion of Honor. *Home:* The Hamlet, overlooking Hudson River, N. Y. (railway station: Lanecliff, Westchester County). Retired from the stage, 1928.

Excerpt from New York World *story of Mr. Drury Lane's announced retirement from the stage (1928):*

". . . Drury Lane was born backstage in a second-rate stock theater, the Comus, in New Orleans during the period in the Lane fortunes when Richard was 'at liberty' and Kitty was forced to return to the boards for the purpose of supporting them and the coming child. . . . Her unfortunate death in childbirth being caused by her exertions before the footlights, the child . . . born prematurely in her dressing-room after the first act. . . .

". . . so that Drury Lane was virtually reared on the stage, dragged from theater to theater by his struggling father, living in cheap quarters from hand to mouth. His first words were theatrical; his nurses actors and actresses; his education dramatic. . . . Taking small rôles as soon as he could walk . . . Richard Lane died in 1887 of pleurisy-pneumonia, his last words a hoarse admonition to his sixteen-year-old son: 'Be an actor.' But even Richard's aspirations for his son fell far short of the heights to which the young Drury eventually rose. . . .

". . . His peculiar name, he said recently, having been deliberately chosen by his parents because of the great theatrical tradition surrounding the hoary Drury Lane Theatre. . . .

". . . said that his retirement is being caused by a growing deafness in both ears—a condition which has now become so aggravated that he is no longer able to differentiate to his own satisfaction between the varying tonal qualities of his voice. . . .

". . . The only exception to Mr. Lane's decision to forsake his beloved rôles is a curious one. On April 23rd of each year, he says, he will perform 'Hamlet' on the full stage of his private theater on his Hudson estate. He has reverently chosen this date because it is the commonly accepted anniversary both of Shakespeare's birth and death. It is interesting to recall that Mr. Drury

Lane has played this rôle more than five hundred times to record houses all over the English-speaking world."

Excerpt from article in Country Estates, *describing Mr. Drury Lane's estate, The Hamlet:*

". . . The estate itself is constructed in the purest Elizabethan architectural tradition, consisting of a huge manorial castle surrounded by a miniature village in which Mr. Lane's personnel abide. Each house in the village is a faithful replica of an Elizabethan cottage, with characteristic thatched roof, peaked gables, etc. All are appointed with modern conveniences, which are cleverly disguised so as not to disturb the period feeling. . . . Splendid gardening; for example, hedgerows imported by Mr. Lane's experts from rural England. . . ."

Excerpt from Raoul Molyneux's critique in La Peinture, *Paris, 1927, of the oils portrait of Mr. Drury Lane, by Paul Révissons:*

". . . just as I saw him on my last visit. . . . The tall spare frame, quiet and yet somehow vibrant, the shock of pure white hair worn low on the neck, the gray-green penetrating eyes, the perfectly regular—almost classic—features, so expressionless at first glance and yet so capable of lightning mobility. . . . He is standing uncompromisingly, as erect as Charlemagne, his right arm draped with the inevitable black cape, his right hand resting lightly on the knob of his famous blackthorn stick, his black straight-brimmed felt hat on the table beside him. . . . This eerie effect of darkness accentuated by his somber clothing . . . yet lightened by the queerest feeling that this man has but to flick a finger and all the habiliments of the modern world will tumble to his feet, leaving him a brilliant figure out of the past. . . ."

Excerpt from letter of Mr. Drury Lane to District Attorney Bruno of New York County dated September 5, *193—*:

"I am taking the liberty of intruding upon the duties of your office by attaching a rather lengthy analysis, compiled entirely by myself, concerning the current police problem of who killed John Cramer.

"My data came completely from what I have been able to glean from the sometimes unsatisfactory newspaper articles on the case. Nevertheless, when you examine my analysis and solution I think you will agree with me that the juxtaposition of certain facts leads to only one tenable conclusion.

"Please do not take this as a presumption on the part of an aging and retired man. I have become intensely interested in crime, and my services are at your command in any future case in which the solution seems impossible or obscure."

Telegram received at The Hamlet, September 7, 193—:

CONFESSION SUBSTANTIATES YOUR REMARKABLE SOLUTION OF CRAMER CASE STOP MAY INSPECTOR THUMM AND I CALL TOMORROW MORNING TEN THIRTY TO OFFER SINCERE THANKS AND ALSO TO SECURE YOUR OPINION ON LONGSTREET MURDER

WALTER BRUNO

THE TRAGEDY OF X

WITH GRATITUDE TO

"TOM" MAHONY

WHO HAS BROUGHT MR. DRURY LANE

BACK FROM THE DEAD

Dramatis Personæ

HARLEY LONGSTREET, *a broker*

JOHN O. DEWITT, *his partner*

MRS. FERN DEWITT

JEANNE DEWITT

CHRISTOPHER LORD, *her fiancé*

FRANKLIN AHEARN, *a neighbor*

CHERRY BROWNE, *an actress*

POLLUX, *an actor*

LOUIS IMPERIALE, *a visitor from abroad*

MICHAEL COLLINS, *a politician*

LIONEL BROOKS, *a lawyer*

FREDERICK LYMAN, *a lawyer*

CHARLES WOOD, *a conductor*

ANNA PLATT, *a secretary*

JUAN AJOS, *consul from Uruguay*

DISTRICT ATTORNEY WALTER BRUNO

INSPECTOR THUMM

DR. SCHILLING, *Medical Examiner*

MR. DRURY LANE

QUACEY, *his familiar*

FALSTAFF, *his major-domo*

DROMIO, *his chauffeur*

KROPOTKIN, *his director*

HOF, *his scenic designer*

Witnesses, Officers, Officials, Servants, Attendants, Etc.

Scene: NEW YORK CITY AND ENVIRONS

Time: THE PRESENT

Act I: *Scene 1*

THE HAMLET. TUESDAY, SEPTEMBER 8. 10:30 A.M.

BELOW, SHIMMERING in a blue haze, was the Hudson River; a white sail scudded by; a placid steamboat waddled upstream.

The automobile pushed its way along the narrow winding road, rising steadily. Its two passengers looked out and up. Far above, framed in cloud, were unbelievable medieval turrets, stone ramparts, crenelated battlements, a queerly ancient church-spire. Its needlepoint rose out of a sturdy forest of green.

The two looked at each other. "I'm beginning to feel like the Connecticut Yankee," said one, shivering slightly. The other, large and square, growled: "Knights in armor, hey?"

The car slammed to a stop at a quaint rude bridge. From a thatched hut near by stepped a ruddy little old man. He pointed wordlessly at a swinging wooden sign above the door which said, in old English characters:

No Trespassing
The Hamlet

The large square man leaned out of the automobile window and yelled: "We want to see Drury Lane!"

"Yes, *sir.*" The little old man hopped forward. "And your admission cards, gentlemen?"

The visitors stared and the first man shrugged. The large man said sharply: "Mr. Lane expects us."

"Oh." The bridgemaster scratched his gray poll and disappeared into his hut. He returned in a moment, briskly. "I beg your pardon, gentlemen. This way." He scuttled forward to the bridge, manipulated a creaking iron gate, stood back. The car rolled over the bridge, picking up speed on a clean gravel road.

A short drive through the green oak forest and the car emerged into a spacious clearing. The castle, a sleeping giant, sprawled before them, staked to the Hudson hills by puny granite walls. A massive iron-hasped door swung back groaning from the wall as the car approached; and another old man stood aside, tugging at his cap and smiling cheerfully.

They were on another road winding through a riot of cultivated gardens, guarded from the driveway by mathematically precise hedges and punctuated by yew trees. To right and left, off side lanes, gabled cottages rose from the gardens, dipping into gentle swales like houses out of fairyland. In the center of a flower garden near by water dripped from a stone Ariel. . . .

They came at last to the stronghold itself. Again, on their approach, an old man anticipated their coming and a monstrous drawbridge clanked forward over the sparkling waters of a moat. The immense oak-and-iron door beyond the drawbridge, twenty feet high, opened on the instant; an astonishingly rubicund little man attired in twinkling livery stood there, bowing and smiling and scraping as if he were enjoying a vast secret jest.

The visitors, eyes wide with amazement, scrambled from their vehicle and thundered across the iron bridge.

"District Attorney Bruno? Inspector Thumm? This way, please." The pot-bellied old servitor repeated his calisthenic welcome and trudged cheerfully before them into the sixteenth century.

They stood in a manorial hall of a vasty awesomeness. Hugely beamed ceilings. Winking metal-armored knights. Pegged old pieces. On the farthest wall, dominating even that Valhalla, leered a gargantuan mask of Comedy and on the opposite wall frowned a twin mask of Tragedy; they were carved out of time-bitten oak. Between them, from the ceiling, hung a prodigious candelabra of wrought iron, its giant candles outwardly innocent of electrical wiring.

Out of a door set in the farthest wall now stepped a queer figure from the past, a hunchbacked ancient—bald, bewhiskered, wrinkled, wearing a tattered leather apron like a blacksmith. The District Attorney and Inspector Thumm looked at each other and the Inspector muttered: "Are they *all* old men?"

The old hunchback came spryly forward to greet them. "Good day, gentlemen. Welcome to The Hamlet." He spoke in clipped and creaking tones, grotesquely as if he were unaccustomed to speaking at all. He turned to the old man in livery and said: "*Whisht*, Falstaff," and District Attorney Bruno opened his wide eyes even wider.

"Falstaff . . ." he groaned. "Why, it's simply impossible. That *can't* be his name!"

The hunchback ruffled his whiskers. "No, sir. He used to be Jake Pinna, the actor. But that's what Mr. Drury calls him. . . . This way, please."

He conducted them back across the booming floor to the same little portal from which he had come. He touched the wall; the door slid open. An elevator in this courtier-haunted place! Shaking their heads, they entered the cubicle followed by their guide. They were whisked upward; the elevator softly stopped; another little door popped open at once, and the hunchback said: "Mr. Lane's private apartments."

Massive, massive, old. . . . Everything was old and flavored and redolent of Elizabethan England. Leather and oak, oak and stone. In a fireplace twelve feet wide, topped by a solid beam bronzed by age and smoke, a small fire was burning. Bruno, his brown eyes alert, was suddenly grateful for the heat; the air was slightly chill.

They sank into great old chairs at their guide's gnomish gesture, crossing glances of wonder. The ancient stood very still near the wall, grasping his beard; then he stirred and said, quite clearly: "Mr. Drury Lane."

Involuntarily the two men rose; a tall man stood regarding them from the threshold. The hunchback was bobbing his head now, a weird grin on his leathery old face. In spite of themselves, and to their own helpless consternation, the District Attorney and the Inspector found themselves bowing too.

Mr. Drury Lane strode into the room and extended a pale muscular hand. "Gentlemen. I'm delighted. Please sit down."

Bruno looked deeply into gray-green eyes of utter quietude; he began to speak and was startled to observe the eyes drop sharply to his own lips. "Good of you to receive Inspector Thumm and myself, Mr. Lane," he murmured. "We—well, we don't know quite what to say. You have an amazing estate, sir."

"Amazing at first glance, Mr. Bruno, but only because it presents to the twentieth-century eye, surfeited with severe angles, an anachronistic quaintness." The actor's voice was serene, like his eyes, but richer, it seemed to Bruno, than any voice he had ever heard before. "On closer acquaintance you will grow to love it, as I do. The Hamlet, one of my colleagues once said, is a backdrop, a scenic effect with the proscenium arch of these lovely hills as a frame. But for me it lives and breathes, a chunk out of the best of old England. . . . Quacey!"

The hunchback stepped to the actor's side. Lane's hand strayed to the ancient's hump. "Gentlemen, this is Quacey, my inseparable familiar and, I assure you, a genius. He has been my make-up man for forty years."

Quacey bobbed again and in some manner mysteriously warm the two visitors sensed the link of mellow kinship between these completely antitypical individuals. So Bruno and Thumm began to speak at once; and Lane's eyes flickered from the lips of one to the lips of the other, and the expressionless lines of his face curved into the merest smile. "Separately, please. I am quite deaf, you see. I can read only one pair of lips at a time—a latter-day accomplishment of which I am very vain."

They stammered apologies and while they settled themselves in their chairs Lane pulled another, surely the great-grandfather of all old chairs, from before the fire and sat down facing them. Inspector Thumm noticed that Lane had set his chair so that the firelight fell on his visitors' faces, leaving his own features in shadow. Quacey had effaced himself; out of the corner of his eye Thumm barely saw that he was crouched, motionless, a gnarled brown gargoyle, in a chair against the farthest wall.

Bruno cleared his throat. "Inspector Thumm and I both feel, Mr. Lane, that we're presuming a bit in coming to you this way. I should never have sent my telegram, of course, if you hadn't solved the Cramer case for us in that really astounding letter of yours."

"Scarcely astounding in its essence, Mr. Bruno." The slow resonant voice came from the depths of the coronal chair. "My action is not entirely unprecedented. You will recall the series of letters Edgar Allan Poe sent to the New York newspapers offering a solution of the Mary Rogers murder. The truth, it seemed to me on analysis of the Cramer case, was obscured by three facts which had nothing at all to do with the solution. Unfortunately, you gentlemen went off on these tangents. You wished to consult me on the Longstreet murder?"

"Are you sure, Mr. Lane, that the Inspector and I—— Well, we know how busy you are."

"I shall never be too busy to dabble in the most elemental form of drama, Mr. Bruno." The voice was colored now with the faintest animation. "It was only after my forced retirement from the stage that I began to realize how theatrical life itself can be. The boards are restrictive, cramping. The creatures of a play are, in Mercutio's evaluation of dreams, 'children of an idle brain begot of nothing but vain fantasy.'" The visitors stirred at the magic that had leaped into Lane's voice. "Creatures of life, however, in their moments of passion present the larger aspects of drama. They can never be 'as thin of substance as the air and more inconstant than the wind.'"

"I see," said the District Attorney slowly. "I see now. Yes, it's quite clear now."

"Crime—the crime of violence induced by mastering emotion—is the highest refinement of the human drama. Murder is its own peculiar climax. All my life, in company with my distinguished brothers and sisters of the fraternity"—he smiled sadly—"Modjeska, Edwin Booth, Ada Rehan, and all those glorious others—I have been interpreting synthetic emotional climaxes. Now I intend if I can to interpret the real thing. I think I can bring to this pursuit a rather unique equipment. I have murdered on the stage countless times; emotionally I have suffered the agony of plotting, the torture of conscience. I have been, among others perhaps less noble, Macbeth, and I have been Hamlet. And, like a child viewing a simple wonder for the first time, I have just realized that the world is full of Macbeths and Hamlets. Trite, but true. . . .

"From obeying the jerk of the master's strings, I now have the impulse to pull the strings myself, in a greater authorship than created drama. Everything fits so nicely; even my unfortunate affliction"—a lean finger touched his ear—"has contrived to sharpen my powers of concentration. I have only to close my eyes and I am in a world without sound and therefore without physical disturbance. . . ."

Inspector Thumm looked bewildered; he seemed immersed in an emotion foreign to his practical nature. He blinked and wondered if this was—and scoffed inwardly—hero-worship.

"You see what I mean," the voice drove on. "I have understanding. I have background. I have insight. I have observation. I have concentration. I lay claim to deductive and detective powers."

Bruno coughed. Those disturbing eyes fastened themselves on his lips. "I'm afraid, Mr. Lane, I'm afraid that our little problem is quite beneath the—well, the dignity of your detective ambitions. It's really just a plain case of murder. . . ."

"I'm disposed to think that I haven't made myself clear." The voice was brimming with humor now. "'A plain case of murder,' Mr. Bruno? But—exactly! Why should I require a fantastic one?"

"Well," said Inspector Thumm suddenly, "plain or fancy, it's a puzzler, and Mr. Bruno thought you'd be interested. Did you read the newspaper stories on the case?"

"Yes. But they're confused and meaningless. I prefer to approach the problem with an unetched perception. Please give me a scrupulously detailed account, Inspector. Describe the people involved. Relate the surrounding circumstances, no matter how apparently irrelevant or insignificant. In a word, tell me everything."

Bruno and Thumm exchanged glances; Bruno nodded and Inspector Thumm's ugly face screwed itself into a narrative expression.

The vast walls faded away. The fire, as if operated by a cosmic rheostat, dimmed. And The Hamlet, Mr. Drury Lane, the tang of old things and old times and old people fused and were submerged under the gruff tones of the Inspector.

Scene 2

A SUITE IN THE HOTEL GRANT.
FRIDAY, SEPTEMBER 4. 3:30 P.M.

ON THE previous Friday afternoon (ran the story from the facts related by Inspector Thumm and interpolations occasionally contributed by the District Attorney), two people sat closely embraced in the sitting-room of a suite at the Hotel Grant, steel-and-concrete hostelry on the corner of Forty-Second Street and Eighth Avenue, in New York.

They were man and woman—the man, Harley Longstreet, tall, middle-aged, of powerful body ravaged by years of dissipation, unhealthily crimson face, dressed in rough tweeds; the woman, Cherry Browne, musical comedy star, a brunette with Latin features, black flashing eyes, arched lips; a woman bold and passionate.

Longstreet kissed her with wet lips and she cuddled in his arms. "I hope they never come."

"So you like the old boy's lovin'?" The man disengaged himself and flexed his muscles with the pride of the athletic male gone to seed. "They'll come, though—they'll be here. When I tell Johnny DeWitt to jump, believe me, sister—he jumps!"

"But why drag him here with that frosty bunch of his if they don't want to come?"

"Because I like to see the old buzzard squirm. He hates my guts, and I love it. To hell with him."

He dumped the woman unceremoniously from his lap, crossed the room, and poured himself a drink from one of an array of bottles on a sideboard. The woman watched him with feline laziness.

"Sometimes," she said, "I can't figure you out. What you get out of tormenting him is beyond me." She shrugged her white shoulders. "Well, that's your affair. Drink hearty!"

Longstreet grunted, threw his head far back, poured the drink down his throat. For the fraction of an instant his head remained that way when the actress continued in an indifferent voice: "Is Mrs. DeWitt coming, too?"

He tossed the whisky glass to the sideboard. "Why not? Now don't go harping on her again, Cherry. I've told you a hundred times there's nothing between us and there never was."

"Not that I care." She laughed. "But it would be just like you to steal his wife, too. . . . Who else is coming?"

He grimaced. "A prize bunch. God, how I love to see DeWitt pull that long pious face of his! There's his side kick out in West Englewood, this fellow Ahearn—regular old woman, always complaining about his belly. Belly!" he regarded his own slight paunch in a bleary way. "These straight-living preachers always seem to have floating guts; none of that for Longie, darling! Then there's little Jeanne DeWitt, and she hates me, too, and her daddy'll make her come, and it will be one sweet party. Especially when her Frank Merriwell boy-friend, Kit Lord, shows up."

"Why, he's an awfully nice boy, Harl."

Longstreet glared. "Sure. Nice boy. He's a prig, that's what he is. Nosey busybody. Can't stand that milk-faced kid around the office. I should have made DeWitt kick him out that time. . . . Oh, well." He sighed. "Then there's another—he'll give you a laugh. A Swiss cheese-eater." He laughed unpleasantly. "Louis Imperiale. I've told you about him. Friend of DeWitt's in the States on business. . . . And, of course, Mike Collins."

Cherry jumped up at the sound of a buzzer and hurried to the door.

"Pollux, old-timer! Come in!"

The arrival, a flashily dressed, oldish man with a dark face, carefully pomaded thinning hair, and a sharply waxed mustache, put his arms around the woman. Longstreet struggled to his feet and made a threatening noise in his throat. Cherry Browne blushed, pushed the newcomer away, and began to fuss with her hair.

"Remember my old pal Pollux?" Her voice was gay. "Pollux, the Great Pollux, Master Mind-Reader of the Age on the two-a-day. Shake hands, you two."

Pollux limply complied and made at once for the sideboard. Longstreet shrugged and returned to his chair, but rose immediately as the buzzer sounded again and Cherry opened the door to admit a small party of people.

A little slender middle-aged man with gray hair and a brush-gray mustache came in first, hesitantly. Longstreet's face brightened; he strode forward, exuding cordiality. He boomed greetings, squeezed the little man's hand. John O. DeWitt colored and half-closed his eyes with pain and nausea. Physical opposites, they were in striking contrast: DeWitt reserved, lined with worry, and apparently in a constant state of fluctuating determination and apprehension; Longstreet heavy, assured, arrogant, masterful.

DeWitt shrank from Longstreet as the big man brushed by him to receive the other members of the party.

"Fern! This is a nice surprise."—This to a faded stoutish woman of Spanish type, with the barest traces of a vanished beauty on her lacquered face; DeWitt's wife. Jeanne DeWitt, a petite brownish maid, nodded coldly; she pressed closer to her escort, Christopher Lord, a tall blond young man. Longstreet ignored him completely and pumped the hands of Ahearn and Imperiale, a middle-aged Latin of large physique meticulously dressed. "Mike!"

Longstreet bounded forward and clapped the back of a broad man who had just slouched through the door. Michael Collins was a brawny Irishman with porcine eyes and an apparently fixed expression of hostility. He grunted a greeting and eyed the others dangerously. Longstreet grasped his arm; his eyes glittered. "Now don't crab this party, Mike," he whispered hoarsely. "I told you I'd get DeWitt to fix things up. Go over there and take a bracer—do you good."

Collins jerked his arm free and without a word lurched toward the sideboard.

Waiters appeared. Ice chimed in amber glasses. The DeWitt party were for the most part silent, strained—polite but uncomfortable. DeWitt himself sat on the edge of a chair, pale and impassive, sipping mechanically from a tall glass. But his knuckles were white about the glass.

Longstreet swooped Cherry Browne, demure and suddenly shy, into the curve of one great arm and yelled for attention. "Friends! You all know why you're here. Gala occasion for old Harley Longstreet. 'Fact, for the whole firm of DeWitt & Longstreet an' all their friends and well-wishers!" His voice was a little thick now; his face more brickish than before, his eyes pinpoints. "Have the honor to present to you—future Mrs. Longstreet!"

There was a conventional murmur. DeWitt rose and bowed, stiffly, to the actress, shook Longstreet's hand perfunctorily. Louis Imperiale strode forward and, gallantly, bent over the actress's manicured fingers, touching them with his lips as his heels clicked in military fashion. Mrs. DeWitt, seated beside her husband, gripped her handkerchief and made a ghastly attempt to smile. Pollux staggered from the sideboard and put his arm clumsily about Cherry's waist. Longstreet shoved him away without ceremony, and he returned to the sideboard, muttering drunkenly to himself.

The women admired an enormous flashing diamond on the actress's left hand. More waiters invaded the room, armed with tables and crockery. . . .

They ate lightly. Pollux fumbled with the dials of a radio. There was music, and spiritless dancing. Only Longstreet and Cherry Browne were gay; the big man romped like a child, caught Jeanne DeWitt in a playful embrace. Blond Christopher stepped between them coolly and the young couple danced away. Longstreet chuckled; Cherry was at his elbow, sweet, perilous. . . .

At 5:45 Longstreet silenced the radio and excitedly shouted: "Arranged a little dinner party at my place in West Englewood. F'got to tell you about it. Surprise, hey? Surprise!" he roared. "All invited. Mus' come. You too, Mike. An' you, there, Pollux, or what's-your-name—you can come 'long an' read our minds or something." He consulted his watch owlishly. "C'n make reg'lar train if we start now. C'mon, everybody!"

DeWitt protested in a strangled voice that he had made other arrangements for the evening, that his own guests . . . Longstreet glared. "I said everybody!" Imperiale shrugged and smiled; Lord regarded Longstreet with contempt—a faint puzzled light glowed in his eyes as he turned to look at DeWitt. . . .

At 5:50 exactly, the entire party left Cherry Browne's suite, strewn with débris, bottles, napkins, glasses. They crowded into an elevator, emerged downstairs in the hotel lobby. Longstreet bellowed for a boy, ordered a late newspaper and taxicabs.

Then they were on the sidewalk—outside the Forty-Second Street exit of the hotel. A doorman whistled desperately for taxicabs. The thoroughfare was jammed with crawling vehicles; overhead thunderclouds raced in a blackening sky. Weeks of dry hot weather gave way suddenly to a vicious downpour of rain.

When the deluge came, it came with such unexpectedness and force that the welter of pedestrian and vehicular traffic became a scrambled, jumpy, wriggling panorama of frenzied motion.

The doorman signaled wildly, looked back over his shoulder at Longstreet with comical despair. The party scurried for the shelter of a jewelry-shop awning nearer the corner of Eighth Avenue.

DeWitt edged close to Longstreet. "Before I forget. About Weber's complaint. Don't you think we ought to do what I suggested?" He poked an envelope at his partner.

Longstreet, right arm about Cherry Browne's waist, took a silver spectacle-case from the left pocket of his coat, jammed the case back into the pocket as he disengaged himself from the woman, and adjusted the eyeglasses to his nose. He took a typewritten letter from the envelope, skimmed through it negligently while DeWitt waited with half-closed eyes.

Longstreet sniffed. "Nothing doing." He flipped the letter

back toward DeWitt; it eluded the little man's clutch and fluttered to the wet sidewalk. Pale as death, DeWitt stooped and picked up the letter.

"Weber can like it or lump it. I won't change my mind. That's final, and don't bother me about it any more."

Pollux whooped: "Here comes a Crosstown. Let's grab it!"

In the snarl of traffic before them a red-faced, snub-nosed street-car was nudging its way. Longstreet snatched off his glasses, returned them to the case, and the case to his left pocket, leaving his hand there.

Cherry Browne was crushed against his great body; he waved his right hand. "Hell with cabs!" he shouted. "Let's take the car!"

The street-car squealed to a stop. A swarm of people, drenched and fighting mad, made for the opening back door. The Longstreet party dashed into the throng, struggling for entrance, Cherry Browne still clinging to Longstreet's left arm, Longstreet's left hand still in his pocket.

They reached the steps. The conductor's hoarse voice cried: "Lively! 'Board!"

The rain soaked their clothes.

DeWitt was squeezed between the ample bodies of Ahearn and Imperiale. They fought their way up, Imperiale cavalierly attempting to guide Mrs. DeWitt. He craned back now to Ahearn, crinkling his eyes with something of humor . . . saying *sotto voce* that this was the queerest party he had ever had the honor—diable!—to attend.

Scene 3

THE FORTY-SECOND STREET CROSSTOWN.
FRIDAY, SEPTEMBER 4. 6 P.M.

THEY WERE on the rear platform now, stifled in the hot wet crush, having managed by vigorous use of elbows and knees to push past the conductor's station. Longstreet towered near the inside step leading into the interior of the car, Cherry Browne releasing his left arm at this moment to follow as best she could the rest of the party.

The conductor had finally been able, while exercising his lungs and shoving passengers forward into the car, to swing shut the double yellow doors. The car, the back platform were freighted to capacity. People waved their fares, but the conductor did not accept money until the doors were tightly shut and he had signaled the motorman to proceed. A disappointed horde was left outside, huddled miserably in the rain.

Longstreet swayed with the rocking motion of the car, a dollar bill clutched in his right fist above the heads of his fellow-passengers on the rear platform. The interior was choking; the humidity, the windows closed throughout, induced an uncomfortable feeling of suffocation.

The conductor wriggled about, shouting commands still, and grabbed the bill from Longstreet's hand. The crowd was pushing and struggling, and Longstreet growled like an infuriated bear; but he finally received his change and began to shoulder his way after his party. He found Cherry Browne ahead of the others halfway through the car; she grasped his right arm and snuggled closer. Longstreet reached for a strap.

The car edged on toward Ninth Avenue in a downpour that roared more deafeningly with every foot of the tangled way.

Longstreet thrust his hand into his pocket and felt about for his spectacle-case. A moment of this, and with a sudden curse he snatched his hand from the pocket, bringing out the silver case. Cherry said: "What's the matter, Harl?" Longstreet uncertainly examined his left hand: the palm and underskin of the fingers were bleeding in a number of places. His eyes wavered, his heavy face twitched, and he breathed in a little nasal gust. "Must've scratched myself. What in the world could've . . . ?" he began thickly. The car lurched, staggered, and stopped; people fell irresistibly forward. Instinctively Longstreet groped for a strap with his left hand, and Cherry held on to his right arm for support. The car jerked forward again a few feet. Longstreet dabbed heavily at his bleeding hand with a handkerchief, returned the cloth to his trousers, extracted his glasses from the case, dropped the case into his pocket, and made as if to open the folded newspaper he held tucked under his right arm—all in a sort of growing fog.

The car had stopped at Ninth Avenue. A clamoring crowd had pounded on the closed doors, but the conductor shook his head. The rain was falling in increasing torrents and the car had crawled on again.

Longstreet suddenly released the strap, dropping the unread

newspaper, and felt his forehead. He was panting and groaning like a man in great pain. Cherry Browne hugged his right arm in alarm, turned as if to call for help. . . .

The car was between Ninth and Tenth Avenues now, stopping, starting, stopping, starting in the maze of traffic before it.

Longstreet gasped, stiffened convulsively, widened his eyes like a frightened child, and collapsed—a pricked balloon—across the lap of a young woman sitting directly before him.

A heavy-set man of middle age standing on Longstreet's left, who had been leaning over and talking with the young woman—a rather pretty brunette heavily rouged—angrily yanked at Longstreet's trailing arm. "Get up out of there, you! Where the hell do you think you are?" he shouted. But Longstreet merely slid from the lap of the young woman and slumped across their feet to the floor.

Cherry screamed, once.

Dead silence for an instant, then a growing hubbub as necks craned and the Longstreet party pushed their way toward the spot. "What's the matter?" "Longstreet!" "He's under!" "Drunk?" "Watch her—she's fainted!"

Michael Collins caught the actress as she reeled.

The rouged young woman and her burly escort, frightened now, were white and speechless. The girl jumped up, clutched the man's arm, stared with horror down at Longstreet crumpled on the floor. "Well, my God," she shrieked all at once, "why doesn't somebody do something? Look at his eyes! He's—he's . . ." She shuddered and buried her face in her escort's coat.

DeWitt stood stonily by, his small hands clenched. Ahearn and Christopher Lord struggled with the heavy body of Longstreet and managed to haul him into the girl's vacated seat. A middle-aged Italian quickly rose and helped stretch the recumbent man on the seat. Longstreet's eyes were staring; his mouth was partly open; he was gasping weakly; light flecks of foam dribbled from his lips.

The growing uproar penetrated well forward into the car. A shouted order, and the crowd parted sufficiently to allow a heavy-set policeman with sergeant's stripes on his sleeve to hustle his way through. He had been riding on the front platform with the motorman. The car had come to a stop by this time, and both motorman and conductor hurried to the spot.

The sergeant roughly shoved the Longstreet party aside and leaned over Longstreet. The body stiffened again, and then became quite rigid. The sergeant straightened up, scowling. "He's dead. Uh-huh!" He had caught sight of the dead man's left hand. More than a dozen tiny trickles of coagulating blood laced the skin of fingers and palm from as many tiny pricks, each swollen a little. "Murdered, looks like. Keep away now, the pack of you!"

He eyed the members of the party with suspicion. They were huddled together now, as if for mutual protection.

The sergeant roared: "I don't want anybody to get off this car—get me? Stay put! Here, you." He beckoned the motorman imperiously. "Don't move this car a foot. Get back to your station. *Keep* those doors and windows shut—understand?" The motorman disappeared. The sergeant yelled: "Hey, conductor! Run down to the corner of Tenth Avenue and tell the traffic cop on duty there to phone the local precinct and tell the traffic cop to make sure it gets to Inspector Thumm at headquarters. Got that straight? Here—I'll let you out myself. I ain't taking any chance on somebody giving me the slip through the open door."

He escorted the conductor to the rear platform, operated the lever which opened the double doors, and closed them the instant the conductor had stepped out into the rain. The conductor headed for Tenth Avenue on the run. The sergeant glowered at a tall hard-looking passenger on the platform. "You watch that no one touches these doors, Bud—see?" The passenger nodded happily, and the sergeant thrust his way back to Longstreet's body.

A bedlam of cursing, horn-tooting traffic had piled up behind the street-car. The frightened passengers could see people endeavoring to press their faces to the streaming windows. The tall hard-looking passenger shouted: "Hey, Sarge, there's a cop wants to get in back here!"

"Wait a minute!" Back plodded the sergeant and opened the doors himself to admit a traffic officer, who saluted and said: "I'm on duty at Ninth. What's the trouble, Sergeant? Need help?"

"Looks like a bump-off here." The sergeant closed the doors and gestured significantly to the tall passenger, who again nodded. "Guess I'll need you, Officer. Put in a call already for Inspector Thumm and the precinct. You go forward to that front door and see that no one gets on or off. Watch those doors."

They pushed forward together, the newcomer hurling people aside in his effort to reach the forward platform.

The sergeant stood, arms akimbo, over Longstreet's body and glared about him. "Well, who's first?" he demanded. "Who was sittin' in these seats?" The young woman and the middle-aged Italian began to speak at the same time. "One at a time. What's *your* name?"

The girl quavered: "Emily Jewett. I—I'm a stenographer going home from work. This man—he fell into my lap a while ago. I got up and gave him my seat."

"How about you, Mussolini?"

"I'm Antonio Fontana. I see-a nothing. This-a man, he fall, an' I get up an' give-a him my seat," replied the Italian. "This dead man—he was standin' up?"

DeWitt thrust his way forward. He was perfectly calm. "Here, Sergeant, I can tell you exactly what happened. This man was Harley Longstreet, my business partner. We were going in a party——"

"Party, huh?" The sergeant eyed them all sourly: "Some party, I'd say. Nice and friendly. You better save your breath, Mister. Inspector Thumm'll get it out of you. Here comes the conductor with another cop."

He hurried back to the rear platform. The conductor, water streaming from the visor of his cap, was hammering on the rear doors. A policeman stood by his side. The sergeant opened the doors himself, admitted them, and closed the doors at once.

The policeman touched his cap. "Morrow reporting. On duty at Tenth Avenue."

"Oke. I'm Duffy, Sergeant, 18th Precinct," said the sergeant gruffly. "Call headquarters?"

"Yep, and the precinct, too. Inspector Thumm and local men will be here any minute. Inspector said for you to take the car to the Green Lines carbarn at Forty-Second and Twelfth. He'll meet you there. Says not to touch the body. I also called for an ambulance."

"He doesn't need that any more. Morrow, you stay here at this door and don't let anybody get out."

Duffy turned to the tall hard-faced man on the rear platform. "Did anybody try to make a getaway, Bud? Was that door opened at all?"

"Nope." And a chorus of assent from other passengers.

Duffy plowed his way to the front of the car. "Motorman! Take 'er to the end of the line. Park in the Green Lines carbarn. Snap into it!"

The motorman, a red-faced young Irishman, mumbled: "That

ain't our barn, Sergeant. This is the Third Avenue Railways line. We ain't——"

"Scram, will you?" said Sergeant Duffy disgustedly. He turned to the Ninth Avenue traffic officer. "Clear the way with your whistle, you—what's your name?"

"Sittenfield, 8638."

"Well, you're responsible for that door, too, Sittenfield. Anybody try to get away?"

"No, Sergeant."

"Anybody try to get out before Sittenfield got here, motorman?"

"Nope."

"All right. Shoot."

He returned to the body as the car lumbered forward. Cherry Browne was moaning softly; Pollux was patting her hands. DeWitt, his face set in grim lines, stood—almost as if he were on guard—over the dead body of Longstreet.

• • • • •

The car crashed into the huge shed of the New York Green Lines barn. A large group of men in plainclothes stood silently watching it come in. Outside the rainstorm splashed and roared.

A giant of a man with gray hair, a heavy jaw, and sharp gray eyes—set in a face of almost pleasing ugliness—hammered on the back door. Officer Morrow shouted, inside the car, to Sergeant Duffy. Duffy appeared, looked out, recognized the gargantuan physique of Inspector Thumm and pounded the door-lever sideways. The double doors folded back. Inspector Thumm clambered aboard, signaled Duffy to close the doors, made a sign to his waiting men outside, and forged into the interior of the car.

"Nice how'd ya-do," he said. He looked down casually at the dead man. "Duffy, what's it all about?"

The sergeant whispered into Inspector Thumm's ear. Thumm remained quite unconcerned. "Longstreet, hey? The broker . . . Well, who's Emily Jewett?"

The girl stepped forward under the wing of her burly escort, who glared belligerently at the Inspector.

"You say you saw this man collapse, Miss. Did you notice anything unusual before he fell?"

"Yes, sir!" said the girl in an excited voice. "I saw him put his hand into his pocket to get his eyeglasses. He must have scratched himself, or something, because he pulled his hand out and I saw it was bleeding."

"Which pocket?"

"His left-hand coat pocket."

"Where did this happen?"

"Well, it was just before the car stopped at Ninth Avenue."

"How long ago was that?"

"Well," said the girl, screwing up her hair line eyebrows, "we took about five minutes coming here since the car started again, and about five minutes from the time he fell down to the time the car started and, well, it must have been only a few minutes—two or three—between the time he scratched his hand and the time he keeled over."

"Less than fifteen minutes, hey? Left-hand pocket." Thumm thudded to his knees and, taking a flashlight from his rear trouser pocket, grasped the material of the dead man's open patch-pocket, pulled the pocket wide, and directed the pencil of light into the interior. He grunted with satisfaction. Putting down the flashlight, he produced a large penknife and with the utmost caution slit the stitching along one side of Longstreet's pocket. Two objects gleamed in the ray of the flashlight.

Without taking them from the slit pocket, Thumm examined them. One was a silver spectacle-case. He looked up for a moment; the dead man was wearing eyeglasses, now slightly awry on his blue-red nose.

The Inspector returned his attention to the pocket. The second object was a peculiar one. It was a small ball of cork, one inch in diameter, riddled with at least fifty ordinary needles, the tips of which projected from the cork a quarter-inch all around, making the total diameter of the weapon an inch and a half. The tips of the needles were stained with a reddish-brown substance. With the point of his penknife Thumm prodded the cork and turned it around. The needle-tips on the other side were similarly stained—it was a tarry, sticky substance. He leaned forward and sniffed vigorously. "Smells like stale tobacco," he muttered to Duffy, who was watching over his shoulder. "I wouldn't touch this barehanded for a year's salary."

He straightened up, explored his own pockets, and produced a small pair of pincers and a packet of cigarettes. He dumped the cigarettes into his pocket. Manipulating the pincers, he managed to get a firm grip on the needled cork. Lifting it out of Longstreet's pocket gingerly, he slipped the ball of cork into the empty cigarette-packet. At a low word to Duffy, the sergeant left, returned in a moment with the article Thumm had commanded—a newspaper—and the Inspector wrapped the cigarette-packet in a half-dozen thicknesses of paper. He handed the package to Duffy.

"That's dynamite, Sergeant," he said grimly, standing up. "Handle it that way. You're responsible for it."

Sergeant Duffy stood stiffly erect, holding the package at arm's length.

Inspector Thumm, ignoring the tense glances of the Longstreet party, went forward. He questioned the motorman and the passengers who were standing close to the front doorway. He made his way back through the car and repeated this procedure with the conductor and passengers on the back platform. Returning, he said to Duffy: "Here's luck, Sergeant. Not a soul left this car since it started at Eighth Avenue. Since this bird got on. . . . Tell you what. Send Morrow and Sittenfield back to their posts; we've got plenty of men here. Post a cordon outside; I want this car cleared."

Duffy, still holding the deadly package, went rearward. He let himself out of the car; the conductor immediately closed the doors behind him.

Five minutes later the doors at the rear were opened again. From the iron-shod step outside to a stairway across the floor of the carbarn extended two lines of police and detectives. Inspector Thumm had weeded out the members of the Longstreet party; they trooped silently from the car in single file and were escorted through the cordon into a private room on the second floor of the building. The door of the private room was closed, and a policeman took up his station outside. Inside, two detectives watched the party.

With the disappearance of the Longstreet party, Inspector Thumm superintended the exodus of all other occupants of the car. They filed, a long shambling line, through the same cordon into a large general room on the second floor, guarded by a half-dozen detectives.

Inspector Thumm now stood, alone, in the deserted car—alone with the sprawled dead figure on the seat. He stood thoughtfully regarding the contorted face, eyes still open to the glaring lights, pupils oddly dilated. The clang of an ambulance outside roused him. Two young men in white hurried into the barn, herded by a short fat man wearing old-fashioned gold-rimmed eyeglasses and a dinky gray cloth hat of ancient vintage, its brim rolled up behind and pulled down in front.

Thumm worked the lever of the back door and leaned out. "Dr. Schilling! This way!"

The short fat man, Medical Examiner of New York County, puffed into the car followed by the two internes. As Dr. Schilling bent over the dead man, Inspector Thumm carefully put his hand into the left patch-pocket and took out the silver spectacle-case.

Dr. Schilling straightened. "Where can I take this stiff, Inspector?"

"Upstairs." Thumm's eyes twinkled with grim humor. "Dump him in that private room up there with the rest of the party. That," he said dryly, "ought to be interesting."

He swung off the car as Dr. Schilling superintended the removal of the body. Thumm beckoned a detective. "Something I want you to do at once, Lieutenant. Have this car gone over with a fine-comb. Collect every piece of junk in it. Then go over the routes the Longstreet party and the other occupants of the car took in passing through the cordon. I want to make absolutely sure that nobody dropped anything. You know! A good job now, Peabody."

Lieutenant Peabody grinned and turned on his heel. Inspector Thumm said: "Come on with me, Sergeant," and Duffy, still holding the newspaper-wrapped weapon tenderly, smiled in a sickly way and followed the Inspector to the staircase leading up to the second floor.

Scene 4

PRIVATE ROOM IN A CARBARN.
FRIDAY, SEPTEMBER 4. 6:40 P.M.

THE PRIVATE room on the upper floor of the carbarn was a large, bare, dismal place. A continuous bench flanked the four walls. The Longstreet party sat about in varying attitudes of misery and strain, but all were silent.

Dr. Schilling, preceding the two internes bearing the dead man on a stretcher, entered the room immediately behind Inspector Thumm and Sergeant Duffy. He commandeered a screen and the three doctors disappeared with the stretcher behind it. Not the slightest sound interrupted this rite, conducted with the utmost cheerfulness by the Medical Examiner. The Longstreet party, as if by an unspoken command, thereafter kept their heads turned away from the screen. Softly, Cherry Browne began to cry, leaning against Pollux's trembling shoulder.

Inspector Thumm clasped muscular hands behind his back and surveyed the party with quiet, almost disinterested speculation. "Now that we're all here in a nice private room," he began pleasantly, "we can have a sane talk about this thing. I know everybody here is upset, but not too upset to answer a couple of questions." They sat like schoolchildren, gazing up at him. "Sergeant," the Inspector continued, "you told me that some gentleman here had identified the dead man as Harley Longstreet. Who was that?"

Sergeant Duffy pointed to the motionless figure of John DeWitt sitting beside his wife on the bench. DeWitt stirred.

"I see," said Inspector Thumm. "Now, sir, suppose you tell me what you began to tell the sergeant in the car.—Be sure to get all this, Jonas," he said to one of a group of detectives at the door. The man nodded, pencil poised over a notebook. "Now, sir. What's your name?"

"John O. DeWitt." Determination, self-assurance had crept into his bearing, into his voice. Inspector Thumm noticed a quick flash of surprise on the faces of several of the party; DeWitt's manner seemed to please them. "The dead man was my business partner. Our firm is DeWitt & Longstreet. Brokers, Wall Street."

"And who are these ladies and gentlemen?"

DeWitt quietly introduced the other members of the party.

"Now, what were you all doing on that street-car?"

The frail little man recited in a dry, precise way the facts leading up to the boarding of the Forty-Second Street Crosstown, the engagement party, what took place there, Longstreet's invitation to spend the week-end at his home, the departure from the hotel, the sudden storm, the decision to take the car to the ferry.

Thumm listened noncommittally. As DeWitt concluded, he smiled. "Nicely told. Mr. DeWitt, you saw that peculiar cork of needles I took from Longstreet's pocket in the car. Have you ever seen it before? Or heard of the existence of such a thing?" DeWitt shook his head. "Anyone else here?" All shook their heads. "Very well. Now listen carefully, Mr. DeWitt. Are the following facts true? While you, Longstreet, and the others waited on the corner of Forty-Second and Eighth under the awning, you showed Longstreet a letter. He put his *left* hand into his *left* pocket, extracted his eyeglass-case, took out the glasses, and put his hand into his pocket again to return the case. Did you notice anything happen to his left hand? Did he cry out? Did he pull his hand out fast?"

"Not at all," replied DeWitt composedly. "You are apparently attempting to fix the exact period during which the weapon was slipped into his pocket. Positively not at that time, Inspector."

Thumm turned to the others. "Anybody notice anything wrong?"

Cherry Browne said in a thin tearful voice, "Nothing was wrong. I was right beside him and if he had stuck himself I would have known it."

"Good. Now then, Mr. DeWitt, when Longstreet finished reading the letter, he once more put his hand into his pocket to take out the case, stowed away his glasses and again—for the fourth time—put his hand into that pocket, on this last occasion to return the case. Did he cry out then, or make any sign that he was pricked?"

"I am willing to swear, Inspector," replied DeWitt, "that he made no outcry or sign of any kind."

The others nodded their heads in unanimous agreement.

Thumm rocked a little on his heels. "Miss Browne," turning to the actress, "Mr. DeWitt says that immediately after returning the letter, he saw Longstreet and you dash for the car, and that you held your fiancé's left arm from then until you both got into the car out of the rain. Is that true?"

"Yes." She shivered a little. "I was pressed up close to him, hanging on his left arm. He—he had his left hand in the pocket. We were that way until—until we were on the rear platform."

"Did you see his hand at all on the platform—his left hand?"

"Yes. When he took it out of his pocket to look for change in his vest pocket and didn't find any. Just after we got on the car."

"His hand was clear—no pricks on it, no blood?"

"No."

"Mr. DeWitt, let me see that letter you showed your partner."

DeWitt took from his breast pocket the muddied envelope and handed it to Inspector Thumm. Thumm read the letter—the grievance of a customer named Weber complaining that he had ordered stock sold at a certain time for a certain price, but that DeWitt & Longstreet had not followed instructions, and that he, Weber, had lost a considerable sum of money as a result. The letter demanded a refund of this loss, claiming that the negligence was the firm's. Thumm returned the letter to DeWitt without comment.

"These facts, then, are substantially correct," he resumed. "In other words——"

"The weapon," went on DeWitt tonelessly, "must have been slipped into Longstreet's pocket while he was *on* the car."

The Inspector grinned without humor. "That's it exactly. He had put his hand into his pocket four times on the corner. As they crossed over to board the car, you yourself saw Miss Browne pressed against Longstreet's left side, and Longstreet's own hand was in that all-important left pocket. If anything was wrong then, both you and Miss Browne would have noticed it. In the car Miss Browne saw his hand, and it was all right. Then the needled cork was not in his pocket before he boarded."

Thumm scratched his jaw, ruminating. Then, shaking his head, he strode up and down before the party, questioning each one as to his or her physical position in the vehicle in relation to Longstreet. He discovered that all were grouped loosely, shifting and swaying with the motion of the car and the restless movements of the passengers. He clamped his lips together but showed no other sign of disappointment.

"Miss Browne, why did Longstreet take out his glasses in the car?"

"I think he wanted to read his paper," she replied wearily. DeWitt said: "Longstreet always consulted the final stock quotations in his late paper on the way to the ferry."

"And it was when he took out his glasses that he cried out and looked at his hand, Miss Browne?" asked Thumm, nodding.

"Yes. He seemed surprised, annoyed, but nothing more. He began to examine his pocket, as if to see what had caused the pricks, but the car lurched badly and he grabbed for a strap. Then he said he had just scratched himself. But he was pretty groggy, it seemed to me."

"But he put on his glasses anyway, and read the stock page?"

"He started to open his paper, but he never finished. He—he collapsed before I could realize what was happening."

Inspector Thumm frowned. "Read the stock page on the car every night, hey? Any *special* reason he might have had, Miss Browne, to look at his paper tonight? After all, it wasn't the politest thing to do. . . ."

"Perfectly ridiculous," interrupted DeWitt again, in cold tones. "You don't know—or didn't know—Longstreet. He'd do anything he pleased. What *special* reason, as you express it, could he have had?"

But Cherry Browne, beneath the traces of tears, was looking thoughtful. "Come to think of it," she said, "there might have been a special reason, at that. Only this afternoon he called for a paper—it wasn't the final, I don't think—to see what a certain stock was doing. He might——"

Thumm clucked encouragingly. "That's the stuff, Miss Browne. And what was the name of the stock, do you know?"

"I think . . . It was International Metals." She stole a swift look at the portion of the bench where Michael Collins sat sullenly studying the dirty floor. "And Harley said, when he saw that International Metals had dropped a lot, Harley said Mr. Collins might need help on short notice."

"I see. Collins!" The bulky Irishman grunted. Thumm regarded him with curiosity. "So you're in on this party, too. I thought the Income Tax Department kept you busy. . . . Collins, where do you come in on this deal?"

Collins bared his teeth. "I'm not sure this is any of your business, Thumm. But if you must know, Longstreet advised me to buy in heavy on International Metals—he'd been watching the stock for me. And hell, the bottom just dropped out of it today."

DeWitt had turned and was regarding Collins with frank surprise. Thumm said quickly: "And did you know about this transaction, Mr. DeWitt?"

"Certainly not." DeWitt faced him squarely. "I'm astonished to hear that Longstreet advised buying Metals. I foresaw its collapse last week and strongly advised a number of my personal customers against buying in."

"Collins, when did you first hear about the drop in Metals?"

"About one o'clock today. But look here, DeWitt, what do you mean you didn't know about Longstreet's information? What kind of lousy firm do you run anyway? I'm——"

"Take it easy," said Inspector Thumm. "Just take it easy, Son.

Did you speak to Longstreet between one o'clock today and the time you saw him at the hotel?"

"Yes," ominously.

"Where?"

"At the Times Square branch of the firm. Early afternoon."

Thumm again rocked on his heels. "No words, I suppose?"

"Oh, for God's sake!" shouted Collins suddenly. "You're barking up the wrong tree, Thumm! What the hell are you trying to do—pin this thing on *me?*"

"You haven't answered the question."

"Well—no."

Cherry Browne screamed. Inspector Thumm whirled as if he had been shot. But he saw only the cheerfully fat little figure of Dr. Schilling emerging from behind the screen in his striped shirt-sleeves. A brief glimpse of Longstreet's rigid dead face . . .

"Let's have that thingamajig—that cork, or whatever it is, the boys told me about downstairs, Inspector," said Dr. Schilling.

Thumm nodded to Sergeant Duffy; Duffy handed the package with an expression of immense relief to the Medical Examiner; who took it, humming, and disappeared again behind the screen.

Cherry Browne was on her feet now, eyes wild and face writhing like a nightmarish Medusa's. Her initial reaction had worn off; the sudden sight of Longstreet's livid clay had brought on a purposeful, somehow cunning hysteria. She brandished her finger at DeWitt, ran forward and clutched his lapels, shrieked into his blanched face: "*You* killed him! *You* did it! *You* hated him! *You* killed him!" The men had risen, pale; Thumm and Duffy sprang forward and pulled the screaming woman away. Throughout DeWitt stood like stone. The color drained out of Jeanne DeWitt's face; her lips tightened and she advanced tigerishly on the actress. Christopher Lord blocked her path, began to soothe her in a low voice. She sat down again, staring horrified at her father. Imperiale and Ahearn with serious faces took their places at DeWitt's side, like a guard of honor. Collins sat belligerently in his corner. Pollux was on his feet now, whispering rapidly into Cherry Browne's ear. She calmed gradually, began to cry. . . . Only Mrs. DeWitt had not turned a hair; she surveyed the scene with bright, unblinking, inhuman eyes.

Inspector Thumm towered above the quivering woman. "How did you come to say that, Miss Browne? How do you know Mr. DeWitt killed him? Did you see Mr. DeWitt put that cork into Longstreet's coat?"

"No, no." She moaned, shaking from side to side. "Oh, I don't know, I don't know. I only know he hated Harl, hated him like poison. . . . Harley told me so dozens of times——"

Thumm snorted, straightened, and looked hard and significantly at Sergeant Duffy. Duffy gestured to the detective writing in the notebook. The man opened the door; his partner stepped further into the room. And while Pollux bent over Cherry, solacing her with some magical words of his own, Inspector Thumm snapped: "Everybody stay right here until I get back," and strode through the open doorway followed meekly by Jonas, the detective with the notebook.

Scene 5

General Room in A Carbarn.
Friday, September 4. 7:30 p.m.

Inspector Thumm proceeded directly to the general room in the barn. He entered upon a grotesque scene—men and women standing, sitting, squirming, chattering, expressing impatience, fear, discomfort. The Inspector grinned at one of the detectives in charge and stamped loudly for attention. There was a concerted rush in his direction; they panted and objected, protested, questioned, swore. . . .

"Stand back!" roared Thumm in his best parade voice. "Now get this straight. No complaints, no suggestions, no excuses. The quieter you people are the sooner you'll get out of here.

"Miss Jewett, I want you first. Did you see anyone put anything into the pocket of the man who was killed—I mean while he was standing in front of you?"

"I was talking with my escort," said the girl, moistening her lips, "and it was pretty hot and——"

Thumm snarled: "Answer the question! Yes or no?"

"No. No, sir."

"If anyone *had* slipped something into that pocket, would you have noticed?"

"I don't think so. My friend and I were talking . . ."

Thumm turned abruptly to the heavy-set man—graying, with a harsh almost malevolent face—who had pulled Longstreet's arm when he had collapsed in the car. He was, he said, Robert Clarkson, bookkeeper. No, he had noticed nothing, despite the fact that he had been standing next to Longstreet. Yes, on his left side. Clarkson's heavy face lost its evil shading; he paled suddenly with apprehension and his loose mouth worked comically.

The middle-aged Italian, Antonio Fontana—a swarthy, thickly mustached man—who said he was a barber returning from work, could add nothing to what had already been said. He had been reading an Italian newspaper, *II Popolo Romano,* during the entire trip.

The conductor, questioned next, revealed himself as Charles Wood, Number 2101, in the employ of the Third Avenue Railways for five years. He was a tall burly red-haired man of perhaps fifty. He had seen the face of the dead man, he said, and remembered his having got on the car, one of a party of people who boarded at Eighth Avenue. This man, he said, had paid fares for ten people out of a dollar bill.

"Did you notice anything funny when this bunch got on, Wood?"

"Nope. The car was full, and I had all I could do to close the doors and collect fares."

"Ever see this man on your car before?"

"Yep. He's been getting on pretty often at that time of day. Been a regular customer for years."

"Know his name?"

"Nope."

"Recognize anybody else in the dead man's party as one of your regular passengers?"

"Seems to me I saw another man, a weak little guy. Gray-haired, sort of. I've seen him come on pretty steady with the guy that was bumped off."

"Do you know *his* name?"

"Can't say I do. Nope."

Thumm stared at the ceiling. "Watch yourself now, Wood. This is important. I want to be absolutely sure. This bunch got on at Eighth, you say. You closed the doors. All right. Now, did anybody get on or off *after* Eighth?"

"No, Chief. We were full up, and I didn't open the doors even at the corner of Eighth Avenue. So nobody got on. And no one got off either at my end—goes without saying. Don't know about the front. Guiness, my partner, prob'ly knows about that. He's the motorman."

Thumm singled out of the crowd the broad-shouldered Irish motorman. Guiness, Number 409, said that he had worked on the line for eight years. No, he had never seen the dead man before, he thought. "But then," he added, "I ain't in as good a spot as Charley here to notice passengers."

"You're sure about that?"

"We-ell, I guess maybe his face looked a little familiar at that."

"Did anyone get off the front after Eighth Avenue?"

"Didn't even open the doors. You know the line, Inspector. Most every passenger on the Crosstown heads for the terminal, to take the ferry over to Jersey. All business places along there. And then Sergeant Duffy can tell you. He rode front with me—goin' off duty, hey Sergeant? Lucky he was on the car at that."

Thumm scowled, but it was a scowl of pleasure. "Then, boys, the doors weren't opened, back or front, after Eighth Avenue?"

"That's right," replied Guiness and Wood.

"Fine. Stand by." The Inspector turned away and began to question other passengers. No one, it seemed, had seen anything slipped into Longstreet's pocket, or anything else of a suspicious nature. Two passengers offered vague statements, but their conjectures were so obviously the result of heated imaginations that Thumm turned away in disgust. He ordered Detective Jonas to take the names and addresses of all present.

At this moment, Lieutenant Peabody panted into the general room under the burden of a burlap bag full of débris.

"Any luck, Lieutenant?" asked Thumm.

"Just junk. Take a look." He dumped the contents of the bag to the floor. Scraps of paper, torn dirty newspapers, empty cigarette packets, the grimy stub of a leadless pencil, burnt matches, half a bar of squashed chocolate, two ragged time-tables—the usual accumulation. Not a trace of cork or needles, or articles in any way connected with cork or needles.

"We went over that car and the cordon routes with a fine-comb, Inspector. Dry as a bone. Whatever this bunch had on 'em when they left the car is still on 'em."

Thumm's gray eyes glinted. He was the most widely publicized Inspector in the New York Police Department. He had fought his way up from the ranks quite literally by the easy spring of his muscles, his well developed reflexes, the common sense in his brain, and the unmistakable authority in his voice. He was a stubborn master of police routine, a man of action. . . . "Only one thing to do," he said, working his jaws slightly. "Search every son-of-a-gun in this room."

"You're looking for——?"

"Cork, needles, anything that's out of place or out of character. And if anybody squawks, paste him one. Get busy."

Lieutenant Peabody grinned, went out of the room, returned in a moment with six detectives and two police matrons, jumped on a bench and shouted: "Line up, everybody! Women on one side, men on the other! No arguments! The quicker you are, the quicker you'll get home!"

For fifteen minutes Inspector Thumm leaned against a wall, a cigarette in his mouth, watching a scene that had more humorous aspects than serious. Women ranted in shrill voices as the muscular hands of the matrons passed impersonally over them, turning out their pockets, exploring their purses, digging into the lining of their hats and the soles of their shoes. Men submitted with better grace, but sheepishly. As each individual was released, Detective Jonas jotted down name, business address, and home address. Occasionally Inspector Thumm's eyes drilled into the faces of those passing out—searching, questioning. One man the Inspector halted peremptorily after he had passed Jonas. This man, a small, pale, clerkish fellow, was wearing a faded overgarment. The Inspector motioned him to step aside and take it off—it was a tan gaberdine trenchcoat. The man's lips were blue with fear. Thumm explored every crevice of the coat, returned it to its owner without a word, and the man skipped out of the room in an ecstasy of relief.

The room emptied rapidly.

"Nothing doing, Inspector." Peabody was dejected.

"Search the room."

Peabody and his men now swept up the débris of the general room, poked in corners and under benches. Thumm straddled the pile of rubbish from the burlap bag, knelt and prodded it with his finger.

Then he looked at Peabody, shrugged, and left the room quickly.

Scene 6

The Hamlet. Tuesday, September 8. 11:20 a.m.

"Please understand, Mr. Lane," interpolated District Attorney Bruno at this point, "that Inspector Thumm is giving you every possible detail. Many of them, such as sidelights on previous conversations, we discovered subsequently. Most of them, in fact, we are not concerned with; they're unimportant. . . ."

"My dear Mr. Bruno," said Mr. Drury Lane, "nothing is unimportant. How trite and how true that is! Nevertheless, an excellent account so far." He stirred in his great armchair, stretching his long legs before the fire. "A moment, please, before you resume, Inspector."

In the uneven light of the flames, and despite the shadows, the two men saw him close his eyes peacefully. His hands were clasped lightly in his lap; no muscle moved in his pale pleasant face. The silence of the traditional past descended on those high dark walls, in that chamber out of another age.

From his dusky corner Quacey, like an old parchment, rustled. Bruno and Thumm craned. The ancient hunchback was chuckling softly.

They looked at each other, only to start at the sound of Drury Lane's measured, flexible, organ voice.

"Inspector Thumm," he said, "there is only one point so far on which I am not entirely clear."

"And what's that, Mr. Lane?"

"The rain, according to your recital, commenced while the street-car was between Seventh and Eighth Avenues. At the time the Longstreet party boarded the car, at Eighth Avenue, the windows, I believe you said, were tightly closed. You meant *every* window?"

Inspector Thumm's ugly face went blank. "Of course, Mr. Lane. No question about it. Sergeant Duffy was positive."

"Admirable, Inspector." The rich voice purred on. "And every window was tightly closed from that period on?"

"Absolutely, Mr. Lane. In fact, it was raining harder when the car got to the barn than before. Those windows were closed every minute of the time after the storm broke."

"Better and better, Inspector." The deep-set eyes under their even gray brows sparkled. "Please continue."

Scene 7

PRIVATE ROOM IN A CARBARN.
FRIDAY, SEPTEMBER 4. 8:05 P.M.

INSPECTOR THUMM's account indicated that events had moved rapidly after the other occupants of the car had been released.

Thumm returned to the private room in which the Longstreet party sat miserably waiting. Louis Imperiale, the perfect gentleman, rose at once and bowed, precisely, his heels clicking together in that absurdly military fashion.

"My dear Inspector," he said in his nicest manner, "please forgive my presumption, but I'm sure we are all in need of nourishment, no matter how little inclined we may be to eat. Don't you think that some provision should be made, at least for the ladies?"

Thumm looked about. Mrs. DeWitt sat, still rigidly, on her bench with half-closed eyes. Jeanne DeWitt leaned on the broad shoulder of Lord; both were pale. DeWitt and Ahearn were engaged in a passionless, low-voiced discussion. Pollux sat well forward, hands clasped between his knees, whispering steadily to Cherry Browne, whose set face and clenched teeth destroyed every vestige of her prettiness. Michael Collins had buried his face in his hands.

"All right, Mr. Imperiale. Dick, run downstairs and rustle some grub for the folks."

A detective accepted a bill from Imperiale and left the room. The Swiss returned to his bench, with the self-satisfied look of a man who has done his work well.

"Well, Doc, what's the verdict?"

Dr. Schilling was standing before the screen putting on his coat. His tattered cloth hat perched grotesquely atop his bald pate. He crooked his finger; Inspector Thumm crossed the room; and the two men went behind the screen to stand over the dead man. One of the young ambulance-doctors was sitting on the bench beside the body, writing scrupulously on a report-blank. The other was paring his fingernails and whistling softly.

"Well, sir," began Dr. Schilling jovially, "this is a nice job. A very nice job. Death from respiratory paralysis, but that's a detail." His left hand flew up and with his pudgy right he began to count off on his fingers. "Number one, the poison." He bobbed his head in the direction of the bench; the weapon had been unwrapped and lay, innocently enough, at Longstreet's stiff feet. "The needle-ends around the ball of cork are fifty-three in number. Their tips and their eyes, projecting from the cork, were dipped in nicotine—nicotine in I think a concentrated form."

"I thought I smelled stale tobacco," muttered Thumm.

"*Ja.* You would. The fresh pure product is a colorless and odorless oily liquid. But in water or on standing it soon becomes dark brown and you can smell the characteristic tobacco odor. Undoubtedly this *verdammte* poison was the direct cause of death. Nevertheless, we shall conduct an autopsy to make sure that there was nothing else. The poison was introduced into the body by direct method—the needles pricked the palm and fingers in twenty-one places, the poison made immediate entry into the bloodstream. From what I understand death did not ensue for a few minutes. That means that this man was a heavy tobacco-user. Unusual tobacco tolerance.

"Number two, the weapon itself." Down went another fat finger. "A prize for your police museum, Inspector. So insignificant, so simple, so unique, so deadly! The product of an ingenious mind.

"Number three, probable source of the poison." The third finger fell. "Thumm, my friend, I don't envy you. Unless this poison was secured through legal channels, it will be untraceable. Pure nicotine is hard to buy, and if I were a poisoner I wouldn't get it from a chemist. It would be possible, of course, to distill it from an enormous quantity of tobacco, which normally has a nicotine content of four per cent. But how are you going to trace a nicotine-cooker? The easiest way is to buy a can of——" Dr. Schilling mentioned a well-known liquid insecticide, "and you have nicotine without much trouble. It has a thirty-five per cent content to begin with, and by evaporation you would get just such a resinous sticky mess as the needles are smeared with."

"I'll send feelers out along the regular channels anyway," said Thumm glumly. "How long would it take for this poison to act, Doc?"

Dr. Schilling pursed his lips. "It shouldn't take more than a few seconds ordinarily. But if the nicotine were not wholly concentrate, and Longstreet were a very heavy smoker, it would have taken three minutes or so, as it did."

"I guess it was the nicotine, all right. Anything else?"

"Well, I am not overfastidious myself, Inspector, but this man was in a frightful physical condition," replied Dr. Schilling. "Faugh! But I'll tell you more about his insides after my autopsy—I'll have it tomorrow. Nothing else here, Inspector; the boys will take this gentleman away. The wagon's outside."

Inspector Thumm wrapped the needled cork in its sheath of cigarette-packet and newspaper, and returned to the Longstreet party. He gave Sergeant Duffy the weapon and stood aside as the two internes carried the blanket-covered body out on a stretcher, followed by a beaming Dr. Schilling.

Again that deathly silence as the body was borne past.

The detective had found no difficulty, it seemed, in securing food; they were unwrapping sandwiches and munching with slow jaws, and sipping from containers of coffee.

Thumm signed to DeWitt. "As Longstreet's partner you're probably best equipped to tell me about his habits, Mr. DeWitt. The conductor has often seen Longstreet on his car. How do you account for this?"

"Longstreet in matters of routine was extremely methodical. Particularly," said DeWitt acidly, "about the time he left the office. Frankly, he wasn't much interested in long hours or hard work; he left most of the plugging to me. Our main offices are downtown on Wall Street, but we've always made a habit of returning to our main branch at Times Square after Wall Street closing, and leave there for West Englewood. Longstreet generally quit the branch office the same time every day, a little before six. He always made the same train on the Jersey side. I suppose it was habit that made him regulate the time of our party's departure from the hotel today, so that we could make the usual train. That accounts for our being on the same car."

"I understand that you took this car yourself rather frequently."

"Yes. When I didn't stay late at the office, I often went back to West Englewood with Longstreet."

Inspector Thumm sighed. "How is it neither of you seems to have used an automobile in business hours?"

DeWitt smiled grimly. "It's a nuisance in New York traffic. We have our cars wait for us at the Englewood station."

"Just how methodical was Longstreet in other matters?"

"Very methodical, Inspector, in little things; although in his personal life he was inclined to be reckless and undependable. But he always read the same newspaper, always consulted the final stock reports in the paper on the way to the ferry, as I've told you. Wore the same type of clothing on business days, smoked only one brand of cigars and cigarettes—he was a terribly heavy smoker—yes, in most details he could be depended upon to follow fixed habit. Even," and DeWitt's gaze was frosty, "to coming into the office at noon."

Thumm eyed DeWitt casually. He applied a match to another cigarette and asked: "Did he *have* to wear eyeglasses for reading?"

"Yes, for close work especially. He was a vain man, thought glasses marred his personal appearance, and therefore dispensed with them for street wear and social functions wherever possible, even though the lack of glasses inconvenienced him. He was forced to wear them for reading, though, not only indoors but outdoors."

Thumm put his hand on DeWitt's small shoulder in a friendly way. "Let's be frank about this thing, Mr. DeWitt. You heard Miss Browne accuse you of killing Longstreet. Of course that's nonsense. But she said over and over that you hated him. Did you?"

DeWitt moved, and somehow Thumm's large hand contrived to fall from the broker's shoulder. And DeWitt said coldly: "I am innocent of my partner's murder, if that is what you mean by frankness."

Thumm stared long and steadily into DeWitt's clear eyes. Then he shrugged and turned to the other members of the party. "Everybody here will please meet me at the Times Square office of DeWitt & Longstreet tomorrow morning at nine o'clock for further questioning. There will be no exceptions, ladies and gentlemen."

They rose wearily and shuffled toward the door. "One moment, please," continued the Inspector. "Naturally I'm sorry, but you'll all have to submit to a personal search. Duffy, get one of the matrons for the ladies here."

They gasped, and DeWitt in an angry tone expostulated. Thumm smiled. "Certainly no one here has anything to conceal?"

The procedure in the general room a few minutes before was now repeated under Thumm's eye. The men were uneasy, the women flushed and irate. Mrs. DeWitt broke her silence of hours to snap a swift word in Spanish at the broad chest of the Inspector. He raised his eyebrows and waved his arm at the matron with finality.

"Names, addresses," came Jonas's droning voice at the door as they began to file out after the search.

Duffy looked depressed. "Not a thing, Chief. No sign of needles, corks, or anything else fishy."

Thumm planted his feet solidly in the center of the room, frowning and chewing his lips. "Search the room," he said harshly.

The room was searched.

When Inspector Thumm left the carbarn in the midst of his men he was still frowning.

Scene 8

Offices of DeWitt & Longstreet.
Saturday, September 5. 9 a.m.

The undercurrent of tension did not break surface as Inspector Thumm crossed the floor of the branch office of DeWitt & Longstreet on Saturday morning. Clerks and customers looked up at his windy passage, startled; but apparently business was being conducted in the normal way. Thumm's men, already on the scene, interfered with nothing. They loitered quietly, and that was all.

In the private office at the rear marked *John O. DeWitt* the Inspector found the entire Longstreet party of the night before assembled under the vigilant eye of Lieutenant Peabody. Sergeant Duffy's big blue back braced the glass door marked *Harley Longstreet*—leading to an adjoining office.

Thumm looked them over without enthusiasm, growled a greeting, beckoned Detective Jonas, and they entered the Longstreet sanctum. There Thumm found, nervously perched on the edge of a chair, an interesting young lady—a large, well-cushioned brunette, good-looking in a vaguely cheap way.

Thumm sank into the swivel chair before the one large desk

in the office. Jonas sat down in a corner, pencil and notebook ready. "I suppose you're Longstreet's secretary?"

"Yes, sir. I'm Miss Platt. Anna Platt. I worked for Mr. Longstreet for four and a half years as a sort of confidential secretary." Anna Platt's straight nose was unfashionably red at the tip; her eyes were very damp. She dabbed at them with a limp handkerchief. "Oh, it's terrible!"

"Sure, sure," said the Inspector with a mirthless grin. "Now cut out the weeps, Sister, and let's get down to business. You look like the sort of gal who would know her boss's business pretty thoroughly. And his private affairs, too. Tell me—how did Longstreet and DeWitt get along?"

"They didn't. They were always squabbling."

"And who usually won these battles?"

"Oh, Mr. Longstreet! Mr. DeWitt always objected when he thought Mr. Longstreet wrong, but then he always gave in finally."

"What was Longstreet's attitude toward DeWitt?"

Anna Platt twisted her fingers. "I suppose you want the truth. . . . He bullied Mr. DeWitt all the time. He knew that Mr. DeWitt was the better business man and he didn't like it. So he just bore down on Mr. DeWitt and got things his own way, even if he was in the wrong and it cost the firm money."

Inspector Thumm's eyes wandered up and down the girl's figure. "You're a smart girl, Miss Platt. We're going to get along. Did DeWitt *hate* Longstreet?"

She lowered her eyes demurely. "Yes, I think he did. I think I know why, too. It's an open scandal that Mr. Longstreet"—her voice hardened—"had been having an affair with Mrs. DeWitt, a serious affair. . . . And I'm sure Mr. DeWitt knew about it, although I never heard him refer to it to Mr. Longstreet or anyone else."

"Did Longstreet love DeWitt's wife? How is it that he became engaged to Miss Browne?"

"Mr. Longstreet didn't love anyone but himself. But he had scores of affairs all the time, and I suppose Mrs. DeWitt was just one of them. I guess, like all women, she thought he was crazy about her and no one else. . . . I'll tell you one thing, though," she went on, in a tone she might have employed to discuss the weather. "You'll be interested in this, Inspector—is it? Mr. Longstreet once made advances to Jeanne DeWitt right here in this room and there was an awful argument, because Mr. Lord came in and saw what was happening and knocked Mr. Longstreet down. Then Mr. DeWitt came in quickly and they sent me away. I don't know what happened later, but it seemed to be patched up. This was a couple of months ago."

The Inspector appraised her coolly; this was a witness after his own heart. "Very nice, Miss Platt. Very nice indeed. And do you think Longstreet had some sort of hold on DeWitt?"

The girl hesitated. "I'm not sure. But I do know that every once in a while Mr. Longstreet demanded large sums of money from Mr. DeWitt, 'personal loans,' he'd say with a nasty laugh, and he'd get them every time. In fact, only a week ago he asked Mr. DeWitt for a loan of twenty-five thousand dollars. Mr. DeWitt was awfully mad; I thought he'd have apoplexy. . . ."

"I shouldn't wonder," murmured Thumm.

"They had quite a fuss in here. But he gave in, as usual."

"Any threats?"

"Well, Mr. DeWitt said: 'This can't go on much longer, and he said that they had to have an understanding once for all or they'd both go to the wall."

"Twenty-five grand," said the Inspector. "My God, what did

Longstreet do with all that dough? This office alone must have given him a big income."

Anna Platt's brown eyes flashed. "Mr. Longstreet could spend money faster than anyone you ever saw," she said in a malicious tone. "He gambled, lived high, played the races, the market—he lost pretty nearly all the time. He certainly ate up his own income in no time and when he ran short he'd hit Mr. DeWitt for one of those 'loans.' Loan! He's never given a cent of it back, I'm sure. Why, I've been calling up his bank regularly to explain overdrawn checks. He cashed his bonds and real estate securities long ago. I'll bet he hasn't left a penny."

Thumm drummed thoughtfully on the glass-topped desk. "So DeWitt never got his money back and Longstreet was a sugar-daddy sucker. Well, well!" He stared at her, and she dropped her eyes suddenly in confusion. "Miss Platt," he went on pleasantly, "we're both grown people, and neither of us believes the nice story about the stork. Was there anything between *you* and Longstreet? You strike me as being a free-and-easy sort of secretary."

She jumped up angrily. "What do you mean!"

"Sit down, Sister, sit down." Thumm grinned as she sank back into the chair. "I thought so. Now, how long did you live with him?"

"I didn't live with him!" she snapped. "We just went around together, for about two years. Do I have to sit here, just because you're a cop, and be insulted? I'm a respectable girl, I'll have you know!"

"Sure, sure," said the Inspector soothingly. "Do you live with your parents?"

"My parents live upstate."

"I thought so. I suppose he promised to marry you, too? Of

course. Just another good girl gone wrong. Threw you over for Mrs. DeWitt, did he?"

"Well . . ." She was wavering, studying the tiled floor sullenly. "Well—yes."

"But you're a smart gal nevertheless," continued Thumm with another admiring panoramic survey of her figure, "Yes, sir. To have had an affair with a guy like Longstreet, be given the air, and still keep your job—that's genius, Honey."

She said nothing; if she felt that he was trying to bait her she was clever enough to refuse the bait. Thumm hummed a little tune, studied her carefully shingled hair in silence. When he spoke again, it was in a different tone on different matters. He learned from her that on Friday afternoon, before Longstreet had left the office for Cherry Browne's apartment at the Grant, Michael Collins had dashed into the office, purple with rage, and had accused Longstreet of double-crossing. DeWitt had been out at the time. The accusation was based, said Anna Platt, on Longstreet's advice to Collins to plunge on International Metals. Collins had demanded with a curse that Longstreet make good the fifty thousand dollars Collins had irretrievably lost on the stock. Longstreet had seemed disturbed but had pacified the Irishman by saying: "Don't worry, Mike, and leave everything to me. I'll see that DeWitt pulls you through." Collins had demanded further that Longstreet settle the matter with DeWitt at once; but since DeWitt was out, Longstreet had invited Collins to the engagement party later, promising to speak to DeWitt there at the first opportunity.

Anna Platt had nothing else to offer. Inspector Thumm excused her and summoned DeWitt into Longstreet's office.

DeWitt was chalky but self-possessed. Thumm said directly:

"I'm going to repeat a question I asked you last night, and I insist on an answer. Why did you hate your partner?"

"I refuse to be bullied, Inspector Thumm."

"Then you won't answer?"

DeWitt pressed his lips together.

"Very well, DeWitt," said Thumm, "but you're making the biggest mistake of your life. . . . How did Mrs. DeWitt and Longstreet get along—good friends, were they?"

"Yes."

"And your daughter and Longstreet—there was nothing between them of an unpleasant nature?"

"You're insulting."

"Then your family and Longstreet got along quite smoothly?"

"Look here!" shouted DeWitt, rising suddenly. "What the devil are you driving at?"

The Inspector smiled and kicked DeWitt's chair with one huge foot. "Take it easy. Sit down. . . . Were you and Longstreet equal partners?"

DeWitt subsided, eyes bloody. "Yes," he said in a smothered voice.

"How long were you in business together?"

"Twelve years."

"How did you two happen to team up?"

"We made our fortunes in South America before the War. Mining venture. We returned to the States together and continued our affiliation in the brokerage business."

"You've been successful?"

"Quite."

"Then why," continued the Inspector in the same pleasant way, "if you were both successful and had fortunes to begin with, did Longstreet borrow money from you continually?"

DeWitt sat very still. "Who told you that?"

"I'm asking the questions, DeWitt."

"This is ridiculous." DeWitt bit a gray strand from his stiff mustache. "I loaned money to him occasionally, but these were purely personal affairs—trivial sums. . . ."

"Do you call twenty-five thousand dollars a trivial sum?"

The frail little man twisted in his chair as if it had burned his hide. "Why—that wasn't a loan. It was something personal."

"DeWitt," said Inspector Thumm, "you're lying in your teeth. You've been paying Longstreet a great deal of money. You haven't been repaid, probably never expected to see your money again. I want to know why, and I'll know if——"

DeWitt sprang from the chair with a shout; his face was contorted and purplish-white. "You're exceeding your authority! This thing had nothing to do with Longstreet's death, I tell you! I——"

"No melodramatics. Wait outside."

DeWitt's mouth remained open; he was gasping for breath. Then he shrank within himself, his rage dissipating; he squared his shoulders, shook himself, and left the room. Thumm watched him, puzzled; the man presented contradictory sides. . . .

He called for Mrs. Fern DeWitt.

The interview with Mrs. DeWitt was short and sterile. The woman—faded, bitter, defiant—was as peculiar as her husband. She seemed to be nursing a deep and warping emotion. No, she knew nothing, nothing at all. She coldly denied any relationship other than mere friendship with Longstreet. She scoffed at the insinuation that Longstreet had been attracted to Jeanne DeWitt. "He was always interested in more mature women!" she said icily. As for Cherry Browne, Mrs. DeWitt knew nothing about her, she said, except that she was "a scheming low actress," that Longstreet had been infatuated by a pretty face. Did she have any suspicion that her husband, Mr. DeWitt, was being blackmailed? Oh, no! How silly. . . .

Thumm silently cursed. This woman was a virago; she had vinegar in her veins. He hammered at her, threatened her, tried to cajole her. But aside from eliciting the fact that she and DeWitt had been married for six years, and that Jeanne DeWitt was DeWitt's daughter by a former marriage, Thumm discovered nothing. He dismissed her.

As the woman rose to go, she took from her handbag a vanity-case, opened it, and began to powder her already heavily powdered face. Her hand trembled; the mirror of the case shivered into fragments on the floor. Her aplomb fled; she paled beneath the rouge. Her hand flew to her breast, making the sign of the cross; with horror in her eyes she muttered, *"Madre de Dios!"* In the same instant, however, she recovered herself, flashed a guilty look at Inspector Thumm, minced around the broken glass, and hurried out. Thumm laughed, picked up the fragments, tossed them on the desk.

He went to the door and called Franklin Ahearn.

Ahearn was a large man, well preserved for his age; he carried himself erectly. Good humor lurked at the corners of his mouth. His eyes were gentle and bright.

"Sit down, Mr. Ahearn. How long have you known Mr. DeWitt?"

"Let me see . . . Since I have lived in West Englewood. Six years."

"How well did you know Longstreet?"

"Not well at all, Inspector. True, we all lived in the same general locality; but I am a retired engineer and have had no business relations with either man. However, DeWitt and I took to each other at once—I'm sorry to say I didn't like Longstreet at all. A deceptive person, Inspector. Bluff, hearty—the usual he-man thing, you know—but inside rotten to the core. I don't know who killed him, but I'll warrant it was because he deserved it!"

"Beside the point," said Thumm dryly. "What did you think of Cherry Browne's accusation last night?"

"Sheer nonsense." Ahearn crossed his legs and looked into Thumm's eyes. "Wasn't that a ridiculous thing to say? Only a hysterical woman would have made such a preposterous accusation. I've known John DeWitt for six years. There isn't a mean or vicious bone in his body; he's generous to a fault, literally a gentle man. He simply wouldn't be capable of murder. And I daresay there's no one outside his family who knows him better than I. We play chess three or four times a week."

"Chess, hey?" Thumm looked interested. "Now, that's something. Good chess-player, are you?"

Ahearn chuckled. "Alas for fame! Don't you read the papers, Inspector? You are speaking to the champion chess-player of these parts. Why, only three weeks ago I won the open tournament for the championship of the Atlantic seaboard."

"You don't say!" exclaimed Thumm. "Glad to meet a champ; I once shook Jack Dempsey's hand. How's DeWitt at the game?"

Ahearn leaned forward, speaking with enthusiasm. "Inspector Thumm, his play for a rank amateur is simply amazing. I've urged him for years to take the game up seriously, enter tournament play. But he's shy, reserved—dreadfully sensitive, you know. Mentally, he's quick as lightning. Plays almost instinctively. Doesn't dawdle over his game. Oh, we've had some interesting chess together."

"Nervous disposition, eh?"

"Very. Quick in everything. He really needs a rest. Frankly, I think Longstreet worried the life out of him, although naturally we've never discussed his business. Now that Longstreet's dead, I'm sure DeWitt will be a new man."

"I guess he will at that," said Thumm. "That's all, Mr. Ahearn."

Ahearn rose with alacrity. He consulted a large silver watch. "Goodness! Time for my stomach-pill." He beamed on the Inspector. "I have a peevish stomach—I'm a vegetarian, you know. The result of eating canned bully in my young days as an engineer. Well, sir, good day."

He strode solidly out. Thumm snorted to Jonas: "If he has stomach trouble I'm President of the United States. Nothing but a hypochondriac."

He went to the door and requested Cherry Browne to come in.

It was a completely altered actress who faced the Inspector across the desk a moment later. She seemed to have recovered her natural gayety of spirits; her face was carefully made up; bluish color tinged her eyelids; she was dressed in modish black. Her answers were decisive. She had met Longstreet at a ball five months before. He had "rushed" her, she said, for several months, and they had decided to announce their engagement. He had promised to "change his will"—she was remarkably sure of this—in her favor, immediately after their engagement. She seemed childishly certain that Longstreet had been a nabob, had left millions.

She caught sight of the broken glass on the desk, and turned her head away with a little frown.

She admitted that her accusation of DeWitt the night before had been prompted by hysteria. No, she had really seen nothing in the street-car and had made the statement because of her "woman's intuition." Thumm grunted.

"But Harley told me ever so often that DeWitt hated him," she insisted in her carefully musical voice. Why? She shrugged, rather prettily.

And favored the Inspector with a deep coquettish look as he held the door open for her.

Christopher Lord stalked into the office. Thumm stood squarely before him and they stared, eye for eye. Yes, Lord said firmly, he had knocked Longstreet down and didn't regret it one bit—the fellow was rotten and had it coming to him. He had tendered his resignation to DeWitt, his immediate superior, but DeWitt had placated him. He had, Lord continued, allowed the matter to drop because he genuinely liked DeWitt and because, on second thought, if Longstreet ever repeated his dirty advances to Jeanne he, Lord, would be on the scene to protect her.

"Lord Fauntleroy stuff, hey?" murmured Thumm. "Well, now. DeWitt strikes me as being a man of forceful character. Why was he so anxious to patch up this affair, which touched his own daughter?"

Lord jammed his big hands into his pockets. "Inspector," he replied shortly, "I'll be damned if I know. It isn't like him at all. In everything except his contacts with Longstreet he's been a keen, alert, independent man of high principles. He's one of the shrewdest brokers on the Street. Immensely jealous of his daughter's welfare and reputation. I should think he would haul off and slap that big ape down at daring to manhandle his daughter. But—he didn't. He temporized. Why, I'll be hanged if I know."

"You'd say, then, that his attitude toward Longstreet throughout hasn't been consistent with DeWitt's character?"

"He certainly hasn't been himself, Inspector."

DeWitt and Longstreet, continued Lord, had quarreled frequently in their private offices. Why? He shrugged. Mrs. DeWitt and Longstreet? The blond young man looked politely off into space. Michael Collins? Lord said that he himself worked under DeWitt and therefore knew little about Longstreet's contacts. Was it possible that DeWitt himself would be ignorant of Longstreet's private advice to Collins? Knowing Longstreet, said Lord, very likely.

Thumm sat down on the edge of the desk. "Did Longstreet ever make another pass at Jeanne DeWitt, young man?"

"Yes," replied Lord grimly. "I wasn't there at the time, but Anna Platt told me about it later. It seems that Jeanne had repulsed Longstreet and run out of the office."

"Did you do anything about it?"

"What do you think I am? Of course I did. I went to Longstreet and laid the law down to him."

"Quarreled?"

"Well . . . We had a damned sizzling conversation."

"That's all," said Thumm abruptly. "Send Miss DeWitt in."

Jeanne DeWitt, however, could add nothing to the testimony with which Detective Jonas was covering page after page of his notebook. She defended her father with spirit. Thumm listened gloomily and sent her back to the adjoining office.

"Mr. Imperiale!"

The tall ample frame of the Swiss filled the doorway. He was dressed with painful correctness; his sleek vandyke beard seemed to impress Jonas, at least, who regarded the man with eyes distinctly awed.

Imperiale's bright eyes fixed themselves on the broken glass on the desk. He made a little *moue* of distaste and turned back to Thumm, bowing courteously. He had been DeWitt's good friend, he said, for four years now, having met DeWitt in Europe when DeWitt was touring the Swiss Alps. They had become interested in each other.

"Mr. DeWitt has been most kind," he said with a flash of his perfect teeth. "Each of the four times since then that I have come to your country on business for my firm, I have been Mr. DeWitt's guest for the duration of my stay."

"What's the name of your firm?"

"The Swiss Precision Instruments Company. I am general manager of the *établissement.*"

"I see . . . Mr. Imperiale, can you offer any explanation of this crime?"

Imperiale spread his well-kept hands. "I have absolutely nothing to offer, Inspector. I knew Mr. Longstreet only superficially."

Thumm dismissed Imperiale. As the Swiss passed through the doorway Thumm's face hardened and he barked: "Collins!"

The big Irishman lurched into the office, his full lips drooping with resentment. His answers to the Inspector's questions were snappish, ill-humored, grudging. Thumm walked up to him, grasped his arm in a vicious grip. "Now you listen to me, you oily son of a politician!" he said. "I've been waiting to tell you this. I know damned well that you tried to pull strings last night to get out of coming here today to testify. But you're here anyway, aren't you? Hell of a public servant, you are! Now you said last night that when you dashed up here, looking for Longstreet to explain that phony tip of his, that you didn't have any words. I let it pass last night, but I'm not accepting that explanation this morning. Give it to me straight now, Collins!"

Collins's body was quivering with suppressed rage. He shook himself savagely free of Thumm's grip. "Smart cop, aren't you?" he snarled. "What do you think I did—kissed him? Sure I bawled him out—may his lousy soul rot in hell! He ruined me!"

Thumm grinned at Jonas. "Got that, didn't you, Jonas?" He turned mildly back to the Irishman. "Had damned good cause to put him away, didn't you?"

Collins broke into an ugly laugh. "Smarter and smarter! I suppose I had that cork full of needles all ready, waiting for the market to drop? Go back to a beat, Thumm; you're too dumb for your job."

Thumm blinked. But he merely said: "How is it DeWitt didn't know about Longstreet's tip to you?"

"That's what I'd like to know," said Collins nastily. "What kind of bucket-shop is this, anyway? But I'll tell you one thing, Thumm." He leaned closer, the cords of his neck livid. "This DeWitt is going to make good that bum steer or I'll know the reason why!"

"Take it down, Jonas, take it down," murmured the Inspector. "This guy is putting the rope around his own neck. . . . Collins, me lad, you invested fifty grand in Metals. Where'd you get all that dough to lose? You can't plunge fifty thousand dollar bills on that measly salary of yours."

"Mind your own business! Thumm, I'll break you for this. . . ."

Thumm's large hand clamped itself on Collins's coat above the chest; he yanked and Collins found his face one inch from Thumm's. "And I'll break your neck if you don't keep a civil tongue in your ugly mug," growled the Inspector. "Now get out of here, heel."

He flung the man away from him and Collins, inarticulate with rage, stamped out of the office. Thumm shook himself, cursed expertly, and called for the dagger-mustached Pollux.

The actor had a lean, wolfish Italian face. He was nervous, and Thumm pinned him with a choleric eye.

"Listen, you!" Thumm ran a broad finger under the edge of

his collar. "I haven't much time to spend on you, and I don't mind telling you so. What do you know about this Longstreet murder?"

Pollux, his eyes glittering sidewise at the broken glass fragments on the desk, snarled to himself in Italian. He was afraid of the Inspector, but bellicose. He said in a flat theatrical voice: "I don't know a thing. You've got nothing on me, or on Cherry either."

"Innocent, hey? Just a milk-fed babe?"

"Listen, Inspector. This Longstreet heel had it coming to him. He would have made Cherry's life miserable. He's known as the prize sucker of Broadway. The wise guys saw this coming, I'm telling you."

"Know Cherry well?"

"Who, me? We're pals."

"Do anything for her, wouldn't you?"

"What the hell do you mean?"

"Just what I said. Beat it."

Pollux flounced from the room, and Jonas came to life, rising and mincing across the floor in excellent pantomime. Thumm snorted, went to the door, and called: "DeWitt! Another minute or two."

DeWitt had calmed. He acted as if nothing had happened. As he crossed the threshold his quick alert eyes fastened on the smashed glass.

"Who broke that?" he asked sharply.

"Notice everything, don't you? Your wife."

DeWitt sat down and sighed. "Very unfortunate. I'll never hear the end of this. She'll blame everything on that broken mirror for weeks."

"Superstitious, is she?"

"Dreadfully so. She's half-Spanish by birth, you know. Castilian mother, and, while her father was Protestant, her mother contrived to bring her up as a Catholic, despite *madre's* own defection from the Church. Fern's a problem sometimes."

Thumm flipped one of the broken slivers off the desk. "I take it you don't believe in such things? I hear you're a pretty hard-headed business man, DeWitt."

DeWitt regarded him with disarming directness. "My friends have been talking, I see," he said softly. "No, Inspector Thumm, I don't believe in that sort of rot."

Thumm said abruptly: "What I really called you in for, DeWitt, was to get your assurance of co-operation with my men and the investigators from the District Attorney's office."

"Don't worry about that."

"You know, we'll have to look into Longstreet's business as well as private correspondence. His bank accounts, and all that truck. You'll see that my operatives posted here will be given every possible assistance?"

"You may depend upon it, Inspector."

"Good enough."

Inspector Thumm dismissed all the waiting members of the group in the outer office, issued some crackling instructions to Lieutenant Peabody and a studious-looking young man who was one of District Attorney Bruno's assistants, and trudged out of the DeWitt & Longstreet offices.

His face was very sad.

Scene 9

THE HAMLET. TUESDAY, SEPTEMBER, 8. 12:10 P.M.

QUACEY THREW small logs on the fire; it spurted up, and District Attorney Bruno studied the physiognomy of Mr. Drury Lane by its flickering light. Lane was smiling faintly. Inspector Thumm had lapsed into silence, frowning.

"Quite all, Inspector?"

Thumm grunted.

Whereupon Lane's eyelids fell; and instantly, by some alchemy of muscular control, he seemed asleep. The Inspector fidgeted. "If there's anything I haven't made clear . . ." His tone implied that even if there *were* something he had not made clear, he was sure the omission would make little difference in the final result. Inspector Thumm was a cynical man.

Bruno chuckled as the long still figure of the actor did not move. "He can't hear you, Thumm. His eyes are closed."

Thumm looked astonished. He scratched his jutting jaw and sat forward on the edge of the tall Elizabethan chair.

Drury Lane opened his eyes, looked quickly at his visitors and, so suddenly that Bruno recoiled, sprang to his feet. He half-turned; the firelight silhouetted his sharp clean profile. "Several questions, Inspector. Has there been a development of interest from Dr. Schilling's autopsy?"

"Nothing," said Thumm despondently. "The nicotine-poison analysis confirmed the Medical Examiner's preliminary report. But we haven't made an inch of progress in tracing the poison or its source."

"And," added the District Attorney—Lane's head jerked toward him by instinct, "neither the cork nor the needles proved traceable. At least we haven't traced them yet."

"Have you a copy of Dr. Schilling's autopsy report, Mr. Bruno?"

The District Attorney produced an official-looking paper and handed it to Lane, who took it closer to the fire and bent over it. His eyes gleamed weirdly as he read; he read aloud, rapidly and disjointedly. "Death from *apnœa*—blood fluid and characteristically blackish in color. Hmm . . . Paralysis of central nervous system, especially area controlling respiration, undoubtedly result of acute nicotine poisoning . . . Lungs, liver show hyperæmia . . . brain shows marked congestion. Hmm . . . Condition of lungs indicates victim possessed decided tobacco tolerance. Certainly heavy tobacco-user. Tolerance lengthened time required to cause death with standard lethal dose, which in non-tobacco addict would kill instantly or in less than one minute. . . . Physical marks: slight contusion of left kneecap probably the result of dying fall. . . . Nine-year-old appendicitis scar. Tip of *annularis,* or ring finger, of right hand missing; probably for twenty or more years . . . Sugar content normal. Abnormal alcohol content of brain. Body that of dissipated man of middle age who once possessed powerful physique, rugged constitution, probably great resistance . . . Hmm. Height six feet one and a half inches; weight *post mortem* two hundred and eleven pounds. . . . And so on and so on," murmured Lane, returning the document to District Attorney Bruno. "Thank you, sir."

He strode back to the fire, leaned against his huge oak mantel. "Nothing was found in the private room at the carbarn?"

"No."

"I assume also that Longstreet's house at West Englewood has been thoroughly gone over?"

"Oh, sure." Thumm was restless now. His eyes gleamed at Bruno in sly, half-humorous boredom. "Nothing there. We did find a lot of correspondence—letters from Longstreet's lady-friends, mostly all dated before March. Receipted and unpaid bills—the usual junk. The servants couldn't give us a lead."

"I take it that his town apartments have also been examined?"

"You take it right. We're not overlooking that bet. We've looked up all his old flames, too, but nothing's come of it."

Lane deliberately surveyed his two visitors. His eyes were serene and thoughtful. "Inspector Thumm, you are entirely satisfied that the needled cork was slipped into Longstreet's pocket in the car and not before?"

Thumm said instantly, "That's one thing we're dead certain of. Not the slightest doubt. Incidentally, I thought you might be interested in the cork itself. I've brought it along."

"Excellent, Inspector! You have anticipated me." The full voice was eager now.

Thumm took from his coat pocket a small glass jar, tightly-covered, and handed it to the actor. "I'd advise you not to open it, Mr. Lane. It's mighty dangerous."

Lane held the jar up to the firelight, studied its contents for a long moment. The cork, riddled with needles whose points and eyes projected on all sides stained darkly, seemed innocent enough. Lane smiled, returning the jar to the Inspector. "A homemade weapon, of course, and—as Dr. Schilling said—an ingenious one. . . . Just before the occupants of the car were ordered out in the carbarn, it was still raining with violence?"

"Sure enough. Coming down in buckets."

"Now tell me, Inspector—were there any laborers on the car?"

Thumm's eyes opened wide; Bruno wrinkled his forehead in astonishment. "What do you mean—laborers?"

"Ditch-diggers. Construction-men. Plasterers. Bricklayers—you know."

Thumm seemed bewildered. "Why, no. They were all office-workers. I don't see . . ."

"And everyone was searched *thoroughly?*"

"Yes," said the Inspector in a scathing tone.

"Believe me, Inspector, casting aspersions on the efficiency of your auxiliaries is furthest from my thought. . . . As a confirmation, sir, once again: Nothing unusual was found on the persons of the occupants of the car, or in the car itself, or in the rooms of the barn after everyone left—anywhere?"

"I think I brought that out, Mr. Lane," replied Thumm coldly.

"Nevertheless—nothing that would seem out of place, considering the weather, the season, the type of persons involved?"

"I don't get you."

"For example—you found no topcoats, evening clothes, gloves—things like that?"

"Oh! Well, one man had a raincoat, but I examined it myself and it was okay as I told you. Otherwise, no articles of the sort you mentioned. I can absolutely vouch for it."

Drury Lane's eyes glistened now; he looked intently from one to the other of his visitors. He stretched to his full height, and the shadow he cast upon the old wall brooded over him. "Mr. Bruno, what is the opinion of your office?"

Bruno smiled wryly. "Obviously, Mr. Lane, we haven't particularly well-defined ideas. The case is complicated by a plethora of motives applying to many figures involved. Mrs. DeWitt, for example, undoubtedly had been Longstreet's mistress, and hated him because he had thrown her over for Cherry Browne. Fern. DeWitt's conduct throughout has been—well, peculiar.

"Michael Collins, whose political reputation is none too savory, is a scheming, unscrupulous man of the hot-headed variety; certainly in his own mind he had incentive.

"Young Kit Lord might in storybook fashion have acted the avenging knight-errant and killed to protect the honor of his lady-love." Bruno sighed. "But taking it all in all, Thumm and I both incline toward DeWitt."

"DeWitt." Lane's lips framed the name judiciously; his eyes were fixed unblinkingly on the District Attorney's mouth. "Please proceed."

"The trouble is," said Bruno with a fretful frown, "there isn't the slightest shred of evidence directly implicating DeWitt—or anyone else for that matter."

Thumm grumbled: "Anyone could have slipped the cork into Longstreet's pocket. Not only a member of his party, but any passenger on the car. By the way, we've investigated the kit and boodle of 'em, and we can find absolutely no connection between Longstreet and any of the other occupants of the car. Nothing at all to go on."

"That," concluded the District Attorney, "is why the Inspector and I have come to you, Mr. Lane. Your really brilliant analysis of the Cramer case, pointing out what was under our noses all the time, made us feel that you might be able to duplicate the feat."

Lane waved his arm. "The Cramer case—elementary, Mr.

Bruno." He stared thoughtfully at his visitors. A shrouded silence enveloped them now; Quacey, perched in his corner, was watching his master with complete absorption. Bruno and Thumm glanced covertly at each other. They both seemed disappointed; the Inspector half-grinned in a jeering way, as plainly as if he had said: "There! I told you so." Bruno's shoulders twitched in the suspicion of a shrug. They looked up simultaneously at the bell-sound in Drury Lane's voice.

"But surely, gentlemen," he was saying, regarding them with gentle amusement, "it must be apparent to you that the course of action is clear."

The quiet words had electric effect. Bruno's jaw dropped; Thumm shook his head slightly, like a fighter attempting to gather his senses after a hard blow.

He jumped to his feet. "Clear!" he shouted. "My God, Mr. Lane, do you realize what you——"

"Peace, Inspector Thumm," murmured Drury Lane. "Like the ghost of Hamlet's father, you start 'like a guilty thing upon a fearful summons.' Yes, gentlemen, the course is clear. If everything Inspector Thumm has told me is true, then I believe the guilt lies in one direction."

"Well, I'll be eternally damned," panted the Inspector. He peered at Lane out of overhung unbelieving eyes.

"Do you mean," asked the District Attorney weakly, "that from Inspector Thumm's mere recital of the facts, you know who killed Longstreet?"

The aquiline nose quivered. "I said—I *believe* I know. . . . You will have to take me on trust, Mr. Bruno."

"Oh!" said both men in one relieved voice. They calmed at once and exchanged significant glances.

"I appreciate your suspicions, gentlemen, but on my word

they are unfounded." Lane's voice became charming, persuasive; he handled it like a rapier. "I prefer for pressing reasons not to commit myself further at this time on the possible identity of your unknown quarry—shall we call him X from now on?—and that, gentlemen, despite the fact that I could make what seems to me a positive disclosure of complicity."

"But Mr. Lane," began Bruno in a sharper tone, "a delay—after all . . ."

Drury Lane stood motionless, in the reddish light like an Indian. The amusement had fled his nostrils and lips now, and his face was carved out of Parian marble. His lips barely moved, but his voice came extraordinarily distinct. "A delay? Dangerous, of course. But not half so dangerous, you will have to take my word for it, as a premature disclosure." Thumm stood sullenly by; he seemed disgusted. Bruno opened his mouth. "Don't press me at this time, please. Now, may I ask a favor of you gentlemen? . . ." The lingering disbelief on the faces of his visitors brought an impatient note into his voice. "Will you send me, by mail or messenger, a clear photograph of your corpse. In the life, of course."

"Oh, all right," mumbled Bruno. He shifted from one foot to the other absurdly like a sulky schoolboy.

"You will also keep me informed, Mr. Bruno," continued Lane in the same unimpassioned voice, "of developments. If," he paused perceptibly, "you have not already regretted consulting me." He regarded them for a moment and something of the old amusement crept back into his eyes.

Both men muttered unconvincing denials.

"Quacey will take any telephoned messages in my presence or absence." Lane reached up above the smoky mantel and jerked a bellcord. The rosy, pot-bellied little old man in livery popped into the room like a genie. "Will you honor me by lunching with me, gentlemen?" They shook their heads emphatically. "Then show Mr. Bruno and Inspector Thumm to their car, Falstaff. Remember that they are to be welcome at The Hamlet at all times. Notify me the moment either or both arrive. . . . Good day, Mr. Bruno." He bowed, a swift inclination of his torso. "Inspector Thumm."

Without a word District Attorney Bruno and Inspector Thumm followed in the wake of the butler. At the door, as if pulled by one string, they paused to look back. Mr. Drury Lane was standing before his old fire in the midst of his old and unbelievable possessions, smiling courteously in farewell.

Act II: *Scene 1*

THE DISTRICT ATTORNEY'S OFFICE.
WEDNESDAY, SEPTEMBER 9. 9:20 A.M.

DISTRICT ATTORNEY Bruno and Inspector Thumm faced each other across Bruno's desk the next morning, two hard-headed men eye to eye with a heckling mystery. The District Attorney's hand played with a neat pile of letters, destroying its neatness; Thumm's squashy nose was eloquent of a cold—and fruitless—morning outdoors.

"Well, sir," said the Inspector in his growling bass, "I'm stymied. Absolutely stymied. Reached a dead end this morning on the poison, cork, and needles. Looks as if the nicotine wasn't bought but was either manufactured privately or distilled from that insecticide Schilling mentioned. We'll never get anywhere there. And as for this Mr. Drury Lane of yours—damned if I don't think we're wasting our time."

Bruno demurred. "Now Thumm, I wouldn't say that. Don't be unkind." He spread his hands. "I think you're underestimating the man. True, he's a queer duck, living in a place like that, surrounded by old fogies, spouting Shakespeare . . ."

"Yeah! Well, I'll tell you what I think," scowled the Inspector.

"I think he's a lot of hot air. I think he's giving us the runaround. I think he made a grandstand play when he said he knew who killed Longstreet."

"Oh, but Thumm! you're being unfair," protested the District Attorney. "After all, he knows he can't make statements like that and expect to get away with 'em. He must know he'll have to make good eventually. No, I'm inclined to think that he knows what he's talking about—really has found a lead somewhere—is keeping quiet for reasons of his own."

Thumm pounded the desk. "Am I dumb, are you dumb? What do you mean—he found a lead? By all that's holy, what kind of lead? There just isn't any! I vote for easing him out of the picture. Christ, yesterday you thought the same way. . . ."

"Well, I can change my mind, can't I?" snapped Bruno. Then he looked sheepish. "We mustn't forget how nicely he pointed out our oversight on the Cramer mess. And if there's the slightest chance of getting help in this damned business, I'm not overlooking it. Then too, I can't very well give him the gate after inviting his co-operation. No, Thumm, we'll have to go through with it; he can't do any harm. . . . Anything new?"

Thumm bit a cigarette in half. "Collins. Making trouble again. One of my men just found out that Collins visited DeWitt three times since Saturday. Of course, he's trying to collect from DeWitt. Well, I'll keep tabs on him, but that's DeWitt's affair. . . ."

Bruno began idly to open the letters before him. Two he tossed into a desk-basket for filing; the third, a letter in a cheap plain envelope, brought him to his feet with an exclamation. Thumm's eyes narrowed as Bruno's eyes swept through the letter.

"Good God, Thumm!" shouted Bruno. "If this isn't the sweetest break—! Well, what is it?" he snarled at his secretary.

The secretary tendered a card, and Bruno snatched it and read it. "He does, does he?" he muttered in quite a different voice. "All right, Barney. Send him in . . . Stick around, Thumm. There's something extraordinary in this letter. But first let's see what this Swiss bird wants. It's Imperiale calling."

The secretary opened the door for the tall square figure of the Swiss business man, who entered smiling. Imperiale was attired, as usual, in meticulously correct morning clothes, a fresh flower in his lapel, stick tucked under his arm.

"Good morning, Mr. Imperiale. What can we do for you?" Bruno was deliberate; but the letter he had been reading had disappeared. He clasped his hands on the edge of his desk. Thumm grunted a greeting.

"My respects, sir. Good morning, Mr. Thumm." Imperiale sat down carefully in a leather chair by Bruno's desk. "I shall not take a moment, Mr. Bruno. I have," he said politely, "concluded my business affairs in America. I am ready to return to Switzerland."

"I see." Bruno looked at Thumm; and Thumm glowered at Imperiale's broad back.

"I had already booked passage on this evening's boat," said the Swiss with a slight frown, "and ordered my luggage called for by the express people, when one of your *gendarmes* appeared out of nowhere at my host's home and forbade me to leave!"

"To leave Mr. DeWitt's house, Mr. Imperiale?"

Imperiale shook his head with the merest trace of impatience. "Oh no! To leave the country, he said. He would not allow my luggage to be removed. This is very disturbing, Mr. Bruno! I am a business man; my presence is urgently required by my firm in Berne. Why am I delayed in this way? Surely——"

Bruno tapped his desk-top. "Now listen to me, Mr. Imperiale. I don't know how they do things in your country, but you don't seem to realize that you are involved in an American murder investigation. A *murder* investigation."

"Yes, I know, but——"

"There are no buts, Mr. Imperiale." Bruno rose. "I am sorry, naturally, but you will have to remain in this country until the murder of Harley Longstreet is cleared up, or at least an official decision reached. Of course, you may move from DeWitt's house and go elsewhere—I can't prevent you from doing that. But you'll have to remain within call."

Imperiale rose and stiffly stretched to his full height; his face lost its pleasantness and became ugly. "But I tell you my business will suffer!"

Bruno shrugged.

"Very well!" Imperiale clapped his hat on his head; his face was as red as the flames of Mr. Drury Lane's fire. "I shall immediately call upon my consul, Mr. Bruno, and demand satisfaction. Do you understand? I am a citizen of Switzerland and you have no right to detain me! Good day!"

He bowed infinitesimally, stormed toward the door. Bruno smiled. "Nevertheless, I'd advise you to cancel your passage, Mr. Imperiale. No sense in losing all that money. . . ." But Imperiale was gone.

"Well," said Bruno briskly, "that's that. Sit down, Thumm, and take a look at this." He produced the letter from his pocket and spread it before the Inspector. Thumm glanced at once at the bottom of the sheet—there was no signature. The letter was written in rusty black ink on cheap ruled stationery, in a plain undisguised hand. It was addressed to the District Attorney:

> I am one of the people on the street-car car when the man Longstreet was murdered. I have found out some-

> thing about who killed him. I am willing to give this information to you, Mr. District Attorney, but I am very much afraid that the murderer knows I know, and I think I am being watched.
>
> But if you will meet me, or send somebody to meet me Wednesday night at eleven o'clock, P.M., I will tell what I know. Mett me in the Weehawken ferry waiting-room at that time. You will know who I am. I will disclose myself. Please for my sake don't make a holler, Mr. District Attorney. Don't tell any outsiders about this letter, for the murderer may find out I have talked and I will be killed for doing my duty to the State.
>
> You will protect me, won't you. When I see you Wednesday night you will be glad I met you. *This is important.* [Heavily underscored.] I am going to watch myself until that time. I don't want to be seen talking to a cop in the daytime.

Thumm handled the letter gingerly; he placed it on the desk and scanned the envelope. "Postmarked Weehawken, N. J., last night," he muttered. "Full of fingerprints from dirty fingers. One of those Jerseyites on the car. . . . Well, Bruno, I'll be damned if I know what to think. Might be a crank letter and then again it mightn't. That's the hell of these things. What's your idea?"

"Hard to say." Bruno stared at the ceiling. "It sounds as if it might be a lead. I'll be there all right, just in case." He swung to his feet, began to pace the room. "Thumm, I have a hunch this is going to be good. The fact that this bird, whoever he is, didn't sign his name to the letter rings true. He's incoherent, puffed up high with his coming importance, and above all trembling in his boots about the possible consequences of his revelation.

Then, too, the letter displays the usual elements—it's voluminous, repetitious, nervous—witness the misspelling of 'meet' and the omission of the cross-bars on some of the t's. No, the more I think about it the more I'm inclined to like it."

"Well . . ." Inspector Thumm was dubious. Then he brightened. "This ought to knock Mr. Drury Lane off his pins, anyway. Maybe we won't need his blasted advice after all."

"Suits me, Thumm. We can stand a quick prosecution." Bruno rubbed his hands together contentedly. "Tell you what. Get in touch with District Attorney Rennells of Hudson County over the river and make the necessary arrangements to have Jersey police watch the Weehawken terminal. Damn this constant fuss about jurisdiction, anyway! No uniformed men, Thumm—all plainclothes. You'll be there?"

"Try and stop me," said Inspector Thumm with grim inelegance.

As Thumm slammed the door, District Attorney Bruno picked up one of the telephone instruments on his desk and put in a call for The Hamlet. He waited peacefully, almost happily, until his buzzer sounded. "Hello! The Hamlet? Mr. Drury Lane . . . District Attorney Bruno calling . . . Hello! Who is this?"

A shrill quavering voice answered: "This is Quacey, Mr. Bruno. Mr. Lane is right here by my side."

"Oh yes. I forgot—he can't hear." Bruno's voice expanded. "Well, tell Mr. Lane that I have news for him."

He heard Quacey's old voice repeating the message word for word.

"He says 'Indeed!'" came Quacey's squeak. "And, sir?"

"Tell him that he's not the only one who knows who killed Longstreet," said Bruno triumphantly.

He listened intently while Quacey repeated this to Lane, and heard, startlingly clear, Lane's remark: "Tell Mr. Bruno that is news, quite literally. Has he had a confession?"

Bruno explained to Quacey the contents of the anonymous letter. Silence from the other end of the wire, then Lane's voice, unhurried and unperturbed.

"Tell Mr. Bruno I am so sorry not to be able to converse with him directly. Ask him if I may be present tonight at this meeting."

"Oh, by all means," said Bruno to Quacey. "Er—Quacey, did Mr. Lane seem at all surprised?"

Bruno heard the oddest chuckle over the wire—the well-fed ghost of a chuckle. Then Quacey's quaking voice, brimming with sly fun: "No, sir, he seems quite pleased with the turn of events. He has often said that he always expects the unexpected. He——"

But District Attorney Bruno with a short "Good-bye!" had replaced the receiver on its hook.

Scene 2

THE WEEHAWKEN FERRY.
WEDNESDAY, SEPTEMBER 9. 11:40 P.M.

THE LIGHTS of midtown New York, on clear nights a pattern of bright stitches against black sky, on Wednesday night had almost completely blurred away in a blanket of fog which had persisted throughout the day and into the dark. From the ferry piers on the New Jersey shore nothing could be seen across the river except an occasional smeared point of electric light and a gray wall of forbidding mist over the water. Ferry boats loomed suddenly out of nowhere, ablaze on lower decks from stem to stern; ghostly small vessels felt their way up and down the river. Foghorns blared warning on all sides to cautious river traffic; but even these sounds were smothered by the fog.

In the vast barnlike structure, the waiting-room behind the Weehawken ferries, a dozen men were grouped, for the most part silent and watchful. In the midst of the group stood the stocky Napoleonic figure of District Attorney Bruno, nervously consulting his watch at ten-second intervals, pacing the hollow floor like a maniac. Inspector Thumm prowled about the big room, looking sharply at the doors and the infrequent newcomers. The room was almost empty.

Quite alone, apart from the group of detectives, sat Mr. Drury Lane, at whose quaint figure waiting ferry and railroad passengers sent wondering, sometimes amused glances. He sat with utter placidity, two white hands clasping their long digits about the knob of a thick, murderous-looking blackthorn stick between his knees. He wore a long black Inverness coat, cape falling free about his shoulders. On his thick hair was a straight-brimmed, black felt hat. Inspector Thumm, looking his way from time to time, thought he had never seen a man so superficially oldish, from his dress and hair, and yet, from his face and figure, so surprisingly young. The still features, chiseled and strong, might have been those of a man of thirty-five. His self-possession was stimulating and arresting; it was not that he ignored the curiosity of passersby—he was serenely unconscious of it.

His bright eyes were fixed on District Attorney Bruno's lips.

Bruno came over and sat down restlessly. "Forty-five minutes late already," he complained. "It looks as if we've invited you on a wild-goose chase. Of course, we'll have to see it through if it takes all night. To tell the truth, I'm beginning to feel a wee bit foolish."

"You should be feeling a wee bit worried, Mr. Bruno," said Lane in his precise musical way. "You would have more cause for that."

"You think—" began Bruno with a frown—and stopped, stiffening, as did Inspector Thumm across the room, at the confused sounds of a raucous commotion emanating from the ferries outside.

"What is the trouble, Mr. Bruno?" asked Lane mildly. Bruno's head and ears strained forward. "You couldn't hear that, of course. . . . Mr. Lane, that was a cry of 'Man overboard!' "

Drury Lane was on his feet in one feline movement. Inspector Thumm thundered up. "Trouble on the pier," he roared. "I'm going out!"

Bruno had also risen, indecisively. "Thumm, I'll stay here with some of the boys. Might be a decoy of some kind. Our man may come yet."

Thumm was already pounding toward the door. Quickly, Drury Lane followed. A half-dozen detectives ran after them.

They crossed the splintered wooden flooring outside, paused to determine the direction of the cries. At the farthest end of the roofed pier a ferry boat had come in and was grinding against the side pilings, maneuvering for the iron-shod curved landing-edge. A small number of scattered figures had already leaped the intervening space as Thumm, Lane, and the detectives reached the landing, while others were hurrying out of the terminal. The gold-leaf on the boat's pilot-house above the upper deck read: *Mohawk.* On the north side of the lower deck passengers milled wildly about, leaning over the rail along the bow, peering out of the windows of the starboard cabin-wall into the misty blackness below.

Three ferrymen were shoving their way through the crowd, endeavoring to reach the side. Drury Lane, following in Thumm's wake, suddenly looked at his gold watch. The time was 11:40.

Inspector Thumm sprang to the boat-deck, collaring a thin gnarled old ferryman. "Police!" he roared. "What's happened?"

The ferryman looked scared. "Man overboard, Cap. They say he fell from the top deck just as the *Mohawk* was sliding into the pier."

"Who is he—anybody know?"

"Naw."

"Come on, Mr. Lane," growled the Inspector. "The ferry people will fish him out. Let's see from where he fell."

They began to push through the press at the bow, going toward the door of the cabin. Thumm stopped short with an exclamation, extending his arm. At the south side of the lower deck a slight frail figure was stepping off to the dock.

"Hey there, DeWitt! Just a minute!"

The frail figure, bundled in a topcoat, looked up, hesitated, then retraced his steps. His face was white; he was panting a little. "Inspector Thumm!" he said slowly. "What are you doing here?"

"Little assignment," drawled Thumm, but his eyes were shining with excitement. "And you?"

DeWitt plunged his hand into the left pocket of his coat and shivered. "I'm on my way home," he said. "What's going on here?"

"Might have stayed to find out," said Thumm amiably. "Come along with us. By the way, meet Mr. Drury Lane. Helping out. Lane the actor. Famous man. Mr. Lane, this is Mr. DeWitt, Longstreet's partner." Drury Lane nodded pleasantly; DeWitt's eyes, wandering before, fixed themselves suddenly on the actor's face and recognition leaped into them, something of deference. "This is an honor, sir." Thumm was frowning; the men at his heels waited patiently. He craned about, seeming to search for someone, swearing beneath his breath.

Then he shrugged his shoulders. "Come along," he said sharply, and burrowed forward with his great bulk as the prod.

The interior of the cabin was in a state of panic. Thumm lunged up the brass-tipped stairs amidships, the others following. They ascended into the oval upper cabin, crossed to one of the northern doors, and emerged on the dark upper deck. The detectives, by the strong local illumination of flashlights, examined the deck. Roughly between the center of the boat and the bow, a few feet behind the cleared space at the tip of the boat, and well to the rear of the pilot-house above, Thumm found long, scratchlike, uneven marks. The detectives riveted their lights on the spot; the scratches ran from the criss-crossed iron railing back across the deck to a cubicle, or alcove, at the northwest outer corner of the cabin. This cubicle's western and southern walls were the outside of the cabin; the northern wall was a thin board; there was no eastern wall. The lights were trained inside; the marks on the deck emanated from the interior. There was a tool chest, locked and fixed to one wall, a few life-preservers, a broom, a pail, and other small articles. A chain extended across the middle of the open side.

"Go through it. Get some keys and open that box. Might be something there." Two detectives vanished. "And Jim. Go downstairs and hold everybody on the boat."

Thumm and Lane, with DeWitt trailing along, walked to the rail. Beyond the rail, the floor of the deck extended two and a half feet to the edge of the boat's side. Thumm, flashlight in hand, was scrutinizing the marks on the deck. He looked up at Lane. "Something rummy here, hey Mr. Lane? Heel-scrapings. A heavy object was *dragged* across the deck. A body, by God, and the heels of the shoes made the scratches. Might be murder."

Drury Lane was intently studying Thumm's face in the faint light which reached them from the flash; he nodded.

They leaned over the rail, straining to catch the frenzied scene below. Thumm out of the corner of his eye watched DeWitt. The little broker was calm now, somehow resigned.

A police boat had moored to the pierhead; scurrying figures

of police clambered to the slippery tops of the pilings, making fast. Two powerful searchlights suddenly switched on, illuminating the ferry brilliantly; and the pier stood out in bold relief despite the fog. The upper deck too was now quite bright. Lights swept below the lower deck, delineating every feature of the scene. The floor of the lower deck bellied outward, ground against the loose slimy pilings of the side piers. Nothing was visible below this wooden rampart. Ferry officials and workmen were standing and kneeling atop the pilings, shouting directions to the dim pilot-house above. There was an instant clanking and groaning in the interior of the ferry; it sidled out, edging away from the north pier toward the south pier. Two men in the pilot-house, the captain and pilot, were working furiously to clear away from the watery spot where the body evidently floated.

"Must have been crushed to a pulp," said Thumm in a matter-of-fact voice. Fell from here just as the ferry ground against the piling; probably was smashed right between the boat and the piling, then as the boat moved on it slipped beneath that jutting floor. They're going to have a job. . . Hullo! There's the water, by God!"

Oily scummed water, black and wicked-looking, appeared as the boat groaned sideways. The surface was churned and yeasty. A grappling-iron appeared from nowhere out of the darkness at the top of the pilings; police and ferrymen began to fish for the unseen body.

DeWitt, standing between Thumm and Lane, was absorbed in the grisly operations below. A detective appeared by Thumm's side. "Well?" growled Thumm.

"Nothin' in the chest, Chief. Nor in the alcove at all."

"All right. Just don't step all over these heel-marks on the deck." But his eyes were abstracted; they rested with curiosity on DeWitt. The frail little man was grasping the clammy rail with his left hand; he held his right hand rigidly before him, crooked elbow resting on the rail.

"What's the matter, DeWitt? Hurt your hand?"

The little broker turned slowly and looked down at his right hand with an absent smile. Then he straightened and offered the hand for Thumm's inspection. Lane leaned forward. On the forefinger, extending from the first joint vertically, was a fresh scar an inch and a half long. A thin scab had healed over the wound. "I cut my finger this evening on some apparatus in the Club gymnasium. Before dinner."

"Oh."

"Dr. Morris at the Club fixed me up. Told me to be careful with it. It does pain a little."

DeWitt and Thumm wheeled and leaned over the railing as a long triumphant yell reached their ears from below. Drury Lane blinked, and followed suit. "We've got him!" "Easy there!" A rope snaked down the pilings as the grappling-irons caught on something solid beneath the black surface of the water.

Three minutes later a dripping, limp bundle emerged from the river. Screams came at once from the lower deck—a meaningless murmur and confused shouting.

"Downstairs!" cried Inspector Thumm. As one, the three men turned and made for the door. DeWitt hurried forward across the deck. As he grasped the handle of the door he exclaimed in pain and annoyance. "What's the matter?" asked Thumm hurriedly. DeWitt was frowning over his right hand; Thumm and Lane saw that the wound was bleeding freely. The scar hung loose, torn in several places.

"Shouldn't have used my right hand on the door," groaned the little man. "Cut's opened after all, as Morris told me it would if I wasn't careful."

"Well, you won't die," growled Thumm and brushed by DeWitt, beginning to descend the stairs. He looked back. DeWitt had taken a handkerchief from his breast-pocket and was wrapping his right hand loosely. Drury Lane, muffled to the chin in his cloak, his eyes in shadow, said something pleasant, and the two men followed as Thumm clattered on down the stairs.

They made their way through the starboard lower cabin and found on the front deck outdoors that the salvagers had spread a piece of canvas. The bundle now lay on the canvas, sodden, in a little pool of foul-smelling water. It was the shapeless body of a man, crushed and bloody and mangled beyond recognition. The head and face were pulp; from the peculiar position in which it lay the spine seemed to have snapped; one arm, grotesquely, was flat, pulpy, spread out as if a steam-roller had run over it.

Drury Lane's face was whiter than before; with an effort he kept his eyes on the gruesome remains. Even Inspector Thumm, inured to scenes of bloody violence, made a little sound expressive of distaste. As for DeWitt, he gasped a little and turned his head away instantly, his face almost green. Around them were ferry officials, the ferry captain and the pilot, detectives, police, all morosely regarding the corpse.

From the south side of the boat, in the cabin, came sounds of excitement; the passengers had been herded into the long room under guard.

The body was lying flat on its dead stomach, the lower half curved impossibly backwards and to one side; the grisly head was sidewise to the deck. On the canvas lay a visored black cap, soaked.

Thumm knelt and pushed the body with one hand. It was like

a sack of wet meal, limp and unresisting. He half turned it over; a detective assisted him, and they managed to turn the body face up. It was that of a large burly man with red hair; the features were crushed and unrecognizable. Thumm muttered to himself in surprise: the dead man was dressed in a dark blue coat, pockets edged in a black leather, two rows of brass buttons down the entire length of the front. With suddenly predatory fingers Thumm snatched the cap from the deck—it was a conductor's cap. A shield above the visor bore the metal number 2101 and a metal inscription: *Third Avenue Railways.*

"Is it possible—?" exclaimed the Inspector, and stopped. He glanced sharply upward at Drury Lane, who was bending over and devouring the cap with his eyes.

Thumm dropped the cap and thrust his hand, callously now, into the inner breast pocket of the dead man's coat. His hand reappeared with a shabby soaked leather wallet. He rummaged through it, and leaped to his feet at once, ugly face shining. . . .

"It is!" he cried. He looked around, quickly.

The stocky figure of District Attorney Bruno, topcoat tails flying, was hurrying from the terminal to the ferry; plainclothes men pounded after him.

Thumm whirled on a detective. "Put double guards on that cabin full of passengers!" He stretched hugely, waving the limp wallet. "Bruno! Hurry up! We've got our man!"

The District Attorney broke into a run, sprang to the boat, took in the dead man, the crowd, Lane, DeWitt in one sweeping glance.

"Well?" he panted. "Who do you mean—the writer of the letter?"

"In person," said Thumm hoarsely. He prodded the body with his foot. "Only somebody else got to him first."

Bruno's eyes widened as he looked down again and saw the brass, buttons of the coat, the visored cap on the deck. "A conduc—!" He lifted his hat from his head despite the chill wind and dabbed the perspiration away with a silk handkerchief. "Are you sure, Thumm?"

For answer Thumm eased a water-softened card out of the wallet and handed it to the District Attorney. Drury Lane stepped quietly behind Bruno and examined it over Bruno's shoulder.

It was a round-edged identification-card issued by the Third Avenue Railways Company, bearing the stamped number 2101 and a signature.

The signature was a scrawl, but quite readable. It said: *Charles Wood.*

Scene 3

WEEHAWKEN TERMINAL.
WEDNESDAY, SEPTEMBER 9.11:58 P.M.

THE WEST Shore Railroad waiting-room in the Weehawken terminal was an old drafty two-story structure, huge as a barn out of Brobdingnag. The ceiling was nakedly iron-girdered, the beams crossing each other in a crazy motif. High above the floor, and hugging the second-story walls, ran a platform skirted by a railing. Off this platform were corridors leading to small official chambers. Everything was drab dusty gray-white.

The macerated corpse of Conductor Charles Wood had been borne on its canvas bier, still sopping with river-water, through the echoing waiting-room, then upstairs along the platform to the private office of the stationmaster. The waiting-room itself had been commandeered by the New Jersey police and cleared of railroad passengers. The passengers from the south cabin of the *Mohawk* were escorted, in a buzzing bustle, through lanes of police to the terminal waiting-room where, under guard, they waited the doubtful pleasure of Inspector Thumm and District Attorney Bruno.

The *Mohawk* itself had been chained by Thumm's order to the pier. Consultation of ferry officials resulted in a rapid revision of the ferry schedule; ferries came and went in the fog; railroad service was permitted to continue as usual, except that a temporary ticket-office was installed in the train-shed itself and passengers suffered to entrain through the ferry waiting-room. The abandoned *Mohawk* alive with lights, was black with detectives and police; none except officials and police were permitted to board. In the stationmaster's office upstairs a small group surrounded the recumbent body. District Attorney Bruno busied himself with the telephone. His first call was to the home of District Attorney Rennells of Hudson County. He explained quickly over the telephone that the dead man had been a witness in the New York murder of Harley Longstreet—over which he, Bruno, had jurisdiction—and requested permission to conduct the preliminary inquiry into Wood's death himself, despite the fact that the man had been killed in New Jersey territory. Rennells acquiesced, and Bruno at once notified New York police headquarters. Inspector Thumm grasped the instrument and ordered additional New York detectives.

Mr. Drury Lane was sitting quietly in a chair watching Bruno's lips, the now hard-lipped pallor of John DeWitt—forgotten in a corner—and the cold fury of Inspector Thumm.

As Thumm put down the telephone, Lane said: "Mr. Bruno."

The District Attorney, who had moved to the foot of the corpse and was staring moodily down at its horrible length, twisted his head toward Lane; an odd hope leaped into his eyes.

"Mr. Bruno," said Drury Lane, "have you examined the signature of Wood carefully—the signature of his identification card?"

"What do you mean?"

"It seems to me," explained Lane mildly, "that it is of paramount importance to *prove,* indisputably, the identity of the anonymous letter-writer. Inspector Thumm seemed to think Wood's signature and the handwriting of the letter were the same. But with all deference to the Inspector's opinion, I for one should feel more content if an expert confirmed it."

Thumm grinned nastily. "They're the same, Mr. Lane. Don't fret yourself about that." He knelt by Wood's body and with no more emotion than if he had been handling a stuffed tailor's-dummy he explored the dead man's pockets. He rose at last with two wrinkled, damp pieces of paper. One was a Third Avenue Railways accident-report blank, carefully describing a minor collision with an automobile that afternoon, and signed. The other was a stamped sealed envelope. Thumm tore it open, read it, handed it to Bruno, who ran his eye down the sheet and then turned it over to Lane. It was a request for literature on a correspondence course in transportation engineering. Lane studied the handwriting and signatures of both documents.

"Have you the unsigned note, Mr. Bruno?"

Bruno rummaged in the depths of his wallet and produced the letter. Lane spread the three pieces of paper on the desk to his side, scrutinized them with unwinking concentration. He smiled after a moment and returned them to Bruno.

"I apologize, Inspector," he said. "All three were undoubtedly written by the same hand. And since we know that Wood wrote the accident-report and the letter to the correspondence school, he must also have been our anonymous letter-writer from the identical handwritings. . . . Nevertheless it is important, I think, that an expert corroborate even Inspector Thumm's violent opinion."

Thumm grunted and dropped to his knees again beside the dead man. District Attorney Bruno returned the three documents to his wallet and reached for the telephone once more.

"Dr. Schilling . . . Doc? This is Bruno. In the Weehawken railroad terminal, stationmaster's office. Yes, behind the ferries . . . Right away . . . Oh! Well, finish that and get here as fast as you can. . . . Four o'clock? Then don't bother. I'll have the body taken to the Hudson County morgue and you can pick it up there for examination. . . . Yes, yes, I insist on having you in on it. It's the body of Charles Wood, the conductor of the Longstreet car. . . . Right. 'Bye."

"If I may make a further suggestion," put in Drury Lane from his chair, "Mr. Bruno? It is possible that Wood spoke to or was seen by ferrymen or fellow street-car employees just before boarding the *Mohawk*."

"Excellent hunch, Mr. Lane. They may still be around." Bruno picked up the telephone again and put in a call to the New York side of the ferry-route.

"Bruno, D.A. of New York County, speaking from the Weehawken terminal. There's been a murder here—oh, you've heard it?—and I want co-operation at once. . . . Fine. Send over any ferry employees who may have seen or spoken to Conductor Charles Wood, Number 2101, Third Avenue Railways line, Forty-Second Street Crosstown, this evening. . . . About an hour ago, yes. . . . And while you're doing that, see if you can't pick up one of the car inspectors on duty. I'm sending over a police boat."

Bruno hung up and dispatched a detective with orders to the captain of the police boat moored to the pilings by the *Mohawk*.

"Now!" He rubbed his hands. "Mr. Lane, while Inspector Thumm is examining the body, would you care to go downstairs with me? There's a raft of work to be done."

Lane rose. Out of the corner of his eye he had been watching DeWitt, crouched forlornly in a corner. "Perhaps," said Lane in a serene baritone, "Mr. DeWitt would accompany us? The scene here cannot be anything but unpleasant to him, Mr. Bruno."

Bruno's eyes gleamed behind his rimless glasses. His gaunt face curved into smiles. "Yes, by all means. Come along if you like, Mr. DeWitt."

The little gray broker looked gratefully at Lane's cloaked figure. He followed the two men from the room. They skirted the platform and descended to the floor of the waiting-room.

The District Attorney raised his hand in the hush that fell as they paraded across the floor. "The pilot of the ferryboat *Mohawk.* This way. Want a chat with you. Captain, too."

Two men detached themselves from the group of passengers and trudged to the spot.

"I'm the pilot—Sam Adams." The ferry pilot was a squat powerful man with closely cropped black hair and a bullish face.

"Just a moment. Here, where's Jonas? Jonas!" Inspector Thumm's secretarial detective hurried up, notebook ready. "Take this testimony down. . . . Now Adams, we're trying to get confirmatory identifications of the dead man. Did you see the body when we had it on the ferry-deck?"

"Sure did."

"Have you ever seen the man before?"

"Hundreds of times." The pilot hitched his trousers purposefully. "Sort of friend of mine, he was. 'Course, his head was bashed in and all that, but I'd swear on the Book that he's Charley Wood, conductor on the Crosstown."

"What makes you think so?"

Pilot Adams lifted his cap and scratched his head. "Why—I just know. Same build, same red hair, same clothes—can't tell you exactly how I know—I just know. Besides, I spoke to him tonight on the boat."

"Oh! You saw him then. Where—in the pilot-house? I thought that was against the rules. Tell me the whole story, Adams."

Adams cleared his throat, spat into a nearby spittoon, darted an embarrassed glance at the tall, cadaverous, weatherbeaten man at his side—the ferry captain—and said: "Well, let's see. I know this Charley Wood for years. Been on this run nigh onto nine years, ain't I, Cap'n?" The captain nodded his head judiciously and expectorated with deadly accuracy into the cuspidor. "Charley lives over in Weehawken here, I guess, 'cause he always took the ferry across at 10:45 when he was through with his shift on the car."

"Just a moment." Bruno nodded significantly to Lane. "Did he take the 10:45 ferry tonight?"

The pilot seemed aggrieved. "I'm gettin' to it. Sure he did. Well, anyways, years back he got into the habit of comin' up on the top passenger deck and passin' the time of night, you might say. Haw!" Bruno scowled, and Adams hastened on. "Anyways, if Charley don't come up there and yell to me of nights I'm sorta disappointed. 'Course, nights he was off or stayed over in the City I didn't see him, but most generally he took the *Mohawk*."

"That's very interesting," commented the District Attorney. "Very. But make it snappy, Adams—this isn't a serial, you know."

"Well, ain't I?" The pilot shuffled again, set himself. "Now then. Tonight Charley comes up on the 10:45, top passenger deck, starb'rd, like he always does, and he yells up at me: 'Ahoy there, Sam!' He says 'Ahoy!' mostly 'cause of my bein' a sailor, you see. Just a joke of his. Haw!" Bruno showed his teeth and Adams sobered instantly. "Well, well, I'm gettin' to it," he said hastily. "So I yells back 'Ahoy!' an' I says, 'Lousy fog, ain't it, Charley? Thick as me old lady's brogue!' an' he says, yellin' up at me—I could see him 'most as clear as I see you; he was up right close to the pilot-house an' the lights of the house was shinin' on his face—he says: 'You tell 'em, Sam. Rotten, ain't it?' an' I says, 'How's tricks with you, Charley?' an' he says, 'Well,' he says, 'so-so. Had a collision with a Chevvy this afternoon. Guiness was hoppin',' he says. 'Damn fool woman-driver,' he says, an' says, 'Ain't they hell,' an'——"

Adams grunted in shocked surprise as the sharp elbow of the ferry captain drove with force into his meaty ribs. "Get th' hell on with that yarn, Sam," said the captain. He had a hollow bass voice that reverberated through the room. "Can't ye see th' lubber's gonna pop you one if ye don't make port?"

Pilot Adams whirled on his superior. "You poke me in th' ribs again——"

"Here, here!" Bruno's voice was sharp. "None of that. You're the captain of the *Mohawk*?"

"That's me," boomed the tall cadaverous man. "Cap'n Sutter. Twenty-one years on th' river."

"Were you in the pilot-house while this—er—conversation was taking place?"

"That's my bally-wick, Mister, on a foggy night."

"Did you see this man Wood while he was yelling up at Adams?"

"Ye're tootin', Mister."

"You're sure it was 10:45?"

"Yep."

"Did you see Wood again after his talk with Adams?"

"Nope. Next I saw o' him, he was bein' fished out o' the river."

"You're positive of the identification?"

"I ain't finished," broke in Pilot Adams in a complaining voice.

"He said somethin' else. He said he wasn't goin' to stay on for any extra trips tonight—had an appointment, he did, over in Jersey."

"You're sure of that? Did you hear that, Captain Sutter?"

"Fer once this gabby shark's right, Mister. An' that was Wood—seen him hundreds o' times."

"You said, Adams, that he wasn't going to stay on for 'extra' trips tonight. Was he in the habit of staying on for extra trips?"

"Not a habit, I wouldn't say. But sometimes when he felt good, 'specially in the summertime, he'd take a coupla rides."

"That's all, both of you."

The two men turned, and halted at once at the commanding note in Drury Lane's voice. Bruno rubbed his jaw. "One moment, Mr. Bruno," said Lane pleasantly. "May I ask these men a question?"

"Certainly. Anything and any time you want to, Mr. Lane."

"Thank you. Mr. Adams—Captain Sutter." The two river-men were staring at him open-mouthed—the cape, the black hat, the formidable stick. "Did either of you see Wood leave that portion of the upper deck where he had been standing when he spoke to you?"

"Sure, I did," said Adams promptly. "Got the signal, began pullin' her out. Wood waved his hand at us an' left, goin' back under the roof of the top passenger deck."

"Right," thundered Captain Sutter.

"Exactly how much of the upper deck is visible to you gentlemen from the pilot-house at night, even when your lights are on?"

Captain Sutter speared the spittoon again. "Not much. We can't see under the roof o' the passenger deck a-tall. An' at night, with th' fog, anythin' that's outside th' reflection other pilot-house lights is dark as Davy's locker. Pilot-house's built like a fan, ye know."

"You saw and heard nothing else from 10:45 until 11:40 that might betray the presence of human beings on the upper deck?"

"Say, listen," growled the captain. "Ever try to take a tub crost the river on a foggy night? Believe me, Mister, ye got all ye can do to keep outa th' way of river-traffic."

"Excellent." Drury Lane stepped back. Bruno, brows knit, dismissed the river-men with a nod.

He climbed to the seat of one of the waiting-room benches, shouting: "Now I want all those who saw the body fall from the upper deck to step up here!"

Six people wavered, looked at each other, then with hesitant steps crossed the room to stand uncomfortably beneath Bruno's unfriendly scrutiny. All, as if rehearsed, began to speak at once.

"One at a time, one at a time," snapped Bruno, jumping off the bench. He eyed a rotund little man with blond hair and a paunch. "You—what's your name?"

"August Havemeyer, sir," said the little man nervously. He wore a round clerical-looking hat, a stringy black tie; his clothes were shabby and begrimed. "I'm a printer—goin' home from work."

"Printer going home from work." Bruno rocked on his heels. "All right, Havemeyer, did you see a man's body fall from the upper deck as the ferry docked?"

"Yes, sir. Yes, sir."

"Where were you at the time?"

"I was sittin' in that room on the ferry—that cabin—and I was sittin' on the bench across from the windows," said the German, licking his fat lips. "Just as the boat began to get into the piers between those—those big sticks . . ."

"The pilings?"

"Yes, the pilings. Just then I saw something big and black, it looked like—I sort of got a look at a face but it was all blurry—come falling outside the windows opposite from upstairs somewheres. It—it crunched right away. . . ." Havemeyer wiped a bead of perspiration from his trembling upper lip. "It happened so sudden——"

"And that's all you saw?"

"Yes, sir. I began to yell, 'Man overboard!' and it seems like other people saw it too because everybody began to yell. . . ."

"That's all for you, Havemeyer." The little man retreated in relief. "Now, folks, did everybody see the same thing?"

There was a chorus of assent.

"Anybody see anything else—maybe get a look at the face as it fell past?"

No answer. They looked at each other doubtfully.

"Very well. Jonas! Take their names, occupations, and addresses." The detective stepped into the midst of the group and interrogated the six remaining passengers with bored rapidity. Havemeyer spoke first, furnished his address, and scuttled back into the main body of the crowd. The second was a dirty little Italian dressed in black shiny material, wearing a black official cap—Guiseppe Salvatore, ferry bootblack. He had been shining a man's shoes, facing the windows, he said. The third was a worn bedraggled little old Irishwoman, Mrs. Martha Wilson, returning, she said, from her work as scrubwoman in a Times Square office-building; she had been seated next to Havemeyer and had seen exactly the same thing. The fourth was a large dapper man, Henry Nixon, dressed in a shrieking checked suit—he was an itinerant salesman of cheap jewelry, he said, and had been strolling forward through the cabin when the body hurtled past the window. The last two were young girls, May Cohen and Ruth Tobias, office-workers, returning to their New Jersey homes

"Yes or no?"

"Of course not."

"So you knew him by sight, had never spoken to him, and didn't see him tonight. . . . All right, DeWitt. Now when I stepped on the ferry not long ago you were just leaving. You certainly knew an accident had occurred. Weren't you curious enough to stay and find out what had happened?"

The smile had faded from DeWitt's lips. His face was tight and heckled. "No. I was tired, anxious to get home."

"Tired and anxious to get home," said Thumm exasperatingly. "A good reason, by God. . . . DeWitt, do you smoke?"

DeWitt stared. "Smoke?" he repeated angrily. He turned to the District Attorney. "Mr. Bruno," he cried, "this is infantile. Am I to submit to such a nonsensical inquisition?"

Bruno said in a cold voice: "Please answer the question." Again DeWitt glanced at Drury Lane, again DeWitt looked about helplessly.

"Yes," he said slowly—something terrified had crawled under his tired eyelids—"yes."

"Cigarettes?"

"No. Cigars."

"Have you any with you?"

Silently DeWitt reached into the breast pocket of his coat, produced a rich leather cigar-case, neatly initialed in gold, and handed it to the Inspector. Thumm pulled the top away and, taking out one of the three cigars in the case, examined it minutely. On the cigar was a gilt band lettered *J. O. DeW.* "Private brand, DeWitt?"

"Yes. They're made up specially for me by Huengas of Havana."

"The bands, too?"

"Of course."

"Huengas puts the bands on?" insisted Thumm.

"Oh, piffle," said DeWitt distinctly. "What is the purpose of this inane questioning? There's something deep, dark, and foolish in your mind, Inspector. Yes, Huengas puts the bands on the cigars, boxes them, ships them to me by boat, and so on and so on. May I ask: What of it?"

Without replying, Inspector Thumm restored the cigar to its case and stowed it away in one of his bottomless pockets. DeWitt's face clouded at this wanton appropriation but, straightening his little body defiantly, he said nothing.

"One question more, DeWitt," resumed the Inspector in the most amiable way in the world. "Have you ever offered Conductor Wood one of these cigars—on the street-car or anywhere else?"

"I—see," said DeWitt in a deliberate voice. "I see now." No one spoke. Thumm, whose cigarette drooping from his lips had gone out, was watching the broker with tigerish eyes. "I am finally," went on DeWitt with restraint, "finally checkmated. Eh, Inspector? You play a clever game. No, I have never offered Conductor Wood one of these cigars, on the street-car or anywhere else."

"That's fine, DeWitt, just dandy," chortled Thumm. "Because I've found one of your special-brand, initial banded cigars in the vest pocket of the dead man!"

DeWitt nodded bitterly, as if he had quite foreseen this statement. He opened his mouth, closed it again, opened it and said in a dreary way: "I gather, then, I'm to be arrested for the murder of this man?" Then he laughed—an old man's broken, embarrassing cackle. "I'm not dreaming, I suppose? One of my cigars on the murdered man!" He sank into a nearby chair.

Bruno said formally: "No one has suggested arrest, Mr. DeWitt. . . ."

At this moment a party of men appeared at the door, led by a man in a police captain's uniform. Bruno stopped speaking and questioned the officer with his eyes. The officer nodded and went away.

"Come in, boys," said Thumm in an agreeable voice.

The newcomers trooped into the room shyly. One was the Irish motorman, Patrick Guiness, who had driven the street-car in which Longstreet had been murdered. The second was a lean old man, attired shabbily and wearing a visored cap, who said he was Peter Hicks, ferryman on the New York side. The third was a wind-burned street-car inspector whose station, he said, was at the end of the Crosstown run, just outside the ferry terminal at the foot of Forty-Second Street.

Behind them appeared several detectives, among them Lieutenant Peabody. Sergeant Duffy's broad shoulders loomed behind Peabody. All eyes focused instinctively on the dead body lying on the canvas.

Guiness glanced once at Wood's remains, swallowed convulsively, and turned away with frightened eyes. He looked sick.

"Guiness, will you formally identify this man?" asked Bruno.

Guiness mumbled: "Christ, look at his head. . . . It's Charley Wood, all right."

"You're sure?"

Guiness directed a shaking finger at the left leg of the corpse. The trousers had been ripped and torn by concussion with the side of the ferry and the pilings. The left leg, except for shoe and sock, was nakedly exposed. Part of a long scar was visible on the calf, disappearing where the black sock covered it. The scar curled and twisted—a peculiar cicatrix now livid in death.

"That scar," said Guiness hoarsely. "I've seen it many a time. Charley showed it to me when he first came onto the car-line, even before we both got transferred to the Crosstown. He'd got it in an accident years and years ago, he told me."

Thumm stripped the sock away from the scar, revealing it in its gruesome entirety. It extended from a point immediately above the ankle to just below the knee, curving halfway around the calf. "You're positive that's the same scar you saw?" asked Thumm.

"That's the scar, all right," said Guiness faintly.

"Okay, Guiness." Thumm rose, brushing his knees. "Now you, Hicks, got anything to offer about Wood's movements tonight?"

The wiry old ferryman nodded. "Sure thing, Cap. I knew Charley purty well—used the ferry near every night, gen'ally stopped and spoke to me. Tonight, around ha'past ten, Charley comes into the ferry terminal and as usual we got to talking. Looked a little nervous, now I come to think of it. We jest gabbled a spell."

"You're sure of the time—10:30?"

"Sure I'm sure. I got to keep tabs on the time—them ferries run on schedule, Cap."

"What did you talk about?"

"We-ell," said Hicks, smacking his leathery lips, "we talked, and he was carryin' his bag, and I asked him if he'd been in town the night before as per usual—y'see, sometimes he stayed over in the City and took some clean duds with him—but no, he says, it was jest a second-hand bag he'd bought on his off-time today; handle of the old one'd broke. And——"

"What kind of bag was it?" demanded Thumm.

"What kind of bag?" Hicks pursed his lips. "Hanged if there was anything special about it, Cap. Jest one o' these cheap black handbags you can buy for a buck anywhere. Square, kind of."

Thumm motioned to Lieutenant Peabody. "See if any of the

passengers in the waiting-room downstairs have bags like the one Hicks describes. And get a search started of the *Mohawk* for a bag of that description. Upper deck, pilot-house, and all. Top to bottom. Then have the boys on the police boat search the water—might have been thrown overboard, or maybe it fell overboard."

Peabody strolled out. Thumm turned again to Hicks. Before he could speak, Drury Lane said gently: "I beg your pardon, Inspector . . . Hicks, by any chance was Wood smoking a cigar while you chatted?"

Hicks's eyes widened at this apparitional inquisitor. But he replied, readily enough, "Sure was. Matter of fact, I asked Charley for one. Them Cremos he smoked sorta appealed to me. Anyway, he looks for one in his pockets——"

"His vest pocket, too, I trust, Hicks?" said Lane.

"Yep, vest pockets and all, and he says: 'Nope, guess I'm all out, Pete. I'm smokin' my last one.'"

"Smart question at that, Mr. Lane," said Thumm grudgingly. "You're certain it was a Cremo, Hicks, and he hadn't another of any kind on him?"

Hicks said in plaintive tones: "But I've jest told this gentleman, Cap . . ."

DeWitt did not look up; he sat in his chair as if turned to stone. From his eyes, it was doubtful whether he had even heard the exchange of questions and answers. They were brimming and bloodshot.

"Guiness," said Thumm, "was Wood carrying this handbag when he completed his run tonight?"

"Yes, sir," replied Guiness in a faint voice. "Just as Hicks said. He went off duty at half-past ten for the night. He'd had the bag stowed on the car all afternoon."

"Know where Wood lived?"

"In a rooming-house in Weehawken here—2075 Boulevard."

"Any relatives?"

"I don't think so. Leastways, he wasn't married and as far as I can remember he never said a word about kin."

"There's another thing, Cap," put in Hicks the ferryman. "While Charley and me were talkin', all of a sudden Charley points to a little geezer that gets out of a cab all bundled up, sneaks into the ticket-office, buys a ferry-ticket and, droppin' the ticket into the box, crosses into the waitin'-room and waits for the ferry like he didn't want anyone to see him. Charley says to me, confidential, that the little guy was the broker, John DeWitt, the feller mixed up in the murder on Charley's car."

"What!" roared Thumm. "And you say this was around 10:30?" He glared down at DeWitt, who had roused now and was sitting, forward, hands gripping the arms of the chair. "Go on, Hicks, go on!"

"Well," drawled Hicks maddeningly, "Charley looked kinda nervous when he sees this DeWitt. . . ."

"Did DeWitt see Wood?"

"Reckon not. He stuck in a corner all the time, all by himself."

"Anything else?"

"Well, I had to go 'bout my dooties jest as the ferry boat came in at 10:40. I did see this DeWitt go in through the gate, and Charley says good-bye and goes in too."

"You're positive about the time, now—it was the ferry leaving at 10:45?"

"Aw rats!" said Hicks in deep disgust. "I said that most a hunderd times."

"Step aside, Hicks." Thumm pushed by the ferryman and glowered down upon the broker, who was nervously picking at the fabric of his coat. "DeWitt! Look at me." DeWitt raised his head slowly; the misery in his eyes startled even the Inspector. "Hicks, is this the man Wood pointed out to you?"

Hicks stretched his attenuated neck, studying DeWitt's face judiciously with fish-eyes. "Yep," he said finally. "Yep, that's the little guy. Ready to take my oath, Cap."

"Good enough. Hicks, Guiness, and this man here—car inspector? won't need you now—go downstairs and wait for me." The three men left the room with reluctant steps. Drury Lane unexpectedly sat down, leaning on his stick, surveying the taut features of the broker with melancholy eyes. Far, far in the crystal depths of those eyes' there was a faint puzzlement—a suspension of judgment, a question.

"Now then, Mr. John O. DeWitt," growled Thumm, looming over the little man, "suppose you explain to us how it is you were seen boarding the 10:45 ferry, and yet a while ago you said you took the 11:30 ferry?"

Bruno stirred slightly; his face was grave. "Before you answer, Mr. DeWitt, it is my duty to warn you that anything you may say may be used against you. There is a stenographer here taking down every word. You needn't answer if you don't want to."

DeWitt swallowed hard, ran his thin finger under his collar, made a sorry attempt to smile. "The sad consequences," he murmured, rearing his body, "of flirting with the truth. . . . Yes, gentlemen, I did lie. I took the 10:45 boat."

"Got that, Jonas?" shouted Thumm. "Why'd you lie, DeWitt?"

"That," said DeWitt quietly, "I must refuse to explain. I had an appointment with someone on the 10:45 boat, but the matter was strictly personal and had nothing to do with this ghastly business."

"Well, if you had an appointment to meet someone on the 10:45 boat, why the hell did you stay on until 11:40?"

"Please," said DeWitt, "moderate your language, Inspector. I am not accustomed to being addressed in this manner; and if you persist, I shall absolutely refuse to say another word."

Thumm swallowed a curse, caught a quick glance from Bruno, inhaled deeply, and continued in a less belligerent tone: "All right. Why?"

"That's better," said DeWitt. "Because the person I was waiting for did not show up at the appointed time. I remained on the boat for four trips, suspecting a delay. At 11:40 I gave up and decided to go home."

Thumm snickered. "You expect us to believe that? Who was this person you were waiting for?"

"I'm sorry."

Bruno wagged his finger at DeWitt. "You understand, Mr. DeWitt, you are placing yourself in a most peculiar position. You must realize that your story is very, very thin—under the circumstances we can't accept it without specific information."

DeWitt pressed his lips together, folded his puny arms across his chest, and stared at the wall.

"Well," said the Inspector argumentatively, "maybe you'll tell us how the appointment was made. Any record of it—letter, witness to a conversation?"

"The appointment was made over the telephone this morning."

"You mean Wednesday morning?"

"Yes."

"Your party called *you?*"

"Yes, at my office in Wall Street. My operators keep no record of incoming calls."

"You knew the person who called you?"

DeWitt remained silent.

"And you say," pursued Thumm, "that the only reason you attempted to sneak off the boat was because you were tired of waiting and decided to go back to West Englewood?"

"I suppose," muttered DeWitt, "that I can't expect you to believe that."

The veins on Thumm's neck swelled. "Damned right you can't!"

He grasped Bruno's arm roughly and marched him to a corner. The two men conferred in heated whispers.

Mr. Drury Lane sighed and closed his eyes.

• • • • •

At this moment Lieutenant Peabody returned from the waiting-room with six people in tow. Detectives hurried into the stationmaster's office carrying cheap black handbags, five in number.

Thumm said quickly to Peabody: "Well, what's doing?"

"Here are some bags like the ones you asked me to look for. And," grinned Peabody, "their anxious owners."

"Anything on the *Mohawk* itself?"

"No sign of a bag, Chief. And the police boat boys haven't had any luck on the river so far, either."

Thumm went to the door and roared: "Hicks! Guiness! Come on up here!"

The ferryman and the motorman ran upstairs and into the room, looking frightened.

"Hicks, take a look at these bags. Any one of 'em Wood's?"

Hicks surveyed the luggage on the floor critically. "We-ell, might all be, I reckon. Can't say exactly."

"What do you say, Guiness?"

"It's hard to tell. They're all pretty much the same, Inspector."

"All right. Beat it." The two men left. Thumm squatted on his hard hams and opened one of the bags; Mrs. Martha Wilson, the old scrubwoman, uttered an outraged little gasp and began to sniffle. Thumm pulled out a bundle of soiled working-clothes, a lunch-box and a paper-backed novel. Disgusted, he tackled the next bag. Henry Nixon, the salesman, began an angry protest; Thumm silenced him with a devastating look and ripped open the bag. It contained several cardboard, wool-topped trays covered with cheap jewelry and trinkets, and a pad of order blanks with the man's name imprinted. Thumm threw the bag aside and went to the next one. It revealed a pair of dirty old trousers and some tools. Thumm looked up and saw Sam Adams, the pilot of the *Mohawk*, regarding him anxiously. "Yours?" "Yes, sir." The Inspector opened the other two bags: one, belonging to a huge Negro dock-worker, Elias Jones, contained a change of clothing and a lunch-box; the second, three baby-diapers, a half-filled nursing-bottle, a cheap book, a packet of safety-pins, and a little blanket. They belonged to a young couple, Mr. and Mrs. Thomas Corcoran; the man held a sleepy, surly infant in his arms. Thumm growled and the baby, after one fascinated stare, squirmed in its father's arms, buried its tiny head on his shoulder and began to howl. Its shrill screeching filled the office; one of the detectives tittered. Thumm grinned impatiently and released the six passengers with their luggage. Drury Lane observed with amusement that someone had hurriedly thrown a few empty sacks over the dead man.

The Inspector sent word by one of his men to release Motorman Guiness, the street-car inspector, and Peter Hicks, ferryman.

A policeman came in and rumbled something to Lieutenant Peabody. Peabody groaned. "A lot of nothing on the river, Chief."

"Well, I guess Wood's bag was thrown overboard and sank. Probably never will be found," muttered Thumm.

Sergeant Duffy clumped upstairs, puffing. A sheaf of scribbled papers was clutched in his red fist. "Names and addresses of all those people downstairs, Inspector."

Bruno hurried over and scanned the list of the ferry-occupants over Thumm's shoulder. Both he and Thumm seemed to be looking for something. They went from sheet to sheet, searching. Then they exchanged congratulatory glances, and the District Attorney's lips set hard.

"Mr. DeWitt," he snapped, "you might be interested to learn that of all the people who were in the street-car when Longstreet was done in, *only you* were present on the ferry tonight!"

DeWitt blinked, looked blankly into Bruno's face, and then, with a little shiver, lowered his head.

"What you say, Mr. Bruno," came Drury Lane's cool voice in the silence, "may be true, but I daresay you will never be able to prove it."

"How? What?" stormed Thumm. Bruno frowned.

"My dear Inspector," murmured Lane, "surely you must have noticed that a number of passengers left the *Mohawk* as you and I approached to board it after the hue-and-cry had been raised. Have you accounted for these?"

Thumm blew out his upper lip. "Well, we can hunt for 'em, can't we," he blustered, "and check up that way?"

Drury Lane smiled. "Will you ever be so positive, Inspector, as to be able to make out a legal case? How will you ever know that you have found all of them?"

Bruno whispered to Thumm; again DeWitt peered at Drury Lane with pitiful gratitude. Thumm shook his heavy frame, barked an order to Sergeant Duffy, and the sergeant left.

Thumm crooked his finger at DeWitt. "Come downstairs with me."

The broker rose in silence and preceded the Inspector out of the door.

Three minutes later they returned. DeWitt maintained his silence and Thumm seemed disgruntled. "Nothing doing," he whispered to Bruno. "Not one of the passengers remembers DeWitt's movements long enough to pin anything on him. One man seemed to remember him all by himself in a corner for a minute, but DeWitt says he kept himself pretty much out of sight anyway because of this phony appointment of his. Hell and damnation!"

"But that's a point in our favor, Thumm," said Bruno. "He has no alibi for the period in which Wood's body was being thrown off the top deck."

"I'd a damned sight rather some passenger testified he saw DeWitt coming down those stairs. What'll we do with him?"

Bruno shook his head. "Let's go easy tonight. He's not small pumpkins and we want to be dead sure before we take action. Put a couple of men on him. Though at that he can't very well skip out."

"You're the boss." The Inspector strode over to DeWitt, glared down into his eyes. "That's all for tonight, DeWitt. Go on home. But keep in touch with the D.A."

Without a word John DeWitt rose, smoothed his coat mechanically, adjusted his felt hat on his gray head, looked around, sighed, and trudged out of the stationmaster's office. Thumm signaled at once with a splayed forefinger and two detectives hurried after the broker.

Bruno put on his topcoat. The office buzzed with the conversation of smoking men. Thumm straddled the dead man, bent over and lifted the sacking away from the smashed skull. "You damned fool," he muttered, "you might at least have named this guy X who killed Longstreet in that crazy letter of yours. . . ."

Bruno walked across the room and put his hand on Thumm's bulging biceps. "Come on, there, Thumm, you'll go screwy. Was that upper deck photographed?"

"The boys are doing it now. Well, Duffy?" as the sergeant panted into the room.

Duffy shook his ponderous head. "Not a sign of those escaped passengers, Chief. Couldn't even find out how many there were."

Nobody said anything for a long moment.

"Well, blast this whole lousy case!" yelled Thumm into the humming silence. He whirled on himself like a furious dog chasing his own tail. "I'm going over to Wood's rooming-house with some of the boys, Bruno. Going home?"

"I may as well. I hope Schilling doesn't miss up on that *post mortem*. I'll go back with Lane." He turned around, putting on his hat and looking for the place where Lane had been sitting.

Astonishment spread all over his face.

Mr. Drury Lane had disappeared.

Scene 4

INSPECTOR THUMM'S OFFICE.
THURSDAY, SEPTEMBER 10. 10:15 A.M.

A LARGE man squirmed on a chair in Inspector Thumm's office at Police Headquarters. He toyed with a magazine, pared his nails, chewed a cigar to shreds, looked out of the window at the monotonous murky sky—and jumped to his feet as the door opened.

Inspector Thumm's ugly face was as dark as the weather outside. He stalked in, hurled his hat and coat on a clothes-tree, and plumped into the swivel-chair behind his desk, grumbling to himself. He ignored the large man shuffling before him.

The Inspector opened his mail, snapped orders into an inter-office communicator, dictated two letters to a male secretary, and only then deigned to turn the battery of his hard eyes on the uneasy man before him.

"Well, Mosher, what have you to say for yourself? Before the day is over you may be pounding a beat again."

Mosher stammered: "I—I can explain the whole thing, Chief. I was—I was . . ."

"Talk fast, Mosher. You're talking for your job."

The large man gulped. "I was on DeWitt's tail all day yesterday, like you told me to. I hung around the Exchange Club downtown all evening, saw DeWitt come out at 10:10 and pile into a cab, telling the cabby to drive to the ferries. I got another cab and stayed on his tail. When we swung into Forty-Second at Eighth, my cab-driver got into a jam. We scraped wheels with another buggy and there was a hell of a fuss. I jumped out and got another cab and we beat it like a streak down Forty-Second, but DeWitt's cab was lost in traffic. I knew he was heading for the ferries, so we kept on down Forty-Second and got to the terminal just as a boat pulled out. Had to wait a couple of minutes for the next boat. When we got to Weehawken, I beat it for the West Shore waiting-room, couldn't spot DeWitt, got a time-table, and noticed that a West Englewood local had just pulled out. There wasn't another till after midnight. What the hell could I figure? I thought sure DeWitt made that West Englewood train. So I hopped a bus and drove all the way out to West Englewood. . . ."

"Tough break," conceded Inspector Thumm. His bellicosity had fled. "Go on, Mosher."

The detective drew a long breath of relief. "At that, I beat the local in. So I waited around till the train pulled in, and damned if DeWitt was on it. I didn't know what to do—thought maybe I missed him after all, or that he'd shaken me off when I was tied up in the collision. So I called headquarters to report to you, and King downstairs said you were out on a case, told me to stick where I was and see what happened. So I went out to DeWitt's house and hung around outside. DeWitt didn't get home till 'way after midnight—must have been 3 A.M. or so. Rode up in a cab. And then Greenberg and O'Hallam showed up, on his tail, and they told me about the murder on the ferry, and the rest of it."

"All right, all right. Beat it, and take over from Greenberg and O'Hallam."

A few moments after Mosher hurried away, District Attorney Bruno strolled into Thumm's office. His face was set in worried lines.

He sank into a hard chair. "Well, what happened last night?"

"Rennells of Hudson County got there just after you left the terminal. We went out to that rooming-house with his men. Not a lead, Bruno. Ordinary sort of dump. Found some more samples of his handwriting. Did you see Frick about checking the fist on the anonymous letter with Wood's handwriting?"

"I saw him this morning. Frick says there's no question that the anonymous letter was written by the same hand that wrote the others. That makes it Wood beyond any doubt."

"Well, the samples I found in Wood's room were the same, too, as far as I could tell. Here they are—you might give 'em to Frick just for an additional check-up. That ought to please Lane—the old coot!"

Thumm tossed a long envelope across the desk. Bruno tucked it into his wallet.

"We found," continued Thumm, "a bottle of ink and some note-paper."

"Relatively unimportant now that the handwritings jibe," said the District Attorney wearily. "I've had the samples of ink and paper checked anyway, and they're all the same."

"Good enough." Thumm's paw riffled through a bundle of papers on his desk. "Some additional reports this morning. For instance, there's one on Mike Collins. Operative gave him the works, told him we knew of his secret visits to DeWitt after Saturday. Collins was nasty as usual, but he admitted visiting De-

Witt. Even admitted that he went after the old boy for a settlement on the dough he lost through Longstreet's bum stock tip. DeWitt, he said, turned him down cold—for which I can't blame the old boy."

"Feeling differently this morning about DeWitt?" sighed Bruno.

"What gave you that idea!" snarled Thumm. "Here's another. One of the boys has found that DeWitt used Charley Wood's car twice since Saturday. That was Mosher—he was detailed on DeWitt last night, damn his eyes, but lost the trail when his cab smacked into somebody."

"Interesting. And too bad; in a way. If this man Mosher had been able to keep an eye on DeWitt all evening, things might have been different. He might actually have seen the killing."

"Well, right now I'm more interested in that report on DeWitt's having used Wood's car twice since Saturday," growled Thumm. "Has it occurred to you how Wood might have found out who killed Longstreet? He certainly didn't know it the night of the murder, or he would have said something. Bruno, this two-trip report is important!"

"You mean," said Bruno thoughtfully, "that Wood might have overheard something. . . . Say! Did Mosher find out if DeWitt was with anybody on those trips?"

"No such luck. He was alone."

"Then he might have dropped something that Wood found. Thumm, this will bear looking into." Bruno's face fell. "If only he'd not been so scared when he wrote that note. . . . Well, no use crying over spilt milk. Anything else?"

"That's all I've got. Anything new on Longstreet's office correspondence?"

"No, but I've managed to discover something interesting," replied the District Attorney. "Do you know, Thumm, there's no trace of a Longstreet will!"

"But I thought Cherry Browne said——"

"Looks like some of Longstreet's particularly smooth brand of oil. We've searched his office, his home, those pretty apartments he kept up, his safe-deposit box, his Club lockers, all the rest of it. There's simply no testamentary document. Longstreet's lawyer, that shyster Negri, says Longstreet never made a will through him. And there you are."

"Just rooking Lady Cherry, hey? Like the rest of 'em. Didn't he have any relatives?"

"No trace of kin. Thumm, old boy, the disposition of Longstreet's virtually non-existent estate will be one fine mess." Bruno grimaced. "He left no property, just a parcel of debts. His only asset was his share in the DeWitt & Longstreet brokerage business. Of course, if DeWitt will buy out Longstreet's share, we'll have something tangible. . . ."

"Come in, Doc."

Dr. Schilling, cloth cap perched on his dome—which everyone suspected was bald but no one had ever proved—marched into Inspector Thumm's office. His eyes were red-rimmed and abstracted behind their round lenses, and he was jabbing at his teeth with an unsanitary ivory pick. "Morning, gentlemen. Would you say Dr. Schilling has been up all night? *Nein,* you would not." He sighed himself into one of Thumm's hard chairs. "I didn't get out to that fancy Hudson County morgue until past four."

"Got that autopsy report?"

Dr. Schilling extracted a long piece of paper from his breast pocket, slapped it on the desk before Thumm, rested his head on the back of the chair, and was instantly asleep. His cherubic face relaxed into chubby folds of fat; his mouth popped open, toothpick still dangling; and without preliminary he began to snore.

Thumm and Bruno rapidly read the neatly written report. "Nothing here," mumbled Thumm. "The usual boloney. Hey, Doc!" he roared, and Schilling's round little eyes struggled open. "This isn't a flophouse. Go home if you want to snooze. I'll try to keep the murders down for about twenty-four hours."

Schilling groaned to his feet. "*Ja*, do that," he said, and tottered toward the door. He stopped short; the door had opened in his face and he found Mr. Drury Lane smiling down at him. Dr. Schilling gawped, cackled an apology, and stood aside. Lane stepped into the room and the Medical Examiner went out, yawning mightily.

Thumm and Bruno rose. Bruno smiled sourly. "Come in, Mr. Lane, come in. I thought you had dematerialized last night. Where under heaven did you disappear to?"

Lane folded himself into a chair, nursing his blackthorn stick between his knees. "You must expect drama from an actor, Mr. Bruno. The first principle of effective stage procedure is the dramatic exit. Unfortunately, there was nothing sinister in my vanishment. I had seen what was necessary and there was then nothing to do but return to the sanctuary of The Hamlet. . . . Ah, Inspector! And how do you feel this gray morning?"

"So-so," said Thumm without enthusiasm. "Up early yourself for an old trouper, aren't you? I thought hams—excuse me, Mr. Lane—I thought actors slept until 'way past noon."

"Unkind, Inspector." Drury Lane's fresh clear eyes twinkled. "I am a member of the most active profession since grail-chasing went out of fashion. I was out of bed at six-thirty this morning, swam my customary two miles before breakfast, appeased my always clamorous appetite, examined a new wig Quacey made yesterday and of which he is justly proud, conferred with my director Kropotkin and my scenic designer Fritz Hof, enjoyed my voluminous mail, delved into a fascinating research on the year 1586-7 in connection with Shakespeare—and here it is ten-thirty. A fair beginning, Inspector, to an ordinary day?"

"Sure, sure," said Thumm, striving to speak pleasantly. "But then you retired people haven't the headaches we working people have. For instance—who killed Wood? After all, Mr. Lane, I won't ask you again about this X guy of yours—you know who killed Longstreet already."

"Inspector Thumm!" murmured the actor. "Do you compel me to reply in the words of Brutus? 'I will with patience hear, and find a time both meet to hear and answer such high things. Till then, my noble friend, chew upon this.'" Lane chuckled. "Have you the autopsy report on Wood's carcass?"

Thumm looked at Bruno and Bruno looked at Thumm, and they both laughed, restored somehow to good humor. The Inspector picked up Dr. Schilling's paper and handed it to Lane without comment.

Drury Lane held it high before his eyes, studying the report with grave intentness. It was a laconic document, written with scrupulosity and Germanic flourishes in ink. Occasionally as Lane read he stopped to close his eyes in candid concentration.

The report stated that Wood had been unconscious, not dead, at the time he was thrown overboard. This, it went on, from unmistakable signs of assault on that part of the head which had not been crushed. The theory of unconsciousness, wrote Dr. Schilling, was substantiated by the fact that a small quantity of water was present in Wood's lungs, indicating that the man had been alive for a few seconds after plunging into the water. The inference was, then, continued the report, that Wood had been struck over the head with a blunt instrument, stunning him into unconsciousness, that he had been thrown overboard, had struck the water, still alive, and had in a very short period of time been crushed to death between the side of the *Mohawk* and the loose pilings.

The report went on to state that traces of nicotine in the lungs were not abnormal, being due in all probability to a mild tobacco addiction. That the scar on the left leg was estimated to have been at least twenty years old; it had been an ugly deep curving gash; it had been rather unprofessionally treated. That the slight trace of sugar in the blood was not sufficient to have made the victim diabetic. That there were definite evidences of alcoholism probably induced by strong-liquor addiction in a mild form. That the body was that of a middle-aged man of rugged constitution, with red hair; fingers splayed; nails irregular, indicating manual labor. That there was osseous evidence of a broken right wrist which was quite old and had knit well. That there was a small mole of the birthmark variety on the left hip; a two-year-old appendicitis scar; also evidences of a cracked rib which had been at least eleven years old and had knit satisfactorily. That the body weighed two hundred and two pounds and was six feet and a half-inch tall.

Drury Lane concluded his study of the document and, smiling, returned it to Inspector Thumm.

"Get anything out of it, Mr. Lane?" asked Bruno.

"Dr. Schilling is a meticulous workman," replied Lane. "A most commendable report. It is remarkable that he was able to make such a comprehensive examination of that poor mangled body. And how are your suspicions of John DeWitt faring this morning?"

"Very much interested?" parried Thumm.

"Very much interested, Inspector."

"His movements yesterday," said Bruno quickly, as if this answered the question, "are being traced."

"You are not withholding anything from me, Mr. Bruno?" murmured Lane, rising and settling his cape about his shoulders. "But then, I'm sure you are not. . . . Thank you, Inspector, for having sent me a clear photograph of Longstreet. It may prove useful before the curtain comes down."

"Oh, that's all right," said Thumm in an instantly pleasant tone. "Look here, Mr. Lane, I think it only fair to tell you that Bruno and I both have our minds set on DeWitt."

"Indeed?" Lane's gray-green eyes swept from Thumm to the District Attorney. Then they clouded, and he grasped his stick more firmly. "I shall leave you to your, work, gentlemen. I have myself something of a crowded itinerary today." He strode across the room and turned at the door. "Let me earnestly advise you, however, to take no specific action against DeWitt at this time. We are face to face with a crucial moment, gentlemen. I say 'we'," and he bowed, "literally, believe me."

They shook their heads in a futile sort of way as Lane closed the door gently behind him.

Scene 5

THE HAMLET. THURSDAY, SEPTEMBER 10. 12:30 P.M.

IF INSPECTOR Thumm and District Attorney Bruno had been present at The Hamlet at half-past noon on Thursday, they would have challenged the evidence of their senses.

They would have seen an amorphous Drury Lane—a Lane who was only half a Lane, whose eyes and speech were normal to the Lane composition, but whose dress was ludicrously unlike the normal Lane dress and whose face under the cunning hands of old Quacey was undergoing an amazing transformation.

Drury Lane sat bolt-upright in a hard, straight-backed chair, before a triple mirror that reflected his image in full face, three-quarter face, profile and rear views at different angles. A brilliant bluish-white electric lamp shone directly on his face. The two floor-windows in the room were covered completely by dull-black shades, so that not the tiniest ray of the gray outdoor light penetrated into this chamber of wonders. The hunchback knelt on a bench facing his master, leather apron smeared with rouge and speckled with powder. On a solid table to Quacey's right were scores of pigment jars, powders, rouge pots, mixing pans, delicate almost invisible brushes, bundles of varicolored human hair. Lying on the table was the photograph of a man's head.

They sat under the streaming glare like actors in a tableau out of the Middle Ages. The room they were in might have served as Paracelsus's laboratory. It was large, littered with work-benches and debris; quaint battered old closets with shelves of queer articles stood open; the floor was strewn with wisps of hair and pied with varicolored putties that had been ground into the wood by the ancient's heel. A peculiar apparatus, the caricature of an electric sewing-machine, stood in a corner. Along one wall was strung a thick wire, and from the wire depended at least fifty wigs of different sizes, shapes and colors. In a recess of one wall, each in its separate niche, were dozens of plaster-cast human heads, life-size—Negroid, Mongolian, Caucasian—some with hair, others bald, some with features in repose, others with features contorted into expressions of fear, glee, surprise, sadness, pain, mockery, anger, determination, affection, resignation, evil.

Except for the one giant lamp above Drury Lane's head there was no illumination in the laboratory. Flexible lamps of all sizes were scattered about the room but they were dark now; and the monstrous shadows cast by the single great bulb told a weird story. Lane's figure was motionless; his shadow, large out of all proportion, did not waver on the wall. On the other hand, the small hunched foreshortened figure of Quacey hopped about like a flea, and his shadow mingled and separated from Lane's on the wall with the fluency of dark liquid.

It was all odd, sinister, and somehow theatrical. The steaming open vats in the corner did not seem real; the thick lazy smoke that floated across the walls might have come from the caldrons of the Three Witches—as macabre as *Macbeth* and as pseudo-supernatural. From the story the shadows told, the lean fixed figure might have been that of a person entranced; the quicksilver shadow that of a humped Svengali, a dwarfed Mesmer, a Merlin without his starry robes.

Actually, little old Quacey was in the most matter-of-fact fashion performing his ordinary duty—the metamorphosis of his master by the guileful art of paints and powders and manual skill.

Lane stared at his reflection in the triple mirror—he was dressed in common street clothes of undistinguished cut and a well-worn air.

Quacey dropped back, wiping his hands on his apron. He surveyed his handiwork with critical little eyes.

"The eyebrows are too heavy—a minim too realistically heavy, Quacey," said Lane at last, patting them with his long fingers.

Quacey screwed up his brown gnome's face, cocked his head, shut one eye in the manner of a portrait-painter standing off and evaluating the proportions of his model. "Maybe yes. Maybe yes," he squeaked. "The curve of the left eyebrow, too—it does not droop so much."

He snatched a small scissors hanging from his belt by a cord and began to snip slowly, carefully, at the artificial hair on Lane's eyebrows. "There. That's better, I should say."

Lane nodded. Quacey busied himself again with a palmful of flesh-colored putty, caressing his master's jaw-line. . . .

Five minutes later he stepped back, dropping his scissors, and put his puny hands on his hips. "That's good, for the time. Eh, Mr. Drury?"

The actor studied himself. "We must not fall into the error, you ugly Caliban, of artificializing this particular task." Quacey grinned an elfin grin. Mr. Drury Lane was pleased—that much was self-evident; he used the name Caliban only when he was especially appreciative of Quacey's work. "But—it will do. The hair now."

Quacey retreated to the other side of the room, switched on a lamp and began to eye the wigs on the wire. Lane relaxed in his chair.

"Caliban," he murmured argumentatively, "I am afraid we will never agree on the fundamental."

"Ha?" demanded Quacey, without turning his head.

"The true function of make-up. If you err anywhere in your uncanny manipulation of your tools, it is in the direction of overperfection."

Quacey selected a bushy gray wig from his line, snapped off the lamp and returned to his master. He squatted on the bench before Lane, produced a peculiarly shaped comb and went to work on the wig.

"There can be no such thing as a too perfect make-up, Mr. Drury," said Quacey. "The world is full of poor workmen as it is."

"Oh, I'm not reflecting on your genius, Quacey." Lane was watching the swift movements of the old man's clawed hands. "But I repeat—the superimposed elements of a make-up are in a way the least important. They are, in a manner of speaking, the props." Quacey snorted. "Very well. You do not take into consideration the panoramic instinct of the normal human eye. The average observer gets a mass rather than a detailed impression."

"But," shrilled Quacey heatedly, "that's the very point! For if one of the details is wrong—how shall I say it?—off the key, then there is a disturbance to the eye in the mass impression, and the eye searches out the detail that has disturbed it. So I say—perfect details!"

"Excellent, Caliban, excellent." Lane's voice was warm and affectionate. "You defend yourself well. But the subtlety of the argument evades you. I have never said that the details of a make-up should be so slurred as to call attention to themselves. It is true—the details should be perfect. However, *all* the details aren't necessary! You see my point? The painful correctness of a make-up . . . it's like viewing a seascape with every wave faithfully painted, a tree with every leaf sharp in outline. Every wave, every leaf, every wrinkle on the human physiognomy make for bad art."

"Well, maybe," said Quacey grudgingly. He held the wig up closer to the light, studied it, shook his head, began a rhythmic rite with the hand that held the comb.

"We arrive then at the conclusion that paints, powders, and the other implements of deception contrive to create the *semblance* of a make-up, not the make-up itself. You know that some elements of a face should be accentuated more than others: if you were to disguise me a Abraham Lincoln you would be inclined to emphasize the mole, beard and lips, and subdue the other elements. No, it is life, motion, gesture that make for complete characterization, for realism that convinces. For example, a wax dummy faithful to the last detail of feature and coloring is still an obviously unlifelike object. If the dummy however could move his arms smoothly, talk chromatically with his wax lips, do natural things with his glass eyes—you see what I am driving at."

"It's all right now," said Quacey calmly, holding the wig up to the brilliant light again.

Drury Lane's eyes closed. "That is what has always fascinated me in the histrionic art—to create by movement, voice, gesture the semblance of life, the illusion of a real personality. . . . Belasco had an uncanny grasp on the art of re-creating life, even on the untenanted stage. There was that production in which he managed to bring out the feeling of *coziness* in a set, not trusting his flickering firelight, the peace and quiet of the physical scene, not-satisfied with these products of his scenic-designer. He trussed a cat before each performance so that the little creature could not move; just before the curtain he had the cat released from its bonds; the curtain rose on the intimate scene, the cat got to its feet on the stage, yawned and stretched its protesting muscles before the fire . . . and the audience knew, without a word having been spoken and merely by this simple homely act familiar to all of them, that this was a warm, cozy room. All the art of Belasco's designer could not create that impression so well."

"An interesting anecdote, Mr. Drury." Quacey pressed close to his master and delicately adjusted the wig on Lane's symmetrical skull.

"But he was a great man, Quacey," murmured Lane. "This business of breathing life into manufactured drama—after all, for decades the Elizabethan drama relied on the words of the play and the actor's pantomime to produce the illusion of life. All plays were given on the naked stage—one supernumerary creeping along the boards holding up a shrub, was sufficient to get over the idea that Birnam Wood was come to Dunsinane. And for decades the pit and the boxes understood. Sometimes I think the modern art of staging has overreached itself—that the drama has suffered . . ."

"It's done, Mr. Drury." Quacey prodded the actor's shins. Lane opened his eyes. "It's done, Mr. Drury."

"So it is. Away from the mirror, imp."

Five minutes later Mr. Drury Lane rose, no longer Mr. Drury Lane in dress, appearance, carriage, or air. He was another individual altogether. He stamped across the room and switched on the main light. He was wearing a light overcoat and had jammed a gray fedora hat on his differently arranged gray hair. His lower lip thrust forward. Quacey howled, holding his sides for glee.

"Tell Dromio I'm ready. Get ready yourself."

Even the tone of his voice had changed.

Scene 6

WEEHAWKEN. THURSDAY, SEPTEMBER 10. 2 P.M.

INSPECTOR THUMM stepped off the ferry in Weehawken, looked about, nodded curtly to a New Jersey policeman who, lounging on guard near the entranceway to the deserted *Mohawk*, had snapped erect in salute, and strode through the ferry waiting-room out into the open.

He crossed the cobbled approach to the ferry and began to climb the steep hill which led from the wharves and piers to the top of the precipitous cliffs buttressing the waterfront. Automobiles crept by, feeling their way down the incline as he toiled upward; he turned and studied below him an ever-widening panorama of the river and the turreted city beyond. Then he resumed his ascent.

At the top he approached a traffic officer and in his gruff baritone inquired the way to the Boulevard. He continued on foot across the wide drive and through quiet, shabby, old tree-shaded streets until he reached a busy intersection which proved to be the thoroughfare he sought. He turned north.

He found finally the house which was his destination—Number 2075. It was a wooden frame building, squeezed between a dairy and an automobile accessories store—ill-painted, crumbling, beaten out of shape by the slow blows of time. There was a sagging porch equipped with three ancient rockers and a tottery bench; a mat before the door welcomed visitors in faded script; a yellowed sign on one of the porch-posts pathetically announced *Rooms for Gentlemen.*

Inspector Thumm looked up and down the street, pulled his coat straight, settled his hat more firmly on his head, and mounted the creaky steps. He pressed a bell marked *Housekeeper.* There was a faint jangle from the recesses of this battered hive, and the shuffle of carpet-slippers. The door stirred inward and a carbuncular nose protruded from the crack. "What d'ye want?" demanded a peevish female's voice. Then a deep gasp, a titter, and the door swung inward, revealing a stoutish middle-aged woman in a frumpy housedress—a lady as ramshackle as her establishment. "It's the police gentleman! Come in, Inspector Thumm, come in! I'm so sorry—I didn't know . . ." She babbled excitedly as she attempted to smile, succeeding only in producing a fanged smirk. Standing aside, bobbing, twittering, she allowed the Inspector entrance to her tomb.

"We've had the *awfulest* time!" she was chattering. "Reporter men and men with big cameras all *over* the place all morning! We——"

"Anybody upstairs, madam?" demanded Thumm.

"And he sure is, Inspector! He's still there, clutterin' up my carpets with his cigarette-ashes," the woman shrilled. "I had my picture took four times this morning. . . . And were you wantin' to see that poor man's room again, sir?"

"Take me upstairs," Thumm growled.

"Yes, *sir!*" The old shrew smirked again, lifted her bedraggled skirt delicately with two worn fingers, and waddled up a flight of thinly carpeted stairs. Thumm grunted and followed. A bulldoggish sort of man confronted them on the top step.

"Who's that, Mrs. Murphy?" he asked, peering down in the half-light.

"All right. Keep your shirt on. It's me," snapped the Inspector. The man brightened; he grinned. "Didn't see you good at first. Glad you're here, Inspector. Dull work."

"Anything stirring since last night?"

"Not a thing."

He led the way along the first-floor hall to a rear room, Landlady Murphy shuffling behind. Thumm stopped at the open door.

The room was small and bare. There were cracks in the discolored ceiling, the walls were stained with age, a threadbare carpet covered the floor, the furniture was dilapidated, the plumbing of an open washstand was antiquated, the chintz curtain of the single window had seen fresher days—but there was a clean smell about the room and it seemed well enough tended. An old-fashioned iron bedstead, a chest of drawers standing higher on one side than the other, a heavy little table with a marble top, a wire-braced chair, and a clothes-closet comprised the furnishings.

The Inspector stepped inside and without hesitation walked over to the closet and opened the double doors. Inside, carefully hung, were three worn men's suits; two pairs of shoes, one fairly new and the other with turned up toes, lay on the closet-floor; and on an upper shelf were a straw hat in a paper bag and a felt hat whose silk band was stained with dried perspiration. Thumm swiftly went through the pockets of the suits, searched the shoes and hats, but seemed to discover nothing of interest. His heavy brows contracted, as if he were disappointed in his search, and he closed the closet-doors.

"You're sure," he muttered to the detective, who stood in

the doorway beside Mrs. Murphy, watching him, "that nobody touched anything in here since last night?"

The detective shook his head. "When I'm on dooty, I'm on dooty, Inspector. It's just as you left it."

On the carpet beside the closet was a cheap brown handbag, its handle, broken, dangling by one end. The Inspector opened the bag; it was empty.

He crossed to the bureau and went through its stiff heavy drawers. The bureau contained a few suits of old but clean underwear, a pile of laundered handkerchiefs, a half-dozen soft-collared, striped shirts, a few crumpled neckties, and clean socks rolled into balls.

Thumm turned from the bureau; despite the chill outdoors the room was close, and he dabbed cautiously at his beet-red face with a silk handkerchief. He stood squarely in the center of the room, legs apart, and frowned about. Then he went to the marble-topped table. A bottle of ink, a clotted pen and a cheap pad of ruled notepaper he ignored; but he picked up a cardboard package of Royal Bengal cigars and investigated its interior inquisitively. Only one cigar, which crumbled between his fingers, was in the package. Thumm put the package down, the frown deepening between his eyes, and surveyed the room again.

Above the washstand in a corner was a shelf, with several articles on it. The Inspector strode across the room and stared down at the shelf. A dented alarm-clock which had run down and stopped; a quarter-full pint flask of rye whisky—Thumm took the cork out and sniffed hard—and a glass; a toothbrush; a tarnished metal shaving-case and a few other ordinary toilet articles; a small bottle of aspirin; an old copper ash-tray . . . The Inspector picked out of the tray the fragment of a smoked cigar, examined a torn cigar-label lying in the ashes. It was from a Cremo. Thumm swung about thoughtfully.

Mrs. Murphy's malicious little eyes had followed the Inspector's movements with rapt attention. She said suddenly in her nasal voice: "Ye'll excuse the condition of the room, Inspector. This man here wouldn't let me tidy it."

"Yes, yes," said Thumm. Then he halted abruptly and eyed the landlady with a flicker of interest. "By the way, Mrs. Murphy—did Wood ever have women visit him here?"

Mrs. Murphy snorted, elevating her pimply chin. "If ye weren't a policeman, Inspector, I'd bash ye over the head for that, I'll tell ye! O' course not! This is a respectable house and everybody knows it. I always tell my roomers that the very first thing. 'No lady friends callin',' I says, polite but firm. No nonsense or monkey-business at Mrs. Murphy's!"

"Uh-huh." Thumm sat down in the room's one chair. "So no women came here. . . . Well, how about relatives? Any sisters who might have come here?"

"Now as to that," replied Mrs. Murphy smartly, "I can't blame a man for havin' a sister, ye see. Some of my roomers have sisters visitin' 'em, and aunts and cousins too, but I don't think Mr. Wood did. You see, I always considered Mr. Wood my star roomer. Been with me five years, and never gave no trouble. So quiet, so polite, such a gentleman! Never had no visitors, far's I could see. But then we didn't see him much; he worked from the afternoon till night on the street-car in N'York. 'Course, I don't run a boardin' house—my roomers eat out—so I don't know 'bout his meals. But I'll say this for the poor soul—he paid me regular, didn't bother me, never got drunk—hardly ever knew he was in the house, seems like. I——"

But Inspector Thumm had risen from the chair and turned his

thick back upon her. She stopped short in the middle of a sentence, blinked her batrachian eyelids several times, then glared, sniffed and flounced past the detective out of the room.

"And what a hell-cat she is," remarked the man against the jamb. "I've seen rooming-houses before that allowed sisters, aunts, and cousins." He chuckled bawdily.

But Thumm was paying no attention. He was pacing off the floor, slowly, feeling along the skeleton carpet with one foot. A slight elevation in the flooring at one point, near the border of the carpet, seemed to interest him; he stripped back the carpet and found merely a badly warped board. When he came to the bed he hesitated; but he dropped heavily to his knees and crawled underneath, feeling about like a blind man. The detective said: "Here, Chief—let me help you," but Thumm did not reply; he was tugging at the carpet. The detective sprawled on his belly and sprayed the beams of a pocket flashlight on the area beneath the bed. Thumm muttered with elation: "Here it is!" The detective ripped away the carpet corner, and Thumm pounced on a thin yellow-covered little book. Both men crawled out from under the bed, rather the worse for wear, choking and pounding the dust from their clothes.

"Bankbook, Chief?"

But the Inspector did not reply—he was swiftly turning pages. The book tabulated numerous small deposits of a savings account several years old; there had never been a withdrawal; no deposit had been for more than ten dollars, and the majority were for five; the last entry showed a balance of nine hundred forty-five dollars and sixty-three cents. In the center-spread of the bankbook was a neatly folded five-dollar bill, obviously a last deposit which Charles Wood had been prevented by death from making.

Thumm pocketed the bankbook and turned to the detective. "When do you go off duty?"

"Eight bells. Relief comes on at that time."

"Tell you what." Thumm scowled. "Tomorrow about half-past two call me at headquarters. Remind me that I've got something special for you to do here. Get me?"

"I get you. Phone at 2:30 prompt, I will."

Inspector Thumm strode from the room, descended the stairs—which squealed like porkers at every step—and left the house. Mrs. Murphy was energetically sweeping the porch. She flung herself out of his path with her carbuncular nose indignantly sniffing in a cloud of dust.

On the sidewalk Thumm referred to the cover of the bankbook, looked about, then crossed the Boulevard and walked south. Three blocks away he found the building he was seeking—a small business bank in pretentious marble. The Inspector entered and made his way to the cashier's cage marked *S to Z*. The cashier, an oldish man, looked up.

"You the regular man on this window?" demanded Thumm.

"Yes, sir. What can I do for you?"

"You've probably read about the murder of a man named Charles Wood, a street-car conductor, who lived in this neighborhood?" The cashier nodded at once. "Well, I'm Inspector Thumm of the Homicide Squad across the river, in charge of the case."

"Oh!" The cashier seemed impressed. "Wood was a depositor here, Inspector, if that's what you're after. I recognized his picture in the papers this morning."

Thumm took Wood's bankbook from his pocket. "Now, Mr.—" he glanced at the metal name in the grilled window, "Mr. Ashley, how long have you been on this window?"

"Eight years."

"Serve Wood regularly?"

"Yes, sir."

"I see by this bankbook that he made a deposit once a week—the days of the week vary, but you might tell me whatever you can remember about his banking here."

"There isn't much to tell, Inspector. Mr. Wood came in, as you say, steadily once every week without missing a week as far back as I can remember. Practically always came in at the same time of day—half-past one or two o'clock—I suppose just before he went back to New York for duty, judging from the newspaper report."

Inspector Thumm frowned. "As far as you can recall, did he always make his own deposits? I'm particularly interested in that. Was he always alone?"

"I can't remember ever seeing him with anyone."

"Thanks."

Thumm left the bank and made his way back along the Boulevard to the immediate vicinity of Mrs. Murphy's rooming-house. Three doors from the dairy there was a stationery store. Thumm went in.

The proprietor, a sleepy old man, oozed forward.

"Did you know the man Charles Wood who lived in Mrs. Murphy's up the street and was murdered last night on the ferry boat?"

The old man blinked excitedly. "Oh, yes, yes! He was a customer of mine. He bought cigars and papers here."

"What kind of cigars did he buy?"

"Cremos. Royal Bengals. Those two mostly."

"How often did he come in here?"

"Pretty near every day right past noon, before going to work."

"Every day almost, hey? Ever see him with anybody else?"

"Oh no! He was always alone."

"Did he buy stationery here too?"

"Yes. Once in a great while. Some paper and ink."

Thumm began to button his coat. "How long has he been coming in here?"

The proprietor scratched his dirty white poll. "Four, five years, I guess. Say, you ain't a reporter, are you?"

But Thumm merely walked out. He paused on the sidewalk. Espying a haberdashery a few doors away, he clumped over and into it. He discovered only that Wood had bought a few items of men's wear over a long period. No, Wood always came in alone.

The Inspector emerged, scowling more deeply than ever, and in turn visited a cleaning-and-dyeing establishment, a shoe-repair shop, a shoe store, a restaurant, and a drug store in the neighborhood. All the tradesmen remembered the man as a customer of small but steady patronage over a period of several years. But he had never been accompanied by anyone—not even in the restaurant.

In the drug store Thumm had made additional inquiries: the pharmacist did not recall ever having filled a prescription for medicine on Wood's request, remarking that it was possible that Wood, if he had ever been ill and received a prescription from some physician, might have had it filled in New York. At Thumm's command the pharmacist wrote out a list of eleven physicians in the vicinity and three dentists—all within a radius of five blocks.

The Inspector visited each in turn. At each doctor's office he made the same statement and asked the same question. "You have probably read that a man, Charles Wood, Forty-Second Street Crosstown conductor, was murdered last night on the

Weehawken ferry. He lives in this neighborhood. I am Inspector Thumm, and I am investigating his background, trying to find someone who knows something about his personal life, possible friends, visitors. Did Wood ever come to you for medical treatment, or have you called to his rooming-house when he was ill?"

Four physicians had not read about the murder and did not know the man even by hearsay. Seven had read the newspapers but had not treated Wood and knew nothing about him.

The Inspector, jaw tight, commenced a round of the three dentists on his list. In the first case, to his increasing annoyance, he was compelled to wait thirty-five minutes before he could see the dental surgeon; and when finally Thumm did corner the man in his laboratory, the dentist refused to answer questions before seeing his visitor's credentials. The light of hope in his eyes, Thumm squared himself and roared the man into compliance. The light died away when the man's ultimately grudging statement indicated a total ignorance of Charles Wood.

Neither of the two remaining dentists had even heard of the dead man.

Sighing, Inspector Thumm trudged back to the wide drive at the top of the hill, descended the winding ramp which led to the ferries, and re-embarked for the New York side.

• • • • •

New York

In the City, Inspector Thumm proceeded immediately to the executive offices of the Third Avenue Railway System, plowing through traffic with a look of pained abstraction on his ugly face.

In the edifice that housed the Personnel Department, he inquired for the Personnel Manager and was ushered into a large office. The Personnel Manager was a hard-looking man with worry-lines etched deeply into his face. He hurried forward at once, hand outstretched. “Inspector Thumm?” he asked eagerly. Thumm grunted. “Sit down, Inspector.” The Manager pulled a dusty chair forward and fairly thrust Thumm into it. “I suppose it’s about Charley Wood. Too bad. Too bad.” He sat down behind his desk and decapitated a cigar.

Thumm appraised him coldly. “Checking up on the dead man,” growled Thumm.

“Yes, yes. Terrible thing. Can’t understand it—Charley Wood was one of my best men. Quiet, steady, reliable—perfect employee.”

“So he never made trouble, hey, Mr. Klopf?”

The Manager leaned forward earnestly. “I’ll tell you something, Inspector. That man was a jewel. Never got drunk on duty, everybody liked him in the office here—neat in his reports, one of our honor men—in fact, due for a bigger job, an inspector’s job after five years of the best kind of service. Yes, sir!”

“Regular little Lord Fauntleroy, hey, Mr. Klopf?”

“I wouldn’t say that, I wouldn’t say that, Inspector Thumm,” replied Klopf hastily. “But I’m just saying—we could depend on him. You want a certificate of character, don’t you? That poor fellow worked every working day since he took over the job. He was anxious to make good, I’m telling you! We gave him every chance, too. That’s the motto of our company, Inspector. When a man shows that he wants to get ahead, we push him.”

Thumm grunted.

“I’m telling you, Inspector. He never took time off, never took a vacation, always preferred to work out his vacation time and earn double pay. Why, we’re always getting requests from motormen and conductors for pay-advances. But Charley Wood?

Not him, Inspector, not him! Saved his money—showed me his bankbook once."

"How long had he worked for this company?"

"Five years. Here, I'll check that up." Klopf jumped up and ran to the door. He stuck his head out and yelled: "Hey John! Bring me Charley Wood's record-sheet!"

He walked back to his desk in a moment, a long sheet of paper in his hand. Thumm leaned over the desk, propped on his elbows, reading the record. "There, you see," said Klopf, pointing, "he came with us a little over five years ago, starting on the Third Avenue run on the East Side, was transferred with Pat Guiness, his motorman, at his own request to the Crosstown three and a half years ago—lived in Weehawken and wanted a more convenient run. See that? Not a black mark against him!"

Thumm looked thoughtful. "See here, Klopf, what about his personal life? Know anything about it? Friends, relatives, pals?"

Klopf shook his head. "Well, I wouldn't know much about that, but I don't think so from what I've heard. He was chummy with the men but he never went out with 'em, as far as I know. I guess the closest thing to a friend he had was Pat Guiness. Here, just a minute." He turned the record over. "See that? Record of his application. Next of kin—none. I guess that sort of answers the question, Inspector."

"I wish I could be sure," muttered Thumm.

"Maybe Guiness——"

"Never mind. I'll see Guiness myself if it's necessary." Thumm picked up his fedora. "Well, I guess that's all. Thanks, old man."

The Personnel Manager pumped Thumm's arm effusively, accompanied him out of the office and building, reiterating offers of co-operation. Thumm cut him off sharply, nodded in farewell, and then turned the corner.

He stood there, as if waiting for someone, consulting his watch frequently. Ten minutes passed before a long black Lincoln limousine with drawn curtains rolled up to the curb before him. In the front seat was a lean, grinning young man in livery, who snapped on his emergency brake, jumped out, yanked the rear door open and stood aside, still grinning. Inspector Thumm glanced quickly up and down the street; then he climbed into the automobile. Crouched in a corner, more gnome-like than ever, was old Quacey, dozing serenely.

The chauffeur closed the door, pounced on his seat and the car purred off into traffic. Quacey opened his eyes, popped awake. He saw Inspector Thumm, a very thoughtful Inspector Thumm, sitting utterly still beside him. Quacey's gargoyle of a face suddenly dripped with smiles, and he stooped to open a compartment built into the floor of the car. He sat up, a little red, holding a large metal box, the cover of which, inside, was a mirror.

Inspector Thumm shook his broad shoulders. "A good day's work, Quacey, all things considered," he said.

Whereupon he took off his hat, dipped his hand into the box, rummaged and came up with something. He began vigorously to attack his face with a creamy liquid. Quacey held the mirror before him, offered a soft cloth. The Inspector scrubbed his shining face with the cloth; and lo! when the cloth came away Inspector Thumm had disappeared, not completely perhaps, for shreds of a putty-like substance still clung to his features, but the disguise was sufficiently obliterated to reveal the clean, sharp, smiling physiognomy of Mr. Drury Lane.

Scene 7

The Dewitt House in West Englewood.
Friday, September 11. 10 a.m.

On Friday morning the sun deigned to show his face again, and the long black Lincoln limousine rolled along between quiet residential streets lined with poplars whose leaves made a last flushed effort to catch the yellow light.

Mr. Drury Lane looked out of his car-window and observed to Quacey that West Englewood, at least in its wealthy sectors, had not made the architectural error of building to a pattern. Each residence stood on roomy grounds, a structural unit distinct from its neighbors. Quacey remarked dryly that he much preferred The Hamlet.

They pulled up before a small estate, well kept, with wide lawns hemming a white Colonial house with many ells and porches. Lane, dressed in his inevitable cape and black hat, gripping his blackthorn stick, got out of the car and beckoned to Quacey.

"Me?" Quacey seemed surprised and even nervous. His leather apron, by its temporary banishment, had divested him of his badge of self-possession. He wore a derby, a little black overcoat with a velvet collar, and brand-new sharply sparkling shoes that seemed to pinch his toes, for he winced as he hopped to the sidewalk. Groaning, he followed Lane up the walk to the portico.

A tall old man in livery admitted them, escorting them through shining halls to a large sitting-room in exquisite Colonial taste.

Lane sat down, Quacey hovering behind him, and looked about with approval. "I am Drury Lane," he announced to the butler. "Is anyone at home?"

"No, there's no one, sir. Mr. DeWitt is in the City, Miss DeWitt is out shopping, and Mrs. DeWitt is having a—" he coughed—"a mud-facial, I believe it's called, sir. So——"

"I am delighted." Drury Lane beamed. "And you are——?"

"Jorgens, sir. Mr. DeWitt's oldest servant."

Lane relaxed in the Cape Cod chair. "The very man, Jorgens. I owe you an explanation."

"Me, sir?"

"Mr. Bruno, the District Attorney in charge of the Longstreet case, of which you know, has kindly permitted me to act in the capacity of independent investigator. I——"

The old man's face lost its woodenness. "I beg your pardon, sir, but surely you don't have to explain to *me*. If I may say so, Mr. Drury Lane is . . ."

"Yes, yes," said Lane, with a queer little gesture of impatience. "I appreciate your enthusiasm, Jorgens. Now a few questions, and I should like exact answers. Mr. DeWitt——"

Jorgens stiffened, and the animation went out of his face. "If it's anything disloyal to Mr. DeWitt, sir . . ."

"Bravo, Jorgens. Bravo." Lane's sharp eyes studied the man intently. "And again—bravo. A commendable sentiment. I should have assured you that it is in Mr. DeWitt's best interests that I am here." Jorgens permitted a relieved smile to touch his grayish lips. "To continue. Mr. DeWitt has been brought into the lamentable murder of Mr. Longstreet by virtue of his close relationship with the deceased. It is felt that this very relationship may elicit information helpful in the apprehension of Mr. Longstreet's murderer. Did Longstreet visit here often?"

"No, sir. Very rarely, sir."

"And why was that, Jorgens?"

"I don't exactly know, sir. But Miss DeWitt didn't like Mr. Longstreet, and Mr. DeWitt—well, sir, Mr. DeWitt seemed to be *oppressed* by the presence of Mr. Longstreet, if I make myself clear. . . ."

"Oh, quite. And Mrs. DeWitt?"

The butler hesitated. "Well, sir . . ."

"You would rather not say?"

"I would rather not say, sir."

"For the fourth time—bravo. . . . Quacey, sit down. You'll be tired, old fellow." Quacey sat down beside his master. "Now, Jorgens. How long have you served Mr. DeWitt?"

"Over eleven years, sir."

"Would you say that Mr. DeWitt is a companionable sort of person—a friendly man?"

"Well . . . no, sir. I should say that his only real friend is Mr. Ahearn, who lives near by. Although Mr. DeWitt is really a very pleasant man, sir, when you know him well."

"Then this *ménage* does not customarily house guests?"

"Not very often, sir. Of course, Mr. Imperiale is staying here now, but he's a special sort of friend, too; he has been here three or four times in as many years. Otherwise, Mr. DeWitt entertains very few guests."

"You say 'very few.' I gather, then, that the few guests that do stay here occasionally are clients, perhaps—business guests?"

"Yes, sir. But not many of those either, sir. Just once in a great while. For instance, there was a business gentleman staying here recently from South America."

Drury Lane looked thoughtful. "How recently?"

"He was here for about a month, sir, and left about a month ago."

"Had he ever visited here before?"

"Not to my recollection, sir."

"South America, you say. What part of South America?"

"I don't know, sir."

"Precisely when did he leave?"

"I believe it was on August fourteenth, sir."

Lane was silent for a moment. When he spoke again it was slowly, in a voice rich with interest. "Do you recall if Mr. Longstreet visited here during the period when the South American was in the house?"

Jorgens replied promptly: "Yes, sir. Much oftener than usual. There was one whole evening, the night after Mr. Maquinchao—that was his name, sir, Felipe Maquinchao—came, when Mr. DeWitt, Mr. Longstreet, and Mr. Maquinchao were closeted in the library until well after midnight."

"Of course, you are not aware of the substance of their conversation?"

Jorgens looked shocked. "Oh, no, sir!"

"Naturally not. Stupid question," murmured Drury Lane. "Felipe Maquinchao. An outlandish name. What sort of person was he, Jorgens? Can you describe him?"

The butler cleared his old throat. "He was a foreigner, sir, a Spanish-looking sort of man. Dark and tall and with a little black military mustache. *Very* dark complected, I might say—almost like a colored person or an Indian. He was a funny sort of gentleman, too. He did not talk much nor stay at the house much. He took very few meals with the family, and did not fraternize, so to speak. Some nights he did not return to the house until four or five in the morning; some nights he did not come in at all."

Lane smiled. "And this peculiar guest's peculiar activity had what sort of reaction on Mr. DeWitt, Jorgens?"

Jorgens seemed disturbed. "Why, Mr. DeWitt took Mr. Maquinchao's coming and going quite for granted, sir."

"Do you know anything else about him?"

"Well, sir, he spoke English with a Spanish accent, and he had very little luggage, just a large suitcase. He had many secret conferences with Mr. DeWitt, sometimes with Mr. DeWitt and Mr. Longstreet in the evening. Mr. DeWitt didn't introduce him more than was—ah—socially necessary when other guests gathered for the evening sometimes. And that's about all I know, sir."

"Did Mr. Ahearn seem to know him?"

"Oh, no, sir."

"And Mr. Imperiale?"

"Mr. Imperiale wasn't here at the time. He came a little after Mr. Maquinchao left."

"Do you know where the South American went after he left the house?"

"No, sir. He carried his own suitcase, sir. I don't believe anyone else in the house except Mr. DeWitt knew any more about him than I, sir. Not even Miss DeWitt or Mrs. DeWitt."

"By the way, Jorgens, how do you know he was a South American?"

Jorgens coughed into one parchment hand. "Mrs. DeWitt

asked Mr. DeWitt once in my presence, sir, and Mr. DeWitt said so."

Drury Lane nodded and closed his eyes. Then he opened them and asked distinctly: "Can you recall any other visitor or visitors in recent years who might have come from South America?"

"No, sir. Mr. Maquinchao is the only Spanish gentleman we have ever had here."

"Very well, Jorgens. I am extremely pleased with you. Now will you get Mr. DeWitt on the telephone, tell him you are calling for Mr. Drury Lane, and that I request most urgently a luncheon appointment today."

"Yes, sir." Jorgens went to a taboret, sedately dialed a number and, after a moment, asked for the broker. "Mr. DeWitt? This is Jorgens, sir. . . . Yes, sir. Mr. Drury Lane is here, sir, and asks for a luncheon appointment today. Most urgently, sir. . . . Yes, sir. Mr. Drury Lane. . . . He asked me particularly to tell you it was urgent, sir. . . ."

Jorgens turned from the instrument. "Will the Exchange Club at noon be convenient, Mr. Lane?"

Lane's eyes gleamed. "The Exchange Club at noon will be perfect, Jorgens."

As they entered the limousine outside, Lane said to Quacey—who was now tugging desperately at his collar—"It occurs to me, Quacey, that your observational talents have been wasted these many years. How would you like to turn detective temporarily?"

The car started, and Quacey ripped his collar from his wrinkled neck fiercely. "Anything you say, Mr. Drury. Right now this collar . . ."

Lane chuckled deep in his throat. "Your assignment is merely this—I must apologize for giving you a small task, but then you are a tyro at this game. . . . This afternoon, while I am occupied with various matters of moment, you will get in touch with every South American consul in New York City. You will endeavor to locate a consular gentleman who might have had contact with one Felipe Maquinchao, a South American, tall, dark, mustached, with probably a touch of the Indian and Negro in his blood. A veritable Othello, Quacey. . . . You understand that discretion is called for, Quacey. I should dislike to have Inspector Thumm or District Attorney Bruno discover in which direction I am seeking. *Comprende?*"

"Maquinchao," said Quacey in his rusty squeak. His old brown fingers twined themselves in the strings of his beard. "Now how in the name of the Three Witches do you spell that?"

"For," went on Mr. Drury Lane contemplatively, "if Inspector Thumm and District Attorney Bruno haven't the sense to question John DeWitt's butler, they deserve to be kept in ignorance."

"He talks too much," said Quacey severely, in the manner of a man who spends most of his life listening.

"On the contrary, lump of evil," murmured Mr. Drury Lane, "he talks too little."

Scene 8

THE EXCHANGE CLUB. FRIDAY, SEPTEMBER 11. NOON.

MR. DRURY Lane made a grand entrance, unpremeditated to be sure. It was simply a matter of walking into the leathery atmosphere of the Exchange Club on Wall Street and, *ipso facto,* creating something of a furor. Three men discussing heated golf on a lounge recognized him as if by signal and the Scottish game was obscured in a blur of whispers. The eyes of a colored attendant rolled wildly at sight of the cape. A clerk behind the desk looked startled and dropped his pen. The word spread with the rapidity of a bullish rumor.

Men began to stroll by, attempting to appear unconcerned but glancing curiously at Lane's odd figure out of the corners of their eyes.

Lane sat down with a sigh in a clubchair in the foyer. A white-haired man hurried up and bowed as low as his circumference would permit.

"Good day, Mr. Lane, good day." Lane smiled briefly. "This is an honor, sir. I'm the Chief Steward. Is there anything I can do for you, sir? A cigar, perhaps?"

Lane's fingers rose in a protesting gesture. "No, thank you so much, Steward. My throat, you know." It seemed to be an old ritual for him, because the words, although pleasant, were utterly mechanical. "I am waiting for Mr. DeWitt. Has he come in?"

"Mr. DeWitt? I don't believe he has, Mr. Lane. I don't believe he has." The Steward's tone implied that Mr. DeWitt was to be severely censured for keeping Mr. Drury Lane waiting. "In the meantime I'm entirely at your disposal, sir."

"You're very kind." Lane leaned back and closed his eyes in dismissal. The Steward, looking very proud, stepped back and tampered with his necktie.

At this moment the slight frail figure of John DeWitt hastened into the foyer. The broker was pale; there was something of apprehension on his features, an added strain, a new pressure from within. He obeyed the smiling gesture of the Steward without changing expression and walked quickly across the foyer toward Lane, followed by envious glances.

The Steward said: "Here's Mr. DeWitt, sir," and seemed hurt by Lane's lack of response. It was not until DeWitt motioned him away and touched Lane's hard shoulder that the actor opened his eyes. "Ah, DeWitt!" he said with pleasure, and sprang to his feet.

"Sorry to have kept you waiting, Mr. Lane," said DeWitt constrainedly. "I had another appointment—had to break it—delayed me . . ."

"Not another word," said Lane, whipping off his cape. A uniformed Negro hurried up and took Lane's cape, hat, and stick and DeWitt's coat and hat with the dexterity of a genie. The two men followed the Steward through the foyer into the Club dining-room where a head waiter, roused out of his professional nonchalance, broke out in smiles and conducted them, at DeWitt's request, to a secluded part of the dining-room.

Throughout a light luncheon—DeWitt toyed with his *filet* while Drury Lane ate robustly a solid chunk of roast beef—Lane refused to be tempted into serious discussion. DeWitt made repeated efforts to discover the purpose of Lane's rendezvous; Lane countered with: "Unquiet meals make ill digestions," and let it go at that. DeWitt smiled in a half-hearted way and Lane continued to talk easily, smoothly, as if there were nothing weightier on his mind than the proper method of masticating English beef. He recounted several intimate reminiscences of his early days on the stage, his sentences punctuated with illustrious theatrical names—Otis Skinner, William Faversham, Booth, Mrs. Fiske, Ethel Barrymore; and as they ate, DeWitt's rigidity softened before the smooth pregnant conversation of the old actor, and he found himself listening with enjoyment. Some of the tension left him, and Lane chatted on without seeming to notice.

Over coffee, and after DeWitt had accepted equably enough Lane's refusal of a cigar, Lane said: "I can see, Mr. DeWitt, that you are not by nature a morose or morbid man." DeWitt was startled, but puffed his cigar without replying. "It is not a feat of psychiatrics to read from your physiognomy and recent actions a sad winter's tale—mental depression, chronic perhaps, but alien to your character."

DeWitt murmured: "In some respects I've had a hard life, Mr. Lane."

"Then I was correct." Lane's voice became persuasive; his long hands were flat on the tablecloth, perfectly motionless. DeWitt's eyes were fixed on them, as on a focal point. "Mr. DeWitt, my primary reason for spending an hour in conversation with you is a friendly one. I feel that I should know you better. I feel that, in my own blundering way perhaps, I may be able to help you. I feel, in fact, that you require help of no common variety."

"That's decent of you," said DeWitt drearily, without raising his eyes. "I realize well enough the dangerous position I'm in. Neither the District Attorney nor Inspector Thumm has deceived me in the slightest. I am being constantly watched. I have the feeling that even my correspondence is being tampered with. You yourself, Mr. Lane, have been questioning my servants. . . ."

"Only your butler, Mr. DeWitt, and entirely in your interests."

". . . and so has Thumm. So you see—I know where I'm at. On the other hand, I sense that you're a little different from the police—more human?" He shrugged. "You may be surprised, but I've been thinking of you a good deal since Wednesday night. You stepped into the breach several times in my defense. . . ."

Lane's face was grave. "Would you mind, then, if I asked you a question or two? My concern with this investigation is not official. It is personally motivated, and only with the end in view of getting at the truth. There are some things I must know if I am to make further progress. . . ."

DeWitt looked up swiftly. "Further progress? Have you reached any conclusions already, Mr. Lane?"

"Two fundamental ones, Mr. DeWitt." Drury Lane beckoned a waiter, who ran up excitedly, and ordered another pot of coffee. DeWitt's cigar had gone out; it drooped from his fingers, forgotten, as he stared at Lane's profile. Lane smiled faintly. "I must commit an impropriety and differ from a beautiful lady. A false prediction, Mr. DeWitt! Madame de Sévigné might as well have prophesied the ephemerality of immortal Shakespeare as of immortal coffee." He continued in the same mild tone. "I know who killed Longstreet and Wood, if you would term that progress."

DeWitt paled as if Lane had struck him in the face. The cigar snapped between his fingers. He blinked under Lane's serene gaze and choked back a lump of amazement, fighting for self-possession. "You know who killed Longstreet and Wood!" he said in a strangled voice. "But, my God, Mr. Lane, if you know aren't you going to do something about it?"

Lane said gently: "I *am* doing something about it, Mr. DeWitt." DeWitt did not move. "Unfortunately, we are dealing with literal-minded Justice; she demands tangible instruments of conviction. Will you help me?"

DeWitt did not reply for a long time. His face was tortured now; his eyes frantically sought to penetrate the blank mask of this unusual prosecutor, as if to probe and discover how much he knew, precisely what he knew. Then he said, in the same tight voice: "If I only could, if I only . . ."

"Dared, Mr. DeWitt?"

It was all melodramatic and somehow shoddy. Deep within the actor's body a little worm of repugnance stirred.

DeWitt kept silent. Again he studied Lane's eyes, as if he sought the name of a murderer there. Finally he struck a match and applied it to the dead end of his cigar with unsteady fingers. "I'll tell you what I can, Mr. Lane. But—how shall I say it ?—my hands are—well, tied. . . . There's one thing you simply mustn't ask me—the identity of the person with whom I had an appointment Wednesday night."

Lane shook his head good-humoredly. "You make it doubly difficult, Mr. DeWitt, by maintaining silence on one of the most interesting points in the case. However, we will waive that—" he paused, "for the present. I understand, Mr. DeWitt, that both you and Longstreet made your fortunes in South America, in some mining venture, that you came to the States together and set up a brokerage business requiring considerable capital. I take it, then, that your mine was something of a bonanza. That was before the War, I believe?"

"Yes."

"In what country of South America was your mine located?"

"Uruguay."

"Uruguay. Quite so." Lane half-closed his eyes. "Mr. Maquinchao is a Uruguayan, then?"

DeWitt's mouth opened; his eyes clouded with suspicion. "How do you know about Maquinchao?" he demanded. "Jorgens, of course. The cursed old fool. I should have told him——"

Lane said sharply: "The wrong attitude entirely, Mr. DeWitt. Jorgens, an estimable man and a faithful servant, was willing to give me information solely because he was under the impression that I asked in your interest. You can do no less than emulate him—unless you question my purpose."

"No, no. I'm sorry. Yes, Maquinchao is a Uruguayan." DeWitt was in agony. His eyes fluttered from side to side, the old wildness in them again. "But Mr. Lane, please don't press me about Maquinchao."

"But I must press you, Mr. DeWitt." Lane's glance was naked now. "Who is Maquinchao? What is his business? How explain his unique activity while he was your guest? I am determined, sir, to have the answers to these questions."

DeWitt traced a meaningless pattern on the cloth with a spoon, speaking in a muffled tone. "If you insist . . . Nothing at all out of the ordinary. Purely a business visit, Mr. Lane. Maquinchao is the—the scout for certain South American public utility locations—wanted our office to handle the floating of a bond issue . . . You see, a perfectly legitimate enterprise. I——"

"And did you decide with Mr. Longstreet to help float this bond issue, Mr. DeWitt?" asked Lane without expression.

"Well—we have—we had the matter under consideration." Round and round went DeWitt's spoon, busy with a geometric pattern on the cloth: angles, curves, rectangles, rhomboids.

"You have the matter under consideration," repeated Lane dryly. "Why did he stay so long?"

"Well, surely . . . I'm sure I don't know, unless he visited other financing institutions. . . ."

"Can you give me his address?"

"Why—I don't believe I know exactly. He travels extensively; he's never long in one place. . . ."

Lane chuckled suddenly. "You are a poor liar, Mr. DeWitt. And since I see it is quite futile to pursue this conversation further, let us end it here before you become so entangled in your own mendacity that you will embarrass me as much as yourself. Good day, Mr. DeWitt, and believe me when I say that your attitude is a rude commentary on my vaunted capacity for judging human nature."

Lane rose—a waiter jumped forward as if on springs and grasped the chair. Lane smiled in his direction, examined DeWitt's lowered head, and said in the same amiable voice: "Nevertheless, you are welcome at The Hamlet, my place on the Hudson, at any time when you have changed your mind. Good day, sir."

He moved away, leaving DeWitt in the crushed attitude of a man who has heard sentence of execution passed upon him.

As he threaded his way among the tables, preceded by the head waiter, Lane paused a moment, smiled to himself, and then resumed his march out of the dining-room. Not far from the table at which DeWitt still sat, a man was dining. The man had a red face, looked uneasy, and during the entire conversation between Lane and DeWitt had strained forward, ears cocked, in a shameless attempt to eavesdrop.

In the foyer Lane tapped the head waiter's shoulder. "That red-faced man near the table at which Mr. DeWitt and I were seated—is he a member?"

The head waiter looked disturbed. "Oh, no, sir. A detective. He forced his way in with his badge."

Lane smiled again, pressed a banknote into the man's hand, and walked with leisurely steps to the desk. The clerk pranced forward.

"Will you please direct me first to Dr. Morris, your Club physician, and then to the Club secretary," said Mr. Drury Lane.

Scene 9

THE DISTRICT ATTORNEY'S OFFICE.
FRIDAY, SEPTEMBER 11. 2:15 P.M.

AT 2:15 of Friday afternoon Mr. Drury Lane was walking briskly along Center Street, hemmed in on the one side by the monumental walls of Police Headquarters and on the other by the polyglot mercenaries of lower New York. When he came to the ten-story building, Number 137, in which the County of New York saw fit to house its chief prosecutor, he turned in, crossed a corridor, entered an elevator and was borne aloft.

As always his features were completely controlled and completely expressionless. A lifetime of discipline on the stage had given him such muscular control of his features as an acrobat has of his limbs. But, unobserved now, there was a certain unsuppressed glow in his eyes that was significant. It was a glow of excitement, of anticipation—the fire of a hunter's eyes as he crouches behind his covert, gun poised—the shine and the joy of keen living and keen thinking. Looking into those eyes, it would be impossible for an observer to conjure the man behind them as having led a thwarted or incomplete existence. . . . Something had tapped the juices of his ego, flooding his being with new energy, directing the vital stream into new channels of confidence, vigor, and alertness.

Yet when he opened the door to District Attorney Bruno's outer office, the light had been quenched and he was merely a youngish man dressed in oldish clothes.

Someone spoke guardedly into an inter-office communicator. "Yes, Mr. Bruno." He turned about. "Will you have a seat, sir? Mr. Bruno is very sorry, but he is in conference with the Commissioner. Will you wait?"

Lane said he would, and sat down. He rested his chin on the knob of his stick.

Ten minutes later, while Lane reposed peacefully with closed eyes, the door from Bruno's private office opened and the District Attorney appeared, followed by the tall stout figure of the Police Commissioner. The clerk rose, flustered, as Lane continued to sit in what seemed to be a senile doze. Bruno smiled and tapped Lane's shoulder. The lids flew up, the calm gray eyes became inquisitive, and Lane jumped from the chair.

"Mr. Bruno."

"Good afternoon, Mr. Lane." Bruno turned to the Commissioner, who was regarding Lane curiously. "Mr. Lane—Commissioner Burbage."

"This is an honor, Mr. Lane," boomed the Commissioner, pumping Lane's hand. "I saw you in——"

"I seem to be living, Mr. Burbage, in the shade of my mellow past," said Lane with a disarming chuckle.

"Not at all, not at all! I understand you're as good as ever. Mr. Bruno's been telling me of your newly acquired vocation, Mr. Lane, and some of the revelations you've hinted which are still mysteries to him." The Commissioner wagged his big head. "Mysteries to all of us, I guess. Thumm's been telling me things."

"The idiosyncrasy of an aging man, Mr. Burbage. Mr. Bruno has been more than patient." Lane's eyes crinkled. "You bear for me, Mr. Burbage, an illustrious name. Richard Burbage, the most eminent actor of his time, was one of Will Shakespeare's three lifelong friends." The Commissioner seemed vaguely pleased.

They chatted for a few minutes, Commissioner Burbage excused himself, and Bruno ushered Lane into his private office. Inspector Thumm was hunched over a telephone, his face a study in incredulity. He jerked a heavy eyebrow in greeting, his ear hooked to the receiver. Lane sat down facing Thumm.

"Now listen," said the Inspector. While he had been listening to the voice in the receiver his face had grown redder and redder, until it seemed about to burst from sheer impotent rage. "What in hell are you trying to pull on me? Let me get this straight. . . . Shut up, will you? You say I told you to. Call me at half-past two this afternoon and remind me to give you something to do? You're crazy in the head, man! Or soused! . . . What? I told you *in person?* Hey, wait a minute." Thumm turned from the telephone and glared at Bruno. "This dumbhead, one of my men, has just gone nuts, I tell you. He—hello, hello!" He howled into the speaker. "You helped me *pick up the rug?* What rug, you infernal jackass? Oh, my God. Hold on a minute." He turned to Bruno again. "The case is simply blowing up from lunacy. Operative says I was in Wood's room in Weehawken yesterday poking about. By God, maybe it's on the level! Maybe—here, you!" he cried frantically. "Looks like somebody . . ." and then his eyes focused on Mr. Drury Lane, who was watching him with affectionate amusement. His jaw sagged and intelligence crept into his feverish eyes. A surly grin spread over his face and he growled into the telephone: "Okay. I changed my mind. Just hang around the room." He hung up and turned to Lane, plopping his elbows on the desk. Bruno looked from one to the other in bewilderment. "Well, Mr. Lane, that's one on me, hey?"

Lane's features ironed out. "Inspector," he said gravely, "if I have ever entertained doubts concerning your sense of humor, they are now eternally dispelled."

"What in the world is all this nonsense about?" demanded Bruno.

Thumm slipped a draggled cigarette between his lips. "It's like this. Here's what I did yesterday. I went to Weehawken, interviewed Mrs. Murphy, searched Wood's room, found a bankbook under Wood's carpet, assisted, mind you, by a man who has known me for six years, and then I walked out. It's something of a miracle, when you come to think of it. Because while I was in Weehawken, I was also sitting in my office jawing with you, down here in Center Street!"

Bruno stared at Lane, broke into a laugh. "That's a little unfair, Mr. Lane. And a little dangerous."

"Not at all. There was absolutely no danger," said Lane blandly. "My familiar is the world's premier make-up man, Mr. Bruno. . . . I must humbly ask your pardon, Inspector. My reason for impersonating you yesterday was serious and peremptory. Perhaps my instruction to your operative was a childish prank, but even that was dictated by a desire to inform you, unconventionally to be sure, of the great impersonation."

"Next time you might let me take a look at myself," grunted Thumm. "A dang—" His jaw thrust forward. "Frankly, I don't li— Well, let it go. Let's have that bankbook."

Lane produced the bankbook from beneath his coat; Thumm took it and began to pore over its contents. "It's quite possible, Inspector, that I may exhibit someone to you in the near future who will startle you even more."

Thumm's fingers curled about the five-dollar bill tucked into the bankbook. "Well," he grinned, "at least you're honest." He threw the book to Bruno, who examined it and put it into a drawer.

"My visit," said Lane in a brisk tone, "is induced by more than a desire to see our good Inspector wriggle. I have two requests. The first is for a carbon copy of the complete list of ferry passengers. Have you one that I may take with me?"

Bruno explored the top drawer of his desk and handed Lane a thin sheaf of papers. Lane folded the sheaf and placed it in a pocket. "I should like to receive, too, complete reports on all missing persons in the past several months, and day-to-day reports from now on. Can that be arranged?"

Thumm and Bruno looked at each other; Bruno shrugged, and Thumm wearily transmitted the order by telephone to the Missing Persons Bureau. "You'll have complete reports, Mr. Lane. They'll be sent to you at The Hamlet."

"Very kind of you, Inspector."

Bruno cleared his throat in a hesitating manner. Lane eyed him with friendly curiosity. "The other day," began the District Attorney, "you said you'd like to be informed before we take definite action. . . ."

"The ax falls," murmured Lane. "What precisely?"

"The arrest of John DeWitt for the murder of Charles Wood. Thumm and I are both agreed that we have a case. When the Commissioner heard my story he told me to shoot. It won't be hard to secure an indictment."

Lane looked grave; the smooth skin stretched tightly across his cheeks. "I gather, then, that you and Inspector Thumm believe DeWitt killed Longstreet also?"

"Naturally," said Thumm. "This Mr. X of yours is behind the

whole business. The two crimes were committed by the same hand, no question about it. With motives that fit like gloves."

"A neat phrase," said Lane. "Very neat, Inspector. And when is this step scheduled to be taken, Mr. Bruno?"

"There really is no hurry," said Bruno. "DeWitt can't run away. But we'll probably arrest him within the next day—if something," he added darkly, "doesn't happen in the meantime to change our minds."

"An act of God, Mr. Bruno?"

"Hardly." Bruno smiled wryly. "Mr. Lane, when the Inspector and I outlined the Longstreet case to you at The Hamlet, you said you had arrived at a solution of sorts. Does the arrest of DeWitt correspond with your solution?"

"It is slightly unfortunate," said the actor in a musing tone. "Entirely too premature. . . . You have a case. How strong is it?"

"Strong enough to give DeWitt's attorneys some sleepless nights," retorted the District Attorney. "The State's case against DeWitt will follow this argument, roughly: He was the only passenger on the ferry, as far as can be determined, who boarded at the same time as Wood and was still on the *Mohawk* four trips later, at the time of the murder. A strong point. He admitted trying to leave the ferry directly after the murder. His explanation of his presence for four trips (which at first he denied altogether, as we will stress) is thin and entirely unsubstantiated. His refusal to back up his story of having an appointment is damning; confirmation of our argument that this was just a trumped-up excuse lies in two facts: the 'caller' has not come forward, and the original telephone call cannot be traced. The indication is, therefore, that DeWitt's story of the call and the caller are products of his imagination. How does that strike you so far, Mr. Lane?"

"Plausible as you state it, but scarcely direct evidence. Please proceed."

Bruno's keen face worked, then he looked up at the ceiling and resumed: "The top deck where the murder was committed was accessible to DeWitt—or anyone else on the boat, it is true—and there was no witness who had DeWitt in sight constantly after 10:55 P.M. A cigar which DeWitt admits was his, and which from its brand and band could only have been his, was found on the dead man. He said that he never anywhere before gave Wood a cigar—a seeming defense, but actually we shall construe it in our favor, for it obviates the possibility that DeWitt gave Wood the cigar elsewhere *before* the murder, to account for its being on his dead body."

Lane tapped his hands together in mute applause.

"Furthermore, the cigar was not on Wood's person when he boarded the ferry and therefore must have been given to him on the boat itself."

"*Given,* Mr. Bruno?"

Bruno bit his lip. "At least, that's the reasonable explanation," he said. "As far as the cigar is concerned, I shall offer the theory that DeWitt met Wood on the boat and talked with him—a theory which accounts for DeWitt's admitted four trips and the hour's duration between the embarkation of Wood and DeWitt, and Wood's murder. Then he either offered Wood a cigar, or Wood asked for one while they talked."

"One moment, Mr. Bruno," said Lane amiably. "You believe, therefore, that DeWitt offered Wood a cigar—or Wood asked for it—that DeWitt later killed Wood and completely forgot that on Wood's body was a damning item of evidence directly implicating himself?"

Bruno laughed shortly. "Look here, Mr. Lane, people do all

sorts of foolish things when they commit murder. Apparently DeWitt did forget. He was bound to be highly excited, you know."

Lane waved his arm.

"All right, then," continued Bruno. "We come to motive. Of course, for DeWitt to have killed Wood we must connect DeWitt with the Longstreet murder. Here we have no direct evidence, but the motive-application is certainly clear. Wood had written the police that he knew the murderer of Longstreet. On his way to make this disclosure he was killed—inferentially, to be kept from making this disclosure. There is only one person who would be interested in sealing his lips—the murderer of Longstreet. This means, gentlemen of the jury," went on Bruno in a mocking voice, "that if DeWitt killed Wood, he also killed Longstreet. *Quod erat et cetera.*"

Thumm snapped: "Oh, he doesn't believe a word of what you're saying, Bruno. It's a waste——"

"Inspector Thumm!" said Lane with gentle reproachfulness. "Please don't misinterpret my attitude. Mr. Bruno points out what seems to him an inevitable conclusion. I quite agree with him. The murderer of Charles Wood unquestionably murdered Harley Longstreet. The logical process by which Mr. Bruno arrives at this conclusion, however, is quite another matter."

"You mean," cried Bruno, "that you too think DeWitt——"

"Please, Mr. Bruno, please continue."

Bruno scowled, and Thumm slumped back into his chair glaring at Lane's famous profile. "DeWitt's motive against Longstreet is pretty clear," said the District Attorney after a stormy silence. "There was bad blood between the two men because of the Fern DeWitt scandal, because of Longstreet's lustful advances to Jeanne DeWitt, because, most important of all, Longstreet undoubtedly had been blackmailing DeWitt for a long time, subject matter unknown. In addition, aside from motive and as corroboration, DeWitt more than anyone else was familiar with Longstreet's habit of reading the stock page on the car and taking out his glasses for that purpose, so that he could plan to the minute when Longstreet would prick himself on the needled cork, and so on. As for Wood's stumbling on a clue that pointed to DeWitt's guilt in the Longstreet murder, we know that DeWitt used Wood's car at least twice between the time of the first crime and the time of the second."

"And the exact nature of this 'clue,' Mr. Bruno?" asked Lane.

"We can't be sure on that point, of course," frowned Bruno. "DeWitt was alone on both occasions. But I don't think I'll have to show *how* Wood came to know—the fact that he presumably knew is sufficient for the thread of my argument. . . . As a clinching point, a really powerful phase of the prosecution's case will be this: As far as we know, DeWitt was the *only* person on the street-car at the time of the Longstreet murder *who was also on the ferry* at the time of Wood's murder!"

"And that," growled Thumm, "is a damned good case."

"It's interesting from the legal standpoint," said the District Attorney thoughtfully. "The cigar fact is strong evidence, the other inferences and circumstances implicating DeWitt guarantee a grand jury indictment, and, unless I'm very much mistaken, Mr. DeWitt won't be feeling so spry after the jury gets through with him."

"An intelligent defending attorney could make out a plausible argument the other way," remarked Lane mildly.

"You mean," said Bruno quickly, "that there's no direct evidence that DeWitt killed Longstreet? That DeWitt was decoyed to the *Mohawk* through the agency of someone whose identity he can't disclose for personal reasons, that the cigar was planted on Wood's body—in other words, that DeWitt was framed for Wood's murder?" Bruno smiled. "Of course, that will be the defense, Mr. Lane, but unless the defending attorney produces the author of that call, in the flesh, he's sunk. No, I'm afraid that argument won't hold much water. Don't forget that DeWitt's silence, his unwillingness to talk, unless he radically changes his attitude, will tell severely against him. Even the psychology is with us."

"Listen," said Thumm nastily, "this isn't getting us anywhere. You've heard our side of the story, Mr. Lane. What's yours?" He spoke in the truculent tone of a man who trod firm ground and defied his opponent to attack.

Lane closed his eyes, smiling faintly. When he opened them again, they were very bright. "I find, gentlemen," he said, twisting about in his chair to face both men, "that you make the identical error in your attitude toward crime and punishment that many producers make in connection with drama and its interpretation."

Thumm snickered loudly. Bruno sank back, frowning.

"The error consists chiefly in this," continued Lane genially, hands clasped on his stick, "that you approach your problem in the same manner of the companions of my boyhood trying to gain admittance to the circus—by walking into the tent backwards. Perhaps that is not clear. I can make a pointed analogy from the drama.

"Periodically we so-called artists of the theater are reminded of the immortality of the one dramatic Immortal by some producer's announcement that he will once more stage *Hamlet.* What is the first thing this well-meaning but misguided producer does? He scrabbles about conferring with lawyers and drawing up impressive legal documents, all timed to a nicety with the publicized intention to star the eminent Mr. Barrymore or the great Mr. Hampden in that sorely mangled classic. The emphasis is placed entirely on Mr. Barrymore, or Mr. Hampden. The attraction is Mr. Barrymore, or Mr. Hampden. The public responds in exactly the same manner—they go to view the earnest efforts of Mr. Barrymore or Mr. Hampden and completely overlook the heroic witchery of the play itself.

"Even Mr. Geddes's venture, while it attempted to correct the evil of overemphasizing the star by engaging that excellent young player, Mr. Massey, in the title-rôle, was ill-advised because it mangled the play in another way. That Mr. Massey had never played Hamlet was an inspiration on Mr. Geddes's part, and something of the original intention of the playwright was regained—to exhibit a Hamlet interesting for himself, and not for his reputation as an interpreter. The mangling, by lopping off speeches and directing Mr. Massey so that Hamlet became a downy-faced young man more athletic than philosophic, is another story. . . .

"But this matter of star-emphasis is cruel to the one great playwright of all time. In motion pictures a similar condition persists. Mr. George Arliss plays in the cinema version of a story dramatizing a historical character. Does the public flock to see Disraeli, the character, reanimated magically in the voice and the flesh? Or Alexander Hamilton? Not at all. They flock to see Mr. George Arliss's delightful interpretation of merely another rôle.

"You see," said Drury Lane, "the emphasis is misplaced, the approach is distorted. Your modern system of criminal apprehension is as overbalanced, as profoundly fallacious, as the modern system of glorifying Mr. Arliss or casting *Hamlet* with Barrymore. The producer shapes *Hamlet*, whittles it, changes its proportions, redesigns it to fit Mr. Barrymore, instead of measuring Mr. Barrymore against the original specifications of the piece as fixed in their true proportions by Shakespeare. You, Inspector Thumm and District Attorney Bruno, commit the identical error when you shape the crime, whittle it, change its proportions, redesign it to fit John DeWitt, instead of measuring John DeWitt against the fixed specifications of the crime. Your loose ends, your shavings, your remnants of inexplicable facts and by-facts are the result of this too elastic method of hypothesizing. The problem should be attacked always from the crime itself as an unalterable bundle of facts; and if a hypothesis results in conflicting or opposing loose ends, it is the hypothesis that is wrong. Do you follow me, gentlemen?"

"My dear Mr. Lane." Bruno's forehead was corrugated, his whole manner subtly altered. "It's a brilliant analogy and I don't doubt it's basically true. But, my God, how often can we use the method you suggest? We need action. We're pressed by our superiors, the newspapers, and the public. If a few things are cloudy, it's not because we're wrong but because they're unexplained, perhaps irrelevant, odds and ends."

"A debatable question . . . As a matter of fact, Mr. Bruno," replied Lane abruptly—his face became smooth and enigmatic again, "to depart from this pleasant discussion, I agree with you that the law should take its course. Arrest Mr. DeWitt for the murder of Charles Wood, by all means."

He rose, smiled, bowed, and quickly left the room.

Bruno returned from escorting him to the elevator in the corridor with a worried face. Thumm regarded him from his chair with the characteristic savagery of his expression gone.

"Well, Thumm, what do you think?"

"Damned," said Thumm, "if I know what to think. In the beginning I thought he was a doddering old blowhard, but now . . ." He got to his feet and began to pace the rug. "That spiel of his just a minute ago wasn't the prattling of a feeble-minded old has-been. I don't know . . . By the way, you'll be interested to learn that Lane had lunch with DeWitt today. Mosher reported to me a while ago."

"Lunch with DeWitt, eh? And he didn't breathe a word about it," muttered the District Attorney. "I wonder if he hasn't something up his sleeve regarding DeWitt."

"Well, he isn't cooking up anything with DeWitt," said Thumm grimly, "because Mosher says DeWitt looked like a beaten dog when Lane left."

"Maybe," sighed Bruno, sinking into his swivel-chair, "maybe he's on our side after all. And if there's the ghost of a chance that he'll turn something up, we've got to stick with him and take our medicine. . . . Not," he added with a final scowl, "that it isn't bitter!"

Scene 10

THE HAMLET. FRIDAY, SEPTEMBER 11. 7 P.M.

MR. DRURY Lane, accompanied by a *Kozakŭ* of a man—raw-boned, with blue jowls that shook fiercely at every stride—came into the foyer of his private theater at The Hamlet. The theater led off a corridor parallel to the vast main hall, and was entered through a magnificent wall of glass. The foyer was uncolored by the gilt glories of the average theater. The predominating note was bronze and marble. In its exact center stood a remarkable sculpture. It was a replica in bronze of Lord Gower's famous memorial—Shakespeare seated on a high pedestal; below, at each side, stood figures of Lady Macbeth, Hamlet, Prince Hal, and Falstaff. Beyond the foyer towered a single portal of bronze.

Lane, keenly watching the lips of his gesticulating companion—dwarfing his own tall, slender figure—opened this door; they entered the theater itself. There were no loges, no rococo decorations, no spectacular crystal chandeliers suspended from the high ceiling—no balcony, no sweeping murals.

On the stage a bald-headed young man in a dirty smock was standing on a ladder, brandishing a paint-brush with free vigorous strokes on a back-drop, in the midst of a curious impressionistic scene—an alley lined on both sides with queer distorted habitations.

"Bravo, Fritz!" said Lane clearly, pausing at the rear of the theater to survey the young man's handiwork. "I like that." Despite the fact that the theater was empty, there was not the slightest echo of Lane's voice.

"Now," said Lane, sinking into a seat in the rear row, "attend, Anton Kropotkin. You are inclined to undervalue the potentialities of your countryman's piece. There is real Russian fervor concealed beneath its grotesqueries. To translate the play into English will dilute its Slavic passion. To rewrite the play in terms of Anglo-Saxon background, as you so terrifyingly suggest, would . . ."

The bronze door clanged inward and the tiny humped figure of Quacey shambled into the theater. Kropotkin swung his bulk, and Lane followed the direction of the Russian's eyes. "Quacey. Do you invade the sanctity of the drama?" Lane asked affectionately. Then his eyes narrowed. "You seem tired, poor ugly Quasimodo. What's the trouble?"

Quacey pottered to an adjoining seat, grumbling a greeting to the huge Kropotkin. He said peevishly: "I have had a day—only the good God above has such days. Tired? I am—I am torn to pieces!"

Lane patted the ancient's hand, quite as if the wrinkled cripple had been a child. "And were you successful, gnome?"

A flash of teeth in Quacey's leathery face. "But how could I be? Is that the way these South American consuls serve their countries? It is shameful. All out of town. All on vacation. . . . As it is, I wasted three hours in futile telephone calls and——"

"Quacey, Quacey," said Lane, "acquire the patience of the neophyte. Have you tried the Uruguayan consul?"

"Uruguay? Uruguay?" squeaked the old man. "Don't believe I have. Uruguay? Is that a country in South America?"

"Yes. I believe you will have better fortune there."

Quacey made a face, a very ugly face indeed, punched the big Russian's ribs out of sheer malice, and pattered out of the theater.

"That accursed mouse!" growled Kropotkin. "He keeps my ribs sore."

Ten minutes later, as Kropotkin, Hof, and Lane sat about discussing a new play, the ancient shuffled into the theater again, grinning. "Oh, a noble suggestion, Mr. Drury. The Uruguayan consul won't be back until Saturday, October the tenth."

Kropotkin heaved to his large feet and thundered down the aisle. Lane's brow wrinkled. "Unfortunate," he murmured. "Is he on vacation also?"

"Yes. He's gone back to Uruguay and no one in his consulate can—or is willing to—supply information. The consul's name is Juan Ajos, A-j-o-s. . . ."

"I'll tell you," said Hof thoughtfully, "I'd like to try an experiment with this opus, Mr. Lane."

"Ajos—" began Quacey, blinking.

"Yes, Fritz?" said Lane.

"How about partitioning the stage laterally? The problem is not too difficult mechanically."

"I just had a telephone call—" began Quacey desperately, but Lane was watching Hof.

"It will bear consideration, Fritz," the actor said. "You——"

Quacey was tugging at Lane's arm. He turned his head. "Oh, Quacey! Was there something else?"

"I've been trying to tell you," snapped Quacey. "Inspector Thumm telephoned that he has just arrested John DeWitt."

Lane waved his arm indifferently. "Stupid, but useful. Was there anything further?"

The hunchback polished his bald dome with the flat of his hand. "The Inspector said that he will get a quick indictment but the trial will not come up for about a month. The Court of General Sessions, he said, does not convene before October. Or something like that."

"In that case," said Lane, "we will permit Mr. Juan Ajos to spend his sabbatical in peace. You have earned a rest, Caliban. Off with you! . . . And now, Fritz, let us vivisect this inspiration of yours."

Scene 11

Offices of Lyman, Brooks & Sheldon,
Tuesday, September 29. 10 A.M.

Mrs. Fern DeWitt paced the floor of the reception-room like a leopardess with lashing tail. She wore a suit trimmed with leopard, a turban trimmed with leopard, very odd shoes trimmed with leopard. In her black eyes the wicked ferocity of the leopardess flashed. The aging, carefully lacquered face might have been a totem mask hiding centuries of cruelty. And, beneath the veneer of that face, too, something of elemental fear.

When the reception-clerk opened the door and said that Mr. Brooks would see her now, Mrs. DeWitt was sitting quite still in a chair. The performance had been for her own voluptuous edification only. Smiling thinly, she picked up her leopard-trimmed purse and followed the clerk through a long corridor lined with law books to a door on which was lettered: *Mr. Brooks. Private.*

Lionel Brooks was like his name—leonine. He was large physically, with a heroic shock of blond hair turning gray. He was dressed soberly, and his eyes were filled with dark worry.

"Sit down, Mrs. DeWitt. Sorry to have kept you waiting." She complied stiffly and refused a cigarette. Brooks perched on the edge of his desk and spoke abruptly, gazing off into space.

"You're probably wondering why I've asked you to call. The matter, I'm afraid, has serious implications, and it's a very difficult one for me to broach. You'll understand that I'm merely an intermediary, Mrs. DeWitt."

She said, without moving her artificially red lips: "I quite understand."

Brooks plunged ahead. "I visit Mr. DeWitt every day in his cell. Of course, he is charged with first-degree murder and the law will not release him on bond. He's taking his confinement—well, philosophically. But that's not what I wanted to say primarily. Mrs. DeWitt, your husband commissioned me yesterday to advise you that, if he is acquitted of the murder charge, he will institute divorce proceedings against you immediately thereafter."

The woman's eyes did not waver for an instant; there was no inner shrinking as from an unexpected blow. Something in the depths of her large Spanish eyes began to simmer, and Brooks went on hurriedly.

"He has authorized me to offer you a settlement of twenty thousand a year, Mrs. DeWitt, for the remainder of your unmarried life, if you will not contest the divorce and will assist in consummating it with the least possible publicity and fuss. I feel, Mrs. DeWitt, that under the circumstances—" Brooks stood on his feet and turned his back to go around his desk—"under the circumstances, Mr. DeWitt is making a very generous offer."

Mrs. DeWitt said in a hard voice: "And if I fight the action?"

"He will cut you off without a penny."

The woman smiled a hideous smile, because the flame behind her eyes did not go out and only her lips curved. "It seems to me that both you and Mr. DeWitt are over-optimistic, Mr. Brooks. There is such a thing as alimony, you know."

Brooks sat down and studiously lit a cigarette. "But there won't be any alimony, Mrs. DeWitt."

"That's a strange statement from a lawyer, Mr. Brooks." The rouge on her cheeks burned like fire. "Certainly a cast-off wife is entitled to support!"

Brooks winced at the metallic quality of her voice; she spoke in a detached mechanical manner that was inhuman. "You are not a cast-off wife, Mrs. DeWitt. If you should contest this action and force us to go to trial, you may take my word for it that the sympathy of the Court will be with your husband, Mrs. DeWitt, not with you."

"Please come to the point."

Brooks shrugged. "Very well, if you insist.—Mrs. DeWitt, there is only one charge on which the plaintiff in a divorce proceeding may bring action in New York State. Mr. DeWitt is in possession of proof—I'm sorry to have to say this, Mrs. DeWitt—proof that doesn't have to be manufactured, either, of your infidelity!"

She was very still this time; one eyelid drooped a little and that was all. "What proof?"

"A signed statement from a witness who swears over legal signature that you and Harley Longstreet occupied Longstreet's apartment early on the morning of February eighth of this year, at a time when you were supposed to be visiting for the weekend out of town. You were observed, the statement makes clear, in flimsy nightdress at eight o'clock in the morning, Mr. Longstreet was in pajamas, and at the moment the witness saw you both, you were on terms of unmistakable intimacy. Shall I be more specific, Mrs. DeWitt? Because the sworn statement goes into harrowing detail."

"That's quite enough. Quite enough," she said in a low voice. The flame beyond her eyes was flickering; she had relaxed and was human again, trembling like a callow girl. Then she tossed her head. "Who is this dirty-minded witness of yours—a woman?"

"I am not at liberty to say," snapped Brooks. "I see what you're thinking. You're thinking this is a bluff, or a put-up job." His face had hardened and his tone became cold and impersonal. "I assure you that we are in possession of that document, and we have the witness, a perfectly reliable person, to back it up. I assure you, too, that we can prove this incident in Longstreet's apartment was not the first between you, although it was probably the last. I repeat, Mrs. DeWitt, that under the circumstances Mr. DeWitt is being generous. I advise you from my experience in these matters to accept the offer—twenty thousand a year for the remainder of your unmarried life, if you keep quiet and help us secure the divorce without a blast of notoriety. Think it over."

He rose with finality, towering over her. Hands folded in her lap, she sat staring down at the rug. Then, without a word, she slipped out of the chair and went to the door. Brooks opened it for her, escorted her to the reception-room, pressed the elevator-button, and in silence they waited for the elevator. When it came he said slowly: "I'll expect to hear from you within a day or so—or from your attorney, Mrs. DeWitt, if you decide to retain one."

As if he did not exist she brushed by him and entered the lift. The elevator-boy grinned and Brooks, shaking himself, stood thoughtfully alone.

Roger Sheldon, the junior partner, poked his curly head into the reception-room. He made a face. "Gone, Lionel? How'd she take it?"

"I've got to give her credit. She swallowed it like a major. She has plenty of guts."

"Well, this ought to please DeWitt. That is, if she doesn't squawk. Think she'll fight?"

"It's hard to tell. I have a hunch, though, she knows that Anna Platt's our witness, because the Platt woman says that she thinks Mrs. DeWitt saw her that morning when she peeped into the bedroom. Damn these women!" He stopped short. "Say, Roger," he muttered, "that gives me an unpleasant thought. You'd better detail somebody to watch Anna Platt. I'm none too sure of her honesty of purpose. I wouldn't be surprised if Mrs. DeWitt tries to buy her off, and if she denies that statement on the witness-stand . . ."

They walked down the corridor to Brooks's office, Sheldon said: "I'll put Ben Callum on it. He's good at that sort of thing. How's Lyman coming with the DeWitt case?"

Brooks shook his head. "Tough, Roger, tough. Fred's got a job on his hands. By Christopher, if Mrs. DeWitt only knew what a slim chance DeWitt has of getting off, she wouldn't worry about the action. More chance of becoming a widow than a divorcee!"

Scene 12

THE HAMLET. SUNDAY, OCTOBER 4. 3:45 P.M.

MR. DRURY Lane was strolling through his English gardens, hands loosely clasped in the small of his back, sniffing the flowered air. At his side, brown teeth champing in his brown face, puttered Quacey, a characteristically silent Quacey, for the mood was upon his master, and upon the vagaries of his master's moods Quacey served with the loyalty of an old hound.

"If I seem to complain, monkey," murmured Lane, with-out looking down on the scraggling dome of Quacey, "forgive me. Sometimes I grow impatient. And yet the master of us all had much to say about unhurrying, not-to-be-hurried Time. For example," he continued in the oratorical vein, "'Time is the old justice that examines all such offenders, and let Time try.' And beautiful Rosalind never said truer word. And 'Time shall unfold what plighted cunning hides; who covers faults, at last shame them derides.' Awkward, for a change, but not unpenetrating. And again, monkey: 'The whirligig of Time brings in his revenges,' which is also very true. So you see . . ."

They came to a curious old tree with thick twin-stems, gnarled and gray and above their heads oddly humped. Between the stems a bench had been hollowed and here Lane sat down, motioning Quacey to sit beside him.

"The Quacey tree," murmured Lane. "You see, honored ancient, we have dedicated a monument to your infirmity. . . ." He half-closed his eyes and Quacey sat forward anxiously on the seat.

"You're worried," grumbled Quacey, and grasped his whiskers at once, as if he had uttered an indiscretion.

"You think so?" asked Drury Lane with a sly sidelong glance. "But then you know me better than I know myself. . . . Yet, Quacey, this waiting upon Time is not soothing to the nerves. We stand at an *impasse.* Nothing has happened of a mobile nature and I am asking myself if anything of such a nature is likely to happen. We are watching the development of a human Sphinx. John DeWitt, from a man gnawed by a hidden fear, has become a man braced by a hidden tonic. Who knows what medicine has steeled his soul? I saw him yesterday and he was like a Yogi—aloof, serene, untroubled, seeming to wait for death with the equanimity of the esoteric East. Strange."

"Maybe," squeaked Quacey, "he'll be acquitted."

"Perhaps," continued the actor, "what I took to be resignation may be Roman stoicism. The man has in his roots cells of iron. An interesting character. . . . As for the rest—nothing. I am impotent, and now I'm reduced to the rôle of inactive Prologue. . . . The Missing Persons Bureau has been courteous, but its reports have been as sterile as Pope's pilfering bard. Inspector Thumm informs me with his humorless efficiency—a naïve gentleman, Quacey—that he has investigated the private lives of all the passengers who rode that Charon's ferry, and that their addresses, identities, and backgrounds seem quite in order. Checkmate again. . . . How little it means, after all! So many disappeared from the scene and are unaccounted for, unaccountable. . . . The ubiquitous Michael Collins visits John DeWitt in his legal tomb with the earnestness of a penitent crawling to the cave of Paphnutius—and with no salve to his soul, Quacey. . . . District Attorney Bruno, a much harassed man, informs me through Attorney Lionel Brooks that Mrs. DeWitt has slunk into her lair—preferring, it would seem, neither to accept nor reject at this time the proposal of her husband. A shrewd and perilous woman, Quacey. . . . And my colleague of the illegitimate theater, Miss Cherry Browne, haunts the District Attorney's sanctum with offers of aid in the prosecution's case against DeWitt, having little to tender the prosecutor save her carefully alluring personality—a tangible asset on the witness-stand, no doubt, when it is accentuated by lovely calves and peeping breasts. . . ."

"If it was around April, Mr. Drury," volunteered Quacey after an awed silence, "I'd say you were rehearsing one of the soliloquies from *Hamlet.*"

"And poor Charles Wood," continued Drury Lane, sighing, "has left the sovereign State of New Jersey his immortal legacy, since no one comes forward to claim it—nine hundred forty-five dollars and sixty-three cents. The five dollars in the bankbook, undeposited, will probably molder in the archives. . . . Ah, Quacey, we live in an age of miracles!"

Scene 13

Residence of Frederick Lyman.
Thursday, October 8. 8 p.m.

Mr. Drury Lane's limousine stopped at an apartment house on West End Avenue and a doorman bowed the actor from his car to the foyer.

"Mr. Lyman."

The doorman manipulated a speaking-tube. Mr. Drury Lane was conducted to an elevator, carried skyward, and deposited on the sixteenth floor. A Japanese showed his teeth in greeting and ushered him into a duplex apartment. A rather handsome man of medium height, in dinner clothes, with a round face, a white scar under his chin, a high wide brow and thin hair came forward. The Japanese took Lane's cape, hat, and stick; the two men shook hands.

"I know you by reputation, Mr. Lane," said Lyman, escorting Lane to an armchair in the library. "I needn't tell you it's an honor and a pleasure to receive you here. Lionel Brooks has told me of your interest in DeWitt's case."

He skirted a flat desk heaped with papers and legal books, and sat down.

"I take it you are encountering difficulties in your defense, Mr. Lyman?"

The lawyer slumped sideways in his chair and began fretfully to finger the scar under his chin. "Difficulties?" He moodily surveyed the litter on his desk. "The case is almost impossible, Mr. Lane, although I'm doing my best. I have assured DeWitt repeatedly that unless he alters his attitude he's in for it. And he persists in that devastating clammishness of his. The trial's been on for days now, I can't get a thing out of him, and it looks black enough."

Lane sighed contentedly. "Mr. Lyman, do you expect to have an adverse verdict turned in?"

Lyman looked glum. "It seems inevitable." He spread his hands. "Bruno's been at his persuasive best—he's an infernally clever trial-lawyer—and he's presented a very strong circumstantial case to the jury. I've watched those twelve good men and true, and there's no question but that they're impressed. Idiots, the lot of 'em."

Lane observed that the lawyer's eyes were underscored with dull pouches. "Would you say, Mr. Lyman, that DeWitt's refusal to disclose the identity of his mysterious telephone caller is dictated by fear?"

"Hell, I don't know." Lyman pressed a button and the Japanese stole in bearing a tray. "You'll have something to drink, Mr. Lane, of course? A little *crême de cocoa? Anisette?*"

"No, thank you. Black coffee, perhaps."

The Japanese disappeared.

"I'll tell you frankly, Mr. Lane," continued Lyman, plucking at a paper before him, "DeWitt has puzzled me from the start. I really don't know if he's merely resigned or has something up his sleeve. If it's resignation he's sealed his own fate. I've done my best. Bruno rested for the State this afternoon, as you know, I suppose, and I launch my defense tomorrow morning. I saw Grimm in his chambers after the day's proceedings, and the old man was more reticent than usual. As for Bruno, he's out for blood, or he's pretty confident, because one of my men overheard him saying that the case is in the bag . . . Yet I've always said, from the things I've seen in this law business, that *Bei so grosser Gefahr kommt die leichteste Hoffnung in Anschlag.*"*

"A Teutonism worthy of Shakespeare," murmured Lane. "What have you planned in defense?"

"All I can do is present the alternative of Bruno's argument—that is, the frame-up plea. Of course," said Lyman, "I've already attempted on cross-examination to discredit Bruno in one particular—guying him before the jury on his inability to explain how Wood could have discovered DeWitt's guilt, even considering that DeWitt had been on Wood's street-car twice after the murder. After all, he was in the habit of taking that car, and I made the jury understand that thoroughly. But what was Bruno's weakness does not counteract, I'm afraid, the direct evidence of that cigar on Wood's dead body. That's a hard nut to crack."

Lane accepted a mug of black coffee from the Japanese and sipped thoughtfully. Lyman toyed with his liqueur-glass.

"And that's not all," continued Lyman, shrugging. "DeWitt has been his own worst enemy. If only he hadn't told the police that he had never given Wood a cigar anywhere! I might have been able to cook up a line of defense that would be convincing. And then the way he lied that night . . . Disgusting." He drained the tiny glass. "First he said he was on the ferry for one trip, then admitted having been on for four trips—that fishy story about his caller—to tell you the truth, I don't blame Bru-

* "In so great a danger the faintest hope should be considered."

no for jeering at it in court. If I didn't know DeWitt as I do, I'd disbelieve it, too."

"But you cannot," said Lane quietly, "expect the jury, to accept your personal appraisal of DeWitt in the face of the evidence? Quite so. . . . Mr. Lyman, from your tone this evening it is evident that you anticipate the worst. Perhaps—" he smiled and put down the coffee-cup, "perhaps we can make capital of Goethe's 'faintest hope' by united effort. . . ."

Lyman shook his head. "I don't see how, much as I appreciate your offer of assistance. Legally, my best bet is to attempt to throw so many question-marks at Bruno's circumstantial case that the jury will bring in a verdict of not guilty because of reasonable doubt. It's a long shot, but my best line of attack. With DeWitt stubbornly keeping his mouth shut, any attempt to *prove* his innocence would be so much wasted breath."

Lane closed his eyes and Lyman was silent, studying the heroic head curiously. The actor opened his eyes, and Lyman saw genuine amazement in their gray depths. "Do you know, Mr. Lyman," he murmured, "it is a matter of complete astonishment to me, that not one of the keen minds surveying this case has pierced the veil of nonessentials and seen the—to me, at least—perfectly photographic truth beneath."

Something leaped into Lyman's face—a hope, a haggard wish. "Do you mean," he asked quickly, "that you are in the possession of a pertinent fact of which the rest of us know nothing?—something that will prove DeWitt's innocence?"

Lane folded his hands. "Tell me, Mr. Lyman—do you honestly believe DeWitt did not kill Wood?"

The lawyer murmured: "That's not a fair question."

Lane wagged his head, smiling. "Well, let it go. . . . As for this photographic truth which I mentioned a moment ago, and your instant conclusion that I have discovered something new . . . Mr. Lyman, I know only what Inspector Thumm, District Attorney Bruno, you yourself from your study of the facts and circumstances surrounding the fatal night, could know. I have the feeling that DeWitt, who has a sharp brain, would have seen the truth under different conditions, perhaps where he was not himself the central figure."

Lyman had jumped impatiently from his chair. "For heaven's sake, Mr. Lane," he cried, "what is it? I—Good lord, I find myself actually *hoping* again!"

"Sit down, Mr. Lyman," said Lane kindly. "Listen carefully, make notes if you will. . . ."

"One moment, sir, one moment!" Lyman ran to a cabinet and hurried back with a curious apparatus. "Here's a dictaphone—talk to your heart's content, Mr. Lane. I'll study it all night and shoot the works in the morning!"

Lyman took from a drawer of his desk a black wax cylinder, adjusted it to the instrument and handed Lane the mouthpiece. Lane spoke softly into the dictaphone. . . . At nine-thirty Lane left a jubilant Lyman, all trace of fatigue vanished from his shining eyes, his fingers already clawing for the telephone.

Scene 14

Criminal Courts Building.
Friday, October 9. 9:30 a.m.

Judge Grimm, a small dour old man enveloped in black robes, entered majestically, an attendant pounded with a gavel, a roaring ritual, the rustle and whisper of people, and the fifth day of the trial of John O. DeWitt for the murder of Charles Wood began in a hush that ebbed into the corridors beyond the courtroom.

The room was crowded with spectators. In the enclosure before the Judge's bench, flanking the court stenographer's desk, were two tables. At one sat District Attorney Bruno, Inspector Thumm, and a small corps of legal assistants. At the other sat Frederick Lyman, John DeWitt, Lionel Brooks, Roger Sheldon, and several clerks.

Beyond the railing familiar faces bobbed in the sea of heads. In a corner not far from the jury-box sat Mr. Drury Lane; in the seat next to him the dwarfed figure of Quacey. On the other side of the room, in a group, were Franklin Ahearn, Jeanne DeWitt, Christopher Lord, Louis Imperiale, and Jorgens, DeWitt's butler. Near them were Cherry Browne, a ravishing study in black, and the saturnine Pollux. Michael Collins, biting his lip, sat alone; as did Anna Platt, Longstreet's secretary. And far to the rear, a veil over her face, sat Mrs. Fern DeWitt, inscrutable and motionless.

The preliminaries over, a rejuvenated Lyman rose briskly, stepped from behind the table, glanced cheerfully at the jury, grinned over at the District Attorney, and stated to the Court: "Your Honor, as my first witness for the defense, I call upon the defendant, John O. DeWitt, to take the stand!"

Bruno half-rose from his chair, staring; Inspector Thumm, in the surprised buzz that swept through the courtroom, shook his head in bewilderment. The District Attorney's face, heretofore calmly assured, became intangibly expressive of worry. He leaned over to Thumm, whispering behind his hand: "What the devil has Lyman up his sleeve? Calling the defendant in a murder trial! Giving me a chance to get at him . . ." Thumm shrugged, and Bruno sank back muttering to himself: "Something's in the air."

John O. DeWitt, duly sworn, giving the oath, his name, and address in a quiet, tight voice, sat down in the witness-chair, folded his hands, and waited. There was lethal silence in the courtroom; DeWitt, his puny figure, his self-possessed almost detached manner, were mysterious and imponderable. The jury hitched forward to the edges of their seats.

Lyman said, quite amiably: "Your age?"

"Fifty-one."

"Occupation?"

"Stock-broker. I was, before Mr. Longstreet's death, senior partner in the firm of DeWitt & Longstreet."

"Mr. DeWitt, will you please relate to the Court and the jury the events of the evening of Wednesday, September the ninth, between the time you left your office and the time you reached the Weehawken ferry."

DeWitt said in almost a conversational tone: "I left my branch office at Times Square at five-thirty and took the subway downtown to the Exchange Club, on Wall Street. I went to the gymnasium with the intention of exercising a bit before dinner, perhaps taking a plunge in the pool. In the gymnasium I cut my right forefinger on a piece of apparatus—a long ugly gash which bled immoderately. The Club physician, Dr. Morris, immediately treated the wound, stanching the blood and disinfecting the gash. Morris wanted to bandage the finger, but I didn't think it was necessary, and . . ."

"One moment, Mr. DeWitt," interrupted Lyman blandly. "You say you didn't think it was necessary to bandage the finger. Wasn't it rather that you are sensitive about your personal appearance and . . ."

Bruno leaped to his feet, objecting to the question as leading. Judge Grimm sustained the objection. Lyman, smiling, said: "Was there any other reason for refusing to have your finger bandaged?"

"Yes. I intended to stay at the Club most of the evening, and since the wound had stopped bleeding through Dr. Morris's ministrations, I preferred not to be inconvenienced with an awkward bandage. It would also have necessitated my answering friendly questions about the accident, and I am rather sensitive about these things."

Bruno was on his feet again. Wrangle, roar, shout. . . . Judge Grimm silenced the District Attorney and motioned Lyman to proceed.

"Continue with your story, Mr. DeWitt."

"Dr. Morris told me to be careful of the finger, since a twist or bump would reopen the wound and it would bleed again. I redressed with some difficulty, forgoing my swim, and went to the Club restaurant with my friend Franklin Ahearn, with whom I had made a dinner appointment. We dined, spent the evening in the Club with other business acquaintances of mine. I was asked to join in a game of contract bridge but was forced to refuse because of my hand. At 10:10 I left the Club and was driven by cab to the ferry terminal at the foot of Forty-Second Street . . ."

Bruno was on his feet again, protesting violently to the testimony as "incompetent, irrelevant, and immaterial," demanding that all of the defendant's testimony be stricken off the record.

Lyman said: "Your Honor, the defendant's testimony as given is pertinent and relevant, and important in building up a defense which will prove his innocence of the crime with which he is charged."

A few moments' further discussion, and Judge Grimm overruled the District Attorney's objection, motioning Lyman to continue. But Lyman turned to Bruno and said in an agreeable tone: "Your witness, Mr. Bruno."

Bruno hesitated, scowled, then rose and viciously assailed DeWitt. For fifteen minutes the courtroom was in an uproar, as Bruno badgered DeWitt, attempting to shake his story, to bring out facts relating to Longstreet. To these Lyman inexorably objected and was sustained in every objection. Finally, after a dry reprimand from Judge Grimm, the District Attorney waved his arm and sat down, mopping his forehead.

DeWitt stepped from the stand, paler than usual, and returned to his seat at the defense-table.

"I call as my second witness for the defense," announced Lyman, "Franklin Ahearn."

DeWitt's friend, wearing a look of complete stupefaction, rose from the group in which he was sitting and walked down the aisle and through the gate to the witness-stand. He was sworn in, gave his full name as Benjamin Franklin Ahearn and his West Englewood address. Lyman, hands in his pockets, asked mildly: "You are engaged in what occupation or profession, Mr. Ahearn?"

"I am a retired engineer."

"Do you know the defendant?"

Ahearn glanced at DeWitt and smiled. "Yes, sir, for six years. We are neighbors and he is my best friend."

Lyman said sharply: "Please answer only the question asked. . . . Now, Mr. Ahearn, did you meet the defendant at the Exchange Club on the evening of Wednesday, September the ninth?"

"Yes, everything Mr. DeWitt said is true."

Lyman again said sharply: "Please answer only the question asked." Bruno, who had grasped the arms of his chair, closed his mouth, settled back and kept his eyes on the face of Ahearn, as if he had never seen the man before.

"I did meet Mr. DeWitt at the Exchange Club on the evening stated."

"At what time, and where, did you first see him that evening?"

"A few minutes before seven. We met in the foyer of the dining-room and immediately went in to dinner."

"Were you with the defendant continually from that moment until 10:10?"

"Yes, sir."

"Did he leave the Club and you at 10:10, as he has just testified?"

"Yes, sir."

"Mr. Ahearn, as Mr. DeWitt's best friend, would you say that he is sensitive about his personal appearance or not?"

"I would say—I do say decidedly—that he is sensitive about his personal appearance."

"Then would you say that his decision not to have his hand bandaged was consistent with this trait of his character?"

Simultaneously with Ahearn's hearty, "Undoubtedly!" Bruno objected to the question and answer, and was sustained by the Court, both being stricken from the record.

"Did you notice Mr. DeWitt's hurt finger during dinner that night?"

"Yes. I noticed it even before we went into the dining-room, and I commented upon it. Mr. DeWitt related the story of his accident in the gymnasium and allowed me to examine the finger."

"Then you saw the finger. What was the condition of the wound when you examined it?"

"It was raw and ugly-looking, a long deep gash about an inch and a half long on the underside of the finger. It had stopped bleeding, and the cut had already formed a rudimentary scab of dried blood."

"Did anything occur over the dinner-table or afterward which bears upon this point, Mr. Ahearn?"

Ahearn sat thoughtfully in silence, stroking his jaw. He looked up. "Yes. Mr. DeWitt, I observed, held his right hand rather rigidly all evening, and at the dinner-table used only his left hand for eating purposes. It was necessary for the waiter to cut Mr. DeWitt's chop."

"Your witness, Mr. Bruno."

Bruno strode up and down before the witness-stand. Ahearn waited quietly.

Bruno thrust his jaw out and eyed Ahearn with hostility. "You testified a moment ago that you are the defendant's best friend.

His *best* friend, Mr. Ahearn. You wouldn't perjure yourself for your best friend, would you, Mr. Ahearn?"

Lyman stood up smiling, objected, even as someone in the jury-box tittered. Judge Grimm sustained.

Bruno glanced at the jury as if to say, "Well, you get the idea, anyhow." He turned squarely on Ahearn again. "Did you know where the defendant was going after he left you at 10:10 that evening?"

"No."

"How is it that you did not leave with the defendant?"

"Mr. DeWitt said he had an appointment."

"With whom?"

"He didn't say, and of course I didn't ask."

"What did you do after the defendant left the Club?"

Lyman was on his feet again, wearily smiling another objection. Again Judge Grimm sustained, and Bruno with a little gesture of disgust released the witness.

Lyman came forward confidently. "For my third witness," he said in a deliberate drawl, and glanced at the prosecutor's table, "Inspector Thumm!"

Inspector Thumm started guiltily, like a boy caught stealing apples. He looked at Bruno, and Bruno shook his head. The Inspector lumbered to his feet and, glaring at Lyman, took the oath, thudded into the witness-chair, and sat truculently waiting.

Lyman seemed to be enjoying himself; he glanced in friendly fashion at the jury, as if to say: "You see! I'm not even afraid to call the great Inspector Thumm in defense of my client." He wagged his finger roguishly at Thumm.

"Inspector Thumm, you were in charge of the police investigation on the ferry boat *Mohawk* when Charles Wood was discovered murdered?"

"I was!"

"Where were you standing just before the body was fished from the river?"

"On the upper passenger deck, north side of the boat, at the railing."

"Were you alone?"

"No!" snapped Thumm, tightening his mouth.

"Who was with you?"

"The defendant and a Mr. Drury Lane. Some of my men were on the deck, too, but only DeWitt and Lane were at the rail with me."

"Did you notice at this time that Mr. DeWitt's finger was cut?"

"Yes!"

"How did you come to notice it?"

"He was leaning against the rail, holding his right hand stiffly upward, his elbow on the rail. I asked him what was the matter and he said he had cut himself at his Club that evening."

"Did you observe the cut closely?"

"What do you mean—closely? I saw it—I've just told you that."

"Now, now, Inspector, don't lose your temper. Please describe the appearance of the wound as you saw it at that moment?"

Thumm shot a baffled glance at the District Attorney below, but Bruno's head was resting between his hands, his ears alert. Thumm shrugged and said: "Well, the finger was swollen a bit, the cut looked sort of raw. There was a dried-blood scab formed over the entire length of the cut."

"The *entire* length of the cut, Inspector? The scab was absolutely in one piece, not broken anywhere?"

A look of wonderment crept over Thumm's hard face, and his voice lost its hostile note. "Yes. It looked very stiff."

"Would you describe the cut, then, as fairly well healed, Inspector?"

"Yes."

"Then it was not a *brand-new* cut that you saw? That is, you would say that the skin had not been lacerated *just* before you observed it at the railing?"

"I don't know what you mean exactly. I'm not a doctor."

Lyman pulled his upper lip, smiling. "Very well, Inspector. I'll phrase the question differently. Was the cut that you saw a fresh cut, *just made?*"

Thumm squirmed. "That's a foolish question. How could it be a fresh cut when there was a scab on it?"

Lyman grinned. "Exactly the point, Inspector. . . . Now, Inspector Thumm, please tell the Court and the jury what happened after you noticed Mr. DeWitt's wound."

"The body was grappled at that moment, and we made a dash for the stairway leading down to the lower deck."

"Did anything pertaining to Mr. DeWitt's wound occur as you were doing this?"

Thumm said sullenly: "Yes. The defendant reached the door first and grabbed the knob to open the door for Mr. Lane and me. He sort of cried out, and we saw that the cut on the finger had opened. It was bleeding."

Lyman leaned forward and tapped Thumm's beefy knee, emphasizing each word. "The scab opened and the wound began to bleed *merely from the defendant's grasping the door-knob?*"

Bruno shook his head in a helpless way as Thumm hesitated. Bruno's eyes were tragic.

Thumm mumbled: "Yes."

Lyman continued rapidly. "Did you get a good look at the wound after it began to bleed?"

"Yes. DeWitt held his hand up for a moment while reaching for his handkerchief, and we saw that the scab had split in several places and the blood was oozing from the broken places. Then he wrapped his hand in the handkerchief and we continued downstairs."

"Are you prepared to swear, Inspector, that the bleeding cut you saw at the door was exactly the same cut that you saw, unopened, at the railing a moment before?"

Thumm said resignedly: "Yes. Yes."

But Lyman was persistent. "There was no new cut at all, not even a new scratch?"

"No."

"That's all, Inspector. Your witness, Mr. Bruno," said Lyman with a significant smile at the jury, and he stepped away. Bruno shook his head impatiently and Thumm descended from the rostrum, his face a study in mingled emotions—disgust, astonishment, understanding. As Lyman moved forward again, the spectators on edge with excitement, whispering to each other, the press-staff frantically writing, attendants clamoring for order, District Attorney Bruno slowly turned his head and surveyed the courtroom, as if seeking a face.

Lyman, calm, assured, called Dr. Morris to the witness-stand. The Exchange Club physician, a middle-aged man with an ascetic face, stepped from the audience, took the oath, gave his name as Hugh Morris, and his address, and sat down on the witness-chair.

"Are you a medical doctor?"

"Yes."

"Place of occupation?"

"Official physician at the Exchange Club. On the visiting staff of Bellevue Hospital."

"Your experience as a licensed physician, Doctor?"

"I have been practicing under a New York State medical license for twenty-one years."

"Do you know the defendant?"

"Yes. I have known him for ten years, the period in which he has been a member of the Exchange Club."

"You have heard the testimony of witnesses concerning a cut which Mr. DeWitt suffered on the forefinger of his right hand in the Club gymnasium the evening of September ninth. Is the testimony given so far concerning what happened in the gymnasium correct in every particular, to the best of your knowledge and belief?"

"Yes."

"Why did you warn the defendant to be careful of his finger after he refused to allow it to be bandaged?"

"Because the wound was such that any sudden stricture which would flex the forefinger would reopen the cut. The gash extended across the two upper joints of the forefinger. The normal closing of the hand any time Wednesday night, for example, would have distended the lips of the gash and broken the scab which was bound to form."

"And that was your professional reason for having desired to bind the hand?"

"Yes. For if the wound did open, as was likely from the exposed nature of its locality, it would have the antiseptic protection of the medicated bandage."

"Very good, Dr. Morris," said Lyman quickly. "Now, you have heard the testimony of the preceding witness, describing the condition of the wound and its scab when he saw it at the rail of the boat. Could this wound as the witness, Inspector Thumm, described it have been open, let us say, fifteen minutes before he saw it, Dr. Morris?"

"You mean could the original wound have opened fifteen minutes before Inspector Thumm first saw it, and have appeared as the Inspector described it?"

"Yes."

The physician said with emphasis: "Positively not."

"Why?"

"Had it been opened even an hour before, it could not have been in the condition Inspector Thumm described it—scabrous, unbroken, in one continuous piece, and all stiff and dry."

"Would you say, then, from Inspector Thumm's description, that the wound had not been opened from the time you treated it at the Club until the time the defendant grasped the door-knob on the ferry?"

Bruno was objecting strenuously at the same moment that Dr. Morris coolly replied: "Yes." While the argument raged, Lyman kept glancing meaningly at the jury, who were whispering with some heat. Lyman smiled with serene satisfaction.

"Dr. Morris, could the defendant have grasped and lifted a two-hundred-pound object a few minutes before Inspector Thumm saw his wound at the railing in the condition described, and shoved or hurled it over the railing and beyond the two-and-a-half foot shelf *without opening that wound?*"

Again Bruno had jumped to his feet, perspiring with anger, objecting with all the energy of his lungs. But Judge Grimm overruled him, indicating that the professional opinion solicited was pertinent to the defense argument.

Dr. Morris said: "Absolutely not. He could not have done what you have just described without opening the wound."

With a plain smile of triumph Lyman said: "You may cross-examine, Mr. Bruno."

Another uproar, and Bruno sucked his lower lip and scowled at the physician. He weaved back and forth before the witness-stand like a caged animal.

"Dr. Morris!" Judge Grimm was hammering for silence. Bruno paused until the courtroom was still. "Dr. Morris. On oath, and under guise of your professional knowledge and experience, you have just testified that the healed condition of the defendant's wound as described by a prior witness indicates that the defendant could not have used his right hand to throw a two-hundred-pound object over the rail without opening the cut . . ."

Lyman said without excitement: "Objection, Your Honor. That was not the question to which the witness answered affirmatively. My question included, besides the railing, the two-and-a-half foot shelf which runs along the sides of the *Mohawk's* upper deck."

"Restate the question correctly, Mr. District Attorney," said Judge Grimm.

Bruno complied.

Dr. Morris replied calmly: "'That is what I said 'yes' to, and I would stake my reputation on my opinion."

Lyman, back at the defense-table, whispered to Brooks: "Poor Bruno. He's more rattled than I've ever seen him before. Imagine impressing that point on the jury by repetition!"

But Bruno was not done. He said menacingly: "To which hand were you referring, Doctor?"

"To the hand with the cut finger, the right hand. Of course."

"But the defendant could have used *his left hand* to perform the aforementioned act without opening the wound on his right?"

"Naturally, if he didn't use his right hand he wouldn't open the cut on the right hand."

Bruno looked hard at the jury, as if to say: "You see, all this hullabaloo doesn't mean a thing. Doesn't apply at all. DeWitt could have done it with his left hand." He sat down with an uncertain grin. Dr. Morris began to descend from the stand, but Lyman was already demanding the right to recall the witness. The doctor sat down again, a glint of amusement in his eyes.

"Dr. Morris, you have just heard the District Attorney insinuate that the defendant could have disposed of the body of the deceased by using only his left hand. In your opinion, could the defendant, using only his left hand and handicapped with an injured right hand, have lifted the two-hundred-pound unconscious body of Charles Wood, and shoved or hurled it over the railing and beyond the shelf to fall from the boat?"

"No."

"Why?"

"I have known Mr. DeWitt professionally for years. I know that he is right-handed, for one thing, and that his left arm, as is usual with dexterous persons, is the weaker member. I know that, small, frail, weighing only one hundred and fifteen pounds, he is a weak man physically. I would say, from these facts, that it would be impossible for a one-hundred-and-fifteen-pound man, using only one arm, and that the weaker of the two, to do what you have described with the dead weight of a two-hundred-pound body!"

The noise was deafening. Several newspapermen ran out of

the courtroom. The members of the jury were talking excitedly, nodding their heads. Bruno was on his feet, face purple, shouting, but no one paid any attention to him while court attendants made stentorian efforts to restore order. When the tumult had subsided, Bruno in a gurgling voice asked for an adjournment of two hours to secure further medical opinion.

Judge Grimm snarled: "If there is any repetition of this disgraceful scene during the remainder of the trial, I will have the courtroom cleared and the doors closed! Motion for adjournment granted. Court adjourned until two o'clock this afternoon."

Somebody rapped with a gavel; everyone rose and waited until Judge Grimm had swept out of the room to his private chambers. Then pandemonium broke loose again as feet scraped, voices argued, and the jury retired. DeWitt, his poise ripped off, sat panting in his chair, an expression of incredulous relief on his white face. Brooks was pumping Lyman's hand in congratulation. "Most astounding defense I've heard in years, Fred!"

As the noise swirled about them, District Attorney Bruno and Inspector Thumm sat at the prosecutor's table regarding each other in half-humorous anger. Newspaper reporters had surrounded the defense-table now, and a court attendant was having difficulty extricating DeWitt from the press.

Thumm leaned forward. "Bruno's folly," he grunted. "Well, old hoss, the joke's on you."

"On us, Thumm, on us," snapped Bruno. "You're as much the goat as I am. After all, it's your department to collect evidence, mine to present it."

"Well, I can't deny that," said Thumm grumpily.

"We're the two prize idiots of New York," groaned Bruno, slapping his papers into his briefcase. "You had the facts at your fingertips all the time and never once made the obvious leap to the truth."

"No comeback there," rumbled Thumm. "I'm some sort of nanny, it's true. But after all," he said feebly, "you certainly saw DeWitt's hand wrapped in the handkerchief that night, and you never thought to ask questions about it."

Bruno dropped his bag suddenly; his face flamed. "I'd like to see Fred Lyman take credit for this! Damn it, that's what rankles. Let me hear him open his yap! Why, it's as plain as the nose on your ugly face that——"

"Sure," growled the Inspector. "Lane, of course. The old coot!" he exclaimed softly. "Just plain bamboozled us, by God, and it serves us right for doubting him."

They twisted about in their chairs and looked the emptying courtroom over. Lane was nowhere to be seen. "Must have ducked out," said Bruno disconsolately. "I saw him here before. . . . Well, Thumm, it's our own fault. He warned us not to go through with this in the beginning." He started. "Come to think of it," he muttered, "he seemed willing enough later on to let us prosecute DeWitt. And he had this defense in his hat all the time. I wonder why. . . ."

"Me, too."

"I wonder why he preferred to take chances with DeWitt's life."

"Not much he wasn't," said Thumm dryly. "Not with that defense. He knew he could get DeWitt off. I'll tell you one thing, though." He rose, stretching his simian arms, shaking himself like a shaggy mastiff. "From now on, friend, little Thummy listens to Drury Lane with respect! Especially when he's on the subject of Mr. X!"

Act III: *Scene 1*

A Suite at the Ritz. Friday, October 9. 9 p.m.

Mr. Drury Lane studied the face of his host unobserved. DeWitt stood in a group of his friends, smiling and chattering, making crackling retorts to friendly jibes.

And Mr. Drury Lane glowed with the warm internal satisfaction of the scientist who probes and probes and finds what he is seeking. For John DeWitt illustrated a character-lesson of provocative outline. Within the space of six hours he had changed from a man enveloped in obdurate armor to a man stripped of sorrow—alive, flashing, a wit, an intellectual companion, an amiable host. From the moment that the foreman of the jury, a gulping old man, had waggled his lantern jaws and ground out the swift release, the sesame of "Not Guilty" that swung open the gates of imprisonment, DeWitt with a surge of his thin chest had cast off the armor of his silence.

A retiring man? Not tonight! For tonight there must be celebration, laughter, the chink of glasses, the banquet of deliverance. . . .

The party had congregated in a private suite at the Ritz. In one room a long table loaded with crockery, stemware, and flowers had been set up. Jeanne DeWitt was there, sparkling and rosy; Christopher Lord, and Franklin Ahearn, looming over the frail body of his friend; and Louis Imperiale, the immaculate; and Lyman and Brooks and, by himself, Drury Lane.

DeWitt murmured an apology and slipped out of the chatting group. In a corner, the two men faced each other; DeWitt alertly humble, Lane pleasant and noncommittal.

"Mr. Lane. I haven't had the opportunity. . . . I can't find words to express my—my profound thanks."

Lane chuckled. "I see that even lawyers as hardened as Lyman cannot resist impulsive indiscretion."

"Won't you sit down? . . . Yes, Frederick Lyman told me, Mr. Lane. He could not accept congratulations, he said, which rightfully belong to you. That was—that was a remarkable alignment of facts, Mr. Lane. Remarkable." DeWitt's sharp eyes fluttered.

"Yet perfectly obvious."

"Not so obvious, sir." DeWitt sighed happily. "You can't know how honored I am by your presence. I know how little you care for this sort of thing, how few public appearances you make."

"True," smiled Lane, "but after all beside the point, Mr. DeWitt. You see, I am here. . . . I'm afraid, however, that my presence is not entirely induced by the pleasant company and the earnestness of your invitation." Something dark flitted over DeWitt's face and was gone in the next instant. "For you see it occurred to me that you might have something," Lane's voice became a shadow of its usual robustness, "something to tell me."

DeWitt did not answer at once. He looked about, drinking in the sounds of gayety, the supple beauty of his daughter, the quiet laughter of Ahearn across the room. An attendant in evening clothes was opening the sliding-doors of the banquet-room.

DeWitt turned back and his hand crept to his eyes. He

pressed the lids down, remained in an attitude of thought, of calculation. "I—well, sir, you're uncanny." He opened his eyes to look directly into the grave face of the actor. "I've made up my mind to trust you, Mr. Lane. Yes. It's the only way." An iron note pealed. "I have—it's true—I have something to tell you."

"Yes?"

"But I can't say anything now." The broker shook his head firmly. "Not now. It's a long sordid story, and I don't want to spoil your evening—or my own." His grayish hands twitched. "Tonight—well, it's a special sort of night for me. I've escaped a horrible thing. Jeanne—my daughter . . ." and Lane nodded slowly. Behind the mirror of DeWitt's abstracted eyes there was a vision, he was sure, not of Jeanne DeWitt but of Fern DeWitt. Grief, perhaps: DeWitt's wife was not present, and knowing what he knew, Lane felt certain that in his quiet uncomplaining way DeWitt still loved the woman who had betrayed him.

DeWitt slowly rose. "Won't you come down with the rest of my party tonight, sir? We're all going out to my place in West Englewood—I've arranged a little celebration—if you don't care to stay for the week-end I'll make any further arrangements you may please to command. One night will certainly not . . . Brooks is staying the night, and we can accommodate you as well as him with linen . . ." He added in quite another tone: "Tomorrow morning we can have to ourselves. And then I will tell you—what by some magical quality of intuition you expected me to tell you tonight."

Lane got to his feet and placed his hand lightly on the small man's shoulder. "I quite understand. Forget everything—until tomorrow morning."

"There's always a tomorrow morning, isn't there?" murmured DeWitt. They moved forward to join the others. A soft sickness attacked the pit of Lane's stomach. Banalities. . . . He found himself bored all at once. His face smiled at the group, and while the attendant in evening clothes invited the party to enter the banquet-room, a pinpoint glowed in a chamber of his brain and he found himself thinking: "'Tomorrow, and tomorrow, and tomorrow . . . to the last syllable of recorded time . . .'" It sheened and trembled, vibrated clearly in his head. "'. . . to dusty death." He sighed, found Lyman's arm entwined in his, smiled, and followed the others to the feast.

The party was gay. Apologetically Ahearn ordered a special platter of cooked vegetables; but he had sipped some Tokay and was recounting the details of a strenuous chess-match to Imperiale, who was frankly inattentive, preferring to murmur polished conceits to Jeanne DeWitt across the table. Lionel Brooks's blond head rolled with the lilt of a soft tune being played by a string orchestra concealed behind palms in a corner of the room. Christopher Lord discussed the prospects of the Harvard eleven, one eye cocked on Jeanne at his side. DeWitt sat quietly, enjoying the hum of conversation, the song of the violins, the room, the table, the food, the warmth; and Drury Lane studied him and watched him and made an occasional jest when Lyman, flushed with wine, urged him into speech.

Over demi-tasse and cigarettes Lyman suddenly rose, clapping his hands for silence. He raised a glass.

"As a rule," he said, "I despise the institution of toasts. It's an archaic hangover from the day of bustles, crinolines, and stage-door Johnnies. But there's a good excuse for toasting tonight—toasting a man's deliverance." He grinned down at DeWitt. "The best of health, the best of luck, John DeWitt."

They drank. DeWitt struggled to his feet. "I—" His voice

broke. Drury Lane smiled, but the sickness deepened in his stomach. "Like Fred, I'm a shy man." For no reason at all, they laughed. "But I propose to give you one of us who for decades has been the idol of millions of intelligent people, who has faced countless audiences and yet who, I think, is the shyest of us all. Mr. Drury Lane!"

They drank again, and Lane smiled again and wished he were very far away. He did not rise, said in his thrilling baritone: "I have the profoundest admiration for people who can carry these things off easily. On the stage one learns self-possession; but I have never mastered the art of perfect equanimity in affairs like this. . . ."

"Let's have it, Mr. Lane!" shouted Ahearn.

"I see I must." He rose and his eyes twinkled out of their boredom. "I suppose I should preach a sermon. And since my stock-in-trade is not the abbé's tract but the actor's script, my sermon must of necessity be couched in dramatic terms." He turned directly to DeWitt, sitting silent and alert at his side, and said: "Mr. DeWitt, you have just passed through one of the most harrowing experiences possible to emotional man. To sit before the bar, waiting through interminable years for a verdict, only too humanly fallible, which will mean life or death, is surely society's most subtle punishment. To endure such an eternity with dignity merits you the highest praise. I was reminded of the half-humorous, half-tragic remark of the French publicist Sieyès, when he was asked what he had done during the Reign of Terror. He said simply: *J'ai vécu,*' 'I have survived,' a retort impossible to any but a man of spirit and philosophy." The actor breathed deeply and regarded the company with unmoving features. "There is no virtue greater than the virtue of courage as executed by perseverance. The very triteness of the thought is its guarantee of truth."

They were quite still, but DeWitt was the most motionless of all; he seemed to feel the tide of rich words enter his body and become part of him; he seemed to feel that the words were directed wholly and meaningly and comfortingly to him alone.

Drury Lane tossed his head and said: "Please bear with me if—since you have insisted on my prattling—I bring a somber note into this gay company by leaning on my inevitable reference for all the wisdom that has ever been uttered." His voice lilted, grew stronger. "In one of Shakespeare's not sufficiently appreciated dramas, *King Richard III,* appears a commentary on the better side of a dark soul which, it seems to me, is confounding in its penetration." He cocked a slow eye at DeWitt's bowed head. "Mr. DeWitt," he said, "your experience of the past few weeks has fortunately stripped suspicion of murder from your name. Yet this does not clarify a greater issue, for somewhere about us, lurking in the mists, is a murderer who has already dispatched two human beings into hell or, for their sakes I hope, heaven. How many of us have reflected on the character of this man-killer, the machinery of his soul? For, even if the observation be trite, he has a soul, and if we are to believe our spiritual guides, an immortal one. Too many of us think of a murderer as an inhuman monster without recalling that buried in the depths of ourselves are raw emotional spots which the lightest touch might convert into just such festering foments to manslaughter. . . ."

There was such silence as to make the atmosphere thick, ponderable. Lane continued evenly: "Whereupon we return to Shakespeare's observations on one of his most interesting dramatic characters—the misshapen, bloody King Richard, surely an ogre in human form if there ever was one. Yet what does the all-seeing eye observe? In Richard's own bitter words . . ."

And suddenly he altered, his bearing, his expression, his voice.

It was done so subtly, so unexpectedly that they stared at him almost with fear. Cunning, acerbity, ravaging viciousness, supreme and aged disappointment obscured the pleasant face with sinister lines and shadows. Mr. Drury Lane was quite swallowed up in a new and terrible personality. His mouth writhed open and strangled sounds issued from that golden orifice. "'Give me another horse; bind up my wounds. Have mercy, Jesu!'" The voice rose to a pitiful snarl, torn from an anguished throat. It fell flatly, without emotion, without despair, almost without sound. "'Soft! I did but dream . . .'" They were bewitched, taken out of themselves in a transport of fascination. The voice went on, muttering but clear. "'O coward conscience, how dost thou afflict me! The lights burn blue. It is now dead midnight. Cold fearful drops stand on my trembling flesh. What do I fear? myself? there's none else by; Richard loves Richard; that is, I am I. Is there a murderer here? No . . . Yes, I am. Then fly . . . What, from myself? Great reason why: Lest I revenge. What, myself upon myself? Alack, I love myself. Wherefore? for any good that I myself have done unto myself? O, no! alas, I rather hate myself for hateful deeds committed by myself! I am a villain; yet I lie, I am not. Fool, of thyself speak well: fool, do not flatter . . .'"

The voice tottered on the brink of something foul, caught itself, surged on in a pæan of tragic self-mogrification. "'My conscience hath a thousand several tongues, and every tongue brings in a several tale, and every tale condemns me for a villain. Perjury, perjury in the high'st degree. All several sins, all used in each degree, throng to the bar, crying all, Guilty! Guilty! I shall despair. . . . There is no creature loves me; and if I die, no soul shall pity me; nay, wherefore should they, since that I myself find in myself no pity to myself?'"

Someone sighed.

Scene 2

WEEHAWKEN RAILROAD STATION.
FRIDAY, OCTOBER 9. 11:55 P.M.

AT A few minutes before midnight the DeWitt party entered the West Shore Railroad terminus in Weehawken—the barnlike, gray waiting-room with the naked iron trusses lacing its ceiling, the platform running overhead beside the walls. There were a few people about; in a corner, near one of the doors to the yard, a clerk at the Baggage Room counter drowsed; a man yawned behind the magazine-stand; the long, backed benches were empty.

They entered in a gust of laughter, a party intact except for Frederick Lyman, who had excused himself at the hotel and returned to his apartment. Jeanne DeWitt and Lord ran to the magazine-stand, Imperiale at their heels, smiling, and Lord purchased a huge box of candy, offering it to Jeanne with an exaggerated bow. Imperiale, not to be outdone in gallantry, purchased an armful of magazines and, clicking his heels together, presented them to the girl; rosy, bundled in furs, eyes shining, she laughed and, putting a hand under an arm of each man, led them to a bench where they sat down, chattering and nibbling at chocolates.

The four remaining members of the party strolled to the ticket-window. DeWitt looked up at the big clock above the magazine-stand; its hands stood at 12:04.

"Well," he said cheerfully, "our train doesn't leave until twelve-thirteen—we have a few minutes. Excuse me."

They had stopped at the window; Lane and Brooks dropped back a step, and Ahearn grasped DeWitt's arm. "Here, John, let me." DeWitt chuckled, threw Ahearn's arm off and said to the clerk: "Six single-trip tickets to West Englewood, please."

"There are seven of us, John," protested Ahearn.

"I know, but I have my own regular fifty-trip ticket-book." His face clouded as the clerk shoved six bits of pasteboard through the window. Then he smiled and said dryly: "I suppose I should sue the State for the value of my old trip-book. It expired while I was—" He stopped and said abruptly: "Let me have a new fifty-trip book, too."

"Name, sir?"

"John O. DeWitt, West Englewood."

"Yes, Mr. DeWitt." The clerk tried not to rubber and became extremely busy. A few moments later he pushed under the grating a dated rectangular paper book. As DeWitt took out his wallet and produced a fifty-dollar bill, Jeanne's clear voice rang out: "Daddy, the train's in!"

The clerk made change rapidly and DeWitt, cramming the bills and loose change into his trousers pocket, turned about to his three companions, the six single tickets and the trip-book in his hand.

"Do we have to run for it?" asked Lionel Brooks. The four men faced each other.

"No, we have time enough," replied DeWitt, tucking the tickets and the new book into the upper left pocket of his vest and then rebuttoning his coat.

They made their way across the waiting-room, joined Jeanne and Lord and Imperiale, and went out into the chilly air of the roofed yard. The 12:13 local was in. They walked through the iron-grilled gateway and down the long concrete platform. A few other passengers were following them, straggling along. The last car was dark, and they walked ahead, boarding the second car from the end.

Several strangers sat down in the same car.

Scene 3

THE WEEHAWKEN-NEWBURGH LOCAL.
SATURDAY, OCTOBER 10. 12:20 A.M.

THEY HAD split into two groups: Jeanne, Lord, and the cavalierly Imperiale sat well forward in the car, chattering; DeWitt, Lane, Brooks, and Ahearn took places nearer the center of the coach, in facing seats.

The train was still in the Weehawken terminal when the lawyer, who had been staring at DeWitt with frank eyes, turned his head toward Drury Lane, who sat opposite, and said abruptly: "Do you know, something you said tonight, Mr. Lane, interested me very much. . . . You spoke of the 'interminable years' that are packed into a single moment—the moment during which a man waits at the bar for the jury verdict which will condemn him to death or send him from the courtroom with a fresh lease on life. Interminable years! Dandy phrase, Mr. Lane. . . ."

"An accurate phrase," said DeWitt.

"You think so?" Brooks stole a look at DeWitt's composed features. "It reminded me at the time of a story I once read—I think it was by Ambrose Bierce. A very strange story indeed. It was about a man who was being hanged. In the—the, well, molecular instant before his neck snapped this man saw the details of his entire lifetime projected in his brain. There's your interminable years idea, Mr. Lane, in literature; and I have no doubt it's been treated by many other writers."

"I believe I know the story," replied Lane. DeWitt, at Brooks's side, nodded. "This whole problem of time is relative, as our scientists have been telling us for some years. Dreams, for example—dreams which seem on awakening to have occupied the brain through all the silent hours of the night—are said by some psychologists to occupy in actuality only the last, the borderline moment between the subconsciousness of sleep and the consciousness of wakefulness."

"I've heard that, too," said Ahearn. He was sitting opposite DeWitt and Brooks, and facing forward.

"What I was really getting at," said Brooks—he was looking at DeWitt again—"was the application of this peculiar mental phenomenon to you, John. I couldn't help wondering—I suppose many of us did—just what *your* thoughts were in the instant before the verdict was given, today."

"Perhaps," said Drury Lane gently, "perhaps Mr. DeWitt would rather not say."

"On the contrary." The broker's eyes gleamed; his face was alive. "That moment provided me with one of the most startling experiences of my life. An experience that bears out, I think, both Bierce's principle and the dream-theory which Mr. Lane just mentioned."

"You don't mean to say that your whole life flashed through your mind at that moment?" Ahearn seemed vastly skeptical.

"Oh, no. Something so isolated, so strange . . ." DeWitt slumped against the green cushions, speaking rapidly. "A case of identity. About nine years ago I was called for jury duty in a murder trial here in New York. The defendant was an old hulking wreck of a man, accused of stabbing a woman to death in a cheap boarding-house. It was a case of first-degree murder—the District Attorney proved conclusively that the murder was deliberately planned—and there was no question of the man's guilt. All during the short trial, and even in the jury-room afterward, as we argued his fate, I was haunted by a feeling that somewhere I had seen the defendant before. As people do in such situations, I wrestled mentally with the problem of his identity until I was tired, but I could not recall who he was or where or when I had seen him. . . ."

With blasting and straining and rattling the train started. DeWitt raised his voice a little. "To make a long story short, I concurred in the general opinion that the man was guilty on the basis of the evidence brought out, cast my ballot for conviction, we brought in the verdict, and the man was duly sentenced and executed. I dismissed the entire incident from my mind."

The train ground out of the terminal. No one spoke as DeWitt paused, licking his lips. "Now here's the strange part of it. To the best of my recollection I never once thought of that man or the incident for the nine years that followed. But when, today, the foreman was asked for the verdict which meant so much to me—that ridiculously tiny interval between the last syllable of the official question and the first word of the foreman's official reply—suddenly, and for no reason that I can offer, the face of that executed man, by now crumbling earth, swung before my mind's eye and in the same instant I solved the problem of who he was and where I had seen him—nine years, remember, after I had last been disturbed by it."

"And who was he?" asked Brooks curiously.

DeWitt smiled. "I said it was strange. . . . Twenty years ago or so, at the time when I was wandering about South America, I chanced to be in a place called Barinas, in the Zamora country of Venezuela. One night, on my way to my lodgings, as I was passing a dark alley I heard the sounds of a violent scuffle. I was young then and of a more venturesome disposition, I daresay, than I am now.

"I carried a revolver. I snatched it from the holster and ran into the alley. Two ragged 'breeds were attacking a white man. One of them was brandishing a *machete* over the head of their victim. I fired, the shot went wild, but the two footpads were alarmed, I suppose, and fled, leaving the white man, already slashed in several places, on the ground. As I went over to him, thinking he was badly wounded, he got to his feet, brushed off his dirty bloody ducks, mumbled surly thanks, and swung off, limping, in the darkness. I had caught just a glimpse of his face.

"And this man, whose life I had been instrumental in saving twenty years ago, was the man whom more than a decade later I was instrumental in sending to the electric-chair. Sort of divine dispensation, eh?"

"Worthy," said Mr. Drury Lane in the silence that followed, "of a place in imperishable folk-lore."

The train was pushing through blackness which was dotted here and there by lights—the outskirts of Weehawken.

"But the peculiar part of it," continued DeWitt, "was that, of all things, I should solve that tantalizing mystery while, my own life was in jeopardy! Remember that I'd seen the man's face only once before, so many years ago. . . ."

"One of the most amazing things I've ever heard," said Brooks.

"The human mind is capable of even more amazing things than that, in the instant before death," said Lane. "Eight months ago I saw in the newspapers a press dispatch from Vienna giving the details of a murder there. The facts were these: A man was found shot to death in a hotel room. The Viennese police easily identified him as an unimportant underworld figure who was known to have served as an informer for the police in the past. The motive for the crime was obviously revenge, probably by some criminal against whom the man's tips to the law had operated disastrously. The news dispatch stated that the victim had been living in this hotel for months, rarely leaving his room, even having his meals served there. That he was hiding from someone was apparent. When he was found murdered the remains of his last meal were spread on the table. He had been shot while standing seven feet from this table; a fatal shot but not causing instant death. This was determined by the fact that a trail of blood led across the carpet from this spot to the place where he was found dead, sprawled at the foot of the table.

"There was a peculiar circumstance. The sugar-bowl on the table had been overturned, the granulated sugar was scattered on the cloth, and in the victim's dead hand, tightly clenched, was a handful of this granulated sugar."

"Interesting," murmured DeWitt.

"The explanation seemed simple enough. He had been shot seven feet from the table, had crawled to the table, and by superhuman effort managed to raise himself sufficiently to take a fistful of sugar from the bowl before collapsing, dead, on the floor. But *why?* What was the significance of the sugar? How explain this last desperate act of a dying man? The Viennese police were baffled, concluded the dispatch." Mr. Drury Lane smiled at his audience. "The answer to these provocative questions occurred to me, and I wrote to Vienna. A few weeks later I received a reply from the prefect of police there, saying that the murderer had been arrested before the arrival of my letter, but that my solution had clarified the incident of the dead man and the sugar—which even after the murderer's apprehension had remained inexplicable to the police."

"And what was your solution?" asked Ahearn. "From the meager details I for one can't see a possible explanation."

"Nor I," said Brooks.

DeWitt's mouth was screwed into a weird shape; he was frowning.

"And you, Mr. DeWitt?" asked Lane, smiling again.

"I'm afraid I can't see the significance of the sugar itself," replied the broker thoughtfully. "But one thing seems perfectly obvious. That is, that the dying man was leaving a clue to his assassin's identity."

"Excellent!" cried Lane. "That's it exactly, Mr. DeWitt. Very well—observe. Was the sugar, as sugar, the clue? That is, was the victim indicating that his murderer was—to stretch the point to its most farcical implication—a lover of sweets? On the other hand, did it imply that the murderer was a diabetic? Far-fetched, of course. I did not believe this; for the clue was undoubtedly left for the edification of the police, and it would seem that the dying man would leave a clue on which the police could work with a fair chance of success. On the other hand, what else could the sugar have meant—what does granulated sugar resemble physically? Well, it is a white crystalline substance. . . . I thereupon wrote the Viennese prefect that while the sugar might have indicated that the murderer was a diabetic, the more probable explanation was that the murderer was a cocaine addict."

They were staring at him. DeWitt chuckled, slapping his thigh softly. "Cocaine, of course! A white crystalline powder!"

"The man arrested," continued Lane, "was what our tabloids amusingly refer to as a cocaine fiend. So wrote my official correspondent, and offered many flowery expressions of admiration. Yet it seems to me that the explanation was an elementary one. What interested me was the psychology of the murdered man. He could not have possessed an ordinary intellect. Somewhere within his brain was the spark of ingenuity. He left the only clue to his murderer's identity which was available to him in the brief interval before he died. So you see—there are no limits to which the human mind cannot soar in that unique, god-like instant before the end of life."

"No, that is perfectly true," said DeWitt. "That's an interesting story, Mr. Lane. And despite your dismissal of the deduction as elementary, I think the entire affair is a tribute to your peculiar talent for getting beneath the surface of things."

"Should have been there in Vienna, and he'd have saved the police a heap of trouble," said Ahearn.

North Bergen disappeared in the darkness.

Lane sighed. "I have often thought that the entire problem of crime and punishment would be simplified if human beings, confronted by their potential murderers, could leave a sign, no matter how obscure, to the identity of their nemeses."

"No matter how obscure?" asked Brooks argumentatively.

"Of course, Mr. Brooks. Isn't any sign better than no sign at all?"

A tall burly man, hat pulled down low over his eyes, face white and pinched, had entered the car from the forward end. He lurched over to the four conversing men, leaned heavily against the green diced fabric of a seat-back, swaying with the rock of the train, glowering over them at John DeWitt.

Lane paused, glancing up at him in annoyance. But DeWitt said, in a disgusted voice: "Collins," and the actor regarded the man with newborn interest. Brooks said: "You're drunk, Collins. What do you want?"

"Not talking to you, shyster," said Collins in a thick voice. His eyes were bloodshot and maniacal; they focused with difficulty on DeWitt. "DeWitt," he said with an attempt at civility, "like to see you alone." He pushed his hat back on his head, endeavoring to smile in a pleasant manner. He achieved only the sick mockery of a smile, and DeWitt looked at him with pity and distaste.

Drury Lane's gray eyes' went from Collins's heavy face to DeWitt's delicately lined one, unceasingly, as each man talked.

"Now look here, Collins," said DeWitt in a gentler tone. "I've told you repeatedly that I can't do anything for you on that matter. You know why, and you're making yourself very disagreeable. Can't you see that you're interrupting a private party? Be a good chap and go away."

Collins's mouth was slack. His red-rimmed eyes became bleared and teary. "Listen, DeWitt," he muttered, "you've *got* to let me talk to you. You don't know what this means to me, DeWitt. It's—it's life or death." DeWitt wavered; the others did not look at each other. The spectacle of this man and his naked humility was embarrassing. Collins rushed on, snatching at the faint hope promised by DeWitt's hesitation. "I promise, I swear I won't bother you again if you let me talk to you privately—just this once. Please, DeWitt, please!"

DeWitt measured him coolly. "You mean that, Collins? You won't bother me again? Won't hound me this way?"

"Yes! You can rely on it!" The hope that flared in those bloody eyes was ghastly. DeWitt rose with a sigh, excused himself; and the two men, DeWitt with bent head, Collins speaking rapidly, violently, gesticulating, pleading, peering into DeWitt's averted face—walked up the aisle toward the rear of the car. DeWitt suddenly left Collins standing in the aisle and returned to his three companions.

The broker put his hand into his upper left vest-pocket and took out the single tickets he had purchased in the terminal, leaving the new trip-book in the pocket. He gave them to Ahearn. "Might as well give them to the conductor, Frank," he said. "I don't know how long this pest will take. Conductor will get me later."

Ahearn nodded, and DeWitt retraced his steps to the rear of the car, where Collins stood in an attitude of dejection. He lumbered to life at DeWitt's approach, and again he began to plead. They passed through the doorway to the rear platform, were indistinctly visible for a moment, and then the three men saw Collins and DeWitt cross over to stand on the front platform of the last, dim car, passing from view.

Brooks said: "There's a man who played with fire and got his fingers badly burned. He's through. DeWitt would be a fool to help him."

"Still wants DeWitt to make good Longstreet's disastrous advice, I suppose," remarked Ahearn. "I shouldn't be surprised if John relents, do you know? He's in high spirits and he's liable to make Longstreet's foolishness good out of sheer joy of living."

Drury Lane said nothing; he turned his head and looked toward the rear platform, but the two men were not in sight. At this moment the conductor entered from the forward door, beginning to collect and punch tickets, and the men turned back, the moment of tension gone. Lord referred the conductor to the group of three men in the center of the car, looking around and seeming surprised at DeWitt's absence. The conductor approached: Ahearn offered him the six single tickets, explaining that there was another man in the party who had stepped out a moment and would be back shortly.

"Right," said the conductor, punching the tickets and jabbing them into one of the ticket-holders on the top of the seat in which Ahearn was sitting, and he moved on up the car.

The three men engaged in desultory conversation. The talk petered out in a few moments, and Ahearn, excusing himself, rose, thrust his hands into his pockets, and began to pace up and down the aisle. Lane and Brooks became involved in a discussion of testaments: Lane cited a curious case which he had run across many years before while he was touring the Continent in Shakespearean repertoire; Brooks countered with several instances of ambiguous wills which had raised complicated questions of law.

The train clanked on. Twice Lane turned his head and peered backward; but neither DeWitt nor Collins was visible. A tiny furrow appeared between the actor's eyes, and he sat thoughtfully during a lull in his conversation with Brooks; then he smiled, shook his head as if dismissing the nonsense of his thoughts, and resumed the discussion.

The local staggered to a stop at the station of Bogota, a suburb of Hackensack. Lane stared out of the window. As the train started again, the furrow between his eyes returned, more deeply now. He looked at the dial of his watch. The hands stood at 12:36. Brooks was regarding him with a puzzled expression.

Lane sprang to his feet so suddenly that Brooks uttered a grunt of astonishment. "Please excuse me, Mr. Brooks," he said rapidly. "Perhaps my nerves are ragged, but I can't help feeling extraordinarily disturbed by the failure of DeWitt to return. I am going back there to investigate."

"You think there's something wrong?" Brooks was alarmed. He rose and strode up the aisle with Lane.

"I sincerely hope not." They passed Ahearn, pacing fretfully.

"Anything wrong, gentlemen?" he inquired.

"Mr. Lane thinks there's something funny about DeWitt's absence," snapped the lawyer. "Come along, Ahearn."

Lane in the van, they went through the rear door of their car and stopped short. There was no one on the platform. They stepped across the swaying junction of the two cars; there was no one on the rear platform of the last car either.

They looked at each other. "Well, where the devil could they have gone to?" muttered Ahearn. "I didn't see either of them come back, did you?"

"I wasn't noticing particularly," said Brooks, "but I don't think they did."

Lane paid them not the slightest attention. He went to the glass top of one of the doors and looked out at the rushing black countryside. Then he returned and surveyed the door of the dim, almost indistinguishable rear car. He peered through the glass into the interior; it was evidently an extra coach being hauled to Newburgh, the end of the local line, to be ready for an early morning rush-hour run back to Weehawken. His jaw hardened, and he said distinctly: "I am going in here, gentlemen. Mr. Brooks, will you please hold the door open? There's very little light."

He grasped the knob of the door and pushed. The door responded readily enough; it was unlocked. For a moment as the three men stood there squinting, to accustom their eyes to the almost total absence of illumination, they could see nothing. Then Lane turned his head abruptly, sucked in his breath. . . .

To the left of the door was a walled compartment—the usual cubicle found at the entrance to railroad day-coaches. The front wall of the car and a wall backing up the first seat in the car beyond formed two of the boundaries; on the outer side there was a regular car-window, and opposite it, where Lane stood, the open area. In the compartment, as in other portions of the car, were two long seats facing each other. On the seat opposite the front wall, sitting on the cushions close to the window-wall, head sunk on his breast, was the figure of John DeWitt.

Lane's eyes narrowed in the murk; the broker seemed asleep. Brooks and Ahearn pressing behind, he edged into the area between the two seats and touched DeWitt gently on the shoulder. There was no response. "DeWitt!" he said in a steely rapier voice, shaking the quiet figure. Still no response. But this time DeWitt's head rolled slightly, bringing his eyes into view; then they rolled to rest again. . . .

The eyes, even in the dimness, were the open blank eyes of a corpse.

Lane crouched and his hand hovered about the man's heart.

He straightened up, rubbed his fingers together and backed out of the compartment. Ahearn was shaking like an aspen, staring down at the still shadowy figure. Brooks quavered: "He's—he's dead."

"There's blood on my hand," said Lane. "Please keep that door open, Mr. Brooks; we need light. At least until we can get someone to turn on the proper switch." He stepped past Ahearn and Brooks to the platform. "Please do not touch him. Either of you," he said sharply. Neither replied; they cowered together instinctively, keeping their eyes with a sort of horrified fascination on the dead man.

Looking overhead, Lane located what he sought and stretched his long arm upward. He pulled vigorously several times—it was the emergency signal-cord. With a crashing and grinding of brakes the train slid, jerked, shivered to a stop. Ahearn and Brooks clutched at each other to keep from falling.

Lane stepped across the car-junction and opened the door to the lighted car in which they had been seated. He stood silently for a moment. Imperiale was sitting alone now, dozing. Lord and Jeanne sat close together, heads almost touching. There were several other passengers, most of them napping or reading. The door at the opposite end of the car burst open, and two conductors ran up the aisle toward Lane. Instantly the passengers awoke or dropped their magazines and newspapers, sensing something wrong. Jeanne and Lord looked up, startled; Imperiale got to his feet, a questioning look on his face.

The two conductors rushed up. "Who pulled that emergency?" cried the first, a small choleric old man. "What's the idea, anyway?"

Lane said in a low voice: "There has been a serious accident, Conductor. Please come back here with me." Jeanne, Lord, and Imperiale had run toward them; the other passengers thronged about, asking bewildered questions. "No, please, Miss DeWitt. It would be better if you did not come back with us. Mr. Lord, take Miss DeWitt back to her seat. Mr. Imperiale, you might stay here also." He looked significantly at Lord; the young man paled, then took the bewildered girl's arm and forcibly conducted her back through the car. The second conductor, a tall heavy man, began to push the crowding passengers. "Back to your seats, please. Don't ask questions. Back now. . . ."

Lane, accompanied by the two conductors, returned to the rear car. Brooks and Ahearn had not moved; petrified, they were still staring at DeWitt's body. One of the conductors manipulated a switch in the wall of the rear car and the hitherto dim coach sprang into clear view as the lights flashed on. All three men went into the car, pushing Brooks and Ahearn ahead of them, and the tall conductor closed the door.

The smaller and elder man edged into the compartment and bent over, heavy gold watch dangling from the chain on his vest. His aged finger pointed to the left breast of the dead man. "Bullet-hole!" he exclaimed. "Murder. . . ."

He straightened up and stared at Lane. Lane said quietly: "I should advise you to touch nothing, Conductor." He took a card from his wallet and offered it to the old man. "I have been acting in the capacity of consulting investigator in several recent murder cases," he said. "I have authority, I think, in this matter."

The elder conductor examined the card suspiciously, then handed it back. He took off his cap and scratched his white poll. "Well, I don't know," he said with a touch of exacerbation. "How do I know this isn't a stall? I'm senior conductor on this train, and the law says I'm in charge of it at all times and in any emergency. . . ."

"Look here," broke in Brooks, "this is Mr. Drury Lane, and he has been helping out on the Longstreet and Wood murders. You must have read about them."

"Oh!" The old man rasped his chin.

"Do you know who this dead man is?" continued Brooks, his voice cracking. "It's John DeWitt, Longstreet's partner!"

"You don't say," exclaimed the conductor. He looked doubtfully at DeWitt's half-hidden face. Then he brightened. "Come to think of it, I guess he does look sort of familiar. Been taking this train a long time. Okay, Mr. Lane, I guess you're the boss. What do you want us to do?"

Lane had stood silently during this colloquy, but impatience glittered in his eyes. He snapped at once: "Make sure that all doors and even windows are kept locked and guarded, at once. Instruct the engineer to run this train to the nearest station——"

"There's Teaneck, next stop along the line," volunteered the tall conductor.

"Whatever it is," continued Lane, "make all the speed you can. Arrange to call the New York police—Inspector Thumm, either at headquarters or at his home—and District Attorney Bruno of New York County, if possible."

"Get the stationmaster to do that," said the old man thoughtfully.

"Precisely. And secure authority, whatever authority is necessary, to shunt this train off the main track into a siding at Teaneck. Your name, Conductor?"

"They call me Pop Bottomley," said the old man soberly. "I got you, Mr. Lane."

"Thoroughly understood then, Bottomley," said Lane. "Please attend to these things at once."

The two conductors moved to the door. Bottomley said to his junior: "Now I'm going down to talk to the engineer and you see to the doors. Get me, Ed?"

"Sure thing."

They ran out of the car, making their way through the throng of passengers crowded about the doors of the other car.

There was silence after they left. Ahearn leaned with sudden weakness against the door of the toilet on the other side of the aisle. Brooks put his back to the door. Lane surveyed the mortal remains of John DeWitt somberly.

He spoke without turning his head. "Ahearn, as DeWitt's best friend it will be your unpleasant duty to break the news to his daughter."

Ahearn stiffened, moistened his lips, but left the car without a word.

And Brooks leaned against the door again, and Lane stood

like a sentinel by the side of the dead. Neither spoke, neither moved. From forward cars came faint shouting.

They stood in exactly the same positions when a few moments later the train shuddered the length of its ponderous steel body, and began to crawl on.

Outside, darkness.

• • • • •

A SIDING AT TEANECK. *Later*

The train, lights blazing, lay like a helpless caterpillar in the darkness of the rusty siding near the station of Teaneck. The station itself was alive with scurrying figures. A roaring automobile rushed out of the night and crashed to a stop by the tracks, discharging immediately a number of bulky forms that plunged toward the idle train.

The newcomers were Thumm, Bruno, Dr. Schilling, and a small group of detectives.

They hurried past a knot of men—trainmen, an engineer, yardmen—talking in low voices outside the train in the gashing light of flares. A man held up a lantern, and Inspector Thumm brushed it from his face as the newcomers dashed to the closed exit of the rear car. Thumm pounded with his hard fist on the door; a faint cry of "Here they are!" somewhere from the interior and Conductor Bottomley shoved back the door, clanging it against the catch in the wall. He pulled up the movable iron platform, revealing a flight of iron steps.

"Police?"

"Where's the body?" They swarmed up the steps in the Inspector's wake.

"This way. Rear car."

They burst into the rear car. Lane had not moved. Their eyes went at once to the dead man. Near by stood a local policeman, the Teaneck stationmaster, the junior conductor.

"Murdered, hey?" Thumm looked at Lane. "How the hell did this happen, Mr. Lane?"

Lane moved slightly. "I shall never forgive myself, Inspector. . . . A daring crime. A daring crime." His carved features had aged.

Dr. Schilling, cloth hat far back on his head, topcoat open, dropped to his knees beside the body.

"Touch him at all?" he mumbled, fingers busy exploring.

"Lane. Mr. Lane," said Bruno queerly. "Dr. Schilling's talking to you."

Lane said mechanically: "I shook him. His head rolled to one side, then back again to its original position. I bent over and felt his heart. There was blood on my hand. Otherwise, not a finger has been laid on him."

They were silent then, watching Dr. Schilling. The Medical Examiner sniffed at the bullet-hole, grasped the coat, and tugged. The bullet had pierced the coat through the handkerchief pocket on the left breast, entering the heart directly. The coat gave way with a sticky tearing little sound. "Plop through his coat, vest, shirt, undershirt and heart. Clean wound, all right," announced Dr. Schilling. There was little blood on the garments; a damp ragged red ring about the hole on each piece of clothing. "Dead about an hour, I'd say," continued the Medical Examiner. He consulted his wrist-watch. Then he felt the muscles of the dead arms and legs, grotesquely attempted to flex the dead knee-joint. "Yep, died about 12:30. Maybe a few minutes before. I can't say exactly."

They were staring at DeWitt's frozen face. A horrible, unnatural expression twisted and distorted the features. The expression was not difficult to interpret—it was stark-naked fear, such fear as screwed up the eyes, laid tense ridges of muscle along the jaw, injected into every line an unmanning toxin that banished courage. . . .

Dr. Schilling exclaimed softly. Their eyes tore away from that terrifying dead face and turned in a battery to the left hand of the corpse, held up for their inspection by the doctor. "Look at these fingers," said Dr. Schilling. They looked. The middle finger was twined tightly over the forefinger in a peculiar sign, the thumb and remaining two fingers curved inward in death.

"What the devil—" growled Thumm. Bruno bent lower, eyes starting out of his head. "By God!" he cried, "am I crazy, or seeing things, or what? Why—" he laughed, "it's impossible. Can't be. This isn't Europe in the Middle Ages. . . . That's the protection-sign against the evil eye!"

They were silent. Then Thumm muttered: "Hell, this is like a detective-story. Ten to one there's a Chink with long fangs hiding in the toilet here." No one laughed. Dr. Schilling said: "Whatever it means, it's here to stay." He grasped the two overlapping fingers and struggled until his face crimsoned. He shrugged. "*Rigor mortis.* Stiff as a board. Suppose DeWitt was slightly diabetic, probably didn't know it himself. Anyway, it would account for the rapidity with which *rigor* set in. . . ." He looked up, squinting. "Thumm, suppose you try putting your fingers together this way."

Like mechanical men they stared at the Inspector. Without a word he held up his right hand and with some difficulty managed to slide his middle finger over the forefinger.

"Bear down, Thumm," said Dr. Schilling. "Tight. The way DeWitt has his. Now keep them that way for a few seconds. . . ."

The Inspector exerted pressure. His face flushed a little. "Quite an effort, hey, Thumm?" said the Medical Examiner dryly. "One of the funniest things in my experience. These dead fingers were so tightly linked that they didn't come apart even after death."

"I can't accept that evil-eye explanation," said Thumm stolidly, disengaging his fingers. "It's too damned storybookish. Doesn't hold water, far's I'm concerned. Why—they'd laugh at us!"

"Suggest an alternative explanation," said Bruno.

"Well," growled Thumm, "all right. Maybe the guy that pulled this job fixed DeWitt's fingers that way himself."

"Nonsense," snapped Bruno. "That's an even wilder explanation than the obvious one. Why under the sun should a killer do that?"

"Well, you'll see," said Thumm. "You'll see. . . . And what do you think, Mr. Lane?"

"Must we seek a *jettatore* in this case?" Lane stirred. "I think," he said with infinite weariness, "that John DeWitt took very seriously a careless remark of mine earlier this evening." Thumm began to demand an explanation, but fell silent when Dr. Schilling struggled to his feet.

"Well, that's about all I can do here," said the physician. "One thing is sure. He died instantly."

Lane made his first energetic movement in long minutes. He gripped the Medical Examiner's arm. "You're certain of that, Doctor—instantly?"

"*Ja.* Absolutely certain. The bullet, probably from a .38, penetrated the heart through the right ventricle. It's the only wound, too, incidentally, from this superficial examination."

"His head is all right? There are no other signs of violence—no bruises anywhere?"

"Not one. He was killed by one bullet in his pumper and

nothing else. And believe you me, that was plenty. Neatest hole I've seen in months."

"In other words, Dr. Schilling, DeWitt could not have twisted his fingers into this position during death-throes?"

"Now listen here," said Dr. Schilling with some exasperation. "I just said he died instantly, didn't I? How in God's name could there have been death-throes? A bullet through the ventricle and—*pffft!* out like a light. Dead. Finished. Man's not a guinea-pig, you know. Hell, no."

Lane did not smile. He turned to Inspector Thumm. "I think, Inspector," he said, "that our irascible doctor's opinion goes far to clearing up an interesting point."

"What of it? Suppose he did die on the spot without a whimper? I've seen hundreds of stiffs who'd died instantly. Nothing new about that."

"There is something new about this, Inspector," said Lane. Bruno glanced at him inquiringly, but Lane made no further comment.

Thumm shook his head and shoved past Dr. Schilling. He bent over the dead man and began unhurriedly to search his clothing. Lane altered his position so that he could see both Thumm's face and the body of the dead man. "What's this?" muttered Thumm. He had found in the inside breast pocket of DeWitt's coat a number of old letters, a check-book, a fountain-pen, a time-table and two railroad trip-books.

Lane said coldly: "That is his old fifty-trip book which expired while he was detained in prison, and a new one which he purchased this evening before we boarded the train."

The Inspector grunted, flipped the perforated pages of the old ticket-book. Its edges were dog-eared. On the cover of the book and inside were numerous idle scribblings; some traced the shapes of punch-marks; others traced printed words—geometric designs throughout, an indication of DeWitt's precise mentality. Most of the tickets had been torn out. He examined the new ticket-book. It was intact, unpunched, just as DeWitt had bought it in the terminal, said Lane.

"Who's the conductor here?" asked Thumm.

The old man in the blue conductor's uniform replied: "I am. Pop Bottomley's the name. Senior on this run. What d'ye want to know?"

"Recognize this man?"

"Well," drawled Bottomley, "I was remarkin' to Mr. Lane over here before you came that his face looked kind of familiar. I remember now he's been takin' this train on and off for years, seems like. West Englewood, ain't he?"

"Did you see him on the train tonight?"

"I did not. Wasn't sittin' in my end, where I was collectin' tickets. You see him, Ed?"

"Not tonight, I didn't," said the husky junior conductor timidly. "I know him, all right, but I didn't see him tonight. When I got to that car up forward, there was a party there, and one man, tall feller, handed me six tickets for the party, said there was another one had stepped out for a minute. Never did see him after that."

"You didn't get to him, eh?"

"Hell, I didn't know where he was. Thought he was in the toilet, most likely. Never thought of this dark car. Nobody ever goes in here."

"You say you knew DeWitt?"

"That his name? Well, he took this train pretty often. Remember him, all right."

"How often?"

Ed lifted his cap and patted his bald head thoughtfully. "I don't know, Cap. Can't say how many times. Just on and off, I guess."

Pop Bottomley thrust his energetic little body forward. "Guess I can settle that for you, Mister. Y'see, pardner and I take this midnight run every night, so we can tell how many times this man took our train. Here, lemme have that old trip-book." He snatched the dog-eared book from Thumm's fingers, opened it and held it up for Thumm's inspection. The others crowded around, looking over the Inspector's shoulder. "Now, y'see," said Bottomley officiously, pointing to strips which had bordered the missing tickets, "we take out the ticket on each trip and punch the ticket and stub along the side to make sure. All you got to do is add up the number of circle-marks—they're my punches; see 'em?—and the number of cross-marks—they're Ed Thompson's here—and that'll tell you how many times he took this p'ticular train, because we're the only men on this run. Get me?"

Thumm studied the old book. "Pretty cute at that. Forty punched altogether. Of the forty let's say half covered trips to New York—different punches, eh?"

"Yep," said old Bottomley. "The morning trains—different conductors, and every conductor has a different punch."

"All right," continued Thumm, "that leaves twenty on the trip back to West Englewood nights. Of the twenty—" he counted rapidly, "let's see now, thirteen punched by your partner and you. Thirteen times, then. Means he took this train oftener than the regular commuting train around six. . . ."

"Regular detective, I am," grinned the old man. "You got it, Mister. Punches don't lie!" and he cackled with glee.

Bruno frowned. "I'll wager the murderer knew DeWitt was in

the habit of making this particular train oftener than the regular commuting-train."

"Might be." Inspector Thumm threw back his wide shoulders. "Here now, let's get some other things straight. Mr. Lane, just what did happen here tonight? How did DeWitt happen to get into this car?"

Drury Lane shook his head. "What actually occurred I do not know. But not long after the train left Weehawken, Michael Collins——"

"Collins!" shouted Thumm. Bruno edged forward. "Is Collins in on this thing, by God? Why didn't you say so before?"

"Please, Inspector. A little self-control. . . . Collins either got away or he did not. As soon as we discovered DeWitt's body the conductors made sure that no one could leave the train. Even if he left before the discovery of the body, he cannot run away." Thumm grunted, and Lane in an even tone related what had occurred in the car when Collins pleaded with DeWitt for a final private conversation.

"And they went into this car, hey?" demanded Thumm.

"I said nothing of the kind, Inspector," retorted Lane. "You are assuming that. It may be true, but we saw merely that the two men crossed the rear platform to stand on the front platform of this car."

"Well, we'll find out soon enough." Thumm dispatched several detectives with orders to search the train for the missing man.

"You want to keep the body here, Thumm?" asked Dr. Schilling.

"Let him be," grumbled Thumm. "Let's go up ahead and ask some questions."

They trooped out of the death-car, leaving a detective on guard beside the dead man.

. . . . .

Jeanne DeWitt was crumpled on a seat, sobbing against Lord's shoulder. Ahearn, Imperiale, Brooks sat stiffly stunned.

The car had been cleared of other passengers; they had been removed to the car ahead.

Dr. Schilling moved quietly down the aisle and looked down at the weakly crying girl. Without a word he opened his physician's bag, removed a small bottle, sent Lord for a cup of water, and applied the open bottle to the girl's quivering nostrils. She gasped, blinked, shuddered away. When Lord returned with the water she drank greedily, like a thirsty child. The doctor patted her head and forced something down her throat. In a few moments she had calmed and lay, eyes closed, with her head in Lord's lap.

Thumm sank into one of the green plush seats and stretched his legs. Bruno brooded over him. He beckoned to Brooks and Ahearn, who rose wearily. Both men were white with strain. On being questioned by the District Attorney, Brooks told briefly of the celebration party at the hotel, the trip to Weehawken, the wait in the terminal, the boarding of the train, the approach of Collins.

"How was DeWitt?" asked Bruno. "Cheerful?"

"Never more cheerful in his life."

"I've never seen him happier," put in Ahearn in a low voice. "The trial, the suspense—and then the verdict . . . When I think that he was saved from the electric-chair for this . . ." He shivered.

A flash of anger crossed the lawyer's face. "Certainly the most devastating proof of DeWitt's innocence, Mr. Bruno. If you hadn't arrested him on that preposterous charge, he'd probably be alive today!"

Bruno was silent. Then— "Where is Mrs. DeWitt?"

"She wasn't with the party," said Ahearn shortly.

"This will be good news for her," said Brooks.

"What do you mean?"

"She can't be divorced now," replied Brooks in a dry voice.

The District Attorney and Thumm exchanged glances. "Then she wasn't on the train at all?" asked Bruno.

"Not so far as I know." Brooks turned away. Ahearn shook his head, and Bruno looked at Lane, who shrugged.

At this moment a detective reported with the information that Collins was nowhere to be found.

"Here! Where the devil are those conductors?" Thumm waved the blue-clad men toward him. "Bottomley, did you see a tall red-faced Irishman—remember collecting his ticket tonight?"

"He was wearing," said Lane quietly, "a felt hat pulled rakishly down over his eyes, a tweed topcoat, and he was slightly intoxicated."

Old Bottomley shook his head. "Pretty sure I didn't take his ticket. You, Ed?"

The junior conductor shook his head.

Thumm roused himself. He stamped to the forward coach and began to thunder questions at the few passengers who had been seated in the same car with the DeWitt party. No one recalled Collins, or anything about his movements. Thumm returned and sat down again. "Remember, anybody, if Collins came back through this car?"

Lane said: "I'm sure he did not, Inspector. In all probability he slipped off the train from one of the two platforms in the rear. It would be simple enough to open one of the doors and jump off. I am certain that we stopped somewhere between the time DeWitt and Collins disappeared and the time of the tragedy."

Thumm demanded a time-table from the old conductor and studied it. By comparing various items of schedule, he concluded that it was possible for Collins to have slipped off the train when it stopped at either Little Ferry, Ridgefield Park, Westview, or even Bogota.

"Okay," he said, and turned to one of his men. "Take a couple of the boys and retrace the route through these stations. Pick up Collins's trail. He must have got off at one of 'em and left some kind of sign behind. Report to me by phone to the Teaneck station."

"Right."

"And it doesn't look as if he could have got a train going back to New York at that hour. So don't forget to question the taxi-drivers around the stations."

The detective left.

"Now men," said Thumm to the two conductors, "think hard. Did any passengers get off the train at Little Ferry, Ridgefield Park, Westview, or Bogota?"

The conductors replied promptly that several passengers had detrained at each of the cited local stops, but neither recalled their number or identities.

"Might recognize some of 'em, maybe," drawled Pop Bottomley, "if we saw 'em, but we wouldn't know their names even if they were regular passengers."

"Wouldn't know the others at all," volunteered Thompson.

Bruno said: "You know, Thumm, it would have been possible for the murderer as well as Collins to have slipped off the train at a station without being seen. All anyone had to do was wait until the train stopped at the station, open the door facing not the station but the tracks, and hop off, closing the door behind him from below. After all, there are only two conductors on this train, and they couldn't keep track of every exit."

"Sure. Anybody could have done it. I'd like," growled Thumm, "to run across one bump-off where the murderer is found standing over the body with the gun in his hand. . . . And where the hell *is* that gun? Duffy! Find a revolver in that car back there?"

The sergeant shook his head.

"Search the whole shooting-match. It's possible that the guy who did it left the gun on the train."

"I suggest," said Lane, "that you send men to search the route we have traversed, Inspector. For it is also possible that the murderer threw the revolver from the train and that it fell to the tracks somewhere."

"Good idea. Duffy, take care of that."

The sergeant stumped off.

"Now," continued Thumm, passing one hand wearily over his forehead, "now for the dirty work." He glared at the six members of the DeWitt party. "Imperiale! Step over here, will you?"

The Swiss heaved to his feet and approached with lagging steps. Fatigue had darkened the area of his eyes, and even his vandyke was in a bedraggled state.

"Matter of form," said Thumm with heavy sarcasm. "What were you doing on this trip? Where were you sitting?"

"I sat with Miss DeWitt and Mr. Lord for a time; then, seeing that they preferred to be alone, I excused myself and moved away. I must have dozed off. The next thing I remember, Mr. Lane was standing in the doorway and the two conductors were running past me."

"Dozing?"

Imperiale's eyebrows went up. "Yes," he said with sharpness. "Do you doubt my word? The ferry and trainride had induced a headache."

"Oh, yes," jeered Thumm. "So you couldn't tell us what the others were doing, hey?"

"I am sorry. I was asleep."

Thumm brushed by the Swiss and walked to the seat in which Lord held Jeanne in his arms. He leaned over and tapped the girl's shoulder. Lord looked up angrily; Jeanne raised a tear-stained face.

"Sorry to trouble you, Miss DeWitt," said Thumm gruffly, "but it would help me if you answered a question or two."

"Are you crazy, man?" snapped Lord. "Can't you see she's in a state of exhaustion?"

Thumm stared him into silence. Jeanne whispered: "Anything. Anything, Inspector. Only find—find out who . . ."

"Leave that to us, Miss DeWitt. Do you recall what you and Mr. Lord were doing after the train left Weehawken?"

She looked at him blankly, only half-comprehending. "We were—we were together most of the time. At first Mr. Imperiale sat with us, then he went off somewhere. We talked. And all the time . . ." She bit her lip; tears sprang into her eyes.

"Yes, Miss DeWitt?"

"Kit left me once. I remained alone for a few minutes . . ."

"Left you, did he? That's fine. And where did he go?" Thumm glanced slyly at the young man, who sat in perfect silence.

"Oh, just out that door." She pointed vaguely at the front door of the car, forward. "Didn't say where he was going. Or did you, Kit?"

"No, darling."

"Did you see Mr. Imperiale after he left you and Lord?"

"Once, while Kit was away. I turned around and saw him a few seats back, dozing. I also saw Mr. Ahearn walking up and down. Then Kit came back."

"When was this?"

She sighed. "I don't remember exactly."

Thumm straightened. "I'd like to speak to you aside, Lord. . . . Here, Imperiale! Or Doc Schilling. Will you please sit with Miss DeWitt for a moment?"

Lord rose reluctantly, and the stubby little Medical Examiner took the seat. He began at once to speak to the girl in a conversational tone.

The two men went up the aisle. "Now Lord," said Thumm, "come clean. Where'd you go?"

"It's quite a story, Inspector," replied the young man steadily. "While we were coming over on the ferry I happened to notice something—well, queer. I caught sight of Cherry Browne and that seedy boy-friend of hers, Pollux, on the same boat."

"No kidding!" Thumm nodded slowly. "Hey, Bruno. Come here a minute." The District Attorney complied. "Lord says he saw Cherry Browne and Pollux on the ferry tonight, coming over." Bruno whistled.

"That's not all, either," continued Lord. "I caught sight of them again in the terminal. Near the piers. They were arguing about something. I kept my eyes open after that because—well, it looked damned fishy to me. I didn't see them in the waiting-room, and I watched when we got on the train, although I don't remember seeing them get on, either. Anyway, when the train started I became uneasy."

"Why?"

Lord scowled. "That Browne woman is a tartar. I didn't know what she might be up to, considering the wild accusations she made against DeWitt during the Longstreet investigation. Anyway, I excused myself from Jeanne; I wanted to make absolutely sure they weren't on the train. I looked, and they weren't. So I came back, feeling better."

"Did you look in that rear car?"

"God, no! How could I think they were there?"

"Near what station was this?"

Lord shrugged. "Hanged if I know. I didn't notice."

"Did you see what anyone else was doing when you came back?"

"Well, I seem to recall Ahearn walking back and forth both times, and I remember seeing Mr. Lane and Brooks talking."

"Did you notice Imperiale when they came back?"

"Can't remember."

"All right. Get back to Miss DeWitt; I guess she needs you."

Lord hastened away, and Bruno and Thumm conversed in low tones for a few moments. Then Thumm beckoned a detective on guard at the forward door. "Tell Duffy to search the train for Cherry Browne and Pollux—he knows their faces." The detective went away. In a short time the bulky figure of Sergeant Duffy barged into the car. "Nothing doing, Inspector. They aren't here. And nobody remembers seeing two people of their description."

"All right, Duffy, that makes it your assignment. Get somebody on it right away. Better do it yourself, at that. Shoot back to town and see if you can pick up their trail. The woman lives at the Hotel Grant. If they're not there, try some night-clubs, a couple of Pollux's hangouts. They might be in a speak. Phone me when you get a lead, and stay on it all night if necessary."

Sergeant Duffy grinned and swung off.

"Now then, Brooks." Thumm and the District Attorney walked back up the aisle. Brooks and Lane were sitting together,

Brooks staring out of the window at the trainyards, Lane with his head resting against the back of the seat, eyes closed. They opened and flashed with remarkable brilliancy as Thumm sat down opposite. Bruno had hesitated, then retreated to the van of the coach, going, to the car ahead.

"How about you, Brooks?" asked Thumm heavily. "God, I'm tired. This damned thing routed me out of bed.—Well?"

"Well, what?"

"What were you doing on this trip?"

"I didn't leave this seat until Mr. Lane got up to investigate the continued absence of DeWitt and Collins."

Thumm looked at Lane, and Lane nodded. "That's jake for you, then." He twisted his head. "Ahearn!" The elderly man plodded up. "What were *you* doing all the time after the train started?"

Ahearn laughed without humor. "The ancient game of hide-and-seek, eh, Inspector? Nothing extraordinary. Mr. Lane, Mr. Brooks, and I engaged in general discussion for some time. Then I felt like stretching my legs and got up. Walked around, up and down the aisle. That's all."

"Notice anything? Did you see anyone through the rear door of the car?"

"Frankly, I wasn't watching. I saw nothing suspicious, if that's what you mean."

"Did you see *anything?*" cried Thumm in an exasperated voice.

"Nothing in that direction, Inspector. Nor anything else, for that matter. In fact, I was thinking out a rather unique gambit."

"A *what?*"

"A gambit. A series of chess moves, Inspector."

"Oh. You're the chess shark. Okay, Ahearn." Thumm turned his head to find Lane's gray eyes regarding him with curiosity.

"And of course, Inspector," Lane was saying, "you must question me also."

Thumm snorted. "If you saw anything in this car, you'd tell us. No, you're wrong there, Mr. Lane."

"As a matter of fact," murmured Lane, "I have never felt more humiliated, more abased in my life. To allow this dreadful thing to happen, virtually under my nose. . . ." He regarded his hands thoughtfully. "So near . . ." He looked up. "Unfortunately, I became so absorbed in my pleasant discussion with Mr. Brooks that I noticed nothing. I was increasingly anxious, however, and it was this anxiety that prompted me to get up later and investigate the dark car."

"You didn't keep tabs on everything in this car, I suppose?"

"To my everlasting shame, Inspector, I did not."

Thumm got to his feet. The District Attorney came into the car, leaned against the seat across the aisle.

"I've just been quizzing the other passengers," he said. "No one who was in this car remembers a thing, or recalls who passed up the aisle and who didn't. I never saw such an unobservant bunch. As for the passengers in the other cars, they're useless. Hell!"

"Well, we'll take their names, anyway." Thumm moved away and began to issue orders. The rest of the party kept silent until he returned; Lane was sitting in his habitual attitude of concentration, with closed eyes.

A man ran up to the Inspector. "A lead, Chief!" he cried. "Just got a call from one of the gang that Collins has been traced!"

The heavy air was suddenly surcharged with sparks. "Good boy," cried Thumm. "What's the lay?"

"He was seen at Ridgefield Park. He hired a hack and headed toward New York. One of the boys called from the City, because he figured Collins went back home, and sure enough Collins had got in a few minutes before. Looks like the taxi took him straight home. The boys will get the driver later—he hadn't got back yet. They're watching outside Collins's apartment. Want orders."

"Fine, fine. Is he still on the phone?"

"One of 'em is."

"Tell him to leave Collins alone unless he tries to sneak off. I'll be there myself in an hour or so. But tell him he can give up his shield if that Irish mug gets away!"

The detective hurried out of the train. Thumm pounded the floor with his huge feet, gleefully. Another detective came in. Thumm looked up with anticipation.

"Well?"

The man shook his head. "The boys haven't located that gat yet. It's nowhere on the train. We've pawed all over the passengers, too, and nothing doing. Haven't heard anything yet from the boys searching the tracks down the line. They're trying, but it's dark as hell."

"Keep at it . . . Duffy!" Vast surprise leaped into Thumm's face. For the square figure of Sergeant Duffy, who was supposed to be heading for New York City, lurched into the car. "Duffy! What in God's name are *you* doing here?"

Duffy took off his cap and swabbed his perspiring brow; but he was grinning. "Did a little detective work myself, Chief. I thought, seeing as how this Browne dame hangs out at the Grant, I'd phone the desk there and find out if she was in, before I beat it. Knew you'd be leaving soon—wanted to get the info for you if I could before you headed back."

"Well, well?"

"She clicked, Chief!" roared Duffy. "She's there, and I'll be a three-horned son-of-a-bull if that guy Pollux didn't come in with her!"

"When?"

"Clerk at the desk says they checked in a few minutes before I called, and they both went up to her rooms."

"Were they seen leaving?"

"Nope."

"Good work. We'll stop there on our way to Collins's joint. You beat it to the Grant and keep an eye out. Grab a cab."

As Sergeant Duffy plowed out of the car, he encountered a group of new figures. Men were pouring into the coach, led by a medium-sized tow-headed man. "Here! Where you goin'?" growled Duffy.

"One side, officer. I'm the District Attorney of this county." Duffy cursed and swung off the train. Bruno hurried forward and the tow-headed man shook his hand briefly. He introduced himself as District Attorney Kohl of Bergen County, routed out of bed, he complained, by a message from Bruno. Bruno led Kohl back to the rear car, where Kohl examined DeWitt's now stark body. They became involved in a polite discussion as to legal jurisdiction. Bruno pointed out that while DeWitt had been murdered in Bergen County, his murder was unquestionably related to the Wood killing in Hudson County and the Longstreet killing in New York County. They stared at each other.

Kohl threw up his hands. "The next one, I suppose, will be in 'Frisco. All right, Bruno. It's your case, I guess. I'll help all I can."

They retraced their steps. The cars suddenly became the swirling center of a violent commotion. A New Jersey hospital ambulance discharged two internes, and under the supervision of Dr. Schilling, DeWitt's corpse was carried out of the train. The

Medical Examiner waved a weary farewell and went off with the ambulance.

In the train, the entire company of passengers were herded together, severely lectured by Inspector Thumm, their names and addresses checked; and they were released. A special train for their use had been pressed into service by railroad officials, and roared out of Teaneck.

"You won't forget now," admonished Bruno, as Kohl and he stood talking in the forward car. "You'll look for the passengers who got off before the murder was discovered?"

"I'll do my best," said Kohl gloomily, "but frankly I don't think it will result in anything. The innocent ones will come in, and if there's the guilty one among 'em, he'll stay away. And there you are."

"One other thing, Kohl. Thumm's men are scouting around up the line, along the tracks and roadbed, looking for the revolver on the chance that it was thrown from the train. Will you send Jersey men to relieve them and continue the search? It will be light soon, and they'll be able to see better. Of course, we've had the DeWitt party as well as the rest of the crowd searched, and the gun wasn't found."

Kohl nodded and left the train.

The party reassembled in the forward car. Thumm was struggling into his topcoat. "Well, Mr. Lane," he said, "what do you say about this crime? Does it verify your other ideas?"

"Do you still think," put in Bruno, "that you know who killed Longstreet and Wood?"

Lane smiled for the first time since he had discovered DeWitt's body. "I not only know who killed Longstreet and Wood, but I also know who killed DeWitt."

They stared at him, speechless. For the second time since

Thumm had met Lane he shook his head like a fighter shaking off the effects of a head-blow. "Whew!" he said. "I give up."

"But Mr. Lane," protested Bruno, "let's *do* something. If you know, tell us and we'll nab him. This can't go on forever. Who is it?"

Lane's face dropped into haggard lines. When he spoke it was with some difficulty. "I'm sorry, gentlemen. You must have—odd, isn't it?—faith in me. Believe me when I say it would do not the slightest good to unmask our Mr. X now. You must have patience. I am playing a dangerous game, but haste would be ruinous."

Bruno groaned. He appealed helplessly to Thumm, who was thoughtfully sucking his forefinger. Thumm looked into Lane's clear eyes with sudden decision. "Okay, Mr. Lane. Whatever you say goes with me. I'll fight it out on my side, and I know Bruno will on his. If I'm wrong in you, I'll take my licking like a man. Because I'm absolutely—this is between you and me—up a tree."

Lane flushed—the first sign of emotional response he had exhibited.

"There may be another murder if we let this crazy killer run around loose," said Bruno with a final desperate lunge.

"You may take my word for it, Mr. Bruno." Lane's voice was dryly assured. "There will be no other murders. X is finished."

Scene 4

EN ROUTE TO NEW YORK.
SATURDAY, OCTOBER 10. 3:15 A.M.

DISTRICT ATTORNEY Bruno, Inspector Thumm, and a small army of men climbed into police cars and roared away from the Teaneck siding in the direction of New York.

For a long time the two men sat without speaking, immersed in a welter of spinning thoughts. The black Jersey countryside skimmed by.

Bruno opened his mouth, and the words flew out soundlessly, swallowed up in the thunder of the cut-out. Thumm yelled: "Hey?" and they put their heads together.

Bruno shouted into the Inspector's ear: "How do you figure Lane knows who killed DeWitt?"

"The same way, I suppose," cried Thumm, "that he knew who killed Longstreet and Wood!"

"*If* he knew."

"Oh, he knows all right. The old son-of-a-gun inspires confidence somehow. Can't figure it out myself. . . . Easy enough to see how his mind worked. He probably figures that Longstreet and DeWitt have been on the spot from the beginning, both of 'em. Wood's murder came between as a result of circumstances—to shut him up. That means——"

Bruno nodded slowly. "That means that the motive for these crimes goes 'way back, maybe."

"Sure looks like it." Thumm swore fluently as the driver of the car took a bump in the road without touching his brake. "So Lane says there won't be any more murders—see? Longstreet and DeWitt rubbed out, and there's an end to it."

"Feel sorry for that poor old devil," muttered Bruno half to himself. The same thought was in their minds—DeWitt, in some as yet unseen way sacrificed. . . . They sat in silent communion as the car rushed on.

After a time Thumm took his hat off and pounded his forehead. Bruno gaped.

"What's the matter—feel sick?"

"Trying to figure out that damned finger-sign DeWitt left."

"Oh."

"It's cuckoo, Bruno, plain cuckoo. Can't make head or tail of it."

"How do you know DeWitt *left* it?" demanded the District Attorney. "Maybe it doesn't mean anything. Just an accident."

"You don't believe that. Accident, hell! Did you see me try putting my fingers in that position? Took a lot of strength to keep them overlapped for even thirty seconds. And it's impossible, I'd say, for the fingers to have got together in a spasm, Bruno. Schilling had the same idea, or he wouldn't have made me experiment. . . . Say, listen!" The Inspector shifted in the leather seat to glare suspiciously at the District Attorney. "I thought you were sort of impressed by that evil-eye crack!"

Bruno smiled sheepishly. "Well . . . The more I think about it, the more I'm inclined to dismiss it. It just can't be. It's too fantastic—isn't real, by God."

"Hard to figure, all right."

"Then again, who can tell? Let's suppose—mind you, Thumm, I'm not saying I believe it . . ."

"I get you, I get you."

"Well, let's suppose those overlapping fingers *did* signify the protection-sign against the evil eye. Might as well take all the possibilities into consideration. All right. DeWitt died instantly on being shot; one thing sure, then, the sign must have been made deliberately by DeWitt and *before* he was shot."

"Murderer might have set DeWitt's fingers that way after DeWitt was dead," said Thumm in a disagreeable voice. "As I said before."

"Oh, rot!" cried Bruno. "The murderer didn't leave any sign on the other two—why on this one?"

"All right—have it your way," shouted Thumm. "I was only acting true to form—detective examining all the possibilities, and all that kind of junk."

Bruno paid no attention. "If DeWitt left that sign deliberately—hell, he knew his murderer, all right, and wanted to leave a clue to his murderer's identity."

"So far so good," yelled Thumm. "Elementary, my dear Bruno!"

"Oh, shut up. On the other hand," continued the District Attorney, "about this evil-eye business. DeWitt wasn't superstitious. Told you himself he wasn't. That means . . . Say, Thumm!"

"I get you, I get you," cried the Inspector, sitting up abruptly. "You mean that DeWitt left the sign to indicate *his murderer* was superstitious! By golly—that begins to sound like something! Jibes with DeWitt, too. Split-second thinker, he was. Quick on the trigger, keen business man . . ."

"Do you think Lane has considered that?" asked Bruno thoughtfully.

"Lane?" The Inspector's excitement subsided as if it had been doused with ice-cold water. His thick fingers bruised his jaw. "Well. Now that I think of it, maybe the idea isn't so hot after all. This goddamned superstition business . . ."

Bruno sighed.

Five minutes later Thumm said suddenly: "What the hell is a *jettatore?*"

"Possessor of the evil eye—Neapolitan term, I think."

They lapsed into gloomy silence as the car hurtled on.

Scene 5

The DeWitt House in West Englewood.
Saturday, October 10. 3:40 a.m.

West Englewood was fast asleep under a frosty moon when a large police touring-car passed through the village and took a side road lined with decaying trees. Two State troopers on motorcycles flanked the car. Behind it came another and smaller car filled with detectives.

The cavalcade came to a stop before the driveway leading through the lawns to the DeWitt house. From the large touring-car emerged Jeanne DeWitt with Kit Lord, Franklin Ahearn, Louis Imperiale, Lionel Brooks, and Drury Lane. All were silent.

The troopers cut their motors, pulled the machines back on their stands, and sat their saddles idly, puffing at cigarettes. The detectives swarmed from the smaller automobile and surrounded the party.

"All of you into the house," said one, with an air of authority. "District Attorney Kohl's orders to keep you together."

Ahearn protested; he lived near by, he said, and saw no reason for spending the remainder of the night in the DeWitt house. Lane hung back as the others straggled up the walk to the portico. The detective with the authoritative air shook his head; another man stepped to Ahearn's side. Ahearn shrugged and followed the others; and Lane, smiling faintly, proceeded along the dark walk in Ahearn's wake. The detectives trudged behind.

They were admitted by a half-dressed Jorgens, who stared at them in bewilderment. No one vouchsafed an explanation. The party, followed doggedly by the detectives, went into the large Colonial sitting-room, dropping into chairs with varying expressions of hopelessness and fatigue. Jorgens, buttoning himself with one hand, lit electric lamps with the other. Drury Lane sat down with a sigh of relief, nursing his stick and watching the others with bright eyes.

Jorgens hovered over Jeanne DeWitt. The girl was sitting on a sofa encircled by Lord's arm. The butler said timidly: "I beg your pardon, Miss Jeanne . . ."

She murmured "Yes?" in a voice so strange that the old man took a step backward.

But he said: "Has anything happened? These men . . . I beg your pardon, but where is Mr. DeWitt?"

Lord said gruffly: "Oh, go away, Jorgens."

The girl said clearly: "He's dead, Jorgens. Quite dead."

Jorgens's face went ashen; he remained in the same stooping attitude like a man entranced. Then he glanced about uncertainly as if to corroborate this appalling intelligence, saw only averted faces or stony eyes from which all emotion had been drained by the remorseless events of the night. Without a word, he turned to go.

The detective in charge blocked his way. "Where's Mrs. DeWitt?"

The old butler regarded him blankly out of bleared, rheumy eyes. "Mrs. DeWitt? Mrs. DeWitt?"

"Yes. Come on—where is she?"

Jorgens stiffened. "Upstairs asleep, I think, sir."

"Was she here all evening?"

"No, sir. No, sir, I think not."

"Where'd she go?"

"I'm afraid I don't know, sir."

"When did she get in?"

"I was asleep, sir, when she came in. She had evidently forgotten her key, for she rang until I came down."

"Well, well?"

"She came in about an hour and a half ago, I should judge, sir."

"Don't you know exactly?"

"No, sir."

"Just a minute." The detective turned to Jeanne DeWitt, who had sat up during this conversation, listening almost with eagerness. The detective seemed puzzled by the peculiar expression on her face. He said, with a clumsy attempt at graciousness: "I guess— Would you want to tell Mrs. DeWitt what happened, Miss? She'll have to know, and besides I want to talk to her. District Attorney Kohl's orders."

"*I* tell her?" Jeanne threw her head back and laughed hysterically. "*I* tell her?" Lord shook her gently, murmuring in her ear. The wildness fled from her eyes and she shuddered. She said, in a half-whisper: "Jorgens, call Mrs. DeWitt down here."

The detective said eagerly: "Never mind. I'll get her myself. Here, you—show me where her room is."

Jorgens shuffled out of the room, followed by the detective.

No one spoke. Ahearn rose and began to pace the floor. Imperiale, his coat still on, bundled it more securely about him.

"I think," said Drury Lane amiably, "it would be wise to light a fire."

Ahearn stood stock-still, looking around the room. He shivered suddenly, as if he had just felt the chill in the air. He glanced about in a helpless way, hesitated, then went to the fireplace, knelt and with trembling hands occupied himself in starting a fire; a little heap of logs crackled after a moment. Firelight leaped along the walls. When he had the fire going to his satisfaction, Ahearn rose, dusted his knees and resumed his pacing. Imperiale took his coat off. Brooks, buried in the depths of an armchair in a far corner, hitched the chair closer to the fire.

They all raised their heads suddenly. A confusion of voices floated through the doorway and the warming air. Stiffly, unnaturally, they held their heads that way—watching, waiting for something to happen in the curiously detached manner of statuary. Then Mrs. DeWitt glided into the sitting-room, followed by the detective and the hesitating, still dazed Jorgens.

Her gliding motion, unnatural as their manner, unreal as the tempo of a dream, nevertheless released them from the spell of horror and the evil night. They relaxed; Imperiale rose and made a formal little bow; Ahearn grunted, tossing his head; Lord's arm tightened about Jeanne's shoulders; Brooks went to the fire. Only Drury Lane remained in the same pose, a man handicapped by deafness, head cocked alertly and eyes sharp for the slightest move that might be significant of sound.

Fern DeWitt was clothed in an exotic dressing-gown hurriedly wrapped about her nightdress; her hair, still gleaming black, streamed over her shoulders. She was more beautiful now than in the light of day: the lacquer was stripped from her face and the firelight softened the marks of age. She paused uncertainly, her eyes much like Jorgens's, and looked around. When they came to Jeanne, they contracted oddly and she crossed the room to bend over the girl's exhausted body. "Jeanne, Jeanne," she whispered. "I'm so—so . . ."

The girl replied in a crystal voice, without raising her head or looking at her stepmother. "Please go away."

Fern DeWitt recoiled as if Jeanne had slapped her; without another word she turned to leave the room. The detective, who had been standing behind her watching closely, barred her way. "A couple of questions first, Mrs. DeWitt."

She stopped, helplessly. Imperiale hurried forward with a chair, and she sank into it, staring at the fire.

The detective cleared his throat in the heavy, palpable silence. "What time did you get in tonight?"

She sucked her breath, in. "Why? Why? You don't . . ."

"Answer the question."

"A few minutes after—two."

"That is, about two hours ago?"

"Yes."

"Where were you?"

"Just driving."

"Driving." The detective's voice was crude with suspicion. "Anybody with you?"

"I was alone."

"What time did you leave this house?"

"A long time after dinner. About seven-thirty. I took my own car and drove, drove . . ." Her voice trailed away and the detective waited patiently. She moistened her dry lips and began again. "I drove to the City. After a time I found myself in the Cathedral . . . St. John the Divine."

"On Amsterdam Avenue and 110th Street?"

"Yes. I parked my car and went in. Just sat there for a long time, thinking . . ."

"What's the idea, Mrs. DeWitt?" demanded the detective in a rough tone. "Do you mean to tell me you went clean to uptown New York just to sit in a church for a couple of hours? When did you leave the Cathedral?"

"Oh, what's the difference?" Her voice rose to a shriek. "What in the world is the difference? Do you think *I* killed him? You do—I know you do, all of you, sitting here this way, watching me, judging me . . ."

She began to weep, hopelessly, her magnificent shoulders heaving.

"What time did you leave the Cathedral?"

She sobbed a little then, choked back the tears, and said brokenly: "About half-past ten or eleven o'clock, I don't remember."

"And then what did you do?'"

"I just drove and drove and drove."

"How'd you get back to Jersey?"

"By the Forty-Second Street ferry."

The detective whistled, stared at her. "Came all the way downtown in heavy New York traffic again? Why? Why didn't you cross by the 125th Street ferry?"

She said nothing.

"Come on now," said the man brutally. "You've got some explaining to do."

"Explaining?" Her eyes were dull. "I have nothing to explain. I don't know why I came downtown. I was just driving, thinking . . ."

"Yeah, thinking." He glared now. "What about?"

She rose, draping her gown about her. "I think you are carrying this just a bit too far. Certainly my thoughts are my own? Let me pass, please. I am going to my room."

The detective stepped before her and she stopped short, the color fading from her cheeks. "No, you don't—" he began, when Drury Lane said pleasantly: "Really, I think Mrs. DeWitt is perfectly right. She is under a strain and it would be only kindness to question her further—if it is necessary—in the morning."

The detective screwed his eyes at Lane, coughed, stepped aside. "All right, sir," he growled. He added grudgingly: "Excuse me, lady."

Fern DeWitt disappeared, and again the party lapsed into apathy.

• • • • •

At a quarter after four Mr. Drury Lane might have been observed at a curious business.

He was alone in the library of the DeWitt house. His Inverness was thrown over a chair. His tall trim figure paced off the room methodically, eyes roving, hands prying and searching. In the center of the room was a large walnut desk, carved and old. Lane went through the drawers one by one, sorting papers, examining records and documents. Apparently he was dissatisfied; because he left the desk and for the third time turned to a wall-safe.

He tried the knob again; the safe was locked. He turned away and slowly, carefully went through tier upon tier of books, looking between shelves and volumes, opening a book here and there.

When he had completely examined the books, he stood musing. His bright eyes strayed to the wall-safe again.

He went to the door of the library, opened it and peered about. One of the detectives was lounging in the hall. The man looked about quickly.

"Is the butler still downstairs?"

"I'll see." The detective walked away and returned shortly with a shuffling Jorgens.

"Yes, sir?"

Drury Lane leaned against the jamb of the library door. "Jorgens, old fellow, do you know the combination of the library safe?"

Jorgens started. "I? No, sir."

"Does Mrs. DeWitt know it? Or Miss DeWitt?"

"I don't think so, sir."

"Odd," said Lane pleasantly. The detective was slouching off down the hall. "And how is that, Jorgens?"

"Well, sir, Mr. DeWitt . . . Well." The butler seemed at a loss. "It's queer, sir, but Mr. DeWitt for years has kept that safe sort of to himself. There's a bedroom safe upstairs in which Mrs. DeWitt and Miss DeWitt keep their jewels But this one in the library . . . I think only he and Mr. Brooks, his attorney, knew the combination."

"Brooks?" Drury Lane was thoughtful. "Will you have him come here, please."

Jorgens moved away. When he returned, it was with Lionel Brooks, gray-blond hair tousled, eyes red and sleepless.

"Want me, Mr. Lane?"

"Yes. I understand that only you and DeWitt knew the combination of the library safe, Mr. Brooks." An alert look swam into Brooks's eyes. "May I have it, please?"

The lawyer stroked his chin. "A rather unusual request, Mr. Lane. I don't know that ethically I have the right to give you the combination. And legally . . . This places me in a peculiar position. You see, the combination was given to me by DeWitt a long time ago. He told me that he didn't want a record kept about the house, and if anything should happen to him he preferred that the safe be accessible only through official channels. . . ."

"You amaze me, Mr. Brooks," murmured Lane. "Under the circumstances, I am more determined than ever to open the safe. You know, of course, that I possess the requisite authority. Would you transmit the combination to the District Attorney?" He was smiling, but his eyes probed the muscular contractions of the lawyer's jaws.

"If it's the will you want to see," began Brooks weakly, "that's really an entirely official matter. . . ."

"But it isn't the will, Mr. Brooks. By the way, are you aware of the safe's contents? There must be something precious inside to warrant all this mystery."

"Oh, no, no! I've always suspected there was something queer inside, but of course I never presumed to ask DeWitt."

"I think, Mr. Brooks," said Lane in quite another voice, "that you had better give me the combination."

Brooks hesitated, averted his eyes. . . . Then with a shrug he murmured a series of numerical symbols. Lane watched his lips gravely, nodded, and without another word retreated into the library, shutting the door in Brooks's face.

The old actor hurried across the library to the safe. He manipulated the dial for some time. When the heavy little door swung open, he paused expectantly, examining its interior without disturbing anything. . . .

Fifteen minutes later Mr. Drury Lane slammed the door of the safe shut, twirled the dial, and returned to the desk. In his hand was a small envelope.

Lane sat down in the desk-chair and studied the face of the envelope. It was addressed in longhand to John DeWitt, was post-marked Grand Central Station, New York City, and had gone through the general post-office on June third of the current year. Lane turned the envelope over; there was no return address.

Carefully he inserted his fingers into the ragged end of the envelope and extracted a single sheet of common notepaper. Like the envelope, it was written in script. The ink had been blue. It bore a date at the top of the sheet; June second. It opened with the abrupt salutation: Jack!

The message itself was laconic:

> June 2nd.
>
> Jack!
>
> This is the last time you will hear from me by letter.
>
> Every dog has his day. Mine will come soon.
>
> Get ready to pay. You may be first.

The letter was signed, without benefit of conventional closure: *Martin Stopes.*

Scene 6

A Suite in The Hotel Grant.
Saturday, October 10. 4:05 a.m.

Sergeant Duffy's preposterous back was pressed against the panels of the door leading into Cherry Browne's suite, and he was talking guardedly to a worried-looking man of girth when Inspector Thumm, District Attorney Bruno, and their men strode down the corridor of the twelfth floor, in the Hotel Grant.

Duffy introduced the worried-looking man as the hotel detective; and the hotel detective looked even more worried at the glint in Thumm's eye.

"Anything?" asked Thumm in an ominous voice.

"Quiet as mice," mumbled the hotel detective. "Quiet as mice. Won't be any trouble, now, will there, Inspector?"

"Not a peep out of them," said the sergeant. "I guess they must have gone to bed."

The hotel man immediately assumed a shocked expression. "We don't allow that sort of thing."

Thumm growled: "Any other exit from this apartment?"

"That door." Duffy wielded his beefy arm. "And 'course there's the fire-escape. But that's covered from downstairs. Got a man on the roof, too, just in case."

"Scarcely necessary, it seems to me," objected Bruno. He seemed uneasy. "They won't try to get away."

"Well, you never can tell," said the Inspector dryly. "All set, boys?" He glanced up and down the corridor; there was no one about except his own men and the hotel detective; two men had strolled over to the adjoining door. Without further preliminary Thumm rapped on the panels of the door.

There was no sound from the interior of the suite. Thumm set his ear against the door, listened for a moment, then knocked thunderously. The hotel detective opened his mouth to protest, closed it again, and began to patrol the carpeting nervously.

There was a long delay, but this time a little murmur of noise made itself faintly audible to the Inspector's ear. He smiled grimly and waited. Then the *click!* of an electric switch somewhere in the interior, a whispering shuffle, and the tumbling sounds of a bolt being withdrawn. Thumm glanced warningly at his men. The door opened a scant two inches.

"Who is it? What do you want?" It was Cherry Browne's voice, a nervous voice with uncertain accents.

Thumm wedged his large shoe into the crack of the door, prying it open. He placed his hamlike hand against the panels, pushed, and the door gave grudgingly. In the light of the room a very beautiful and very apprehensive Cherry stood, wrapped in lacy silken negligee, her tiny bare feet thrust into satin mules.

She uttered the ghostliest gasp at the sight of Thumm's face, retreating instinctively. "Why, it's Inspector Thumm!" she said in a weak voice, as if Thumm's substantial presence were not self-evident. "What's the—the trouble?"

"No trouble, no trouble at all," said Thumm heartily, but his eyes were roving. He was standing in the sitting-room of the actress's suite; it was in some disarray; on the sideboard an empty gin-bottle and an almost empty bottle of whisky; a litter of half-smoked cigarette-butts, a woman's pearl-beaded evening bag on the table; unwashed glasses, an overturned chair . . . Her eyes went from the Inspector's face to the doorway; they widened at the sight of Bruno and the silent men in the corridor outside.

The door leading into the bedroom was closed.

Thumm smiled. "Let's go, D.A.—you men stay outside," and the District Attorney walked into the room, shutting the corridor-door behind him.

Some of the woman's natural self-possession returned; color came back into her cheeks, and one hand strayed to her hair.

"Well!" she said, "this is a fine time to disturb a lady. What's the idea, Inspector?"

"Can it, Sister," said Thumm pleasantly. "You alone?"

"What's that to you?"

"I said—are you alone?"

"It's none of your rotten business."

Grinning, while Bruno leaned against the wall, Thumm crossed the room to the other door. The actress uttered a little cry of dismay and ran after him, intercepting him, placing her back against the bedroom door. She was angry; her luminous Spanish eyes flashed. "You've got a sweet nerve!" she cried. "Where's your warrant? You can't——"

Thumm placed his large hand on her shoulder, brushed her from the door . . . It opened in his face and Pollux stepped out, blinking in the light.

"All right, all right," said Pollux in a cracked voice. "No sense in getting nasty. What the hell's up?"

He was attired in clinging silk pajamas; his careful diurnal veneer had vanished. His thin hair stuck up from his head as if greased; his needle-pointed mustache drooped sadly; unhealthy sacs, the color of graphite, curved under his protruding eyes.

Cherry Browne tossed her head, salvaged a cigarette from the litter on the table, struck a match, puffed hungrily, and sat down, legs swinging. Pollux merely stood still; he seemed conscious of the miserable figure he presented and shifted from one foot to the other.

Thumm appraised him dispassionately, looking from one to the other. No one said a word.

The Inspector said, in the charged silence: "Now suppose you two love-birds tell me where you were tonight."

Cherry sniffed. "Who wants to know? Suppose you tell us why you've suddenly taken such an interest in my affairs."

Thumm thrust his hard red face close to hers. "Now listen, Sister," he said without heat, "you and I will get along fine—fine, see?—if you don't act Park Avenue. But get tough and I'll break every bone in that pretty body of yours. Answer me, and cut the society stuff!"

His eyes were like agates, boring into hers. She giggled a little. "Well . . . After the show tonight Pollux met me and we—and we came here."

"That's hooey," said Thumm. Bruno observed that Pollux was frowning, trying to signal the woman across Thumm's shoulders. "You got in around 2:30. Now where were you?"

"Well, what are you so steamed about? Sure we came here. I didn't want to say we went right from the theater to the hotel. I mean—I didn't *mean* to say it. We went to a speakeasy on Forty-Fifth Street. *Then* we came here."

"You weren't on the Weehawken ferry tonight by any chance, were you? A little before midnight?"

Pollux groaned. "You, too!" snapped Thumm. "You were there, and both of you were seen in the ferry landing on the Jersey side."

Cherry and Pollux looked at each other in a kind of despair. The woman said slowly: "Well, what of it? Anything wrong in that?"

"There's plenty wrong with it," growled the Inspector. "Where were you two going?"

"Oh, just taking a ferry-ride."

Thumm snorted in disgust. "My God," he said, "are you just dumb, or what? Expect me to believe *that?*" He stamped one foot. "I'm sick and tired of this beating around the bush, Sarah. You were on that ferry, and you got off on the Jersey side because you were following the DeWitt party!"

Pollux muttered: "We'd better give it to 'em straight, Cherry. It's the only way."

She glared at him with contempt. "You poor, white-livered sissy. There you go, spilling the beans like a scared brat. We didn't do anything wrong, did we? They haven't got anything on us, have they? Then what are you yapping about?"

"But Cherry—" Pollux was wincing; he spread his hands.

Thumm let them bicker. For some time he had been eyeing the pearl-beaded evening bag on the table. Now he plucked the bag to him and hefted it speculatively. . . . The bickering stopped as if by magic. Cherry watched that heavy hand go up and down, up and down. . . . "Give me that," she said thickly.

"Pretty heavy upholstery in this bag, isn't there?" grinned Thumm. "Weighs near a ton. I wonder . . ."

She uttered a little animal cry as his large fingers dexterously flipped the bag open and dipped inside. Pollux paled and took a spasmodic step forward. Bruno quietly left the protection of his wall and went to Thumm's side.

The Inspector's fingers emerged with a diminutive pearl-handled revolver of small caliber. He manipulated the mechanism of the weapon and examined its interior. Three chambers were filled. Thumm wrapped a handkerchief around a pencil and swabbed the barrel; the handkerchief emerged clean. He held the revolver close to his nose and sniffed. He shook his head and threw the weapon on the table.

"I have a permit to own a revolver," said the actress, licking her lips.

"Let's see it."

She went to the sideboard, opened a drawer, and returned to the table. Thumm examined the permit and handed it back to her. She sat down again.

"Now, you," said Thumm to Pollux, "let's have it. You were tailing the DeWitt party. What for?"

"I—I don't know what you're talking about."

Thumm's eyes strayed to the revolver. "You know this gun makes it look bad for little Cherry here, don't you?"

Cherry gulped. "What do you mean?" Pollux's mouth sagged.

"John DeWitt was shot and killed on the West Shore local tonight," said District Attorney Bruno—the first time he had spoken since entering the room. "Murdered."

Their lips repeated the word mechanically; they looked at each other in a dazed, horrified way.

"Who did it?" whispered the woman.

"Don't *you* know?"

Cherry Browne's full lips began to quiver. Pollux surprised Thumm and Bruno by taking his first decisive step—he leaped to the table before Thumm could move and snatched up the revolver. Bruno lunged aside; Thumm's hand shot to his hip-pocket; the actress screamed. But Pollux was not attempting drama; he held the weapon gingerly by the barrel, and Thumm's hand paused at his pocket.

"Look!" said Pollux quickly. His hand trembled as he shoved the grip toward the Inspector. "Take a good look at those bullets inside, Inspector! They're not loaded—they're blanks!"

Thumm took the weapon away. "Blanks they are," he muttered. Bruno observed that Cherry Browne was staring at Pollux as if she had never seen him before.

Pollux's words tumbled over each other in his eagerness. "I changed them myself last week. Cherry didn't know until just now. I—I didn't like the idea of her carrying a loaded gun around. A—a woman's careless about those things."

"Why only three cartridges, Pollux?" asked Bruno. "For all we know there might have been a loaded cartridge in one of the empty chambers."

"But I tell you there wasn't!" cried Pollux. "I don't know why I didn't fill it up. I just didn't. We weren't on that train tonight either. We got as far as the pier and then we turned around and took the next ferry back to New York. Didn't we, Cherry?"

She nodded dumbly.

Thumm rifled the bag again. "Did you buy tickets?"

"No. We didn't even go near the ticket-office, or the train."

"But you *were* following the DeWitt party?"

A little nerve in Pollux's left eyelid began to jump, comically. The rapidity of its quiver increased. But Pollux snapped his mouth shut like a turtle. The woman lowered her eyes and stared at the rug.

Thumm went into the dark bedroom. He came out again,

empty-handed, and searched the sitting-room with ruthless efficiency. No one said anything. Finally, he turned his back on them and clumped heavily to the door. Bruno said: "Be on call at any time. No funny business, either of you," and followed Thumm out of the room into the corridor.

The waiting men looked expectant as Thumm and Bruno emerged. But the Inspector shook his head and forged ahead to the elevators, Bruno trailing alone wearily.

"Why didn't you take the revolver?" asked Bruno.

Thumm jabbed a horny forefinger at the button. "And what good would that do us?" he said grumpily. The hotel detective pressed behind, the worried look on his face more pronounced than ever. Sergeant Duffy shouldered him aside. "No good at all. Doc Schilling said the wound was made by a .38. The only gun in that place is a .22."

Scene 7

MICHAEL COLLINS'S APARTMENT.
SATURDAY, OCTOBER 10. 4:45 A.M.

NEW YORK was unbelievable in the dark glow of the false dawn. The police car rushed, unhindered, through streets as black and deserted as mountain trails, unseen except for an occasional cruising cab, headlights staring.

Michael Collins lived in a fortress on West Seventy-Eighth Street. As the police car slid to the curb, a man detached himself from the shadows of the house. Thumm jumped out, followed by Bruno and the detectives, and the man said: "He's still upstairs, Chief. He hasn't been out of the place since he came in."

Thumm nodded and they streamed into the lobby. A uniformed old man at a desk gaped. They shook a sleeping elevator-boy into wakefulness, and he rushed them upward.

On the eighth floor they got out of the elevator; another detective appeared and significantly pointed to a door. They gathered round, quiet, and Bruno with a sigh of excitement consulted his watch. "Everything covered?" asked Thumm in a matter-of-fact voice. "He's liable to be rambunctious."

He stepped to the door and pressed the bell-button. A distant trill came to their ears. Instantly they heard the scuffle of feet and a man's voice cried hoarsely: "Who's there? Who is it?"

Thumm bellowed: "Police! Open the door!"

A short silence, then: "You'll never get me alive, damn you!" in a strangled shout, another scuffling of feet and, sharp and clear as the snapping of a frozen branch, a revolver-shot. Then the sound of something heavy falling.

They leaped into frenzied action. Thumm took one step backward, inhaled deeply, and hurled himself at the door. It was solid, formidable. Sergeant Duffy and another man, a hard-muscled individual, stepped back with Thumm and the three men crashed into the door with the impact of a battering-ram. It shivered, but held. "Again!" yelled the Inspector. . . . Under the fourth assault the door gave with a grinding scream and they tumbled headlong into a long dark hall. At the end of the hall there was the doorway to a room which was fully illuminated.

On the threshold, between hall and room, lay the pajama-clad figure of Michael Collins. By his right hand was a dull-black revolver, still smoking.

Thumm scrambled forward, heavy shoes scraping the parquet. He landed on his knees beside Collins with a thud, placed his head to the man's chest.

"He's still alive!" he shouted. "Get him into that room!"

They lifted the inert figure and carried it into the lighted room, a living-room, dumping it on a divan. Collins's face was ghastly: his eyes were closed, his lips drawn back in a wolfish snarl, and he was breathing in huge gulping pants. Along the right side of his head nothing but matted hair and dripping blood was visible; the whole side of his face was dyed red, and the blood had splattered down to his right shoulder, soaking and spreading into the pajama-cloth. Thumm's fingers touched the wound and were instantly crimson. "Didn't even penetrate his thick skull," he growled. "Just plowed alongside his head. Fainted from the shock, I guess. Lousy aim. Get a doctor, somebody.... Well, Bruno, it looks like the end."

A man ran out. Thumm crossed the room in three strides and picked up the weapon. "It's a .38, all right," he said with satisfaction. Then his face fell. "Only one shot fired, though. The one he tried to kill himself with. Wonder where the bullet went?"

"Right in this wall," volunteered a detective. He pointed to a spot on one wall at which the plaster had spattered.

As Thumm probed for the bullet, Bruno said: "He ran toward the living-room from the hall and fired as he ran. Bullet went clean across the room. He fell on the threshold when he missed." Thumm scowled at the flattened leaden pellet in his fingers. He put it into his pocket, wrapped the revolver carefully in his handkerchief and handed it to a detective. There was a hubbub from the eighth floor corridor; they turned to find a small mob of scantily clad people staring fearfully into the apartment.

Two men went out. In the *mêlée* that ensued, the detective who had been commissioned to summon a physician shoved his way through the crowd, followed by a distinguished-looking man dressed in pajamas and robe, carrying a black bag.

"You a doctor?" demanded Thumm.

"Yes. I live in this house. What seems to be the trouble?"

He did not catch sight of the still figure on the divan until the detectives stood aside. Without another word the physician dropped to his knees. "Water," he said after a moment, his fingers flying. "Warm." A man went into a bathroom and returned with a panful of steaming water.

Five minutes of deft ministration, and the physician rose. "Just a bad scratch," he said. "He'll come to in a moment." He had swabbed the wound, sterilized it, and shaved the entire right side of the head. With perfect unconcern, after a second cleansing, he sewed the lips of the wound together and bandaged the head. "He'll need further attention soon, but this will do temporarily. He'll have an ugly headache and a good deal of pain. He's coming to now."

A hoarse, hollow groan and Collins shuddered; his eyes rolled open, filled incredibly with tears as intelligence slowly crept into them. "He'll be all right," said the physician indifferently, closing his bag.

The physician left. A detective grasped Collins's armpits and hauled him to a semi-sitting position, stuffing a pillow under his neck. Collins groaned again and one bloodless hand strayed to his head, felt the bandage, dropped helplessly to the divan.

"Collins," began the Inspector, sitting down beside the wounded man, "why did you try to commit suicide?"

Collins moistened his lips with a dry tongue; he was a fearful, grotesque object, the right side of his face a smear of dried blood. "Water," he mumbled.

Thumm glanced up, and a detective brought a glass of water, holding Collins's head gingerly while the Irishman gulped and sniveled over the cool liquid. "Well, Collins?"

Collins panted: "You've got me, haven't you? You've got me, haven't you? I'm ruined anyway . . ."

"Then you admit it?"

Collins began to say something, stopped, nodded, looked startled, and raised his eyes suddenly with something of his old ferocity. "Admit what?"

Thumm laughed shortly. "None of that now, Collins. Don't play the innocent victim stuff. You know damned well what. You killed John DeWitt, that's what!"

"I—killed—" Collins began blankly; then his body writhed as he strove to sit up; he sank back under the pressure of Thumm's hand on his chest, crying wildly: "What the hell are you talking about? *I* killed DeWitt? Who killed him? I didn't even know he was dead! Are you crazy? Or is this a frame-up?"

Thumm looked puzzled. Bruno stirred and Collins's eyes rolled toward him. Bruno said soothingly: "Now look here. Evasion won't do you a bit of good, Collins. When you heard it was the police coming after you, you yelled: 'You'll never get me alive,' and attempted to kill yourself. Is that the last speech of an innocent man? A moment ago you said: 'You've got me, haven't you?' Isn't that an admission of guilt? It won't help you to lie. You've acted like a guilty man."

"But I didn't kill DeWitt, I tell you!"

"Then why did you seem to expect the arrival of police? Why did you try to commit suicide?" Thumm demanded harshly.

"Because . . ." Collins caught his underlip between his strong teeth and peered at Bruno. "That's my business," he said in a sullen voice. "I don't know anything about a killing. The last time I saw DeWitt he was very much alive." He groaned as a spasm of pain flicked across his heavy features; he put his head between his hands.

"Then you admit seeing DeWitt tonight?"

"Sure I saw him. Plenty of witnesses to that. I saw him on the train tonight. Is that where he was killed?"

"Stop stalling," said Thumm. "How'd you happen to be on the Newburgh local?"

"I followed DeWitt. I admit it. Followed him all evening. When he and the rest of his bunch left the Ritz I trailed 'em to the station. I've been trying to see him for a long time, even when he was behind bars. I bought a ticket and got on the same train. As soon as it started I went up to DeWitt—he was sitting with his lawyer Brooks and two other men, Ahearn was one of them—and I pleaded with him."

"Sure, sure, we know all that," said the Inspector. "What happened after you left the car and went out on the platform?"

Collins's bloodshot eyes were staring. "I asked him to make good Longstreet's bum tip on the market. Longstreet had put the skids under me. It was DeWitt's firm, and he was responsible. I—I needed that dough. DeWitt wouldn't listen. He just said no, that he was . . . Oh, hell, he was hard as nails." Choked rage crept into his voice. "I almost got down on my knees to him. But it was no go."

"Where were you standing at this time?"

"We'd crossed over to the other platform, the platform of the dark car. . . . So then I decided to get off the train; I was through. We were pulling into a place called Ridgefield Park. The train stopped, I opened the door on the tracks side and jumped down. Then I reached up and closed the door again, and crossed the tracks. I found out there was no train for the rest of the night going back to the City. So I hunted up a cab and came right back here, so help me God."

He sank back on the pillow, breathing heavily. "Was DeWitt still on that back platform when you jumped out?" demanded Thumm.

"Yes. He watched me, damn his soul. . . ." Collins bit his lip. "I was—I was sore at him," he faltered. "But not sore enough to commit murder—my God, no. . . ."

"You expect us to swallow that?"

"I'm telling you I didn't kill him!" Collin's voice rose to a scream. "When I was on the tracks and pulling the door to, I saw him wipe his forehead with a handkerchief, put the handkerchief back into his pocket and open the door of the dark car. He went inside. Why, God only knows. I saw him, I tell you!"

"Did you see him sit down?"

"No. I was off the train then, I told you."

"Why didn't you go through the lighted car and get off by the door opened by the conductor, ahead?"

"I didn't have time. The train had already stopped at the station."

"So you were sore at him, hey?" said the Inspector. "Quarreled?"

Collins cried: "Are you *trying* to pin this on me? I'm being on the up and up, Thumm. I told you we had words of a sort. Sure I was in a huff. Who wouldn't be? So was DeWitt. He stepped into that dim car to cool off, likely. He was excited enough."

"Did you have your revolver with you, Collins?"

"No."

"*You* didn't go into that dim car, did you, mug?" asked Thumm.

"Christ, no!" shouted the Irishman.

"You said you bought a ticket in the terminal. Let's see it."

"It's in my overcoat in the hall closet." Sergeant Duffy went to the clothes-closet in the hall, fumbled about, and returned in a moment with a small bit of pasteboard.

Thumm and Bruno fingered it. It was a West Shore Railroad single-trip ticket, unpunched. It designated a local trip from Weehawken to West Englewood.

"How is it it wasn't collected by the conductor, mug?" demanded Thumm.

"He hadn't got to us by the time I left the train."

"Oke." Thumm rose and stretched his arms, yawning prodigiously. Collins sat up; some of his strength had returned; he fumbled in the jacket of his pajamas for a cigarette. "Well, Collins, I guess that's about all now. How do you feel?"

Collins mumbled: "A little better. Head aches like fury."

"Well, I sure am glad you feel better," said Thumm heartily. "That means we won't have to call an ambulance."

"Ambulance?"

"Sure. Get up and get dressed now. You're coming back to headquarters with us."

Collins let the cigarette fall out of his mouth. "You—you tagging me for that murder? I didn't do it, I tell you! I've told you the truth, Inspector—honest to God. . . ."

"Rats. Nobody's arresting you for DeWitt's bump." Thumm winked at Bruno. "We're just holding you as a material witness."

Scene 8

Consulate of Uruguay.
Saturday, October 10. 10:45 a.m.

Mr. Drury Lane strolled through Battery Park, cape fluttering like a black cloud behind him, striking his stick vigorously against the walk and sniffing the sharp salt air. There was a smell and tang of sea about, and the morning sun warmed his face pleasantly. He paused along the Battery wall to watch a corps of gulls dash to the surface of the oily swell, pecking at floating orange-peels. Out to sea a low-slung slanting liner crept through the water. A Hudson River excursion-boat uttered a startling cry. The wind freshened, and Drury Lane sniffed again, and drew his cape snugly about him.

Sighing, he looked at his watch and turned away. He crossed the park, walking toward Battery Place.

Ten minutes later he was seated in a severe room, smiling across a desk at a small dark Latinical man dressed in a morning coat. A fresh flower gleamed in his lapel. Juan Ajos was a twinkling sort of person with brilliant teeth in his brown face, lively black eyes and a delicate mustache.

"Such an honor, Mr. Lane," he was saying in perfect English, "as our poor Consulate scarcely merits. When I was a young attaché I remember you . . ."

"Kind of you indeed, Señor Ajos," replied Lane. "But you have just returned from your sabbatical and no doubt can spare only a moment. I am here in a peculiar capacity. Perhaps you heard of a series of murders in this city and its environs while you were in Uruguay?"

"Murders, Mr. Lane?"

"Yes. There have been three recently of, I might say, an interesting nature. I have unofficially been aiding the District Attorney's investigation. My private researches have turned up a provocative clue which may or may not be pertinent. I have reason to believe that you may be able to assist me."

Ajos smiled. "Anything in my power, Mr. Lane."

"Have you ever heard the name Felipe Maquinchao? A Uruguayan?"

A remarkably lucid light came into the dapper little consul's eyes. "Our sins come home to us," he said lightly. "So, Mr. Lane, you inquire about Maquinchao. *Sí.* I have met and talked with the good señor. What is it concerning him that you would like to know?"

"How you came to meet him and anything about him that you consider interesting."

Ajos spread his hands. "I shall tell you the whole story, Mr. Lane, and you shall judge for yourself whether it is pertinent to your investigations. . . . Felipe Maquinchao is a representative of the Uruguayan department of justice, a very valued and trusted man."

Lane's eyebrows went up.

"Maquinchao came several months ago from our country to New York, sent by the Uruguayan police on the trail of an escaped convict from the great Montevideo prison. The convict was a man named Martin Stopes."

Mr. Drury Lane sat very quietly. "Martin Stopes. . . . You interest me more and more, Señor Ajos. And how is it that a man with the Anglican name of Stopes was incarcerated in a Uruguayan prison?"

"I myself," replied Ajos, tenderly sniffing at the flower in his lapel, "am familiar with the case only as it was transmitted to me by Maquinchao, the agent. He brought with him complete transcriptions of the case-history and an intimate personal knowledge."

"Go on, sir."

"It seems that in 1912 a young prospector, a man of geological training and considerable technical education, Martin Stopes, was sentenced by a Uruguayan court to life imprisonment for the murder of his young wife, a native Brazilian. He was convicted on the overwhelming evidence of three men, his prospecting partners. They had their mine inland, a rather long water-journey from Montevideo through jungle. The partners testified at the trial that they had witnessed the murder and were forced to beat and bind Stopes in order to bring him to justice by boat from the interior. The body of the murdered woman they brought with them, in horrible condition from the heat of the atmosphere, and Stopes's daughter, a two-year-old child. The weapon was also produced—a *machete.* Stopes gave no defense. He was temporarily deranged, dazed, incapable of speaking in his own behalf. He was duly convicted and sent to prison. The child was placed by the Court in a Montevideo convent.

"Stopes proved to be an exemplary prisoner. He recovered slowly from his unbalanced mental state, seemed to accept his confinement with resignation, and gave no trouble to his keepers. Neither did he fraternize with his fellow-prisoners."

Lane asked quietly: "Did the motive for the crime come out during the trial?"

"Curiously enough, no. The only conjecture as to motive the partners could make was that Stopes killed his wife during an argument; the three partners testified that they were not in the shack before the murder, that they heard screams and ran in just in time to see the man cleave the woman's skull with the *machete*. He was, it seems, a man of passionate temper."

"Please continue."

Ajos sighed. "In the twelfth year of his imprisonment Stopes confounded his jailers by executing a daring escape. The escape was of such a nature that it had obviously been planned down to its last detail over a period of many years. Would you care to hear these details?"

"Scarcely necessary, Señor."

"He disappeared as if the earth had swallowed him. The whole of the South American continent was scoured, but there was no trace of him. It was generally thought that he had made his way into the deep interior, the terrible jungles, and perhaps perished there. So much for Martin Stopes. . . . A cup of Brazilian coffee, Mr. Lane?"

"No, thank you."

"Perhaps you will permit me to brew for you our delicious Uruguayan beverage, *yerba maté?*"

"No, thank you. Is there more to Maquinchao's story?"

"*Sí.* Meanwhile the three partners, according to official records, had sold out their mine, a rich one, during the Great War. It seems that the mine produced manganese ore of a rare quality, and manganese became very precious during the war in the manufacture of munitions. The sale of the mine made them wealthy men, and they returned to the United States."

"Returned, Señor Ajos?" asked Lane with a peculiar inflection. "Were they Americans?"

"I am desolated. I have forgotten to tell you the names of the partners. They were Harry Longstreet, Jack DeWitt, and—let me see—*sí!* William Crockett. . . ."

"One moment, sir." Lane's eyes were glittering. "Do you know that two of the men murdered here recently were the partners of the firm of DeWitt & Longstreet?"

Ajos's black eyes popped. "*Dios!*" he cried. "That is news indeed. Then their premonitions were . . ."

"What do you mean?" asked Lane swiftly.

The consul spread his hands. "In July of this year the Uruguayan police received an unsigned letter, postmarked New York, and which later was admitted by DeWitt to have been sent by himself. This letter stated that the escaped convict Stopes was in New York, and suggested that Uruguay investigate. Naturally, although the government had changed hands, immediate action was taken after reference to the old files, and Maquinchao was assigned to the case. Working with me, and since he suspected that only one of the old partners would have cause to send such information to Uruguay, Maquinchao looked them up and discovered that Longstreet and DeWitt actually lived in the City, in fact in eminent positions. He had endeavored to trace William Crockett, the third partner in the old mining enterprise, but without success. Crockett had dropped out of the triumvirate when the three men returned to North America, either because of a quarrel or because he wanted freedom to spend his riches—I really do not know which. Perhaps neither is correct. Of course, this is all conjecture."

"So Maquinchao approached DeWitt and Longstreet," prompted Lane gently.

"Exactly. He approached DeWitt, disclosed his information and produced the letter, and after some hesitation DeWitt confessed that he was its author. He invited Maquinchao to live at his home while in the country, and to use it as a sort of headquarters from which to operate. Maquinchao naturally sought first of all to discover how DeWitt knew that Stopes was in New York. DeWitt showed the agent a letter, signed by Stopes, threatening DeWitt's life——"

"One moment." Drury Lane took out his long wallet and extracted the letter which he had found in DeWitt's library safe. He handed it to Ajos. "Is that the letter?"

The consul nodded emphatically. "Yes, for Maquinchao showed it to me in a subsequent report, and then returned it to DeWitt after making a photographic copy.

"DeWitt, Longstreet, and our operative had many conferences in West Englewood. Maquinchao of course had intended to secure the co-operation of the American police at once, for he was virtually helpless alone. But both partners urged him to keep the story from the police, pleading that it would reach the newspapers, the old story of their humble beginnings and the sordid murder-trial would come out. . . . The usual sort of thing. Maquinchao did not know what to do, consulted me, and we decided because of their position to acquiesce to their plea. Both men, they said, had received similar letters sporadically over a period of some five years, all from New York. They had torn up the letters, but DeWitt grew very apprehensive over the last, which was more threatening than the others, and had preserved it.

"To make a long story short, Mr. Lane, Maquinchao spent a month in vain searching, reported his failure to me and to the partners, washed his hands of the entire affair, and returned to Uruguay."

Lane was thoughtful. "And you say no trace of this man Crockett was ever found?"

"Maquinchao learned from DeWitt that Crockett had parted company with them after leaving Uruguay, without giving an explanation. They heard from him periodically, they said, chiefly from Canada, although both maintained that they had not been in communication with him for six years."

"Of course," murmured Lane, "we have only the word of two dead men for this information. Mr. Ajos, do the records contain any mention of the fate of Stopes's infant daughter?"

Ajos shook his head. "To a certain point only. It is known that she left, or was taken away from—which, is not clear—the Montevideo convent at the age of six. Nothing has ever been heard about her since."

Mr. Drury Lane sighed, rose, and towered above the little consul by his desk. "You've done yeoman service to the cause of justice today, Señor."

Ajos grinned through his white teeth. "I am so happy, Mr. Lane."

"You can, if you will," continued Lane, adjusting his cape, "do justice an even greater service. If it is possible, you might cable your government for a telephotograph of Stopes's fingerprints, to be followed by a telephotograph of the man's face, if there is such a camera record, and a complete description. I am also interested in William Crockett, if you can secure similar information concerning that gentleman. . . ."

"It shall be done immediately."

"I take it your enterprising little nation has modern scientific facilities?" smiled Lane. They walked to the door.

Ajos looked shocked. "Naturally! The photographs will be transmitted on as excellent equipment as you may find anywhere."

"That," said Mr. Drury Lane, bowing, "will be most satisfactory." He emerged into the street and headed toward the Battery. "Most satisfactory," he repeated in a little mental hum.

Scene 9

THE HAMLET. MONDAY, OCTOBER 12. 1:30 P.M.

INSPECTOR THUMM was conducted by Quacey through winding corridors to a concealed elevator, which shot them like a moon-missile through the interior of the main turret of The Hamlet to a small landing high in the tower. Thumm followed Quacey to a stone staircase which looked as ancient as the Tower of London, and up the curved ambulating steps to an iron-bolted oaken door. Quacey struggled with the hasp and heavy bolts, succeeding in freeing them, and pushed open the door with a loud exhalation of aged breath. They stepped out on the solid-stone battlemented roof of the tower.

Mr. Drury Lane lay, almost nude, on a bearskin, arms shading his eyes from the sun high overhead.

Inspector Thumm stopped short and Quacey grinned himself away. The Inspector could not conceal his stupefaction at the bronzed vigor, the firm youthfulness and muscularity, of Drury Lane's figure. His lean sprawling body, hairless except for a faint golden down, brown, hard and smooth, was that of a man in the prime of life. The shock of white hair on his head was a startling incongruity when the eye traveled the full length of that clean hardy body.

The actor's only concession to modesty was a white breech-clout. His brown feet were naked, but a pair of moccasins lay near the rug. A padded deck-chair stood to one side.

Thumm shook his head sadly and drew his topcoat a little more snugly about him. The October air was keen; a brisk wind blew about the tower's head. He strode forward, closer to the recumbent figure; the skin was perfectly smooth, he saw, untouched by gooseflesh.

Some alert intuition caused Lane to open his eyes; or perhaps it was the projection of Thumm's shadow as the Inspector stood over him. "Inspector!" He sat up, instantly awake, hugging his slim hard legs. "A splendid surprise. Please excuse the informality of my attire. Draw up that deck-chair. Unless, of course," he chuckled, "you would care to discard your swathings and join me on the bearskin. . . ."

"No, thanks," said Thumm hastily, sinking into the chair. "In this wind? No, thanks." He grinned. "It's none of my business, I suppose, but how old are you anyway, Mr. Lane?"

Lane's eyes crinkled in the sun. "Sixty."

Thumm shook his head. "And I'm fifty-four. I'd blush—I give you my word, Mr. Lane—I'd blush to take off my duds and show you my body. Why, I'm a flabby old man compared with you!"

"Perhaps you haven't had the time to take care of your body, Inspector," said Lane lazily. "I have both the time and the opportunity. Here—" he waved his hand at the delicate toy-like panorama, "here I can do as I please. The only reason I decorate my middle in the manner of Mahatma Gandhi is that old Quacey is something of a prude and would be inexpressibly shocked if I did not conceal the ah—more personal elements of my nakedness. Poor Quacey! For twenty years I have been trying to persuade him to join me in these solar orgies. You should see *him* in the altogether! But then he is a very old man. I don't believe he himself knows exactly how old."

"You're certainly the most remarkable man I've ever met," said Thumm. "Sixty . . ." He sighed. "Well, sir, things are looking up. I've come down to report new developments—one particularly."

"Collins, I take it?"

"Yes. I suppose Bruno told you what happened when we broke into Collins's apartment early Saturday morning?"

"Yes. The doltish fool attempted suicide. So you are holding the man, Inspector?"

"For dear life." Thumm was grim. "In a way," he said sheepishly, "I feel like a raw rookie. Here I am, telling you about something while we're feeling around in the dark; and you, I suppose, know the whole thing."

"My dear Inspector, for a long time you were antagonistic to me. You felt that I was pretending to knowledge I did not possess. A natural feeling. You still do not know whether my silence is that of compulsion or deception, and yet you exercise a new faith. A compliment of vast proportions, Inspector. We are in this hideous mess together, now and until it is cleared up."

"If it will be," said Thumm gloomily. "Well, as far as Collins is concerned, here's the dope. We've dug back into his history and we've discovered just why he's been so anxious to recoup his market losses. He's been embezzling the State's money on his income-tax job!"

"Really?"

"That's the ticket. To date he's appropriated a hundred thousand or more, there's no telling now exactly how much. That's no chicken-feed, Mr. Lane. It seems he's been 'borrowing' the State's money to play the market. Well, he lost, got in deeper and deeper, and took a last fifty grand at the time Longstreet tipped him off to plunge on International Metals. That was his grandstand play—an attempt to make good his former losses and cover his embezzlements. It seems that there's been a hint of what was going on, and an investigation under cover started to check over the bookkeeping of the Bureau."

"Collins forestalled direct investigation, Inspector? How was he able to do this?"

Thumm pressed his lips together. "Pie for him. He's been falsifying the records, staving off discovery for months. Then, too, he swings a lot of cheap grafting political influence. But his back was up against the wall. He couldn't stall any longer."

"A remarkable sidelight into human character," murmured Lane. "This man, choleric, strong-willed, of passionate temperament, his life probably a succession of juggernaut impulses, his career probably strewn with the political corpses of his enemies . . . this man begging on his knees, as Bruno told me! A broken man, Inspector. Completely, devastatingly demoralized. He is already atoning to society for his crime."

Thumm did not seem impressed. "Maybe. Anyway, we have a pretty strong case against him—circumstantial again, but what the hell. Motive? Equally strong against both Longstreet and DeWitt. In revenge for what he thought was a double-cross by Longstreet, he kills Longstreet. When, desperate, faced with ruin, with nothing to lose, he hears DeWitt's refusal to cover up Longstreet's bum steer, he kills DeWitt. As far as circumstances are concerned, they favor Collins as the criminal in the murder of both partners, and don't contradict the possibility of his having murdered Wood. He might easily have been one of the ferry passengers who escaped when the *Mohawk* docked. We're checking up his movements for that night, and Collins can't furnish an alibi. . . . Then again, when he comes to trial, Bruno can present the evidence of Collins's guilty conduct when we broke in on him—his shout, attempted suicide . . ."

"In court, under the magic of the District Attorney's oratory," commented Lane with a smile, stretching his long lean arms, "I have no doubt but that Collins will appear the guilty man. But have you considered, Inspector, the possibility that when Collins heard the police at his door, at five o'clock in the morning, his frenzied mind leaped to the conclusion that his depredations on the State's funds had been discovered, and that he was to be arrested for embezzlement or grand larceny? This would account, considering his state of mind, for his attempted suicide and his statement that you would never 'get' him alive."

Thumm scratched his head. "That's just what Collins said when we confronted him this morning with that embezzlement charge. How did you know?"

"Pshaw, Inspector, that was almost childishly obvious."

"It seems to me," said Thumm soberly, "that you think Collins told the truth there. You don't believe he's our man, eh? As a matter of fact, Bruno sent me confidentially to ask your opinion. You see, we want to indict him on the murder charge. But Bruno's had his fingers burnt once, and he doesn't care to go through the experience again."

"Inspector Thumm," said Drury Lane, rising to his bare feet and expanding his brown chest, "Bruno will never convict Collins of the DeWitt murder."

"I guessed you'd say that." Thumm made a fist and stared at it glumly. "But look at the position we're in. Have you been reading the papers? See the razzing we're getting for pulling a dud on the DeWitt charge? They've raked it up and linked it with the DeWitt murder, and we can't show our faces to the newspaper boys. Between you and me, it looks as if my job is at stake. The Commissioner had me on the carpet this morning."

Lane looked at the distant river. "If I felt," he said gently, "that it would do you and Bruno any good, don't you think I would tell what I know now? But the game is in its final period, Inspector; we're very near the whistle. As for your job . . . I scarcely think the Commissioner will demote you when you deliver the fettered murderer to him."

"When *I* . . ."

"Yes, Inspector." Lane leaned his bare body against the rough stone of a parapet. "Now tell me what else is new?"

Thumm did not reply at once. When he spoke, it was almost diffidently. "I don't mean to push you, Mr. Lane, but for the third time since I know you you've made a positive statement about these crimes. How are you so *sure* that Collins can't be convicted?"

"That," said Lane mildly, "is a long story, Inspector. On the other hand, we have reached the point where it is high time for me to prove as well as pose. I think I shall be able to prick your case against Collins this very afternoon."

Thumm grinned. "Now you're talking, Mr. Lane! I feel better already. . . . Developments? Plenty. Doc Schilling has had his precious autopsy on DeWitt and extracted the bullet. It's from a .38 as he opined from the first. Point number two is sort of disappointing. Kohl, the D.A. of Bergen County, hasn't been able to trace the passengers who got off the train before the discovery of the body. And neither his men nor ours have been able to locate the revolver anywhere along the tracks or roadbed. Of course, it's Bruno's opinion that Collins's gun did the job; we're having a micro-photographic study made of the bullet from DeWitt's body to compare with a discharged bullet from Collins's revolver. Even if they're different, though, it won't prove Collins's innocence, because he might have used a different gun on DeWitt. At least that's Bruno's argument. Bruno's theory is that Collins, if he did use a different gun, could easily have taken the revolver back with him in the cab that night and thrown it into the river while the cab was on the ferry going to New York."

"An interesting coincidence," murmured Lane. "Go on, Inspector."

"Well, we checked the back-trail to the cab-driver who took Collins to New York, to see if he used the ferry and if Collins got out of the cab on the ferry. The driver didn't know whether Collins had or not. He did testify that Collins took his cab just as the local was pulling out of the Ridgefield Park station. So much for that.

"The third development isn't a development at all. We haven't found a solitary item of interest in our investigation of Longstreet's business and personal files.

"Number four is damned interesting, though. Because on examining DeWitt's files at his office we made a remarkable discovery. Found the canceled vouchers—two checks a year for the past fourteen years—made out to a chap by the name of William Crockett."

Lane did not stir. His gray eyes took on an almost hazel tinge as he watched Thumm's lips. "William Crockett. Hmm . . . Inspector, you are the harbinger of generous news. For what amounts were the checks, and through what bank or banks had they been canceled?"

"Well, not one of them was for less than fifteen thousand dollars, although the amounts varied. They were all cashed in the same bank—the Colonial Trust of Montreal, Canada."

"Canada? More and more interesting, Inspector. And how were the checks signed—were they personal signatures of De-Witt, or firm checks?"

"No, they seemed to be firm checks; they were signed by both DeWitt and Longstreet. We thought of that, too. We thought it might have been some blackmail stunt against DeWitt. Well, even if it was, both partners were in on it. There's no record in the office of the reason for the semi-annual checks; they were applied fifty-fifty against the personal drawing-accounts of the two men. The tax records are all right, too—we checked there."

"Did you investigate this Crockett?"

"Mr. Lane!" said Thumm reproachfully. "The Canadian people must think we're crazy. We've hounded them ever since we discovered the vouchers. Funny thing there. The investigation through Montreal revealed that a man named William Crockett—of course, each check was endorsed by him . . ."

"There were no counter-endorsements? Each endorsement was in the same handwriting?"

"Absolutely. As I was saying, we found that this Crockett had been depositing the checks through the mail from various places in Canada, and drawing against these deposits by check. He spent his dough, evidently, almost as fast as he got it. The bank could give no description of Crockett and no clue to his present whereabouts, except that statements and vouchers were requested to be mailed to a general post-office box in Montreal.

"Well, we lost no time in that direction. We investigated the post-office box and didn't find out a solitary thing of value. Nobody could remember how long before anyone had called at the box, although it was empty at the time we had it searched. We swung back on the trail at the DeWitt & Longstreet office and found that the checks themselves had all originally been mailed to the same general post-office address. No one in the office knows who William Crockett is, what he looks like, or why he's been getting the checks. And as far as the postal box is concerned, it's paid for by the year and always a year in advance—also by mail."

"Irritating," murmured Lane. "I can imagine how disgruntled you and Bruno must have been."

"We still are," grumbled the Inspector. "The more we looked into it, the more mysterious it got. A fool could see that this guy Crockett was keeping in the dark."

"Perhaps he was keeping in the dark, as you say, more at the instigation of DeWitt & Longstreet than from his own desire."

"Say, that's an idea!" exclaimed Thumm. "Never thought of that. Anyway, it's a toss-up what all this Crockett business means. Maybe it has nothing to do with the murders—that's what Bruno thinks, and he certainly has plenty of precedent on which to base his opinion. I've never seen a murder-case in which the main issue wasn't all tangled up in false and unimportant trails. Then again, it might really mean something. . . . If Crockett were blackmailing the two of 'em, then we've got a motive for murder."

"How do you reconcile that statement, Inspector," smiled Lane, "with the pleasant fiction of the goose that laid the golden eggs?"

Thumm scowled. "I'll admit the blackmail theory is funny. In the first place, the last check-voucher was dated only last June, so evidently Crockett got his semi-annual dough in the regular way. Why then should he kill the goose that lays the golden eggs, as you say? Especially since that last check was for the biggest amount of all."

"On the other hand, Inspector, to follow out your blackmail theory, Crockett might no longer have had a goose to kill. Suppose this June check was to have been the last of the series? Suppose Crockett had been informed by DeWitt and Longstreet that there were to be no further checks at all?"

"There's something in that. . . . Of course, we looked for records of correspondence with this Crockett, but there just weren't any. That doesn't prove anything, because naturally they could have got in touch with him without leaving a trace."

Lane shook his head lightly. "Somehow, I cannot subscribe to the theory of blackmail purely on the facts you present, Inspector. Why should the amounts vary so? Blackmail would generally take the form of standardized amounts."

Thumm muttered: "And that makes sense, too. As a matter of fact, the June check was for seventeen thousand, eight hundred and sixty-four dollars. How's that for a round figure?"

Lane smiled. He cast a last longing look at the tiny thread of the Hudson River that twinkled through the tops of the trees below, breathed hugely, and slipped his feet into the moccasins.

"Come along downstairs, Inspector. We have reached the point where I must 'crown my thoughts with acts.' Therefore—'be it thought and done'!"

They moved toward the tower stairs. Thumm grinned at the naked flesh of his host's chest. "By God!" he said, "you've got even me going, Mr. Lane. Never thought I'd cotton to quotations like that. This Shakespeare lad had horse-sense, didn't he? I'll bet that mouthful was from *Hamlet.*"

"Before me, Inspector." They stepped into the half-light of

the turret and began to descend the curving stones. Lane smiled behind Thumm's broad back. "I suppose that was a valiant deduction from my terrifying habit of citing the Dane. But you're wrong, Inspector. It was *Macbeth.*"

• • • • •

Ten minutes later the two men were seated in Lane's library. Lane, a gray dressing-gown thrown over his bare body, was consulting a large map of New Jersey while Inspector Thumm looked on in utter obfuscation. The roly-poly, roast-beef-and-pudding figure of Lane's butler, the euphemistically-nicknamed Falstaff, was disappearing through an archway rimmed with books.

After several moments of unswerving concentration on the map, Lane pushed it aside and turned to face Thumm with a smile of sheer satisfaction. "The time has come, Inspector, to make a pilgrimage. A pilgrimage of some importance."

"We're off at last?"

"Oh, no—not the last pilgrimage, Inspector," murmured Lane. "Perhaps the penultimate pilgrimage. Again you will have to take me on faith, Inspector. I am beginning, I fear, to question my own powers since the DeWitt murder which, while I might have foreseen it, I could not have prevented by any direct method. . . . You see, I make excuses for myself. DeWitt's death . . ." He was silent, and Thumm gazed at him curiously. Then he shrugged. "We play on! My instinctive sense of the dramatic prevents me from spoiling a perfect climax for you. Do as I suggest and, provided the fates are with us, I can furnish excellent evidence that will cause your case against Collins to collapse. This will naturally disturb our good friend the District Attorney, but we must protect the living. Telephone from here at once to the proper authorities, Inspector. Have a squad of men meet us as soon as possible this afternoon at Weehawken. Among them must be men equipped with dragging apparatus."

"Dragging apparatus?" Thumm was dubious. "Dragging . . . For deep water? A body?"

"I should say that your men be prepared for any contingency. Ah, Quacey!"

The diminutive wigmaker, his old leather apron bound about his tiny waist, had trudged into the library bearing a large manila envelope. Under his disapproving gaze—he saw Lane's nudity beneath the dressing-gown—Lane took the envelope with eager fingers. It bore a consular imprint.

"A message through Uruguay," he said gayly to Thumm, who looked blank. He tore open the envelope, extracting several stiffly backed photographic prints and a long letter. He read the letter and threw it on the desk.

Thumm could not disguise his curiosity. "Is that a photo of a set of fingerprints, or am I seeing things, Mr. Lane?"

"These, Inspector," replied Lane, waving the photographs in the air, "are telephotographs of the fingerprints of a most interesting gentleman named Martin Stopes."

"Oh, I beg your pardon," said Thumm instantly. "I thought it had something to do with the case."

"My dear Inspector, these *are* the case!"

Thumm regarded Lane with the hypnotized stare of a light-blinded rabbit. He licked his lips. "But—but," he spluttered, "these are *what* case? These murders we're investigating? My God, Mr. Lane, who in the name of glory is Martin Stopes?"

Lane did the impulsive thing; he circled Thumm's thick shoulders with one arm. "I have the advantage of you there, Inspector. I shouldn't have laughed—it was a boorish thing to do. . . . Martin Stopes is the X we have been seeking—the man responsible for removing Harley Longstreet, Charles Wood, and John O. DeWitt from the face of the good earth."

Thumm gulped, blinked, shook his head in the characteristic dazed way. "Martin Stopes. Martin Stopes. Martin Stopes, murderer of Longstreet, Wood, DeWitt . . ." He rolled the name on his tongue. "Why, my God!" he burst out, "I've never even heard of him! His name's never even come up in the case!"

"And what's in a name, Inspector?" Lane replaced the photographs in the manila envelope. Thumm stared at them as if they were precious documents; his fingers hooked unconsciously. "What's in a name? My dear Inspector, you have had the pleasure of *seeing* Martin Stopes many, many times!"

Scene 10

NEAR BOGOTA. MONDAY, OCTOBER 12. 6:05 P.M.

HOURS OF search found Inspector Thumm looking very depressed indeed. Strong as his faith had grown in the divinatory or logical powers of Mr. Drury Lane, it had not been able to withstand some rude shocks. Their little company equipped with queer instruments that resembled relics of the Spanish Inquisition, had all afternoon been disturbing the turgid depths of various New Jersey streams crossing the path of the West Shore Railroad. Inspector Thumm, as successive attempts with the dragging apparatus proved sterile, pulled a continuously longer face. Lane had said nothing; he directed the physical aspects of the search, contenting himself with suggestions of watery spots likely to produce whatever he was seeking.

It had grown quite dark by the time the wet and weary party of men reached a stream near the town of Bogota. Men were dispatched on errands; the magic of Inspector Thumm's authority secured additional apparatus. Strong searchlights were set up near the tracks and played upon the quiet water. A scoop-like iron object, which had been in constant use all afternoon, was again brought into play. Lane and a disconsolate Thumm stood side by side watching the mechanical movements of the workmen.

"Like looking for a needle in a haystack," grumbled the Inspector. "Absolutely not a chance of finding it, Mr. Lane."

As if Thumm's pessimistic statement had aroused the pity of the gods of chance, there came at this moment a shout from one of the men operating a rowboat twenty feet from the roadbed. The shout cut off Lane's reply. Another searchlight was trained on the boat. The scoop had come up with its usual complement of slime, vegetation, gravel and mud, but this time something winked and shone in the powerful rays.

With a cry of triumph, Thumm scrambled recklessly down the slope, followed more sedately by Lane.

"Is it— What is it?" roared the Inspector.

The rowboat edged toward him, and the operator's muddy hand held out the glittering object. Thumm looked up at Lane, who had reached his side, with something like awe. Then he shook his head and began to examine the find.

"A .38, no doubt?" asked Lane mildly.

"That's what it is, by God!" cried Thumm. "Boy, luck sure is with us today! Only one empty chamber, and I'll bet dollars to doughnuts that when we fire a bullet through this barrel the bullet-markings'll jibe with that one we took out of DeWitt!"

He fondled the wet weapon tenderly, wrapped it in a handkerchief and put the thing into his coat pocket.

"Come on, boys!" he yelled to the miserable crew. "We've got it! Pack the stuff away and go on home!"

He and Lane marched back along the tracks toward one of the several police-cars which had driven them about all afternoon.

"Well, sir," said Thumm, "let me get this straight. Now here we find a gun of the same caliber as was used in killing DeWitt, in a body of water over which the train passed that night. From the location of the find, it isn't hard to see that the gun was thrown out of the train after the murder into the water. By the murderer."

"There is another possibility," said Lane. "That the murderer got off the train before or at Bogota, walked on or back, as the case might be, to that stream and threw the revolver into it. I am merely," he said, "pointing out the possibility. That the revolver was hurled from the train is by far the likelier theory."

"You think of everything, don't you? Well, I'll agree with you there. . . ."

They had reached the police-car now and rested gratefully against the black door. Lane remarked: "In any event, the discovery of the revolver where we found it definitely eliminates any opportunity of securing a conviction of Collins."

"You mean that Collins now has a perfect out?"

"Judiciously phrased, Inspector. The local pulled into the Ridgefield Park station at 12:30. Collins secured a taxicab before the train was out of sight—this is important. From that point on his alibi is fixed by the taxi-driver, who was taking him in the opposite direction from the train—toward New York. The revolver could not have been thrown from the train into the stream before 12:35, the time the train passed over the stream. Even if the revolver were thrown into the stream by a person on foot, he could not have reached the stream before the train, naturally. But Collins could not possibly have walked or driven to the stream, thrown in the weapon, and returned to the Ridgefield Park station before the train was out of sight! There is a distance of approximately a mile between Ridgefield Park and the stream, two miles up and back. True, it is conceivable, for example, that the revolver was hurled into the stream long after the murder-period; that Collins might have come back hours later and done this would not be impossible under ordinary circumstances. But the circumstances are extraordinary. For the cab took Collins directly to his New York apartment, and his movements were covered from that moment. *Ergo*—exit Mr. Collins."

Thumm's voice rose triumphantly. "I knew you'd overlooked something, Mr. Lane! You're dead to rights in that argument—Collins himself couldn't have thrown the gat into the stream. *But how about an accomplice?* Suppose Collins killed DeWitt, handed the gun to an accomplice, beat it off the train, and told the accomplice to throw the gun into the water from the train five minutes after he himself had left it. That would be damned smart figuring, Mr. Lane!"

"Now, now, Inspector, don't excite yourself," said Lane with a smile. "All along we have been discussing the *legal* aspect of the Collins case. I have not overlooked the possibility of an accomplice. Not at all. It is sufficient that I ask you—who is this accomplice? Can you produce him before the Court? Have you anything except a glossy theory to offer the jury? No, I am afraid that Mr. Collins cannot be convicted of DeWitt's murder in the face of the new evidence."

"That's right," said Thumm, his face gloomy again. "Neither Bruno nor I have the slightest idea who the accomplice might be."

"If there *is* an accomplice, Inspector," said Lane dryly.

The crew had straggled up and Thumm climbed into the police-car. Lane followed, the other car filled up, and the caravan headed back toward Weehawken, a trailer carrying the apparatus.

Thumm sat immersed, from the expression on his face, in an

eddy of bitter thoughts. Drury Lane relaxed, stretching his long legs. "You see, Inspector," he continued, "even from a psychological standpoint the argument of an accomplice is weak."

Thumm groaned.

"Let us work along the theory that Collins killed DeWitt, had an accomplice, gave the weapon to the accomplice and instructed him to throw the revolver out of the train five minutes after Collins had dropped off at Ridgefield Park. So far, so good. The hypothesis is based solely on the presumption that Collins is building for himself an air-tight alibi; in other words, the revolver is to be found along the route at a point five minutes beyond the place where Collins is known to have turned back in the opposite direction.

"But Collins has no alibi if the revolver is not found at the point five minutes beyond his dropping-off place. Therefore, if Collins planned all this, he had to make absolutely certain that the revolver was *found.* Yet we discover the weapon in a stream, where but for the grace of God it might have lain until doomsday. How can we reconcile the theory of Collins's manufactured alibi with the fact that every effort was apparently made to keep the revolver from being found at all? You will say, I suppose"—although Thumm's expression indicated no desire to speak—"that it might have been an accident that the revolver landed in the stream, that the accomplice threw it out of a window intending it to land along the roadbed. *But* if he intended the revolver to be found in support of Collins's alibi *would he throw it twenty feet out of the train?* For that is where we found it—at a point in the stream twenty feet from the tracks.

"No, the accomplice would merely *drop* the revolver out of the window, where it could not possibly land anywhere but on the roadbed, insuring its later discovery."

"In other words," muttered Thumm, "you've proved clearly that the gun wasn't meant to be found. That eliminates Collins, all right."

"So it does, Inspector," murmured Lane.

"Well," remarked Thumm with a helpless snort, "I'll admit it beats me. Every time Bruno and I get our mitts on somebody we think is X, you spoil our party. It's getting to be a habit, by God. Now the case is more complicated than ever, as far as I'm concerned."

"On the contrary," said Mr. Drury Lane, "we have pushed it very near the end."

Scene 11

THE HAMLET. TUESDAY, OCTOBER 13. 10:30 A.M.

QUACEY STOOD at a telephone in his wiggery establishment at The Hamlet. Mr. Drury Lane sprawled in a chair near by. The dark shades were drawn up at the windows, and the weak sunlight spattered in.

The ancient was speaking in his creaky voice. "But Mr. Bruno, that's what Mr. Lane says. Yes, sir. . . . Yes, tonight, at eleven P. M., you are to meet Mr. Lane here and bring Inspector Thumm and a small squad of police with you. . . . One moment, please." Quacey snuggled the speaker to his bony little breast. "Mr. Bruno wants to know if the men are to be in plainclothes, Mr. Drury, and what's the idea, he says."

"You may inform the District Attorney," drawled Lane, "that the men are not to be in uniform and that the idea is a little excursion into New Jersey. Tell him that we shall take the West Shore train bound for West Englewood on a most important mission connected with the case."

Quacey blinked, and obeyed orders.

• • • • •

11 P.M.

Inspector Thumm, perhaps by virtue of his more intimate acquaintanceship, was the only member of the police party which gathered that night in the library of The Hamlet to appear completely at ease. Mr. Drury Lane was not in evidence, and District Attorney Bruno sank into an old chair with an irritable exclamation.

The fat little body of Falstaff bowed and scraped itself into Bruno's consciousness. "Well?"

"Mr. Lane's regrets, sir. Will you wait a few moments, he says."

Bruno nodded without enthusiasm. Thumm chuckled to himself.

While they waited the men's eyes traveled with curiosity about the vast room. The ceiling was very high, and three of the walls were covered from floor to ceiling by open bookshelves holding thousands of volumes. Library ladders stood braced against the upper shelves. A quaint balcony ran completely around the room; two winding flights of iron steps gave access to it at two corners. Bronze signs engraved in Old English catalogued the books—a circular desk at one end of the room was evidently the sanctum of a special librarian, although the desk was now unoccupied. On the fourth wall there were some curious items; Bruno rose impatiently from his chair and began to wander about. He saw a stiffly varnished, glass-covered old chart in the center of the fourth wall; the curlicued inscription in the lower left-hand corner established it as a map of the world dated 1501. A collection of Elizabethan costumes, each in a separate case, lined the wall on the floor. . . .

They all turned as the door of the library opened suddenly and the wizened figure of Quacey slipped into the room. He held the door wide, an expectant grin on his old gnarled face.

Through the arching doorway strode a tall, burly, ruddy-faced man who regarded them truculently. He had a powerful chin, but his cheeks sagged slightly and there were unmistakable signs of dissipation around his eyes. He was dressed in a tweed suit—a rough tweed with wide sporty trousers and a sackcoat. He jammed his hands into the flapless pockets and glowered at them.

The effect of his appearance was instantaneous and dynamic. District Attorney Bruno froze to the floor, blinking his eyes rapidly as if he could not credit the intelligence their nerves flashed to his brain. But if Bruno was startled, Inspector Thumm was affected in a subtler, profounder way. His rocky jaw trembled like a child's; it dropped and wagged slightly. His eyes, normally hard and cold, blazed with a feverish horror. He opened and shut them quickly several times. The color had quite fled his face.

"Holy Mother of God," he whispered hoarsely. "Har—Har—Harley Longstreet!"

The others dared not move a muscle. The ghost at the door broke the silence with a subterranean chuckle that sent a chilled spark down their spines.

"'O, that deceit should dwell in such a gorgeous palace!'" said Harley Longstreet.

In the splendid voice of Mr. Drury Lane.

Scene 12

THE WEEHAWKEN-NEWBURGH LOCAL.
WEDNESDAY, OCTOBER 14. 12:18 A.M.

AN ODD journey . . . History, the unimaginative jade, repeated herself. The same locale, the same black night, the same time, the same clack and clatter of iron wheels.

Eighteen minutes past midnight found the police party which Mr. Drury Lane had mustered seated in one of the rear cars of the Weehawken-Newburgh local train, clanking along between the Weehawken terminus and North Bergen. Aside from Lane, Thumm, Bruno, and the accompanying squad there were few people in the coach.

Lane sat swathed in a bundling topcoat, a wide-brimmed felt hat pulled over his face, so that his features were concealed. He sat beside Inspector Thumm by the window, his head turned to the pane, speaking to no one and apparently either asleep or absorbed in some mental problem. Neither the District Attorney, sitting opposite, nor the Inspector said a word; both men were very nervous. The tension had transmitted itself to the detectives sitting about them; they talked little and sat like ramrods. They seemed to be waiting for an active climax of whose very nature they were in ignorance.

Thumm was restless. He glanced at Lane's averted head, sighed, and got to his feet. He tramped heavily out of the car. Almost at once he returned with an excitement-flushed face. He sat down and leaned forward, whispering to Bruno. "Something queer. . . . Just spotted Ahearn and Imperiale in the forward car. Think I ought to tell Lane?"

Bruno searched the muffled head of Lane. He shrugged. "I guess we'd better let him handle everything. He seems to know what he's doing."

The train shuddered to a stop. Bruno looked out of the window; they had arrived, he saw, at the North Bergen station. Thumm consulted his watch—the time was exactly 12:20. In the misty light of the station a few passengers could be discerned getting on the train. Lanterns swung, the doors banged shut, the train trundled on again.

A few moments later the conductor appeared at the forward end of the coach and began to collect and punch tickets. When he reached the police party he grinned in recognition; Thumm nodded sourly and paid for the fare of the party in cash. The conductor took from his outside breast pocket a number of standard cash-fare duplex tickets, placed them neatly together, punched them at two places and, ripping the tickets in half, handed Thumm one set, depositing the duplicate set in another pocket. . . .

Mr. Drury Lane, the somnolent, or the thoughtful, chose this instant to spring startlingly into life. He rose, whipped off the concealing hat and coat, and turned squarely about to face the conductor. The man stared blankly. Lane plunged his hand into one of the patch-pockets of his sackcoat, produced a silver case and, snapping it open, took out a pair of eyeglasses. He did not put them on, merely regarded the conductor with a reflective, curious preoccupation. The face—strong, pouchy, dissipated—seemed to enthrall the conductor.

It affected him strangely. His hand had stopped in mid-air, holding his ticket-punch. He took in the details of this grim figure confronting him, at first uncomprehendingly, then with a rush of terrified intelligence. His mouth popped open, his tall burly figure sagged, the winy coloring of his face vanished in a flood of dead-white. Out of his mouth came a choked sound, a single word: "Longstreet . . ." And as he stood there, petrified, physically incapable of nervous activity, the artificial lips of Harley Longstreet smiled and his right hand, dropping the silver case and the eyeglasses, in an effortless movement went again into his pocket and came out clutching something dull and metallic. . . . A pounce forward, a tiny click, and the conductor tore his eyes away from that smiling face to look down stupidly, dazedly at the pair of handcuffs on his wrists.

Whereupon Mr. Drury Lane smiled again, this time down at the bleak unbelieving faces of Inspector Thumm and District Attorney Bruno, who had watched the brief tableau in unbreathing silence, powerless to move. Fine lines appeared on the foreheads of both men; they looked from Lane to the conductor, who was cowering now, moistening his lips with a trembling tongue, leaning against the back of the seat—broken, ashamed, pathetically unable to believe the evidence of his eyes as he stared at the manacles on his wrists.

And Mr. Drury Lane said calmly to Inspector Thumm: "Did you bring the inking-pad as I requested, Inspector?"

And Thumm without a word took a tin-covered inking-pad from his pocket and a tablet of white paper.

"Please take this man's fingerprints, Inspector."

And Thumm struggled to his feet. Still unbelievingly, he complied. . . . Lane stood by the side of the stricken conductor, who like him leaned against a seat; and while Thumm grasped the man's nerveless hand and proceeded to press it on the pad, Lane picked up from his seat the discarded topcoat, searched one of the pockets, and brought forth the manila envelope he had received on Monday. As Thumm applied the conductor's slack fingers to the paper, Lane took from the envelope the Uruguayan telephotographic prints and studied them with a chuckle.

"Finished, Inspector?"

Thumm handed Lane the wet impression of the conductor's fingertips. Lane held the paper side by side with the photographic prints, cocking his head critically at the whorls. Then he returned the wet impression to the Inspector, together with the photograph.

"What would you say, Inspector? You've compared thousands of these, no doubt."

Thumm scanned them carefully. "They look the same to me," he muttered.

"Identical, of course."

Bruno faltered to his feet. "Mr. Lane, who—what——?"

Lane grasped the arm of the manacled man in a not unfriendly manner. "Mr. Bruno, Inspector Thumm, allow me to introduce one of God's most unfortunate children, Mr. Martin Stopes——"

"But——"

"—alias," continued Lane, "Conductor Edward Thompson of the West Shore Railroad——"

"But——"

"—alias an unknown gentleman on the ferry boat——"

"But I don't see—"

"—alias," concluded Lane in an amiable way, "Conductor Charles Wood."

"*Charles Wood!*" spluttered Thumm and Bruno together. They turned to stare at the cowering figure of their prisoner. Bruno whispered: "*But Charles Wood is dead!*"

"Dead to you, Mr. Bruno, and dead to you, Inspector Thumm. But to me," said Mr. Drury Lane, "very much alive."

BEHIND THE SCENES

The Explanation

THE HAMLET. WEDNESDAY, OCTOBER 14. 4 P.M.

AND AS it was in the beginning, there was the Hudson River far below, and a white sail, and a waddling steamboat. As it had done five weeks before, the automobile wound up the road, rising steadily with its burden of Inspector Thumm and District Attorney Bruno toward the fragile beauty of The Hamlet, set in its forest of russet like a delicately colored castle out of a fairy-tale.

Five weeks!

Far above, the cloud-framed turrets, the ramparts, the battlements, the needlepoint of the church-spire. . . . And then the quaint little bridge and the thatched hut and the ruddy little old man pointing to his swinging wooden sign. . . . The creaky old gate, the bridge, the gravel road ever winding upward, the oak forest now red-brown, the stone wall of the castle grounds. . . .

They crossed the drawbridge and were met at the oak portals by Falstaff. Into that manorial hall out of past ages, under seasoned old ceiling-beams, by knights in armor and the massive pegged furniture of Elizabethan England. Under the incredible masks and the gargantuan candelabra, and there was the bald bewhiskered little Quacey. . . .

In the pleasant warmth of Mr. Drury Lane's private apartments, toes toasting at the fire, the two men relaxed. Lane was in a velveteen jacket, and he looked very handsome and youthful in the reflection of the flinging flames. Quacey squeaked gibberish into a little microphonic instrument in the wall and soon Falstaff appeared in the rosy flesh, beaming over a trayful of glasses filled with some aromatic concoction of liqueurs; and there were *canapés* that disappeared under the shameless forays of Inspector Thumm.

"I suppose," remarked Mr. Drury Lane when they sat, replete and comfortable, before the fire and Falstaff had returned to his culinary caverns, "I suppose you gentlemen seek the explanation of the verbal acrobatics in which I have, I fear inconsiderately, been indulging during the past weeks. It can't be another murder so soon!"

Bruno murmured: "Hardly, although you may be sure, from what I've seen in the past thirty-six hours, that I shouldn't hesitate to consult you about one if there were one to consult you about. A little involved, but you get my point. Mr. Lane, both the Inspector and I are eternally grateful for—I'll be damned if I know how to express it."

"To put it another way," said Thumm with a grumpy smile, "you've saved our jobs."

"Fudge, foam, and fiddlesticks." Lane dismissed the subject with a gentle wave of his hand. "The papers have informed me that Stopes has confessed. Somewhere, somehow, one of them got wind of my part in the affair, and I have been besieged all day by utterly implacable reporters. . . . Has anything interesting come out of Stopes's confession?"

"Interesting to us," said Bruno, "but I suppose—although I'll be hanged if I know how—I suppose you know the substance of his confession."

"On the contrary." Lane smiled. "There are a number of items in connection with Mr. Martin Stopes on which I am completely at sea."

Both men shook their heads. Lane did not explain; he urged Bruno to relate the story told by the prisoner. When Bruno began from the beginning—the obscure and enthusiastic young geologist in Uruguay in 1912—Lane did not comment. He seemed curious about certain details, however, and by adroit questioning elicited information which his conversation with Juan Ajos, the Uruguayan consul, had not brought out.

He learned that it had been Martin Stopes himself who in 1912 had discovered the manganese mine, while he and his partner Crockett were prospecting in the wild interior. Because the two men were penniless and needed capital to work the mine, they had taken in as additional partners on smaller percentages two other prospectors—Longstreet and DeWitt, introduced to young Stopes by Crockett. Stopes in his confession made it painfully clear that the crime he had been accused of subsequently—the murder of his wife by *machete*—was committed by Crockett. Crockett had attacked Stopes's wife one night in a drunken lust, while Stopes was at the nearby mine; and when she resisted, he had killed her. Longstreet, the ring-leader, had seized the opportunity and concocted the plan whereby the three were to accuse Stopes of the murder; and, since no one knew that the mine legally belonged to Stopes, they took over the mine themselves—it had been unregistered. Crockett was pliable at this time; he was shaken by his crime and accepted the plan eagerly. DeWitt, Stopes said, was a man of softer fiber; but he was dominated by Longstreet and forced by threats to join the conspiracy.

The shock of his wife's death, the realization of his partners' perfidy had unbalanced the young geologist. It was not until after his conviction and imprisonment that he regained his normal faculties; and then he realized that he was helpless. From that moment, then, his thoughts, the thrust of his ambitions and aspirations, were diverted into a bitter desire for revenge. He had been willing, he confessed, to spend the rest of his life in executing an escape and killing the three scoundrels. By the time of his escape he had aged considerably; the rigors of close confinement had taken toll of his features, although his body was as strong as ever. He felt reasonably certain that when the time for vengeance came, he would not be recognized by his intended victims.

"These things, however," concluded Bruno, "aren't nearly so important to us now, Mr. Lane, as the—to me, at least—almost supernatural way in which you solved the case. Just how in the world did you arrive at such an uncanny solution?"

"Supernatural?" Lane shook his head. "I do not believe in miracles, and certainly I have never performed any. What success I was able to achieve in these fascinating investigations was the direct issue, in a manner of speaking, of straight thinking out of observation.

"I might begin by a generalization. For example, of the three murders with which we were confronted, the simplest was the first. You're surprised? But the circumstances attending Longstreet's curious demise permitted of incredibly damning logic. You will recall that I came to know of these circumstances in an ordinarily unsatisfactory way—by hearsay. Not having been on the scene of the crime, I deliberated under the handicap of no personal observation. I will say, however"—and he inclined gravely toward the Inspector—"that Thumm's account was so straightforward and detailed that I was able to visualize the component elements of the drama as clearly as if I had been present myself."

Drury Lane's eyes were brilliant. "In the street-car murder one inference was indisputable; it stood out at once, and I cannot to this moment comprehend how its self-evidence escaped the intelligence of both of you. Namely, that the nature of the weapon was such as to make it apparent that *it could not be handled with the bare hand without the handler pricking himself with the poisoned needles with fatal results to himself.* You, Inspector, were zealously careful to keep from picking up the needled cork—so much so that you used a pair of pincers and later sealed the cork in a glass bottle. You showed the weapon to me, and I saw at once that the murderer *must* have used some sort of protective covering for his hands and fingers both in transporting the weapon to the car and then in manipulating it during the operation of slipping it into Longstreet's pocket. I say, I *saw* this at once; actually, even if I had not seen the cork, you had described it so accurately that I could not miss the obvious point.

"The natural question then arose: What is the common form of protective covering for the hand? And the natural answer was: A glove, of course. How did this satisfy the murderer's requirements? Well, a glove would suit his purpose *practically*—it has a tough texture, affording complete protection especially if it is made of leather; and being an accepted article of clothing it is more inconspicuous than a hand-covering of an unusual nature. In a well-planned crime we have no reason to believe that a murderer would manufacture a *strange* protective covering when an ordinary glove would fulfill his needs even better; and what is more to the point, would, if seen or found, remain relatively inconspicuous and non-suspicious. The only article which might serve as a glove and yet not be manufactured or suspicious, would be a handkerchief; but a handkerchief wrapped around a hand would be clumsy, conspicuous and, more important, would not afford *certain* protection against the poisoned needles. It also occurred to me that the murderer might have employed the same method as did Inspector Thumm—that is, manipulated the needled cork with pincers. But a little thought convinced me that such a method, while it would have kept the murderer's own skin from the poisonpricks, would on the other hand have entailed a delicacy of manipulation too uncertain in the light of the circumstances—a jammed street-car, very little freedom of manual movement, and what was necessarily a strictly limited period of time in which to work.

"I felt certain, then, that when the murderer slipped the needled cork into Longstreet's pocket, *he must have worn a glove.*"

Thumm and Bruno looked at each other; Lane closed his eyes and proceeded in a low unaccented tone. "Now we knew that the cork was dropped in the pocket *after* Longstreet boarded the car. This was brought out by testimony. We also knew that from the moment Longstreet boarded the car, the doors and windows remained shut, with two exceptions which I shall discuss in a moment. It was indisputable, too, that the murderer must have been one of the occupants of the car later examined by the Inspector; since from the time Longstreet and his party got on the car, *no one left* with one exception, and this person left by Sergeant Duffy's own order and returned.

"We also knew from a thorough search of all the occupants of the car, including the conductor and motorman, that no glove was found on the persons of the occupants in the car or in the rooms in which these people were later questioned at the carbarn; and you will remember that when they went from the car to these rooms it was through cordons of police and detectives, who found nothing over this route when it was subsequently searched. Please recall, Inspector, that I specifically asked you at the termination of your recital whether gloves, among other things, had been found; and you replied in the negative.

"In other words: Although the murderer was still in the street-car, there was the peculiar situation of an object, which must have been used in the commission of the crime, not being found *after* the commission of the crime. It could not have been thrown out of a window; no window was open from a period even prior to the boarding of the Longstreet party. It could not have been thrown through a door, because Duffy himself opened and closed the doors on the only occasions when they were used after the crime and noted nothing of this nature, or he would have mentioned it. The glove could not have been destroyed or mutilated, or some remains would have been found and reported. Even had it been passed to an accomplice, or secretly to an innocent person, it would have been found; since the accomplice could have disposed of it no better than the murderer, or it would have been discovered on the innocent party's person during the search later.

"How, then, did this ghostly glove disappear?" Drury Lane sipped contentedly from a mug of steaming coffee, which Falstaff had served to his master and guests a moment before. "I was mentally titillated, I assure you, gentlemen. Speaking of miracles, Mr. Bruno, I was confronted with one then; but being something of a skeptic, I proceeded to explain away this vanishment by mortal means. For I had eliminated all but one means of disposal; the last remaining means, by the old logical law, must therefore have been the medium of disappearance. If the glove could not have been *thrown* out of the car, and yet it left the car, it could have left only on the person of someone who himself left the car. *But only one person left the car!* That was the conductor, Charles Wood, sent by Sergeant Duffy to summon Officer Morrow and notify headquarters of the tragedy. When Officer Sittenfield, who had run up from his Ninth Avenue traffic post, was admitted, he was let in by Duffy, and he did not leave the car. Neither did Officer Morrow when he finally arrived at Conductor Wood's behest. In other words, while two personalities, both policemen, *boarded* the car after the murder, no one but Charles Wood *left* the car after the murder. That he returned was of course irrelevant to the progress of the argument.

"So that I was forced to conclude: Improbable, wild, hectic as it seemed, Charles Wood, conductor of the streetcar, had taken the glove from the scene of the crime and disposed of it somewhere. It struck me at first as strange, naturally; but the argument was so rigorous and uncompromising that I was forced to accept the conclusion."

"Perfectly wonderful," said the District Attorney.

Lane chuckled and went on. "Charles Wood, then, having taken the glove from the car and disposed of it, was either the murderer himself or an accomplice of the murderer, from whom in the crush of the crowd he had received the glove for disposal.

"You will recall that at the conclusion of Inspector Thumm's story I said that the course of action was clear, but abstained from elucidation. The reason was that I could not have known at that time beyond a doubt that Wood was the murderer; there was always the possibility that he was an accomplice. But of his guilt in one capacity or the other I was convinced, since had the glove been slipped into his pocket by the murderer without Wood's knowledge—that is, if Wood were innocent of deliberate complicity—the glove would have been found on him when he was searched, or found by Wood himself and reported to the police. In other words: Since the glove was not reported by him or found on his person, he must have deliberately disposed of it when he was out of the car summoning Officer Morrow. This is guilt, either if he was disposing of it for himself or for someone else."

"Pretty—pretty as a picture," muttered Thumm.

"There was a psychological check-up," continued Lane amiably, "on the logical indication of Wood's guilt. Naturally, he could not have anticipated being granted the opportunity to leave the car and dispose of the glove. No, he must have weighed his chances and accepted the possibility of having the glove found on him if there were a search and he had had no opportunity to throw it away. But here was one of the most subtle elements of the murderer's plan! For even if the glove *were* discovered on Wood, even if *no other glove* were found on the car, as actually transpired, he would still feel reasonably secure against suspicion; since it is normally expected that a conductor, even in the heat of summer, when others do not ordinarily wear or carry gloves, will use a glove in the performance of his duty. As a conductor, handling money all day long, he possessed the psychological advantage of knowing that a glove on his person would be taken for granted. This line of corroborative reasoning also convinced me that my original idea about the glove was absolutely sound; for if Wood could not have anticipated the opportunity to dispose of his hand-covering, he would have used the most ordinary article, like a glove. A handkerchief would be found stained with the poison.

"Another point. Wood could not have planned his crime for rainy weather, which forced him to close the windows and doors;

rather he must have planned it for fair weather. In fair weather he would have had ample opportunity to dispose of the glove by throwing it out of an open window or door, and the police would surely reason—he could depend on it—that the glove could have been thrown out by anyone on the car. In fair weather, too, people would have boarded and probably left the car along the route with frequency, so that the police would have to consider the possibility that the murderer had escaped. Why, then, in the face of the advantages fair weather would have afforded him, did he choose rainy weather during which to kill Longstreet? This puzzled me for a time; but a little concentration indicated that this particular evening, rainy or not, presented the murderer with an almost unique opportunity; namely, the fact that Longstreet was accompanied by a large party of friends, all of whom would come under direct suspicion. Perhaps the incredible good fortune of this circumstance blinded him momentarily to the complications which would ensue because of the inclement weather.

"As a conductor, of course, he had two advantages which the average murderer would not have had. First, as everyone knows, a conductor's coat contains leather-lined pockets in which change is kept; and one of these afforded absolute safety to himself while keeping the weapon handy until he was ready to use it. Probably for weeks he had kept that needled cork, already dipped in poison, ready in his pocket. Second, as a conductor he could be certain of an opportunity to drop the weapon into his victim's pocket, since everyone who boards a car *must,* in cars of the Forty-Second Street Crosstown type, pass by the conductor. This was made even more favorable by the great crowd around the rear platform during the rush-hour. Two additional confirmations of a psychological nature, it seemed to me, in the consideration of Wood's guilt. . . ."

"Uncanny," said Bruno at this point. "Positively weird, Mr. Lane. For Stopes's confession bears you out in every particular, and I know that you've had no conversation with him. Specifically, Stopes says that he manufactured the needled cork himself, and procured the poison in the way Dr. Schilling so cleverly postulated in his autopsy report—from an insecticide purchasable in open market and evaporated until the sticky mass containing a high percentage of pure nicotine was left; whereupon he dipped his needles into the mass, and there he was. He dropped the weapon into Longstreet's pocket while Longstreet was detained at the rear platform waiting to pay the fares for his party and receive his change. He also says, in further confirmation, that he had intended to kill the man on a fair-weather evening, but when he saw Longstreet appear with such a large private party, he could not resist the temptation to involve as suspects Longstreet's friends and enemies, despite the rain."

"Triumph of mind over matter, as the professors say," volunteered Thumm.

Lane smiled. "A graceful compliment from an admittedly material person, Inspector. . . . To continue. You see, then, that at the conclusion of your story to me I was certain of Wood's complicity, but whether he was the murderer or merely an accomplice or tool of a second and unknown person I did not know. This was, of course, before the arrival of the anonymous letter.

"Now, unfortunately, none of us knew that Wood was the author of that letter, and when by comparison of handwritings we did discover this fact, it was too late to prevent the second tragedy. At the time the letter arrived, it appeared to be the communication of an innocent witness who had accidentally come into possession of dangerously vital knowledge and meant to inform the police even at risk of his own life. When later I saw that

Wood himself, who I knew was *not* an innocent witness, had written that letter, the letter on analysis could only have meant: One, that as the murderer himself he was giving the police a false trail leading *away* from himself by implicating an innocent person; or two, that as accomplice Wood meant to give up the real murderer, or at the real murderer's instigation meant to frame an innocent person.

"But there was something wrong here. *Wood himself was murdered.*" Lane placed the tips of his fingers together and closed his eyes again. "In the light of this inconsistency, I was forced to retrace my steps and re-analyze the two interpretations of the letter.

"The most pressing problem was this: If Wood were the murderer of Longstreet (not an accomplice), why then was he himself murdered on the *Mohawk,* and who murdered him?" Lane smiled reminiscently. "This problem was productive of interesting thoughts. For I saw at once that there were three possibilities: one, that Wood had an accomplice despite the fact that he himself was the murderer, and the accomplice killed him—in which case either the accomplice was afraid Wood meant to frame him for the Longstreet murder, or reveal the accomplice as the instigator though not the killer. Or two, that Wood was working alone, had no accomplice, was intending to frame an innocent person, and was killed by this innocent person. Or three, that Wood was killed by an unknown for reasons in no way connected with the Longstreet murder."

Lane continued swiftly. "I analyzed each possibility thoroughly. The first case—implausible. Because if the accomplice was afraid Wood meant to frame him for the Longstreet killing, or to reveal him as instigator of the crime, it would be more to the accomplice's advantage to let Wood remain alive; since in case one I was assuming that Wood was the killer himself. In the event of a frame-up, the accomplice could throw the original guilt back on Wood; whereas, if he killed Wood, he was making himself a murderer, on top of being an accessory to the first murder, and would in this event have less chance of going scot-free and no chance of turning State's evidence.

"The second case—similarly implausible. For first of all the innocent party would probably not know in advance of Wood's intention to frame him by the ruse of informing the police that the innocent party had killed Longstreet; and second, even if he did know, he certainly would not *commit* murder to protect himself from being *falsely accused* of murder.

"The third case, that Wood was killed by an unknown for reasons unknown, was a possibility, but a remote one, since it would entail an amazing coincidence—the juxtaposition of unrelated motives.

"A peculiar thing happened here, gentlemen." Lane stared into the fire for a moment, then closed his eyes again. "From this analysis, and since I was pursuing the investigation along lines of strictest logic, I was forced to conclude that the interpretation was wrong—that Wood was not himself the murderer of Longstreet. The three possibilities I had examined were all implausible—most unsatisfactory.

"So I allowed myself to be carried along with the main stream of my argument. I examined the second possible interpretation—that Wood, not the murderer of Longstreet, was an accomplice of the murderer, that by his letter he meant to give up the real murderer. This theory made the subsequent assassination of Wood quite understandable. It would indicate that the real murderer had discovered Wood's intention to squeal, and had killed Wood to prevent him from divulging the real murderer's identity. A perfectly logical deduction, and there was nothing to show that I was in error.

"But I was not yet out of the bulrushes; I was in fact becoming more and more mired in the swamp of reasoning. For, if this hypothesis was correct, I was forced to ask myself: Why should Wood, an accomplice and therefore accessory to the Longstreet murder, come to the police with his traitorous story? He could not have expected, if he revealed the identity of the murderer, to conceal his own part in the affair; either he would be forced to reveal it on police questioning, or the murderer himself on being apprehended would reveal it out of desperate retaliation. Then why, why, in spite of certain danger to himself, did Wood choose to disclose the murderer's identity? The only answer—a sound but vaguely unsatisfactory one—was that, regretting or fearing the consequences of his complicity in the Longstreet murder, he meant to protect himself by turning State's evidence.

"At this point in the pursuit of the argument there was no question of choice. The most plausible explanation for Wood's murder in the face of his letter to the police and his own guilty connection with the Longstreet murder was that he was killed by the real murderer because he intended to turn traitor."

Lane sighed and stretched his legs nearer the firedog. "In any event, my course of action was clear, in fact inevitable; I must investigate Wood's life and background in an effort to find a clue to the identity of the person for whom he acted as accomplice—the person who would himself be the murderer, if two criminals and not one were involved.

"This investigation provided the turning-point of my problem. Apparently fruitless at first, a new field was opened up almost by chance, and I was astounded by what . . . But let me begin in the proper place.

"You will recall, Inspector, that I took the inexcusable liberty of impersonating you when I went to Wood's rooming-house in Weehawken. My purpose was not Machiavellian; invested with your personality and authority, I could pursue lines of inquiry unhampered by the necessity of explanation. I did not know definitely where or for what to look. I examined the room, and everything I found was in perfect harmony. The cigars, the ink and papers, the bankbook. There was Wood's crowning touch, gentlemen! He actually left a bankbook and forfeited what must have been to him a considerable sum of money, merely to lend color to the illusion he was creating! I went to the bank; the money was there, untouched. The rate of deposit was regular and in no way open to suspicion. I consulted tradesmen of the neighborhood, endeavoring to find something, anything which might disclose some clue to a possible secret connection in the man's life, someone he may have been seen with. There was nothing, nothing at all. I visited neighborhood doctors and dentists, and this interested me. Apparently the man had never consulted a physician. I asked myself why, remembered that he possibly had consulted one in New York—a pharmacist pointed this out—and dismissed the fleeting suspicion for the moment.

"When I visited the Personnel Manager of the streetcar company, still on the trail of I knew not what, quite by chance I became aware of a monstrous, incredible, and yet increasingly intriguing fact. You will remember that the autopsy report on the corpse of the man murdered on the *Mohawk,* identified as Wood, included mention of a *two-year-old* appendicitis scar. Yet, when I examined the company records of Wood's employment and spoke with the Manager, I discovered that *Wood had worked every working day for five years preceding his murder, without vacation.*"

Lane's voice throbbed; Bruno and Thumm sat forward, mesmerized by the exultation on the actor's face. "But how in the name of all the patron saints of drama was it possible for Wood to have been operated upon for appendicitis two years before his death and yet to have worked every working day for five years before his death? An appendicitis operation, as everyone knows, calls for at least ten days' stay in the hospital—and that is a rare minimum. Most persons are kept away from their work for from two to six weeks.

"The answer was as uncompromising as the ambition of Lady Macbeth—a discrepancy which proved beyond the shadow of a doubt that the body found and thought to be Wood's—the body with the two-year-old appendicitis scar—*was not Wood's at all.* But this meant—and how my eyes opened at the newly discovered terrain!—this meant that Wood was not murdered, that a deliberate attempt had been made to make it *appear* as if he had been murdered; in other words, that *Wood was still alive.*"

In the cathedral silence that followed, Thumm sighed with an oddly synthetic excitement; and Lane smiled as he continued in a low swift pursuit of his thought. "At once all the elements of the second murder rearranged themselves in orderly rows. The incontrovertible fact that Wood was still alive indicated that the letter which he had sent in his own handwriting was a blind; that it was meant to *prepare* the police for Wood's apparent murder; that there was no intention from the beginning to divulge anyone's identity as the Longstreet murderer; that the police, finding Wood murdered after he had promised to divulge the killer's identity, could only believe that this murderer had killed Wood to seal his mouth forever; whereas in this way Wood completely effaced himself from the scene, making himself appear an innocent man killed by a murderer still unknown. The letter and the deception in the identity of the corpse in the water were therefore clever means of putting the police wholly off the scent of the real criminal, Wood himself.

"And what other channels did this all-important deduction open for speculation! For the reason Wood effaced himself in the second crime was that he *had* to disappear, as will be obvious when we come to the third crime, where he faced the possibility of being called as a witness in the character of Edward Thompson, and called simultaneously with the witnesses in the first crime, as Charles Wood—and how could he be two personalities at the same time in the same place? Another point: Wood's plan for self-effacement literally killed two birds with one stone—he not only killed himself as Charles Wood, but he also killed an unknown—the man whose dead body was found dressed in Wood's clothes on the ferry.

"To proceed along this last line. The body supposed to be Wood's had a peculiar scar on the calf of one leg, and red hair; other features being so mauled and smashed as to be useless for identification. Now we know that Wood had red hair and, from Motorman Guiness, that Wood had an identical scar on his leg. But the body found was not Wood's. The red hair might have been a coincidence, but the scars plausibly could not. Wood's scar then must have been false—and false for at least five years, the period of his service with the car company, since he showed the scar to Guiness immediately after going to work on the car. Then he planned to be the superficial counterpart of the man who was to be killed on the *Mohawk* in at least two particulars—hair and scar—so that when the body was found it would seem to be Wood's without question. Then the plan of the ferry-boat crime must have been of at least five years' duration. But since the ferry-boat crime was the result of the Longstreet murder, then Longstreet's murder must also have been planned five years or more before.

"Another conclusion: Since Wood was seen boarding the ferry and was not killed, as supposed, he must have escaped from the ferry in disguise. He might have been one of those who slipped off the boat before Thumm gave instructions to hold everyone, or . . ."

"As a matter of fact," interrupted Bruno, "your correlative supposition is the true one. Actually, he was one of those who were detained on the boat. Stopes says he was Henry Nixon, the jewelry salesman."

"Nixon, eh?" murmured Drury Lane. "Very clever. The man should have been an actor—he had an instinctive gift for assuming alien personalities. I never did know whether Wood was on the boat after the murder or not. But now that you tell me he was posing as Nixon the salesman, the facts tenon nicely. As Nixon the salesman he carried off the ferry the cheap handbag which as Wood the conductor he had carried onto the ferry. He needed the handbag because of the necessity of transporting the salesman-disguise, a blunt instrument with which to stun his victim, weights with which to sink the victim's own clothing in the river. . . . Very clever indeed. As an itinerant salesman his lack of a permanent address and his absence at odd times, if he were superficially investigated, would be accepted as conforming with his trade. Furthermore, by retaining the handbag, which had also been stocked beforehand with trinkets—he was wearing the salesman's clothing, having thrown the victim's clothing away plus the weights and the blunt instrument—he made his rôle natural and convincing. He had even gone to the length, I recall, of having order-blanks printed with his assumed name, and a lodging place where he was known to have stopped sporadically in the past was prepared. His personality as Nixon also accounts for Wood's purchase of a new handbag, for he could not carry off the boat, as the salesman, the old handbag which would be easier to identify as having been Wood's. He even went to the length of breaking the handle of his old bag, to make the deception complete. Altogether, I must say, a brilliantly thorough means of preparing for the contingency of not being able to escape from the boat before the police detained everyone; for of course he could not have foreseen the opportunity to slip off the boat before the hue-and-cry, or risked it in his plan."

"I'll be damned, Mr. Lane," muttered Thumm, "if I've ever heard anything like it. I'll tell you the truth—in the beginning I thought you were an old fossil bluffing your head off. But this—Lord, it isn't human!"

Bruno licked his thin lips. "I'm inclined to agree with you, Thumm, because knowing the whole story as I do, even at this point I can't see how Mr. Lane got anywhere on that third murder."

Lane held up one white hand; he was laughing openly now. "Gentlemen, please. You embarrass me. As for the third murder—I haven't finished with the second!

"For I said to myself at this point: Is Wood still only an accomplice, or is he the murderer himself? Before I discovered that the ferry corpse was not Wood's, the indications pointed to the former. Now the pendulum swung back to the latter.

"There were three definite psychological reasons for the reborn theory that Wood himself killed Longstreet.

"The first was: Wood had planted on himself for five years certain characteristics of an unknown man in order to prepare for that man's murder—certainly this is the action of an active murderer, not a mere tool.

"The second: The sending of the warning letter and the deliberate deception in identity leading to Wood's self-effacement were more the indications of a murderer's scheming than of a pawn's.

"The third: All the events, circumstances, deceptions were planned obviously to insure the safety of *Wood*—certainly again the premeditated actions of a central figure rather than of an accessory.

"In any event, the situation at the end of the second murder was this: Wood, killer of Longstreet and an unknown man, had attempted to efface himself from the scene by the coruscating method of seeming to be murdered himself, and was still alive after having deliberately involved John DeWitt in this seeming murder of himself."

Drury Lane rose and pulled the bellcord by the mantel. Falstaff materialized in the room and was commanded to fetch another caldron of hot coffee. Lane sat down again. "Patently, the next question was: Why should Wood have framed DeWitt with the cigar after decoying him to the ferry?—for it followed that since Wood was the conniver, it had been somehow through his instrumentality that DeWitt had been lured to the boat. Either because DeWitt's strong motive against Longstreet made him the most natural suspect in the eyes of the police, or—and this was important—because Wood's motive against Longstreet *also applied to DeWitt.*

"In the latter event, if the frame-up were successful and DeWitt were arrested, tried but acquitted, there was every reason to expect that the murderer would attempt to consummate his original scheme by attacking DeWitt. This," and Lane accepted another mug from Falstaff's pudgy hand, gesturing toward his guests, "this was why I was willing to allow DeWitt's trial to be prosecuted, despite my knowledge of his innocence. For so long as DeWitt was in danger of conviction by the legal method, he was physically safe from an attack by Wood. You were puzzled, no doubt, by my peculiar attitude; it was really paradoxical, for by plunging DeWitt into one danger I staved off another and more certain danger. At the same time, I gave myself the advantage of a breathing-spell, a period of quiet during which I could chew the cud of my thoughts, perhaps unearth evidence which would lead to the apprehension of the murderer. Don't forget that I had not the slightest idea of what form Wood was taking. . . . There was another advantage, too; for I hoped that the seriousness of DeWitt's predicament—on trial for his life—would force him to reveal facts which I knew him to be withholding, facts which were undoubtedly linked with the man who called himself Wood and the lurking, still obscure motive in the background.

"With the case going against DeWitt, however, imperiling his life, I was forced to step in and bring out the argument concerning DeWitt's wounded finger, although I was no further advanced at that time than before. I should like to point out here that had I not been in possession of the facts concerning DeWitt's wound, I should never have allowed you to prosecute him; if you were bull-headed, Mr. Bruno, I should have been compelled to reveal all I knew.

"With acquittal, DeWitt's personal danger became an immediate consideration." Lane's face clouded, and his voice became troubled. "I have tried many times since that night to convince myself that I was not to blame for DeWitt's death. Apparently I had taken all precautions. I consented with alacrity to accompany him to his West Englewood domicile, even intending to stay the night there; I could not foresee how completely I might be fooled. In extenuation of myself, I must confess that I did not expect Wood to attack DeWitt the very night of the day the poor man was acquitted. After all, since I did not know the new identity Wood was taking, or where he was, I considered that he had weeks, months in which to find his opportunity to kill DeWitt. But Wood turned out a greater opportunist than I knew. He found his opportunity the very first night of DeWitt's acquittal, and he seized it. In this Wood outsmarted me, did the utterly unexpected. When Collins approached him I could scent nothing wrong, because I knew Collins was not Wood. However"—there was a touch of self-reproach in his luminous eyes—"I cannot really claim victory in this affair. I was not sharp enough, not fully enough alive to the potentialities of the murderer. I am still, I fear, an amateur man-hunter. If ever I have the opportunity to investigate another . . ." He sighed and pressed on. "Another reason for my acquiescence to DeWitt's invitation that night was that he promised to reveal information of importance to me next morning. I suspected then—and now I am sure—that he meant at last to reveal the true story of his background, the story Stopes told you in his confession, the story which, by following the trail of DeWitt's South American visitor—never heard of *him*, I'll wager, Inspector!—I learned anyway. This trail in turn led to Ajos, the Uruguayan consul . . ."

Bruno and Thumm were regarding him in amazement. "South American visitor? Uruguayan consul?" spluttered Thumm. "Why, I never even heard of them!"

"Let's not discuss that now, Inspector," said Lane. "Actually, the vital result of my discovery that Wood had executed a deception in identity and was still alive, was that it swung the probabilities from Wood's being a mere accomplice to his being the brilliant murderer himself, maneuvering the complicated segments of a series of crimes of many years' planning in an imaginative, daring, and nearly flawless manner. On the other hand, while I was convinced of this, I had not the remotest notion of where to look for him. Charles Wood, as Charles Wood, I knew to be wiped from the face of the earth; in what incarnation he would next appear I could only conjecture fruitlessly. But that he would appear I was sure, and that was what I was waiting for.

"Which brings us to the third murder."

Lane refreshed himself from the steaming mug. "The very rapidity of the DeWitt murder, combined with certain other elements, indicated clearly that this crime also was a well-planned one—probably planned simultaneously with the first two.

"My solution of the DeWitt murder hinged almost wholly upon the fact that DeWitt had purchased a new fifty-trip ticket-book in the presence of Ahearn, Brooks, and myself while we waited for the train in the West Shore waiting-room that night. If DeWitt had not done so, there is no telling whether the case would ever have been brought to a satisfactory *dénouement*. For, despite my knowledge of the identity of the murderer of Longstreet, I should never have known in what disguise Stopes committed the murder of DeWitt.

"The primary point was the *location* of this ticket on DeWitt's person. In the terminal he had placed it in the upper left pocket of his vest, together with the single tickets which he purchased for the others of the party. When he left with Collins later to go to the rear car, he took from that same upper left vest pocket the single tickets and handed them to Ahearn; and I saw that he did not remove the new ticket-book from its original vest pocket. But when DeWitt's corpse was searched by our Inspector here, I noticed with astonishment that the new ticket-book was no longer in the upper left vest pocket, but now reposed in the inside breast pocket of the coat!" Lane chuckled sadly. "DeWitt had been shot through the heart. The bullet had pierced the coat on the left side, the upper left vest pocket, the shirt, and the underclothing. The conclusion was elementary: at the time he was shot the book was not in the upper left vest pocket, for if it had been it would have contained a bullet-hole, whereas when we found it the book was unpunctured, indeed unmarked in any way.

"I asked myself immediately: How account for the fact that the ticket had been removed from one pocket to another *before* DeWitt was shot?

"Recall the condition of the body. DeWitt's *left* hand formed some sort of sign by the overlapping of his *medius,* or middle, finger and his index finger. Inasmuch as Dr. Schilling affirmed that DeWitt had died instantly, the overlapping fingers indicated three vital conclusions: First, that DeWitt made the sign before he was shot—there were no death-throes. Second, that, since he was right-handed and the sign was made with his left hand, therefore his right hand was occupied when he decided to make the sign. Third, that since the sign he made required a conscious physical effort, it must have been made for a definite purpose connected in some way with the murder.

"Now mull over this third point. If DeWitt had been a superstitious man, the fingers might have denoted the protection-sign against the evil eye, and might have indicated a realization that he was to be murdered and an instinctive superstitious gesture to ward off the 'evil.' But it was known that DeWitt was not superstitious in the slightest degree. The sign, therefore, purposely made, must have related not to himself but to his murderer. This was unquestionably the result of a conversation DeWitt, Brooks, Ahearn, and I had engaged in just a few moments before DeWitt left with Collins. The conversation swung about the last thoughts of dying men, and I related the story of a murdered man who had left a sign to the identity of his murderer before dying. I felt sure, then, that DeWitt, poor fellow, had snatched at this fresh recollection and left a sign for me—for us, I should say—which pointed to the identity of his murderer."

Bruno looked triumphant. Inspector Thumm said excitedly: "Just what Bruno and I figured!" Then his face fell. "But," he said, "even so . . . How the deuce does that apply to Wood? Was he superstitious?"

"Inspector, DeWitt's sign did not point to Wood, or Stopes, in the superstitious sense," replied Lane. "In fact, I should tell you that I never subscribed to that interpretation of the sign. It was too utterly fantastic. What it meant I did not know at the time. In fact, it was necessary for me to solve the case completely before making the connection between the murderer and DeWitt's sign—a connection which I shamefacedly admit stared at me from the first. . . .

"In any event, the only reasonable explanation for the overlapping fingers was that somehow they pointed out the identity of the murderer. But see! Leaving a clue to his murderer's identity proved that DeWitt *knew* who his murderer was, knew enough about his assailant to leave a symbol referring personally to this individual.

"There was an even more cogent deduction in this connection. For whatever the sign of itself meant, its being on the left hand indicated that his right hand, the one he normally used to do everything, was occupied, as I said a moment ago, just before the murder. Now what could this occupation have been? There was no sign of a scuffle; he might have been warding off his murderer with his right hand, but it seemed unlikely that while he was doing this he was simultaneously making a sign with his left—a sign which required conscious physical effort. Was there a better explanation, I demanded of myself? Was there anything about the body that suggested itself as an *explanation* for the occupation of the right hand? Yes, there was!—for I knew that the ticket-book had been moved from one pocket to another.

"I swiftly went through the possibilities. It was conceivable, for instance, that DeWitt moved the book some time before the murder with his own hand—that is, that the transference of the book from one pocket to another had nothing to do with the crime itself. But this would leave the occupation of his right hand during the murder-period still unaccounted for. If I worked on the theory, however, that the book was moved *at the time of the murder,* I explained in one fell swoop why the right hand was occupied, and why the left hand was employed in making a sign which ordinarily would have been made by the right. This seemed to be a fecund theory; it did cover all the facts. Being fruitful, it called for close examination; where did it lead?

"For one thing, it led to this speculation: Why should the ticket-book have been in DeWitt's hand at all at the time he was murdered? Only one defensible explanation—he was intending to use it. Now we knew that up to the time Collins left DeWitt the conductor had not reached them to collect and punch their tickets, for Collins was still in possession of his unpunched ticket when you arrested him in his apartment that night. If the conductor had reached them, Collins's ticket would have been taken from him. Then when DeWitt entered the dim car he had not yet been approached by the conductor for his ticket. Of course, I did not know this that night on the train; it was not until you, Inspector, apprehended Collins that his possession of the ticket came out. But in pursuing my argument I played with the theory that later was confirmed.

"In the light of the hypothesis, later a fact, that DeWitt had not been approached by the conductor by the time he entered the dim car, what would explain most naturally his action in my theory that he produced his ticket-book and held it in his right hand just before his death? The explanation was simple: the approach of the conductor. But both conductors claimed that they did *not* approach DeWitt. Was my theory wrong, then? Not necessarily. *Not if one of the conductors did approach DeWitt, was the murderer, and lied because he was the murderer.*"

Bruno and Thumm was sitting tensely forward, fascinated by the remarkable analysis falling calmly from Lane's lips, enriched by his flexible thrilling voice. "Did this theory plausibly cover all the known facts? It did.

"For, one, it explained why the sign was made with the left hand.

"Two, it explained why and with what the right hand was occupied.

"Three, it explained why the ticket was left unpunched. For if the conductor were the murderer and after killing DeWitt saw the ticket-book in DeWitt's hand, he could not punch it; since the punchmark would leave absolute proof that he was perhaps the last person to see DeWitt alive and would therefore point to his guilt, or at least bring him actively into the investigation of the murder—an undesirable state of affairs for any scheming murderer, naturally.

"Four, it explained why the ticket was found in the inside breast pocket. If the conductor were the murderer, he naturally could not allow the ticket to remain in DeWitt's hand to be found by the police, for exactly the same reason that he could not punch the ticket—its presence at the time of instant death would have indicated the very thing he wished to avoid—that

DeWitt was aware of the conductor's approach and had been killed immediately after. On the other hand, the conductor would prefer not to take away the ticket, since its newness indicated by the perforated date on its cover presupposed the possibility that someone had seen it purchased that very night, and would miss it; and if it were missing it would not be difficult for the police to make the dangerous 'ticket-conductor' mental connection. No, the conductor's best course was to keep himself and suspicion of himself completely out of the scene.

"Now then—what would the conductor do with regard to leaving the ticket on DeWitt's body, since his safest course was not to take it away? He would put it back into one of DeWitt's pockets—reasonable, eh? In which pocket? Well, either he would know where DeWitt usually kept the ticket, or he would look in DeWitt's pockets for an indication of where he usually kept it. Finding the old, expired ticket-book in the inside breast-pocket, what more natural than that he should put the new one into the breast-pocket with the old one? Even if he knew that DeWitt had placed this new book in the vest pocket, *he could not return it to that pocket;* for the vest pocket was in direct line with the course of the bullet already in DeWitt's body, and to replace the ticket in the vest pocket unpunctured by a bullet-hole would make it obvious that it had been placed there after the murder. A police conclusion the conductor again wished to avoid.

"Fifth, as a result of the fourth point—the theory also explained why the ticket-book had no bullet-hole in it. The conductor could not have shot another bullet into the book and expected to hit precisely the spot which would have been pierced had the book been in the pocket at the time of the original shot. In addition, there was danger of a second shot being heard. And to have shot a second time in the car would have left the bullet imbedded somewhere to be found later. And, to cap it all, such a procedure would have been involved, tortuous, time-consuming, and generally foolish on the surface. No, all told, he took the most natural course and what seemed to be the safest.

"So far," Drury Lane went on, "the theory checked in all particulars. Were there confirmations that the murderer was a conductor on the railroad train? One very excellent psychological confirmation. For the conductor on a train is virtually invisible; that is, his presence anywhere on the train is accepted without question, and no one has reason to notice and remember his movements. While the movements of the other members of the party might have, and in some instances were, observed—the conductor could have, as he did, moved through the coaches and into the dim car without leaving a recollection or a trace. In fact, I myself did not observe him, and I was presumably on the alert. He must have passed me to get into that dim coach after Collins left; and yet to this moment I have no recollection of his passing.

"Another confirmation. The disappearance and ultimate recovery of the weapon. The revolver was not found on the train—it was found in a stream over which the train passed about five minutes after the murder. Was it mere chance that dictated waiting five minutes after the murder to throw away the gun—purely by accident, so that it landed most fortuitously in one of the bodies of water along the route? It would have been much safer for the murderer to have thrown the revolver from the train immediately after the commission of the crime. Yet he waited—*why?*

"The theory that he knew, despite the darkness, the exact location of the stream—the best hiding-place for the weapon thrown off the train—indicated that the thrower, to have waited the five minutes and to have had knowledge of the stream's location, must have been extremely familiar with the terrain. Who among the train's occupants was most apt to have had such familiarity? Certainly an employee of the train, which every night passes over the same route at the same time. Engineer, brakeman, conductor . . . A conductor, of course! More confirmation of the conductor theory, though purely a psychological one.

"There was still another confirmation, the most convincing of all, one which definitely pointed to the criminal. But I shall come to that shortly.

"Naturally at the time of the crime, I worked out the reasoning concerning the weapon inversely. I asked myself: If I had been the conductor-murderer, how would I have disposed of the revolver? In such a way as to minimize the chances of its being found? The obvious places—at the side of the track along the roadbed, or on the roadbed itself—I should have discarded, as they would be the first places searched by the police. But, I should have said, the route offers a natural hiding-place which would not only dispose of the weapon but keep it out of sight with no extra effort on my part. The stream! . . . I examined a map of the train-route, spotted all bodies of water within the possible area of disposal, and led the successful search for the weapon."

Lane's voice took on a fresh note. "Now, which of the two conductors had committed the crime—Thompson or Bottomley? Aside from the fact that this part of the train was Thompson's, there was no direct evidence pointing to either man in preference to the other.

"Ah, but wait! For I had deduced a conductor as the murderer in the third crime, and the murderer in the first crime was also a conductor. Was it possible that both conductors were one and the same—that is, Wood? Yes, a very fair possibility. For the murders of Longstreet, the unknown of the ferry, and DeWitt were undoubtedly the work of the same hand.

"But what were the physical characteristics of Wood? Forgetting the red hair and the scar, the first of which could easily have been artificial, and the second of which was unquestionably so—I knew that Wood at least was tall and burly. The old conductor, Bottomley, was small and frail. Thompson was tall and burly. Thompson, therefore, was our man.

"I had arrived then at this point: DeWitt was murdered by Thompson, who, I had every reason to believe, was Charles Wood.

"But who on earth was this Wood-Thompson person? Evidently all three murders had been animated by the same motive, and that motive was a minimum of five years old, probably much older. The next step was plain—to examine the back history of both DeWitt and Longstreet in an effort to uncover someone who had sufficient motive to desire the death of both and plan for years to that end.

"You know now who Stopes was, but bear in mind that at that time I had not the faintest idea of the back history. I did know, from questioning DeWitt's butler Jorgens, that there had been a mysterious visitor from South America stopping at the DeWitt home shortly before—there's a lead, Inspector, in which you must confess to have been outwitted. . . . It seemed a productive trail, and I sought quietly among the South American consuls, ultimately discovering the story from Juan Ajos, consul to New York from Uruguay. That story you know now, but for the first time, to me, it linked Longstreet and DeWitt with *two other men*—Martin Stopes, escaped convict, and William Crockett, who turned out to be a silent third partner of DeWitt & Longstreet. Of the two, Stopes must be Wood-Thompson. His motive was plain—revenge, and was directed equally against all three of the others. So Stopes, I concluded, was the conductor; and Crockett was the man killed on the ferry—a man whom for five years Stopes had been preparing for the slaughter by the device of simulating his red hair and calf-scar so that, when Crockett was found dead, other means of identification being frustrated by the crushed condition of his body, he would be taken for Wood.

"The reason I requested Missing Persons reports, long before I heard the Ajos story and after I had deduced that the body was not Wood's, was that Wood had killed some unknown, and there might be a clue to the unknown's identity in one of these reports. After hearing Ajos's tale, however, I knew the unknown was Crockett. The unknown could not have been a mere human tool unconnected with the other crimes and used merely for his body; for Wood for five years at least had prepared the way by simulating the man's scar and hair. How Crockett was decoyed by Stopes into a position to be murdered, I could not, and still do not, know. Did Stopes explain, Mr. Bruno?"

"Yes," said the District Attorney huskily. "Stopes, who had never written Crockett threat-letters for the specific reason that he wanted Crockett to be ignorant of his handwriting, keeping him unsuspecting, communicated with Crockett in the guise of a discharged bookkeeper of DeWitt & Longstreet, writing that Crockett was being defrauded of a large part of his rightful one-third share of the firm's net, despite the large checks sent Crockett by the two men twice a year. For Crockett, when the three originally returned to the States, insisted on sharing whatever success the other two attained; and rather than have Crockett, a reckless, brutal, irresponsible sort, spill the story of the Uruguayan frame-up, Longstreet and DeWitt consented to his investing one-third of the capital required to swing the business and giving him a third share of their profits. I take it that only DeWitt's insistence prevented Longstreet from reneging through the years. At any rate, the letter went on to say that he, the bookkeeper, had proof of this fraudulency and was willing to sell the proof to Crockett if Crockett would come to New York. He hinted something dire in the wind—evidently to make Crockett believe that his two partners were contemplating giving him up on the old murder-charge. He asked Crockett to watch the personal columns of the *Times* on his arrival. Crockett fell for the story, came to New York angry and afraid at the same time, found his instructions in the *Times*—namely, to check out of the hotel without fanfare and meet the writer of the letter on the 10:40 ferry to Weehawken, upper deck, north side, being careful to keep under cover. The murder of course took place there."

"Not only that," put in Inspector Thumm, "but Stopes, the cunning devil, told us how he fooled DeWitt. Because it was Stopes who telephoned DeWitt that Wednesday morning posing as Crockett, and commanding DeWitt to be on the lower deck of the 10:40 ferry that night, on the excuse of an urgent matter and accompanied by threats. He cautioned DeWitt to 'be careful' not to be seen—thereby minimizing the chances of DeWitt and Crockett meeting, since he had also cautioned Crockett."

"Interesting," murmured Lane, "for that explains why DeWitt refused to tell with whom he had his appointment; he had to keep quiet about Crockett for fear that Crockett would reveal, in a panic, the sordid details of the Uruguayan back history; and Stopes knew he would keep quiet—a subtle touch to his implication of DeWitt.

"As a matter of fact," continued Lane thoughtfully, "I am continually startled by the extreme versatility and daring of this man Stopes. Remember that these were not *crimes passionels,* impulsive and strictly emotional; they were cold, calculated crimes induced by a motive steeled by years of suffering. The man possesses the seeds of greatness. Examine what he had to do in that second crime. He had to meet Crockett on the upper deck as Wood; to lure him near that cubicle, blackjack him with the blunt instrument from the hand-bag; to change clothes, putting his own on Crockett and arraying himself with a new outfit—Nixon's—from the bag; to throw Crockett's original clothes overboard by the weights from the bag; to wait until the *Mohawk* was pulling into the Weehawken pier and then hurl Crockett's unconscious body overboard, to be ground and crushed against the pilings; to hurry down to the lower deck, unnoticed, as Nixon, and join the hue-and-cry of 'Man overboard!'; all this was the work of a brave man, a brilliant thinker and planner. Of course, the precarious business of changing clothes was simplified by the fact that he took four trips, up and back across the river, to commit the murder, probably using the first three for stunning Crockett, changing clothes, disposing of Crockett's, and so on; and the fact that it was late at night and dark and foggy; and the fact that on the Forty-Second Street-Weehawken ferry, passengers rarely go to the upper deck because of the abbreviated trip across the river; and the fact that he could have worked as slowly as he wished, since he could take eight trips, if necessary, and the police would still be waiting on the Weehawken side."

Lane touched his throat wryly. "I find myself considerably staled; there was a time when I could give a continuously oratorical performance for hours without feeling the effects. . . . To resume with the reasoning." Briefly, Lane told of finding in West Englewood, on the night of DeWitt's murder, one of the threat-letters Stopes had sent to DeWitt a few months before. Lane produced the letter and handed it to his guests for their examination.

"Of course," he said, "I had already solved the case before I found this; had I not found it, I should still have achieved my solution. For I knew already that Wood and Thompson were the same.

"But the letter was important from a legal standpoint. A glance sufficed to show that the handwriting of Stopes was identical with that of Wood, which I remembered from seeing Wood's note and signature on his street-car identification card. The fact that the handwritings coincided, I must repeat, was not necessary to the deductive solution; it was merely legal confirmation.

"But now I was faced with the prosecutor's aspect of my solution. Knowing that Wood, Stopes, and Thompson were the same man was one thing, but proving it was another. I thereupon requested Juan Ajos to cable his government for a telephotograph of Stopes's fingerprints. When Thompson was apprehended, the first thing I asked you, Inspector, was to take his fingerprints. You did, and Thompson's matched exactly with the telephotographic prints of Stopes. Therefore I had legal proof that Thompson was Stopes, and from the identical handwritings, that Wood was Stopes. Therefore, in the elementary algebraic conclusion, Thompson was also Wood. The case was complete."

He went on with renewed vigor. "There were some loose ends, however. How had Stopes arranged his three personalities—Wood, Nixon, Thompson—so that he was physically able to keep them separate? I confess I am still somewhat at sea on this point."

"Stopes cleared that up, too," said the District Attorney. "In the first place, it wasn't as hard as it looks. As Wood he worked from 2:30 to 10:30 P.M., and as Thompson from 12 to 1:40 A.M. on the short railroad shift, a special job. As Wood he lived in Weehawken for convenience in changing his clothes and disguise before taking up his train duties; as Thompson he lived in West Haverstraw, the last stop of his run, sleeping there the rest of the night and returning to his Weehawken lodgings as Wood by a late morning train. The Nixon personality was flexible, and he used it rarely. As far as the night of the ferry-murder was concerned, Stopes selected that particular night because it was his night off as Thompson! As simple as that! . . . Incidentally, this business of disguise wasn't so terribly complicated, either. He's bald, as you know. As Wood he wore a red wig. As Thompson he was really himself. The Wood personality, a few touches here and there . . . But you know yourself how easy it is. With the Nixon get-up he had more time and could do what he pleased. As I say, he used the personality of Nixon only rarely."

"Did Stopes explain," asked Lane curiously, "how he managed to secure the cigar which he planted on Crockett's body to incriminate DeWitt?"

"That guy," growled Thumm, "explained everything. Except how you solved these damned crimes, and I can hardly believe that yet. He said that a short time before the Longstreet kill, DeWitt had handed him—as Thompson, the train-conductor—a cigar. The way some of these big mucks do. Doesn't mean a thing to 'em—they just hand 'em out. One-buck cigars, too. Stopes kept it fresh."

"Of course," Bruno added, "Stopes wasn't able to explain a good many things. For instance, the cause of the incessant quarrels between Longstreet and DeWitt."

"I fancy," said Lane, "that the proper explanation is simple enough. DeWitt was a reputable enough character with one weak spot in his moral armor. In his younger days he was probably dominated by Longstreet, and came to regret the conspiracy against Stopes into which he had been coerced. I should say that DeWitt tried persistently to break away from Longstreet, in business as well as in social life; and that Longstreet, because of some quirk of sadistic psychology, perhaps, and because DeWitt was a reliable source of extra income, refused, holding the old dreary bloody conspiracy over DeWitt's head. I should not be surprised if Longstreet made it a point to threaten a disclosure of the old story to Jeanne, the apple of her father's eye. In any event, this is undoubtedly the explanation of the two men's bickering, of DeWitt's willingness to finance Longstreet's dissipations, and of DeWitt's acceptance of Longstreet's open insults."

"Rings true," admitted Bruno.

"As for Crockett," continued Lane, "the nuances of Stopes's plot were self-evident. It must have been Crockett who had murdered Stopes's wife; since for Crockett Stopes reserved the most horrible of the three deaths. Although it is true that the crushing of Crockett's features was necessary to Stopes's plan to make the corpse seem his own, or Wood's."

"You remember," said Thumm thoughtfully, "when the telephoto arrived at The Hamlet here, Mr. Lane? That was the first time I heard the name Martin Stopes, and I asked you who the devil the man was. You said that Martin Stopes was responsible for removing Longstreet, Wood, and DeWitt, or something like that. Now, weren't you misleading me when you included Wood in that statement? How in hell could Stopes have killed Wood when he was Wood himself?"

Lane chuckled. "My dear Inspector, I did not say that Stopes killed Wood. I said he was responsible for removing Wood from the face of the earth, which is literally true. By killing Crockett and dressing him in Wood's clothes, he permanently rid himself and the world of the personality of Wood."

The three men sat in silence, ruminating. The fire leaped higher and Bruno saw that Lane's eyes were pacifically closed. Bruno started at the slapping sound of Thumm's great palm against his thigh. "By God!" exclaimed the Inspector. He leaned over and touched Lane's shoulder; Lane opened his eyes. "I knew you left something out, Mr. Lane. Yes, sir! There's one thing I still don't understand, and you haven't cleared it up. That hocus-pocus of DeWitt's fingers. You said a while ago that you never believed the overlapping fingers had anything to do with superstition. Well, what *did* they mean?"

"Careless of me," murmured Lane. "A good point, Inspector, and I am delighted to be reminded of it. A good point, indeed. In many ways the most curious element of the entire affair." His clean profile sharpened, and his voice grew animated. "Until I deduced that Thompson murdered DeWitt, I had absolutely no personal explanation for the overlapping fingers. Of only one thing was I certain: that DeWitt, remembering my story in that last flashing moment of life, had deliberately left the sign as a clue to his murderer's identity. Therefore the sign must have had something to do with Thompson, or my nice little logical structure would collapse. And it was not until I had satisfied myself that I had the true meaning of the sign that I brought myself to arrange Thompson's arrest."

He rose from the armchair in his characteristic way—quickly, smoothly, with no apparent muscular effort. The two men looked up at him. "Before I explain, however, I should like to know if Stopes related exactly what occurred between him and DeWitt before he fired the shot that ended DeWitt's life."

"Well," said Bruno, "his confession made that point clear enough. It seems that he kept his eyes open from the moment the DeWitt party got on the train. He was looking for an opportunity, remember, to catch DeWitt alone. If necessary, he could have waited a year for the precise situation in which he could murder DeWitt unobserved. But when he saw Collins go back with DeWitt and caught sight of Collins, from the car-door ahead, slipping off the train, he knew his opportunity had come. Then he walked through the car in which you were sitting and immediately spied DeWitt sitting where we found him, in the dim coach. He went in. DeWitt looked up, saw the conductor, and instinctively took out his new ticket-book; but in the heat of the moment Thompson did not notice from which pocket DeWitt produced the book. On fire with the realization that here was the final measure of his revenge, Thompson whipped out his revolver and, before DeWitt's horrified eyes, revealed his true identity—Martin Stopes. He gloated, taunted DeWitt, told him what he was about to do, while DeWitt, Stopes said, seemed fascinated by the nickel ticket-punch swinging from a leather cord at Stopes's (or Thompson's) waist. De Witt had become as white as death, sitting very still, saying nothing (he must have been thinking with lightning rapidity, and left the sign at the moment), whereupon Thompson in an uncontrollable outburst of fury, fired. The spasm of rage passed as quickly as it had come; and he realized, as DeWitt's head slumped forward, that DeWitt still held the ticket-book, unpunched, in his right hand. He immediately decided that he could not take the book away, yet he did not want to leave it in DeWitt's hand; so he searched DeWitt's pockets, and put the new book in the breast-pocket with the old. Stopes claims that he did not notice at all that DeWitt had twisted his fingers. He was very much surprised when it was discovered later, after the murder; and to this moment he is as much at a loss as we to explain it.

"Anyway, at Bogota, he opened the door of the dim car, jumped out, and closed the door again, ran forward along the station and boarded a coach ahead. The revolver he had planned to throw into the stream just as you explained it, and for the same reasons."

"Thank you," said Lane gravely. His tall figure was etched in black against the mottled ruddy background of the fire. "Then we return to the fascinating problem of the sign. Thompson and the fingers, the fingers and Thompson. . . . What connection, I asked myself?

"It was not until I recalled a most insignificant fact that I suddenly saw, in a blinding flash of light, the only possible answer to the pestiferous problem. . . ." Lane went on quietly. "Aside from the evil-eye interpretation, which made no sense at all, what else could the twisted fingers mean? Above all, in relation to Thompson?

"I discarded my hitherto blundering method of thought in this connection and took another tack entirely. What was the *physical* significance of the twisted fingers; that is, did the fingers, by their odd position, approximate a specific geometric symbol? A moment's thought revealed an interesting discovery; the geometric symbol approximated most closely by the crossed fingers was undoubtedly an *x!*"

He paused a moment, and a look of comprehension spread over his guests' faces. Thumm crossed his fingers and nodded emphatically.

"But *x*," continued Mr. Drury Lane in a resounding voice, "*x* is the universal symbol of the unknown quantity. Then I was wrong again. For certainly DeWitt had not intended to leave a riddle behind him! . . . But—*x*, *x* . . . I could not forget it, felt intangibly that somehow I was hot on the scent. So I tested the *x* against Thompson. And, gentlemen, the veil fell from these poor mortal eyes, and I remembered that there was one characteristic of Thompson, the railroad conductor, which was distinctly, rigidly an identification-mark of Thompson—as characteristic of this one man as his finger-prints."

Bruno and Thumm regarded each other blankly. The District Attorney corrugated his brow fiercely; Inspector Thumm's fingers crossed and uncrossed with desperation. He shook his head. "I give up," he said in deep disgust. "I guess I'm just dumb. What was it, Mr. Lane?"

For reply Lane explored his wallet once more, this time extracting a long piece of printed paper. He looked at it affectionately, then strode before the fire and placed the paper in Bruno's hand. The two men's heads thumped together as they bent over the slip. "Merely one of the duplex cash-tickets which passed through the hands of Conductor Edward Thompson, gentlemen," said Mr. Drury Lane softly, "at the time when you, my dear Inspector, paid our fares just before his arrest."

And while Lane turned his back to stride to his fire, breathing in the woody perfume of the curling smoke, Thumm and Bruno stared at the final exhibit.

At two spots on the paper—by the side of the printed words *Weehawken* and, lower down, *West Englewood*—were the clean, sharp perforations of Conductor Edward Thompson's cross-mark punch—an *x*.

THE END

DISCUSSION QUESTIONS

- Did any aspects of the plot date the story? If so, which?
- Would the story be different if it were set in the present day? If so, how?
- Did the social context of the time play a role in the narrative? If so, how?
- If you were one of the main characters, would you have acted differently at any point in the story?
- Did you identify with any of the characters? If so, which?
- What skills or qualities make Drury Lane such an effective sleuth?
- If you've read the Ellery Queen novels, how does this compare? Do you think Ellery Queen or Drury Lane is a more skilled detective?
- Did this book remind you of any present day authors? If so, which?

MORE ELLERY QUEEN FROM
AMERICAN MYSTERY CLASSICS

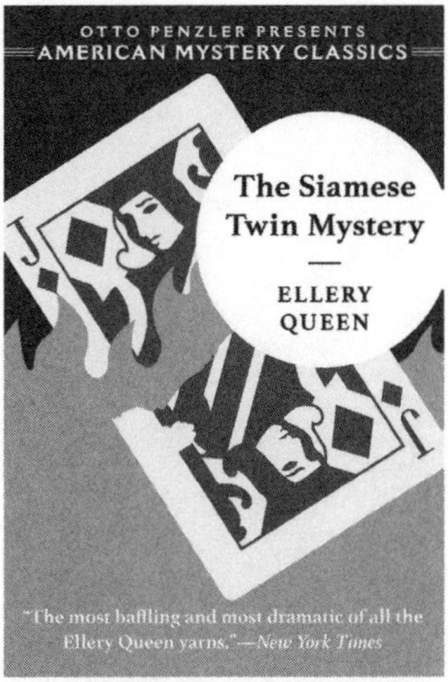